PRAISE FOR A BESTSELLING AUTHOR

"The novels of Noel Hynd stand out like emeralds!"
—*The New York Times Book Review*

PRAISE FOR THE BESTSELLER GHOSTS

"A ghost novel needs to convince unbelieving readers against their will and scare the liver out of them and GHOSTS does this in spades. The atmosphere builds steadily, moving from reality to an utterly convincing realm of the supernatural."

—*Library Journal*

AND NOW PRAISE FOR NOEL HYND'S BESTSELLING NOVEL OF TERROR AND SUSPENSE *A ROOM FOR THE DEAD*

"The chills come fast and hard in Hynd's latest, a riveting blend of ghost story and police procedural. New Hampshire cop Frank O'Hara, approaching 50 and close to retirement, is given a case that duplicates the M.O. of serial killer Gary Ledbetter. But Gary, a "low-rent Lothario" nabbed by O'Hara, was executed months ago. Since then, O'Hara's life has turned to ashes. He's taken seriously to booze, his wife has left him, his partner has committed suicide—and now, deep into another hated winter, something seems to be haunting his house: floors creak, doors slam, an empty rocking chair rocks. A tangle of right-wing state politics, skinhead thieves, and a mysterious young woman lead the cop to a shattering conclusion. Throughout, the atmospherics are excellent and the local color first rate."

—*Publishers Weekly*

NOEL HYND

A ROOM FOR THE DEAD

PINNACLE BOOKS
WINDSOR PUBLISHING CORP.

PINNACLE BOOKS are published by

Windsor Publishing Corp.
850 Third Avenue
New York, NY 10022

The P logo Reg U.S. Pat & TM off. Pinnacle is a trademark of Windsor Publishing Corp.

10 9 8 7 6 5 4 3 2

Printed in the United States of America

for
my good friends
Joan and George Kaczender
with thanks
and appreciation

Et clamor meus
ad te veniat.

And let my cry come
unto Thee.

—Roman Catholic Mass

True love is like seeing ghosts. We all talk
about it, but few of us have ever seen one.

—Francois de Rochefoucauld
1613–1680

Chapter 1

June 6, 1993. Tallahassee, Florida. Four-fifteen A.M. on an ugly, humid morning that was growing uglier by the second. And not because of the weather.

Florida State Correctional Facility. Two burly guards escorted Father Robert Trintino down the long corridor on the second floor. Death Row. Father Trintino stopped at a spot where he had been a dozen times previously.

The priest turned to Correctional Officer Butch Thurman and drew a breath. This was the moment that Trintino had dreaded for months. He had asked God many times to help him through it. He was not sure that God had listened.

Father Trintino calmed himself. Then he waited. Within the command center of the prison, a captain of security fed a combination of numbers into the prison's central computer. In response, the door to cell 211 E. slowly opened.

The portal had a chunky, creaking, unforgiving sound to it, a grudging mechanical noise, combined with a hissing reminiscent of the air brakes on a truck. A blend of old prisons and new, the worst aspects of both.

Father Trintino wore the traditionally turned collar

and a black shirt with short sleeves. He walked slowly into the cell.

The condemned man's name was Gary Ledbetter. Gary was wide-awake, playing solitaire with a fresh deck of Budweiser playing cards. A tray of food, delivered forty-five minutes earlier, remained untouched. Behind him, along the walls, beside his cot, were several books. Classic stuff in several categories: Charlie Dickens to Tommy Pynchon, Steve King to Al Camus. Gary called all the authors by diminutive first names once he had made friends with them. Then again, he had also taught himself French in his first year on Death Row and read Jean Genet in the original. Saint Genet would have gotten off on that one.

Yeah, Gary was a pile of contradictions: a self-educated eighth grade dropout. Well-read and badly spoken, but an intellect among convicted killers. Even played the piano pretty well—played hymns in church when he was a kid down South. But, of course, the prison wouldn't let him touch a piano. Warden's opinion—Gary would make a shiv out of a key or a garotte out of a string. Ledbetter was too damned smart, too damned self-destructive, too bad-assed for his own good. That's the only thing upon which everyone agreed.

Ledbetter was twenty-eight years old and had been in trouble with the law since he was nine. Before age nine, there had been incidents. A number of them. Some involving people. Others involving neighborhood dogs and cats. But no one had ever kept track, except his mother, who quickly *lost* track.

Gary Ledbetter. Stocky, muscular, and occasionally sadistic. Five feet ten, and all seventy inches as mean as a wounded bobcat. A misspent life that the newspapers could latch upon. Could have been a musician. Could have been a novelist. Instead, he liked to murder. He himself confessed that he had a "wicked streak." Gary's own words.

A face you could trust, naturally. Round. Angelic. More contradictions: Off-kilter handsome. Love me or hate me. Love me *and* hate me. Dirty blond hair. The typically bad hairchop of a prison inmate, but still—even after a few dozen months on Death Row—a white trash Adonis. Could have been a fine actor, too. Brooding presence. In a crowded room, all eyes gravitated to him. In a cell, there was no choice.

Gary Ledbetter looked up. Two cobalt blue pilot lights: the kind of eyes that made women trust him. Fall in love. Go willingly to bed with him before he murdered them, the prosecutors of four states had claimed. The owner of that face—of those eyes—had been implicated in the mutilation-murders of five young women up and down the east coast, Maine to Florida. Five unsuspecting girls, each murder a little more calculated and grisly than the preceding one. So the cops said. The newspapers and several police departments had wondered, how many more had there really been?

Gary had an answer. None. *No* other murders. No, sir. And he surely hadn't snuffed the first four, either. Like half of the Death Row inhabitants in the United States, Ledbetter swore he was innocent. The victim of a terrible frame-up. Mistaken identity. Witnesses who were vindictive and wrong. A bunch of liars. *Who me?* Hurt them? No way. Not Gary. "I done some bad things in my life, but I didn't kill no girls. Fact is, I got some good in me. Everybody does."

That's what Gary swore in court.

After a three-day trial for one of the homicides, a jury had taken an hour and fifteen minutes to decide. It didn't believe Gary. Not a damned bit. Hell, the jurors had all read the tabloids, so they knew exactly what they were doing. Given the opportunity, the jurors would have executed Gary several times, each time a little more painfully than the last. The victims' families suggested that electrocution was too good for Gary, after what he had done to those innocent girls.

But, "No, sir," Gary kept insisting. "I never harmed no girls."

Outside the prison there were the usual vigils. On the north side of the main gate there were the softies who believed in Gary's innocence. Among them were the bleeding hearts who felt that capital punishment was inherently cruel and unusual.

South of the main gate there was the redneck cheering section. The execution freaks. The crew who turned out for any good electrocution. Zap Gary, they said. Toast him and roast him. And, hey! Make it slow and painful!

The door closed behind the priest. Father Trintino gazed at Ledbetter. "Good morning, Gary," the priest said. Even he knew that his words, just those two, contained a terrible irony.

Gary tried to place a three of hearts into the four rows of playing cards, then absently looked up at his visitor. A cobalt blue glance that continually unnerved the priest. Sheer, cold, chip-on-the-shoulder malice when Gary didn't smile.

"Good morning, handsome," Gary answered. A voice like velvet to go along with those eyes. Gary continued his game of solitaire without missing a beat.

"I asked you not to call me that, Gary," the priest said. "I'm a pastor."

Ledbetter turned over a series of spades, then clubs. His eyebrows raised over the sequences of the cards.

"Why can't you leave me alone?" Ledbetter finally asked.

"I don't feel you should be alone," Father Trintino said.

Ledbetter shrugged. "Suit yourself," he answered. He turned back to his cards.

The priest found a seat in the cell. From behind a heavy glass in the ceiling, a closed circuit camera monitored the encounter. Outside, the two guards waited. Beneath the NO SMOKING sign, they broke open a pack of unfiltered butts. Behind bars, Joe Camel was one popular dromedary.

Father Trintino was dark and nice-looking. Three decades old. Classic Mediterranean features. Pacino in *Dog Day Afternoon*. Yet his bearing conveyed great understanding and patience. This morning, he was also ill at ease. He knew the condemned man no better now than he had the time he had first visited.

"This is our final meeting, Gary," Trintino said.

"Think I don't know that?"

"You were raised as a Christian, Gary," the priest attempted bravely. "I know this idea has never appealed to you before. But it is never too late to—"

"Forget it, Father. Save your breath."

The priest forged ahead. "It is never too late to make your confession. Or to ask God for His forgiveness."

Ledbetter laughed. "Hell, Father," Ledbetter said. "It was too late for me fifteen years ago, my first felony bust. I knew that this day would come. So what of it? All I bring into this world is misery, so why not let me take myself out of it?"

Father Trintino sighed. He found Ledbetter infuriating.

"It matters to me, Gary," the priest tried.

"Fuck it."

"And you should want to go to God with an unburdened soul."

"My soul *is* unburdened."

"Is it really?"

"Yes." Ledbetter's gaze was as unflinching as a terrier's. It was the priest who finally looked away. "My soul ain't burdened 'cause I never killed no girl," Ledbetter said.

"A court found differently, Gary. There was evidence. Witnesses. Testimony against you."

"Lies."

"I'm sorry. I wish I could believe you, Gary."

"Yeah, right," Ledbetter answered, quickly seizing upon the point. "You come here all these times and you don't believe me no how. So what can I do?"

The priest tried to phrase a response. But Ledbetter forged ahead.

"Let me ask you something, Father," Gary continued, hanging cynically upon the word "Father." "Why did you join the church, anyway? Was it a thing you had for boys?"

"Gary, please don't continue this."

"Answer me," Ledbetter demanded. "Another priest could come. But *you* do. Are you attracted to me?"

"I am not attracted to you."

"Liar. You love me."

Father Trintino experienced a sinking feeling. "Gary, time is short. I'm offering you a final opportunity to accept Christ."

"You're interfering with my damned card game," the prisoner said. "Know how much I had to pay the guards for a new deck?"

"Gary . . ." the priest said, "I have my duties. And there are certain things I have to ask."

Ledbetter was silent for a moment. "Then let's get on with it," he finally said.

The priest pressed his agenda. "Would you like to talk?" he asked. "About life? About Heaven?"

"No."

"Would you like to accept Holy Communion?"

"Of course not." Ledbetter made three final moves with his remaining cards.

"May I pray for you?" Trintino asked.

"Can if you want. Don't matter none to me."

Gary leaned back from his table and smiled triumphantly. He had completed his suites. "Look at that. I did it," he said proudly. A final game of solitaire and he had won.

Now the priest sighed. "Would you like," he asked with some hesitation, "to talk about what's going to happen today?"

Gary turned toward the clergyman. "Are you going to watch my execution?" Ledbetter asked.

The priest eyed him, unblinking. As had happened on previous meetings, the prisoner had read his thoughts.

"Why did you ask me that?"

"Because that's what worries you, isn't it? Having to watch. That bothers you more than coming in here and talking to me."

"No, Gary. That's not the case."

"You're lying, Father. Answer my question."

Father Trintino experienced a sinking feeling. "Are you asking me to be your witness?"

"Wouldn't you like to be?"

"I don't care to see you die."

"Why's that?" Ledbetter demanded.

The priest didn't answer.

"I have the right to ask for a witness," Ledbetter said. "I want you."

"Gary . . ."

"Hey, where's your courage, Father?" Ledbetter taunted, blue eyes narrowing. "This is my time of need. Or does it upset you especially to watch my *cojones* get cooked because—"

"All right, Gary. I'll be your witness."

The prisoner thought about it.

"That's good," Ledbetter said, a taunt in his voice. "I think someone who cares about me should watch them kill me. Cares about me physically, I mean."

The cleric cringed.

"Ever seen anyone killed close up?" Gary asked.

"No."

"Do you find it disturbing?"

"Very."

"Then it should happen no other way. *That's* what death is about, Bobby. Pain and suffering."

The young priest stiffened. "Why did you call me that?"

"Call you what?"

" 'Bobby.' "

"That's your name, ain't it?"

"I was called that as a boy. How did you know?"

The prisoner paused and smiled. "Lucky guess, Bobby." Ledbetter paused and rose to his feet. "Or maybe I can see what a man really likes."

"And what's that?"

Ledbetter stepped to Father Trintino. The priest rose but made no effort to move. Ledbetter inclined gently forward and kissed the other man, squarely on the lips. Father Trintino held still, then an expression of quiet disgust overtook him.

The prisoner smiled.

"There you go, Bobby," said Ledbetter. "An abomination. A sin against your church. And the best part is that it's exactly what you wanted."

"That's not the case, Gary."

"Sure it is."

Trintino turned and rapped on the door. The guards manually opened the cell from the opposite side. One of the guards stepped in. Fresh tobacco smoke followed.

"Bobby?" Ledbetter asked.

The priest paused and waited.

"Hasta la vista, Bobby," the prisoner said. "Be good."

Ledbetter smiled. Father Trintino left. The guard eyed the condemned man belligerently. Then he, too, stepped from the cell.

The priest didn't look back. The door closed behind him, another creaking metal groan.

The guards exchanged a glance as the door closed. Both entertained the same thought. Another hour and they would feel damned good about being rid of Gary Ledbetter.

The predawn glow was on the horizon, the prelude to a hot, sticky, eighty-eight-degree daybreak. Seven minutes later, a Supreme Court justice, considering a final appeal, phoned the prison. The justice told the State to get the job done. Fry Gary as the lower courts had decided. Even Gary's own mother admitted that he was no good. Then dawn came at 5:24 A.M. There was no further possibility for a reprieve.

Guards led Gary Ledbetter from his cell at 5:33 A.M. They took him to the execution chamber. He walked past a row of other convicts on his wing. Most of them banged on their cell doors as he passed, a salute to Gary's final exercise in macho. A calm upright swagger to his own execution. A big, wet, gooey spit in death's eye.

Ledbetter was given an enema, compliments of the State of Florida. Two guards shaved his body hair and washed him with salt water.

Father Trintino appeared again moments before the execution and gave him the last rites of his church. The priest's voice was halting. Ledbetter looked at him and smiled.

"Know the only thing that bothers me, Bobby?" Ledbetter asked.

Trintino waited.

"There are a couple of people who deep down know

this is a fucking joke," he said. "They know I didn't kill no girls. And they didn't do nothing."

"I'm sorry, Gary," the priest said.

Ledbetter looked at the guards. "Tell them to start cranking it up," the prisoner said. He turned back to the priest and rejected the last rites.

Ledbetter offered no resistance as he was shown to the chair. He had no further remarks. No relatives attended. No friends, either. Families of the dead girls also stayed away. A coroner served as witness for Florida. A prosecutor and the warden of the prison were also present.

At 5:59 A.M. Gary Ledbetter was strapped into the electric chair. At 6:00 A.M. the application of the amps and volts began.

Father Trintino watched it happen. He saw the torment as Gary's body coursed with fifty thousand volts of electricity. Ledbetter writhed and kicked. He snarled the most sacrilegious profanities imaginable. The blood vessels in his neck and forehead looked like they would burst.

Trintino watched Gary's eyes. One moment, as Gary fought the surges of electricity, they were focused on the priest. Moments later, they went wide with *something*. It was as if Ledbetter's eyes were focused on this world one second and something beyond human imagination the next.

Then Gary's body spasmed a final time. It kicked and went slack. Gary was dead. The execution had taken forty-five seconds. Officially, it was still six A.M. The air breathed by the witnesses was filled with the odor of burning flesh. There was a trace of smoke in the chamber.

The medical technicians appeared and removed the corpse. But Father Robert Trintino did not move.

First, he was drenched with sweat. But then he had the sensation of something enveloping him. Almost instantly, he felt deeply ill, as if the air pressure in the witnesses' chamber had changed too quickly.

The priest could not move or speak. And he could barely breathe. His wet palm found the gold crucifix near his belt. But his hand seemed to have no feeling. No direction. The stench from the execution—it was vaguely reminiscent of burnt pork—remained in his nostrils, and he had the sensation that something was trying to crush him.

Then the force—or the emotion, or whatever it had been—was gone, as quickly as it had arrived. In looking around him, the priest realized that no one else had felt it. Everyone else was returning to his duty.

Slowly the priest regained his breath. His heartbeat slowed to its normal pace. He attributed the incident to his own personal trauma over what he had seen, what he had smelled. What he had endured these past months with Gary. He told himself that in the future he would prefer to comfort a thousand terminally ill people on their passage to Heaven than witness one more execution of a man destined in the opposite direction. He wondered if he could broach the subject with his bishop without implying that he was somehow unfit for his full duties.

These thoughts followed the clergyman as he quietly lowered his head and walked to the prison parking lot.

Outside, when the announcement was made of Ledbetter's death, the two camps maintaining vigils reacted predictably. Some of the capital punishment opponents cried. The "Fry Gary" camp cheered. Later that morning, Gary Ledbetter's vital organs were "harvested" for transplants. The rest of the prisoner's remains were buried in a local cemetery that afternoon.

That might have been the end of it.

But it wasn't.

About a month after Gary Ledbetter had been executed, Father Trintino was gardening behind his parish house. Late July. A Saturday. He had been working all morning, another bright, hot day.

All of a sudden, Father Trintino was aware of a strange feeling, not too distant from the one he had felt on that horrible morning of June 6 at the state prison. A sense of oppression, bordering on paralysis. But moreover this time, the priest felt there was a set of eyes upon him.

Father Trintino looked around. Then he froze. He saw, or thought he saw, a man standing about twenty feet from him, facing away. The man was of medium height and fair haired. He wore battered jeans and a torn yellow T-shirt.

Father Trintino felt his skin crawl. Then the man in the yellow shirt turned. The priest was sure that it was Gary Ledbetter. He would know that face—those blue eyes!—anywhere. Slowly, a hoe slipped from the priest's hands and fell.

The vision, or the man, or whatever it was, said nothing. It—Gary—only smiled while a bolt of fear overtook Father Trintino.

The priest leaned down to pick up the hoe. He took his eyes off the vision, and then looked back.

Whatever the priest had seen, it was now gone. Trintino quickly told himself that he had been imagining things. There was no one anywhere near him. The priest quickly set his hoe aside and went into the parish house. There he had a glass of cold water and a piece of fruit. When he looked out at the garden, he was relieved not to find anyone.

So, what had he seen? Where had it gone? And, even more challenging, from where had it come?

About an hour later, Father Trintino walked back to the rectory, the vision still preying upon his mind.

He ate in silence. During this evening and the days

that followed, he went through his duties by following habit rather than any inspiration.

He mentioned this sighting to no one. Lesser visions had caused priests to be temporarily relieved from their duties. And Father Trintino was happy in Florida. If only he had seen Christ, he mused, it could have been considered a Revelation. Instead, a vision of Gary Ledbetter was something much darker.

Then, as days passed, as weeks went by, the thought of the vision receded, as did the threat of another one.

Father Trintino never saw Gary Ledbetter again. Which was just fine with him. Gary still preyed upon his conscience in too many ways. Nor was Ledbetter ever too far from his thoughts. But the truth was, Father Trintino had seen him too many times already.

Uneasily, Frank O'Hara slept.

Fitfully, he dreamed.

From somewhere, a restless spirit addressed him.

Ask yourself, what is your greatest fear?

Of what are you truly afraid? What have you done that could return to you to shatter your life? What do you fear the most?

In his dream, O'Hara drifted. He experienced a strange sense of floating, unlike any that had ever come previously. He also had the sensation of being before a large, unopened gate, poised on the threshold of some unprecedented experience.

The voice came again. Silken. Slithery.

Tell me your special terror, Detective Frank O'Hara, and I'll show you something far, far worse.

From somewhere, a long distance away, there was laughter. Manic. Demonic. Insane.

But let us not dwell on your terrors too much. Let us not, because we each know what inevitably will happen.

O'Hara turned abruptly in his sleep. Then there was

a hand on his shoulder in the dark. A firm hand. A man's hand. In his closed bedroom where there should have been no other living, breathing human being.

O'Hara bolted upright in his bed. His eyes flashed open. With both of his arms, he swiped at the hand that he had felt on his shoulder. He flailed at it, forcing it away.

But he couldn't find it. Had it been there at all? He was sure that it had. He groped for a bedside lamp and lit up the room. He scanned an empty, quiet place, presided over by all of his familiar objects.

There was also an echo in the room and in his ears. The same sound that had been in his throat. A reverberation from his heart. His own scream, the one that he had ridden up out of his nightmare.

If it had been a nightmare. *If* it hadn't been reality.

Who the hell knew any more? These things, these black terrors while he slept, were so damned frequent now. And over this hot summer, particularly over the past few weeks, these horrors were growing more intense.

He sat up in bed, his heart kicking in his chest. His bedclothes were wet with perspiration. It was August 1993. Detective Frank O'Hara of the New Hampshire State Police was half scared to death and didn't even know why.

At least, not *exactly* why.

His eyes remained open in the empty bedroom. The dull red light of the clock radio said 4:47 A.M. It was either very late at night or very early in the morning, depending on one's point of view. O'Hara alternated between the two theories. Sometimes from minute to minute.

O'Hara heard something and froze.

Downstairs a creak sounded within the woodwork. Like someone taking a cautious step on old floorboards. Or maybe it was the wood of the old house—

O'Hara's home dated from the 1880s—reacting to summer humidity.

O'Hara rose from bed and listened. There was another creak. He reached to the automatic pistol that he always kept an arm's length from where he slept. In case he ever needed it in a hell of a hurry. A nine-millimeter security blanket.

O'Hara should have felt safe. But lately, and with increasing intensity, he sensed that he wasn't safe. There was *something* out there. Something seeking him. *Stalking* him. But who? Or *what?*

O'Hara was a tortured man. One beset by shadows. By questions. By the uncertainties of the past and the future, not to mention the insecurities of the present.

And he was recently tortured also by phantoms, particularly in the black hours before dawn. Not always. But often enough. Like right now.

Almost twenty years as a police officer, he mused. Two decades of defending the public and now *he* was scared to death.

He lay the pistol across his lap. Subconsciously, his hand fumbled around a night table for a cigarette. Then he realized he hadn't smoked for seven years. Gave it up when a close pal, also a career butt-puffer, was diagnosed with the "Big C" in his throat. Got planted in a cemetery four months later.

O'Hara lay back slightly. He set the gun aside and folded his arms across his chest. In his mind, he recalled those black-and-white pictures of the old American West. Dead outlaws in pine coffins, their arms folded the same way, making two perfect Vs. These days, images of mortality were never far from O'Hara, either mentally or physically.

He sighed. He felt a headache coming on and wondered if he had any more prescription painkillers. Well, maybe he'd settle for a good, stiff drink.

He asked himself what he was afraid of. What *ex-*

actly? He still couldn't place it. Yet he did recognize one thing. Within him was the secret, gnawing, gripping, accelerating fear that follows so many law enforcement professionals to the grave. The fear that out of a past so complicated and complex, so tortured and so disturbing that even he couldn't completely grasp it, out of all this would someday—suddenly!—step an old enemy to demand a moment of reckoning.

And of course this ancient enemy would step forward in an irrational way at a vulnerable moment, a point in time when O'Hara's guard would be down.

Like in the middle of a dark August night. While O'Hara slept.

O'Hara turned on a second lamp in his bedroom. He lay in his bed and let his gaze travel around the room. He listened to his heart pound. The heartbeat was settling now. But O'Hara could feel its vibration through the mattress of his bed.

His eyes attempted to close again. They tried to find some semblance of peace. But there was none. No sooner had Frank O'Hara started to drift off to sleep than the unwelcome voice was back, a serpentine voice that existed in the dim area between sleep and wakefulness.

Hell is a very personal thing, the voice told him. *Same as fear. So I'll ask you once again, Frank: What is it that scares you the most?*

"I don't know!" The voice was a man's. Loud. A blurting shout. O'Hara's.

His eyes flickered open again. His body shook and he breathed hard. More sweat upon his face and chest. He knew that he had been talking in his sleep.

He glanced at the clock radio by his bed. 4:52 A.M. Outside of his house, the New Hampshire countryside was quiet. So was the rural road that passed his front door. Fact was, except for some of the local wood mills that worked around the clock, the entire region slept.

A long minute passed. Then another. O'Hara turned off his room lights. 4:54. A.M.

He turned over in his sleeplessness. He sighed. No one in the room to hear him. Or so he thought. What about the hand he had felt on his shoulder?

A vivid dream? Or had there really been something? Or someone?

Nonsense, he told himself. Utter nonsense. He was alone in his bedroom; he was sure he was alone.

Somewhere in the distance, probably a mile or two away, an airplane travelled the sky. O'Hara focused on the sound of the aircraft engine. The mechanical rumble was almost reassuring in its ordinariness.

He turned again, bunching up the pillow, trying to settle in for comfort.

Crazy thoughts in his half-sleep. Disturbing thoughts. More feelings than tangible ideas. An uneasy sense that something was very wrong. And very dangerous.

He wondered from what dark world did these ideas ascend.

Downstairs, anguishingly, there was another creak on the old floorboards. Just loud enough to accelerate O'Hara's pulse rate again.

Hey! *Was* it the floorboards? Or *did* he have an intruder?

"Fuck it," O'Hara whispered to himself. He would have to go have a look.

He picked up the pistol and checked the clip. Yes, it was loaded. He always kept it loaded.

He moved through his bedroom to the hallway. He glanced toward the two other rooms on the second floor of his home. The rooms looked undisturbed. He didn't bother with them.

He walked slowly down the steps to the front hall of the house. He held his gun aloft as he walked.

Another creak downstairs in the living room. So be it, he told himself. He'd have a confrontation.

He moved as quietly as he could, but the wooden steps moaned under his feet.

He arrived at the base of the stairs. Then he was at the living-room door, his pulse racing. He slid his hand into the room and found the wall switch. He threw on the light.

The room was quiet. No one there. O'Hara stood very still, listened and kept watching. Nothing at all.

Only one thing in the room was moving. There was a walnut rocking chair which O'Hara had picked up a few years earlier at a flea market. It was a comfortable rocker, but off balance. Sometimes, on the uneven floor, it could move slightly by itself.

Like right now. O'Hara's heart raced a little when he saw the motion. The rocker had a suspicious look to it—that gentle easy sway that a rocker would have when someone has just left it. O'Hara put his hand on the chair to stop the motion. The rocker came to a halt and remained still. O'Hara lowered his pistol.

A strange odor was in the air. Yet he couldn't place it. It was something foul and repugnant, and he knew it from somewhere else. A dead rodent decomposing somewhere within a wall?

No, he told himself. This was an odor with a bad association. He sniffed and tried to find it a second time. But strangely it was gone.

A moment passed. O'Hara was quickly convinced that he had imagined the smell.

He sighed, to ease his own anxiety. Then he studied the room a final time. He convinced himself that his fears were foolish. He clicked off the light and walked back upstairs to his bedroom.

He returned to his bed and sat down on the edge of it.

A stillness remained upon the house. Eerie more than peaceful. An image came to him. The stillness was like the moment of silence that precedes a scream. He felt beads of sweat break anew on his brow, and buried his face in his hands.

His whole body ached. His eyes were so tired they stung. His nerves felt like they had been rubbed raw with sandstone.

But worse—much much worse—Frank O'Hara felt his sanity slipping away from him. Midway through his life, events didn't make sense any more.

Yet he knew that he needed help. He knew he had to start pulling things together. He had to protect his own rationality. In his head, he had to create order out of events where there was no order.

Recently, he had found great but temporary solace in alcohol. A nice, comfortable belt here and there. To summon up courage. To get his eyes open for the day. To summon the confidence to go to work. It wasn't a get-drunk type of thing. It was just that a little nip here and there helped him cope.

There was a half-expired pint of bourbon on his dresser. Old Crow. O'Hara opened it. He took a heavy sip and replaced the bottle. He turned on his radio. All he could find was some damnable soft-rock station from Boston. He felt like shooting the radio.

What he really could have used was some jazz. Or some of his favorite: Sinatra. When it came to music, when it came to a way with a song, Sinatra owned the place and everyone else just paid rent.

Yeah, Sinatra. The "Other" Frank. But no station played O'Hara's type of music through the night. Another small touch of isolation for a man who was isolated in many large ways.

No wonder cops have so many heart attacks,

O'Hara said to himself. No wonder cops turn to drink so often. You get to a certain age, you've seen too much, you know too much, you can't make sense of a damned thing. And you're fucking all alone.

He set the bottle back on the dresser and went to his bedroom window, the one in the front of the house that overlooked the driveway. He leaned on the windowsill.

It was past five in the morning now, the radio in the background gently playing music that he hated, but he couldn't deal with silence any more. Friends would have called this insomnia, combined with a general orneriness. A doctor would have talked about an attack of nerves, about free-floating anxiety waiting to settle.

O'Hara called this neither of those. He called it the inevitable. The time when the moment of reckoning was due. But with what? With whom? Himself? An event? *Who?*

He stared out of his window at the night. Dawn would soon break, and O'Hara would wait for it.

"Help," O'Hara muttered aloud. "God damn it! I got to have some help."

He looked back to his dresser, then moved to it.

He found the bottle of bourbon again and this time skipped the niceties. He drew a nice, long belt of it, then a second one. He felt the warm, reassuring surge that the booze so generously gave. Yet the glow of the alcohol was still upon him while he fumbled through the top drawer of the dresser.

He found what he was looking for. A slip of notepaper from state police headquarters.

Upon it, in his own handwriting, was the name and address of a woman he had asked about within his department.

Dr. Julie Steinberg. A clinical psychologist specializing in wacko cop cases.

Dr. Julie. That's what some other cops called her. Professional trust combined with informality. She had a telephone number and an address in Nashua. Some members of O'Hara's department had felt the need for counseling or treatment of depression. She had been helpful to many of them.

O'Hara had inquired about her name and number. A week earlier, a friend had given both to him.

These nights couldn't go on like this, O'Hara knew. Nor could his drinking. It was one vicious circle: He needed the booze to soothe his bankrupt nerves. But eventually there was a rebound effect, where the booze would only soothe his nerves until it started to rattle them by itself. At those times, the last thing he needed was another drink, which was exactly what he wanted.

There had even been some D.T.'s in his career battle with the bottle. Once, following a long undercover stint not long after his wife had left him, he had attempted to drink himself to sleep. Instead of bringing sleep, drunkenness played upon him. As he lay on his bed, he envisioned a large red crab at his feet. The crab crawled up his body, across his bare chest and down his throat as O'Hara screamed for help. No help came. He found himself at the foot of the steps the next morning, bruised and bleeding from a fall, his head pounding as if someone had slammed a car door on it.

If things continued like this, there would be a tragedy on some future night. The formula was already in place: the gun, the alcohol, and the unseen fears. Frank O'Hara was on the path to getting himself in some deep trouble.

Either that or killed. By suicide. By accident. Or by some self-destructive combination of the two.

He put the note upon his wallet. The time had come to call Dr. Steinberg. The next morning, he told himself.

Or at least sometime this week.

He had to have help. Soon. Before the red crab returned. Before he started seeing other things that he knew weren't there.

Meanwhile the night surrounded him. He leaned against the windowsill again. He gazed out at the darkness of the summer night which lay before him like an ancient debt. It was accumulating interest all the time, and, in the end, he suspected it would be hell to pay.

He turned the music off and crawled back into bed. For several seconds, he lay very still, again listening to the silence. As he closed his eyes and felt himself drift back to sleep, a strange notion was upon him.

The smell he had noticed downstairs. The strange acrid scent that he had picked up near the quaking rocking chair. The scent was similar to that of burning flesh. Like a body burned during warfare. Or like an execution.

It was a bizarre notion, he told himself, that he thought he could smell such a thing in his home. Absolutely crazy, with no rational explanation for it whatsoever.

Chapter 2

From the very start, Adam Kaminski sensed something unnatural about Carolyn Hart.

Not that he hadn't seen some strange customers in his time. As a rental agent for several family-owned buildings in Philadelphia, Kaminski had developed an extra sense, a special inner voice that told him when a prospective tenant was a bit "off."

Not that he hadn't acquired this skill through several disastrous experiences.

There had been Mrs. Bernice Ryan, for example, who had rented an apartment on the 800 block of Spruce Street with a "husband" and two children. She had signed a lease, initialed the "No Pets" clause, and paid her security deposit plus the first month's rent. Yet by Christmas her children were gone, so was her husband, and she had come into possession of thirteen cats.

The stench from the kitties was fierce. The tenant across the hall moved out, and eviction proceedings dragged on for fifteen months. Then when Kaminski dug a little deeper, he discovered that Mrs. Ryan had a history of nickel-and-dime litigation—and a talent at it as well. The pussycats, she argued in court, were her "only family." Kaminski finally managed to evict, but she picketed his office for another six months.

And there had also been the Strauss kid, who must have been about twenty-five—approximately Adam Kaminski's age—when he first rented from Adam's family.

Larry Strauss had rented three rooms on the ground floor of a walk-up on Lombard Street, not far from St. Peter's Church. The premises had a front and back entrance. There were also several ground-floor windows.

"I'm jittery about fires," Strauss had explained. "A lot of exits mean a lot of ways to get out. Know what I mean, man?"

"Uh huh," Kaminski answered.

"People get careless, you know," added Strauss.

"Uh huh," Kaminski said again.

Getting out in a hurry obviously had its appeal, but not due to fires. Strauss moved a bed into the living room and even had a dresser—sort of, it was concocted out of mismatched plastic milk crates—in the front hall. The rest of the apartment had been taken up by the warehousing of electronic gadgets, jewelry, and expensive leather coats. Larry's inventory was without any receipts and mostly—the Philadelphia police said when they came to visit one day, equipped with a warrant—removed without paying from some of the finest stores in the city.

Larry Strauss, before he jumped bail in August 1992, called this the storage of personal effects. The D.A. called it a fencing operation. Kaminski called it another costly headache.

And then there was Paula Burns. Of a bad lot, she was Adam's favorite. First, she didn't cost him anything. And second, she fulfilled an emotional need.

Kaminski fancied that he would someday rent to just the "Right Woman," some primal fox with an insatiable libido with whom he could fall in love.

Within several minutes of meeting Paula Burns, he fantasized that Paula was her.

Ah, Paula Burns.

She gave as her employer an accounting firm on Walnut Street. She was fashionably thin, stood about five feet six on a great pair of wheels, and had red curls down her forehead. She usually wore purple lipstick, jeans, and plain blouses. The latter were usually opened to the third button where they revealed the freckles that dotted the tops of her breasts. She did not look, Kaminski told himself, anything like a cruncher of numbers. She looked like a cruncher of men. Adam was anxious to be crunched.

Paula rented a single-unit house, a small brick edifice at 565 South Oswell Street. This particular block of Oswell was a narrow tree-lined lane that intersected with Lombard about two hundred yards west of Broad Street. It was barely navigable by car and hadn't changed much in the last seventy-five years.

"The house is a 'trinity,' " Kaminski explained the day he first showed it to Paula. "Three floors, one large room to each floor. Some people find that very cozy."

"I'm sure I will, too," Paula answered. She signed the lease the same day.

When Paula moved in, she brought with her an assortment of white wicker furniture, large, leafy plants, and a bed big enough for three. She painted the walls of her bedroom a sensuous shade of fuchscia and kept to herself.

Kaminski was thin, bespectacled and balding. He was also a snoop, even after a tenant had moved in. But he was particularly nosy when it came to Paula. She was, after all, the woman of a lifetime.

He put her under a crude sort of surveillance. At first, he just kept an eye on her, keeping track of her comings and goings, occasionally allowing himself to imagine the things they would do together after she admitted that they were in love.

He came around twice in her first month to see if he could perform any carpentry for her. She said no. He learned her hours and managed to be on the sidewalk a half-dozen times when she came and went from the building. She exchanged a pleasant but brief greeting each time, which he took as encouragement, though she never stopped to talk. He learned where she parked her car and made passes at her garage on the off-chance of an encounter.

Then, a few weeks into her tenancy, Kaminski noticed that Paula was not going to "work" until evening. He phoned the employment number that she had placed on her rental application and learned that she had never worked there. So Kaminski reckoned he was more than justified in nosing around a little more.

From a distance of two blocks, he followed Paula one evening. She reported to Benny's Sahara Spa, a concrete-and-neon mob joint with a desert harem motif located on one of the shadier strips of Delaware Avenue. Paying his way inside, Kaminski discovered that Paula's real line of employment was that of a hostess—clad only between the thighs and the navel, and even there not very much. Not that Paula's actual employment wasn't more lucrative than squeezing the blood out of bottom lines at the accounting house. And not that Paula didn't pay her rent on time. She paid quarterly and in advance.

But from Adam's sudden change in attitude, Paula knew he had discovered her true vocation and had most likely caught her act. So henceforth, when they passed on the street, Paula would give him a con-spiratorial wink. Just one wink. One enticing flutter of a mascaraed lash. It turned Kaminski into soft butter and kept him firmly in her camp. A gesture like that from Paula was enough to speed any normal man toward a cold shower.

But inevitably there were police again, this time an investigation from out of state. It stemmed from the sudden demise of a man in Baltimore who went by the name of Antonio Blue.

Blue was either Paula's former boyfriend, ex-husband, current legal husband, or one-time pimp, depending on how those terms were defined. Or maybe Mr. Blue was a modern version of all these things. No one knew exactly, and by the time the story reached Kaminski, Blue wasn't anything anymore. One night as Blue sat in his Buick 225—the automobile was a striking deep blue, naturally—an unknown female who matched Paula's size, shape, and hair color, walked up to his car and popped a bullet in the left side of his head, just above the ear.

This was a case which the local cops could clearly mark as "Civic Improvement." But nonetheless they investigated. Paula hadn't been dancing at Benny's that night, and the "Crabcake City" cops wanted to ask her a few questions about the shooting.

Paula, however, didn't wish to answer. In fact, she was so anxious not to answer that she disappeared, leaving behind her possessions, that high-paying, high-octane job, and Adam Kaminski with a broken heart.

To the young landlord, the emotional strain was nothing new. Women had trampled his feelings before. And he knew they would again until that Right Woman came along.

But from a business angle, the Paula Burns affair was another case altogether. Fully paid tenants didn't usually leave everything behind. The Baltimore cops pushed a business card into his hands and asked if he would call if he heard from her. He promised he would. And he knew he was lying.

Two weeks later he received a letter attached to an American Express money order for the final three months' rent on Paula's lease. She said she wouldn't be returning to Philadelphia. She had gone to stay with her sick mother in Montana and her stuff—the plants, the white wicker, and the big plush bed *à trois*—could be donated to the Salvation Army. Montana or not, the letter was postmarked Miami. Kaminski sighed. He pictured the woman he loved on South Beach, wearing only slightly more than she wore at Benny's, and his spirits sagged a little more. He cashed the check and said nothing to the police. Although he cried inside that his lady love had vanished from his life, who was he not to do her a final favor?

Later that month he put the house on Oswell Street up for rent. Paula's furniture remained. Real estate rented faster with furniture in it. All of which brought Adam Kaminski to Carolyn Hart. And vice versa.

By the time Carolyn appeared in Philadelphia in August 1993, Kaminski was certain that he knew which tenants were trouble and which ones were okay. Particularly women.

Which further brought him to Carolyn Hart. There was something wrong with her. Something not quite right.

Carolyn Hart had replied to an ad in the newspaper. She was specifically interested in the house on Oswell Street. It was a Thursday afternoon, Kaminski would always remember, and she met him on the corner half a block away.

The first thing Kaminski noticed was that initially she wasn't there, then a moment later she was. The second thing he noticed was how pretty she was. Here, he immediately started to think, was a woman who would help him forget Paula Burns.

They walked together to the house that Paula had

evacuated. Adam carried under his arm a sturdy leather portfolio bearing pens, leases, and notepads.

Carolyn was thin and tall. Her skin was astonishingly pale and very pretty, as if she had been confined indoors for an unconscionably long time, or as if she disdained being in the sun. To Adam Kaminski—a well-read, literate sort of swine—she looked like one of those delicate beauties he associated with F. Scott Fitzgerald, the ones who sat around the Plaza Hotel in New York in the 1920s.

But she wasn't one of those. She was flesh and blood, and belonged to the modern world. Or so she gave every indication as they arrived before the house at number 565.

"From the outside, it's very charming," Carolyn said. "How old would it be?"

"About a hundred years," Kaminski answered.

She lowered her eyes, looked back to him and gave him a beguiling smile. "Well?" she pressed gently, covering an awkward moment. "May I see the inside?"

"Of course," he said. He fished a key from his pocket. The front door opened with a creak.

The house was stuffy from disuse. And Paula's furniture didn't show it to its best advantage. But Kaminski had been watering her plants, and the property did have a certain charm.

The first floor was a large single room with a kitchen at the rear and a half bathroom near a staircase. There was also a tiny but cozy garden in the back.

"You new in Philadelphia?" Kaminski asked. They stood in a spot on the first floor that could have been occupied by a small dining table.

"Sort of," she said. "I was here once before."

"*Here? In this house?*"

"No, no. In Philadelphia."

"Really? School? University?"

"I was a little girl," she said. "Don't remember that

much of it. Just passed through. With my parents. I was a Navy brat."

"A Navy 'kid,' " he offered, gently correcting her. "I'm sure you were never a brat."

Carolyn smiled softly. "If you say so," she said.

She stood in the kitchen and gazed out the rear window toward the small garden. The window was large, and sunlight was upon her. Then a cloud must have obscured the sun because shade came across both her and the garden.

Kaminski guessed that she was in her late twenties, but he had been wrong about women's ages before. So she could have been anywhere from twenty-five to thirty-five. Perfect age for him, he mused further. But a tinge of sadness gripped him as he realized that she very well might have a boyfriend.

"Can we go upstairs?" Carolyn finally asked, turning back to him.

"Of course."

Kaminski led the way. He was starting to like her, attached or not.

The second floor was bright and airy. Two of Paula Burns's leafy-palmed plants stood sentry amidst the departed's furniture.

There were two large windows on the front of the room overlooking Oswell Street, and a window of odd proportions and construction, sort of a half-bay effect, overlooking the rear garden. The room was about twelve by fifteen, but gave the impression of being more spacious than its measurements.

"Perfect for reading or relaxing," Kaminski offered. "Or maybe for your television."

Carolyn nodded. She said she didn't own a television, which Kaminski took to be evidence of stellar character.

"You would like living here," Kaminski then volunteered. "The neighbors are very nice. A retired couple on one side. A young family on the other. I can introduce you."

"I keep to myself," Carolyn said.

"That's fine, too. But it's nice to know you have good people around you," Kaminski said. "Never any problems. The block is a very good one. It's a safe area if you're alone."

"Let's look at the top floor," she said.

"Of course."

The second floor was the one with the full bathroom, but the third floor, Carolyn said after Kaminski had led her all the way up, would be her bedroom.

Kaminski stood to one side as Carolyn examined the closets. Kaminski waited patiently, watching her, keeping his thoughts to himself as she poked into the corners of what he hoped would be her bedroom.

Then she turned and gave him a smile. "I like it," she said. "How much are you asking?"

"Seven hundred fifty a month," he said. His voice was firm. But he was ready to bargain.

She surprised him. "Seems like a fair price," she said.

"And you would be . . . ?"

"Living alone?" she asked. "Yes."

"So you're single?"

"No husband, no boyfriend, no roommate. I travel light."

Kaminski nodded. "I guess you do."

"Whose furnishings are these?" she asked.

"The last tenant left them behind," Kaminski said. "I'll have them removed as soon as—"

"Actually," Carolyn interrupted, "I could use them. If you don't *have* to give them away."

"I own the building," Kaminski said in his most accommodating voice. "I don't *have* to do anything."

"Can we go downstairs? I'd like to see the garden."

He let her descend first.

In the garden she said she was entranced by the house. It had a certain hominess ready to emerge, she said. Kaminski bowed very slightly at her comments.

"What do I have to do to be a tenant?" she asked next.

"Same as everyone else," he said. "You fill out an application form."

"An application form?" She made a face.

"Standard procedure."

"Can I see a copy?"

Kaminski opened his leather portfolio and handed her the dreaded sheet of paper. The usual questions probing the details of her life. Name. Date of birth. Social Security number. Job. Personal references.

When she took it in her hand, Kaminski felt a wave of contradictory vibrations. There were some that he liked, but he also noticed something that he recognized as a danger signal. There was something "off" about her which made him wonder why she was passing through Philadelphia in the first place.

But all of this was nuts, he told himself. She was a prospective tenant like any other.

"We insist on the application," Kaminski explained. "The references. Previous landlords." He thought of his parents back in the rental office. They would howl if he veered from the norm.

Carolyn made an uncomfortable expression and said nothing.

"Look," Kaminski said, "if there's been a problem, we try to be understanding."

"That's good."

"You been in some sort of trouble?" he asked.

"You could say that."

"With the law?"

"No. Not with the law."

He looked for something positive. "Current employment?"

"What about it?"

"Do you have a job?"

"I'm looking." Then she added, as if to serve as her own advocate, "I'm trying real hard. Trouble is—"

"You need an address."

"A good address," she corrected.

He glanced again at the application. "Can you tell me where you've been for the last few years?" Kaminski asked.

"No one single place. I've been moving around."

"From where to where?"

"A whole bunch of places," she said. Again the smile. Again the charm.

"Personal references?" he asked.

"I can give you some. But they'd be friends who haven't seen me for several years."

"What did you do?" Kaminski blurted out. "Vanish from the face of the Earth?"

"Sort of," she laughed.

"Why did you do that?"

"I just did."

Kaminski let this sink in. Why, he wondered, did she have to put him on the spot?

"I guess that might be okay in terms of references," he said. "It's a little unusual. But if they check out. . . ."

"The references will check out." She paused and sighed. "I just. . . . Well, I don't want anyone to know where I am."

He blinked. "May I ask why not?"

"You may ask, but. . . ."

Her voice trailed off. She grinned and hunched her shoulders as if she couldn't explain, even if she had wanted to.

"Well, what about those last couple of years?"

"What about them?"

"Where did you work? Where have you been?"

She gave him another plaintive gesture.

"You can't tell me at all?" he pressed.

"I'd only be lying."

"Then tell me the truth."

"You wouldn't believe the truth."

"Test me."

"Sorry." She shook her head.

He shifted uncomfortably and lowered his eyes. Then he raised his eyes again when a nasty thought was upon him.

"You haven't been in jail, have you?" he asked.

"No. Never jail."

"Under arrest?"

"No."

"Declared bankruptcy?"

She shook her head.

"Well," he said, trying hard. "I can't think of anything much worse than jail or bankruptcy."

"Thank you," she said.

A kept woman, Kaminski thought next. Some wealthy old goat had her as his mistress. By God, *that's* what she was! But there was an air of innocence, even purity, to Carolyn Hart that made him dismiss this last notion as quickly as he had seized it.

"Look, I can pay the rent," Carolyn explained. "I hate to say, 'Just trust me.' But that's what I have to say."

Kaminski scratched his head and shuffled his feet. "You're asking me to extend an awful lot on instinct," he said.

"You just said you were very good at that," she said. "I'll stand by your judgment. If you don't want to do this, I'll disappear and you won't see me again."

"You don't have to disappear."

"Well, then . . . ?"

Kaminski seemed to be trapped. She nudged him forward.

"I'll take good care of your house," she said. "You'll never know I was even in it. And I'll be forever grateful."

Kaminski sighed. Here was something new: Someone who was almost begging to be rejected. But other instincts kicked into gear. It was always the applicants who seemed really straight, he reminded himself, who turned into trouble. Like that bitch Mrs. Ryan. And that pricky Strauss kid. And, of course, here was also another female to fall in love with. Someone to replace Paula. Someone who just might be the Right Woman. So. . . .

Kaminski sighed. "I shouldn't do this. But what's life without taking a few chances?" he concluded philosophically.

They sat down together on the back step of the house. He read through the lease with her. A standard one-year agreement.

Kaminski signed for the landlord. Carolyn etched her signature on the appropriate space. She smiled. Her eyes danced.

Adam would remember the moment. Once both signatures were affixed to the document, Carolyn leaned forward gently and kissed him on the cheek. Her touch was very soft, almost like a gust of wind rushing past. He was surprised. And smitten.

The next day, Carolyn stopped by Kaminski's office. She paid her deposit and first month's rent. Kaminski gave her a key and said she could move in. She admitted that she didn't have much.

"I travel light," she said. "Remember?"

"I remember." He paused. "Well, you must at least have a few suitcases or something."

She smiled sweetly and shook her head. "Just a few small things," she answered.

"Carolyn, sometimes you make me nervous."

"There's nothing for you to worry about," she said.

Whenever he received such reassurance was when Adam Kaminski *did* start to worry. But she was so pretty, and he felt that he was off to a good start with her. So later the same day Kaminski smuggled the paperwork—including the unchecked references— past his parents.

Two afternoons later, he walked by 565 South Oswell Street to deliver an executed copy of the lease personally to Carolyn. It was a perfect excuse to come calling.

But she wasn't there, and none of the neighbors recalled seeing her. Kaminski, disappointed, slipped the lease through the mail slot and went on his way.

He remembered later on thinking as he was leaving, that Carolyn Hart was sometimes so ephemeral and fleeting that it was as if she wasn't even there at all.

But of course she *was* there, he told himself. Or she had been. She had left money in his office, and she had signed the lease. He wasn't imagining her. He had *seen* her twice.

He cheered himself. It was absolutely inevitable that their paths would cross again. After all, he had her signature and her personal check. Best of all, she was now his tenant.

And so when he thought about it, Adam Kaminski felt pretty good. There was a lot to love about Carolyn Hart and, the more he thought about it, the more he felt that he was just the type of down-to-earth, stable guy who might appeal to her vagabond spirit.

Chapter 3

Like much in the stark, frozen New Hampshire countryside, the details of Detective Frank O'Hara's life lay beneath the surface, carefully concealed from the world.

Today in Nashua, in the dying hours of an afternoon in late November, even the physical details of O'Hara were hidden, cloaked first by a heavy early season snowfall and then by the clumsy garments of savage New England winters. As O'Hara walked from the state police headquarters to the department's rear parking lot, he wore his own version of civilian attire: a floppy leather fedora, a parka, jeans, work boots, and a pair of leather gloves.

Had anyone been able to discern the actual appearance of O'Hara, they would have seen a rugged, well muscled man in his late forties, amazingly sturdy and agile for his journey into middle age. He had a handsome but craggy face and a shaggy brown-blond mustache that matched the hair on his head. Had anyone probed the spirit beneath the exterior, the examiner would have found something every bit as rugged—and perhaps with as many scars—as the surrounding landscape.

O'Hara paused and did what he frequently did at

this time of the year. He looked angrily at the sky. All that was above him was white with snow.

"This is the last time I will ever experience this," O'Hara told himself. He grimaced as the year's first snow settled upon the hood of his car, the brim of his hat, and the tip of his nose. "And for that, thank God."

The snow, of which he had seen countless tons over nearly twenty years, might have conveyed a benign appearance to the rest of the world, a fitting motif for a cozy New England winter landscape. It was immortalized on postcards, tourist brochures, and maple syrup bottles.

Sure. Kids played in the snow. The Labradors and golden retrievers of his neighborhood in Hancock ran through it, tucked their noses in it and tossed it aloft, spinning it sometimes almost like cotton candy or wet confetti. Tourists skied on it, and more than a few of O'Hara's friends made money plowing it.

Ah, snow. O'Hara hated it.

Snow—particularly heavy snow like this, that fell early in the season—had become a harbinger of glacial winters to come, of ice and sleet storms, of freezing winds, cars skidding into ditches, stray livestock turned into rigid corpses, and pipes busted and hemorrhaging water in basements. And every winter, some poor senior citizen was found frozen in a cabin or a house heated only by a fireplace that had long since died down.

Snow was white death to O'Hara. He had come to associate it with his own resolute march toward the grave. Snow depressed him endlessly. Both his parents had passed away in January. His marriage had ended in February. The two close friends on the police force who had died in the line of duty had been killed in winter, one in February, the other five days before Christmas.

O'Hara pulled his parka closer to him and hurried to a battered old Pontiac with oversized tires and a heart the size of a mountain. "My dinosaur of the highways," he called this clunky old monster. "The thing is, it never stops working," he confided to friends.

He stepped into the Pontiac, fumbled for the key, and found the ignition. His breath appeared in misty intermittent cones before him. The temperature was somewhere in the twenties, with a windchill in the teens. Inside the car, it was every bit as hot.

O'Hara turned the car key. The engine growled stubbornly, like a bear disturbed during midwinter hibernation. The battery, engine, and electrical system were no more enamored of the cold than O'Hara. But after a moment, the dependable old wreck—124,000 miles since he had first purchased it in 1978, but still clanking along—turned over with a snarl. O'Hara gunned the accelerator, then stepped out, leaving the motor running.

O'Hara knocked the accumulated whiteness off his windshield. With a brush and scraper he freed the side and rear windows from snow and ice. Then he slid back into the car.

As he waited a final minute for the engine to warm, he punched the dial of the car radio. No Sinatra anywhere. And surely no Louis Armstrong or Duke Ellington in these godforsaken sticks. So by default, he found a rock station in Boston. Here he was—well within shouting distance of his fiftieth birthday—and he still occasionally listened to the music of his youth, the music of social revolution. It would have to do when Mr. Sinatra was unavailable.

Well, nothing too revolutionary about the golden oldie the DJ in Boston was playing. The station played The Beach Boys. "Good Vibrations." Like hell, good

vibrations on such a day. O'Hara caught the nasty
irony and smiled with it.

It was just such little details of life that O'Hara
focused upon, the cruel little twists and ironies. He
shifted the vehicle into gear. The car obediently surged
forward.

He watched the special "arctic" wipers methodically
throw the snow from his windshield. Already this
looked like a blizzard. He was certain that he would
quickly be called back to work, probably by six in the
evening, for emergency duty.

O'Hara pulled onto Route 3 which snaked out of
Nashua. And suddenly—because he made an effort to
put it out of his mind—the snow didn't bother him
quite as much. It didn't bother him because a wave of
satisfaction came over him.

Today was November 20. His retirement papers had
been processed that morning, sixty days ahead of his
retirement date, just as the state police handbook dic-
tated. He had put in nineteen and three quarters years
on the state police department, the last fourteen years
as a plainclothes detective. Now he was in a position
to walk away as a free, healthy man.

What the hell? Let it snow. He would claim victory
even over the elements of the vicious New Hampshire
winters. He had survived nineteen of them and saw no
reason why he couldn't scratch and claw his way
through a twentieth.

Back in August when those vibrant nightmares
scorched every night, he had finally gone to Dr. Julie
Steinberg, the department shrink. He had come away
with a clearer understanding of himself, an understanding that led him to tender his retirement from the
state police. Now he was at ease with that decision.

He would sell his house and move south while still
relatively young. A man like him, honest, strong, with
excellent law enforcement credentials, would have no

trouble finding a slot as a security specialist of some sort. Not in this crazy world where nothing was secure any more. Snow or no snow, life could have been much worse.

Traffic crept on the snowy highway that led out of the city. The salt and sand trucks were nonexistent. But O'Hara had learned that his best move was to go home, have dinner, perhaps grab a nap, and wait for the inevitable ring of the telephone. Once he was called back to work, he might do twenty hours straight. Thank God it would be reflected in his paycheck.

He arrived at Cooper Road in the town of Hancock, a dead end of middle class houses, some very old, a few very new. This was the street upon which he lived. To either side were homes of younger families, some busy, some with dogs running through the snow, others with children at play on the lawn. Two to three cars, some of them inoperable, jammed each driveway.

From long habit, O'Hara passed these cars in review, checking to make sure all were familiar, and that all had local plates, the numbers of which he had committed to memory. Partly he did this to keep his instincts sharp. But equally, he did this as a policeman's extra level of caution, the same motivation that compelled O'Hara to arrange his living room in a way in which he could sit in a comfortable chair, watch television, sip a drink, and keep an eye on the approach to the house, so that he could see anyone arriving before he, himself, could be seen.

He edged his car as close to his mailbox as possible and picked up the day's bills. Then he turned the Pontiac into his driveway. From a remote unit in his car, he raised his garage door and parked.

He was proceeding as he ordinarily might on such a day when his gaze fell—and froze—upon a pair of boots just outside his kitchen door.

The boots were leather and dry. Yet there was a

puddle of water, meaning melted snow, beneath them. So it passed through his mind that the boots must have arrived since the snow began—more than an hour ago—and that whoever owned the boots hadn't arrived by car because there was none unaccounted for outside. Or at least, there was no car that had remained.

And after his first flash of anxiety had subsided, O'Hara knew that the owner of the boots must have been a man in a similar line of work, one who knew him and his signature pretty well, in order to enter his home.

He also sensed that the intruder was not malevolent. At least not this time. Besides, he thought he had identified the footwear.

Yet a man could never be too sure. For good measure, O'Hara's hand drifted beneath his parka and found the reassuring presence of his automatic pistol. O'Hara kept his hand there as he stepped from the garage into the kitchen.

He thought he heard a radio playing very softly somewhere. And, as he quietly stepped through his kitchen, he could see that a light was on in the living room.

O'Hara continued forward and, with a toe, pushed open the living-room door. The door moved silently.

"Frank?" called an amiable male voice from the living room. "That you?"

"Philip?" O'Hara asked.

O'Hara's hand moved away from his weapon.

Through the light from the front window, past the dormant piano, the form of a large man took shape. The man was standing in the living room near O'-Hara's past-its-prime sound system. Standing, and picking critically through O'Hara's collection of CDs and cassette recordings. O'Hara's musical acquisitions, which ran largely from early Sinatra (Columbia label, big bands) to late Sinatra (Reprise label, 1960s and after), with much middle Sinatra (the best stuff, the Capitol years) in between, did not meet the visitor's approval. Then again, "The Man and His Music," while close to sainthood in O'Hara's pantheon, met the approval of virtually no one whom O'Hara knew personally. Another clear sign to O'Hara that he was a pilgrim among philistines.

"Still listening to all this Mafia music?" the visitor said.

"You don't know class when you see it. Or hear it," O'Hara answered.

"If that dissipated old dago had done a cover of 'Incense, Peppermints,' I do believe you would have bought that, too."

"Yeah," O'Hara answered, "and the song wouldn't have sounded like crap anymore. It would have sounded great with Frank's pipes applied to it. Now leave my 'Old Blue Eyes' collection alone and tell me why I have the pleasure of your company."

As it turned out, the electronic sound came from the television, not a radio, not a CD player.

"I took the liberty of letting myself in," said Philip Reynolds, a friend, a neighbor, and also the assistant chief of police of the local five-man town squad. O'Hara had worked with Reynolds frequently. The local cops and the Staties often washed each other's hand when it came to special assignments. Reynolds and O'Hara had covered each other's back from time to time. O'Hara had once lent his friend a key to the house, which must have been how he had let himself in now.

"So I see," said O'Hara, who now understood why there had been no advance warning of the intrusion. Reynolds lived two houses away. He had walked, and the snow had fallen so resolutely that his bootprints had already been obliterated.

"Well, it's snowing like hell, man. I wasn't about to pitch camp on your doorstep."

"But I'm not sure I know why you've come calling at all, Philip," O'Hara said. "Am I missing something?"

"You're not going to miss anything. Particularly in a snowstorm."

"What does that mean?" O'Hara asked, starting to remove his outer clothing.

"It means that you're the state's numero uno homicide detective. So I'd leave on the hat and parka if I were you," Reynolds answered.

"Oh, Christ Almighty," O'Hara cursed. "The maniacs of this state can't even control themselves in a blizzard?"

"Guess not. And we've got about an hour to drive, and I don't know if the heat is working in my four-wheel."

"An hour to where?"

"Let's just say Captain Mallinson wants to see you."

"Mallinson? *Now?*"

"Frank, would I be here today if 'the Cap' had meant tomorrow morning?"

"What's going on?"

"Does the name Gary Ledbetter bring back any memories?"

A sinking, uneasy pause. The key name in the state's most celebrated murder case of the last fifty years tended to stay with those who had been intimately involved, as O'Hara had.

"Of course it does," O'Hara answered.

"Thought it might."

"So? What of it? Ledbetter went to the electric chair in Florida last summer."

"That's all I'm allowed to tell you," Reynolds said. "And you're to come right away. Hope you don't mind a little spin toward Mount Monadnock. Mallinson wants you to see a crime scene before the press gets wind of it."

"Even in this weather?"

"I told you: Captain's orders."

Quietly, O'Hara cursed again.

It had been a day just like this one, O'Hara found himself thinking next, a day when there had been a heavy snowfall. How long ago had it been? Five years? Six? Time tended to blur past the initial impact of a case. And further, this was not O'Hara's moment for understanding the murkier points of time.

And then he found himself thinking, My God, yes. Fifteen minutes earlier he had been taking refuge in the fact that a lifetime of police work was coming peaceably to a close. And now he was thinking that, yes again, with the advent of the snow anything horrible was possible.

Absolutely anything horrible.

Just past five o'clock, dressed in a fresh and heavier parka, a gift five years earlier from a woman who was no longer his wife, Frank O'Hara was sitting angrily in the drafty cabin of Reynolds's red Ford pickup. And they were bombing along a two-lane rural route at a speed that tempted fate every second.

Actually, there was no speed that actually was safe in such conditions, but Reynolds gravitated toward particularly perilous ones. He owned a concrete foot which, when combined with a truck on a snowy day, made the experience of climbing a mountain road more akin to the experience of flying low through fog in a small aircraft. It was not a question of *if* they would hit something; it was a matter of *when*.

O'Hara glanced at his driver. Reynolds wasn't even wearing a seat belt. So much for the billboards across the state picturing an almighty Aryan-looking state trooper and bearing the words, "Seat Belts Save Lives—We Use 'em."

The road was already covered with five inches of snow and, with the new state austerity—meaning the precipice of bankruptcy—it had no chance of seeing salt, ash, or sand for another day. By then there would be a killer sheet of ice under the white stuff.

They were travelling east, navigating a road that led into the mountains. The cold was so irresistible that it penetrated the cabin of the truck, and the vehicle's heating system, much as Reynolds had warned, was a free spirit unto itself. One moment it worked, the next moment it didn't, and the moment after that it came back with a vengeance and threatened to blow them out of the car. Then it would fail again, only to repeat the cycle.

"You really should get that thing fixed," O'Hara said, indicating the heater. It moaned during the intervals when it worked.

"Got to replace the whole blower motor on the truck," Reynolds answered. "I'd be looking at six hundred dollars, easy."

"Funerals are two thousand bucks," O'Hara said sourly. "And that's with imitation pine."

Reynolds only grinned. He was a man in his late twenties who had not yet grasped the concept of his own potential mortality.

"What I'm trying to tell you," O'Hara tried tactfully, "is that you're driving like an asshole."

"Yeah. I know. That's how I like to drive."

"Fuck it," O'Hara grumbled. Then his spirits sagged a little further as daylight completely disappeared. Now they were at the mercy of the headlights on Reynolds's truck. And the snow was pouring forth so relentlessly that it seemed like a shroud coming down from a malevolent Heaven to obliterate everything living.

They drove on a road that was pristine with the damned stuff, with the snow howling out of the sky and against them. The truck's windshield seemed midway between some movie screen or a kaleidoscope. And Reynolds was a terrible driver, taking turns too quickly, hitting the brake and accelerator too often. For the preservation of his life and his truck, he relied on the bulky chains on his tires. The chains clanked rhythmically and loudly and somehow—idly, as O'Hara stared past the falling snow into the white countryside—O'Hara thought of old ghost stories with clanking chains being dragged through attics. Yet somehow—fate? the chains? good luck?—the pickup stayed on the road.

The truck began to climb a low mountain. They were on a winding road with no guardrails, just a deep ditch on each side. O'Hara consoled himself with the notion that Reynolds's truck had a two-way police radio, so as soon as they were in the ditch they could call for help. This notion reassured O'Hara until Reynolds informed him that only the receiving end of the setup was working. But Reynolds had made a note to have the phone fixed before the first big storm of the year.

"This *is* the first big storm, you dickhead," O'Hara said.

"So I didn't get it done," Reynolds said with a shrug. "It's expensive." The shrug caused Reynolds's hands to leave the wheel for a moment. The car lost its direction momentarily and gave a quiver in the direction of a row of sturdy snowy pines.

O'Hara lunged for the wheel, but Reynolds's hand was there first, correcting the tires.

"We don't have a radio? Is that what you're telling me?" O'Hara asked.

"Cops worked these woods for a hundred and fifty years without radios," Reynolds answered.

"This isn't eighteen eighty," O'Hara said.

"Might just as well be. No radio. Plus when we get where we're going there'll be plenty of radios."

"*If* we get there," O'Hara grumbled.

"What a fucking grouch you're turning into."

"Yeah. Tell me about it."

"I wish to hell you'd just go out and get laid for a change. It would make life more pleasant for all of us."

O'Hara controlled his temper, then suffered silently for a moment. Eventually, he calmed a little.

"I just spent three months seeing the department psychologist," O'Hara said. "Dr. Julie Steinberg. Nice woman. Pretty, smart, thirty-something years old. I should be married to someone like that. Saw her for tension, nightmares, and an urge to start hitting the Jack Daniel's at two each afternoon."

"Yeah. Okay. I know you were going to a shrink, and I know you got your head all straightened out now." Reynolds paused as the tires danced on a curve in the road. "So?"

"So she got me past all that. And you're now undoing it all in one drive through the white fucking countryside."

Reynolds managed a grin. "Frank, this drive ain't nothing compared to what's waiting halfway up this mountain."

O'Hara turned to ask more, but somehow thought better of it. So his eyes found the road again, and he fell silent.

The path grew steeper as they climbed the mountain, and the snow gave no indication of relenting. The yellow headlights from the truck cut a swath through the storm and, incredibly, as they turned into one narrow area, a logging truck with a full load careened recklessly toward them, encroaching on their lane.

O'Hara closed his eyes, waited and braced. He opened his eyes a moment later and was surprised to find himself still alive and intact. Noisily, the truck rumbled past.

O'Hara opened his eyes. Reynolds was looking at him, grinning like a gargoyle.

"Jesus, you're a pile of nerves," Reynolds said.

"Just drive," O'Hara answered. A mild profanity formed a further punctuation mark at the end of his sentence.

From the side window, O'Hara studied the snowfall in the woods beside the road. There was an optical illusion sometimes present during winter storms. By staring long enough into the snow and shadows among the trees, one could often see figures moving.

Human figures in the forests.

"Snow ghosts," the Monadnock Indians used to call them. The spirits of the deceased returned to Earth along with the downfall from the heavens, according to native legend. The spirits remained among the living until the snow melted, which in New Hampshire meant all winter.

If O'Hara looked for the snow ghosts, and unchained his better judgment, he could find them: the dark human figures ducking out from behind one tree and darting to the next. But of course it was nothing more than an illusion, the product of an overactive imagination and a willingness to believe. The D.T.'s without even the thrill of the alcohol.

O'Hara watched them silently for several minutes and was amazed, as he let his imagination go, at how real they looked. He understood how, following the legend, Monadnock warriors had taken these illusions to be enemies stalking them. Sometimes the warriors had pursued the illusions far into the wooded mountains during blizzards, only to be found frozen to death days later.

O'Hara shuddered and returned his attention to within the truck. The heater failed again, this time for a quarter hour.

Yet, after an additional twenty minutes, half frozen, O'Hara and Reynolds arrived at their destination. The latter was a two-room cabin in the middle of nowhere, an unheated wooden structure that was used by campers in the summer. Usually in the winter it was untouched by human hands.

Today it was touched by several human hands. It was ringed by a pair of police cars, plus a jeep which belonged to a local auxiliary. The jeep had oversized tires and a red beacon flashing on its roof.

O'Hara stepped out of the car, felt his foot slide through the fresh snow, then felt his other foot follow. He had been tramping through this white stuff for two decades; yet today he felt as if he were stepping onto the surface of the moon, and the crap underfoot was just about to give way.

O'Hara faced the cabin. A familiar figure hulked into the doorway.

"Talk to me," the figure growled. His usual greeting.

"Hello, Captain," O'Hara said.

"What the fuck took you so long?" answered Captain William Mallinson, head of the homicide division of the New Hampshire State Police.

"There was a little matter of seven inches of snow," O'Hara answered. "I know you didn't notice, but—"

"You're right. I don't see no frigging snow," Captain Mallinson answered. He puffed something that was small, brown, smelled bad, and gave off smoke, indicating that it was on fire. It was some subspecies of tobacco, halfway between a cigar and a cigarette.

When Mallinson wasn't puffing it, he held the stinking, burning, brown object in a gloved hand.

Captain Mallinson was a big, irritable, belligerent, militantly disagreeable man with a ruddy, porky face. His shoulders were slumped, and in his thick winter parka—with two silver captain's bars on each lapel— he looked like one of the smaller, nastier floats from an upcoming Thanksgiving parade in one of the distant cities. On his left side, he wore a Smith & Wesson that looked as if it could have dropped a bull elk.

Mallinson was fifty-seven years old and the head of homicide investigations within the state, a no-nonsense position held by appointment from the commissioner of state police. Fourteen years earlier he had become the youngest captain ever on New Hampshire homicide, a reward for having been a priority case hatchet man for the previous two state police commissioners. Before that, he'd done "gunboat" police work, meeting the state prison bus at the Nashua and Manchester depots and pistol-whipping white trash recidivists into docile parolees. And he had the sour, unforgiving demeanor to underscore all of this: the temperament of an angry warthog. Those who worked for him liked to quip that he was New Hampshire's only *living* heart donor. Yet all the bare knuckle living had taken its toll. Mallinson had already had one heart attack and was hoping to retire before a second one killed him. Even he knew it would probably be a photo finish.

"Does anyone here see any frigging snow?" Mallinson eventually asked the men around him.

Two sergeants standing near their captain didn't see any snow, either. No one else ventured an opinion. To admit seeing snow was an invitation to start shoveling it.

"See? No snow," Mallinson said. "God damn it, I'm the most powerful goddam son of a bitch in this state. When I say there's no snow, there's no snow. O'Hara! Am I right?"

"Right, Cap," O'Hara said. "Nice sunny day. And these aren't pine trees around us, they're palms."

"See?" Mallinson said to the younger men with him. "Here's a veteran detective and *he* doesn't see any snow. Now do you all get the idea?"

"Bet it was a great day for someone to get whacked, huh?" O'Hara suggested.

"You can't imagine," Captain Mallinson said. "Had anything to eat recently?"

"No."

"You're lucky."

Mallinson made a motion of his head to one of his uniformed men, a fresh-faced officer in a blue parka and a fur cap. The young man's name was Samuelson and he looked terrified. Or, as O'Hara read the expression more carefully, horrified.

Samuelson led O'Hara back into the cabin, a crummy, little building containing motel-reject furniture. Clear plastic sheets were spread across the windows from the inside, but a couple of the windows had been broken, so the plastic had been torn and shredded. No telephone. No power. The only lights—the illumination by which O'Hara now saw—were handheld battery-lanterns maintained by the cops, plus a web of trouble lights strung from the police jeep out front.

In the big room, off from what passed as a kitchen, was a door that led to an outhouse which in turn was accessible from outside and inside. To work as a cop in New Hampshire was to never be surprised at what one found in such buildings: from a stripped Ferrari to a cannabis hothouse to a corpse.

Today it was the latter. Everything in sight was frozen, even the odor of death that hung in the air. The stench—a modest pile of decomposing human flesh—

had been so bad that it had permeated the cabin before the big winter freeze set in a few days earlier.

O'Hara recoiled as he and the young cop passed through the first room. He braced himself for what was coming.

"A couple of hikers made the discovery," Samuelson explained. "Sometime after the storm began to break on the mountain. Took them an hour to get down the slopes. Called the report in. Then it took us another hour to locate the cabin. Real bad weather by that time," the young man explained in a low voice.

"Real bad weather," O'Hara agreed.

"Plus this structure is not on any maps," Samuelson said. "No building permit."

O'Hara had already pegged the building as pre-World War Two, with probably a decade to spare. Back in the 1930s the State had built many such cabins as public shelters for hikers and campers, even where there were no trails or campsites. Rural America WPA projects: A make-work wooden assemblage in the middle of nowhere. No one had bothered with building permits. Currently, no one in any state authority even had an accurate guess as to how many structures still existed on public lands: some occupied by squatters, some abandoned for decades.

"What the hell have we got?" O'Hara finally asked. "One corpse or more than one?"

"Just one, sir."

O'Hara had already guessed as much. The stench of frozen decomposition would have been much worse with two.

He and the younger officer stepped into the death chamber. Both gagged. The reek of death was much stronger here, much like a punch in the nose as they entered the room. Both gagged. The young cop studiously avoided looking at the cadaver. O'Hara felt a surge in his stomach. Mallinson had been correct: He was lucky he hadn't eaten.

"Oh, Jesus," O'Hara said. It was as if he had stepped into his past, a horror film, and an abattoir simultaneously.

Before him was a scene out of a warped nightmare. The remains of a woman's torso lay on the bare wooden floor. It was in an advanced state of decomposition, a state that had been halted by the plunging temperatures.

The torso was facedown. Or, more accurately, it would have been facedown had there been a face to have been facing down. And there would have been a face if there had been a head. But there wasn't a head because whatever fiend had done this had decapitated his victim.

But the murderer hadn't stopped there. Or maybe he hadn't started there, either. The victim's right hand had been cut off, too. Then the instrument of death, which appeared to have been a sword, had been laid across the area of the neck where the neck would have joined the head.

The head had been placed on a dresser before the body, much the way something holy would be placed on an altar. At the foot of the dresser was a wooden box. A neat, little, rosewood affair, made up as a tiny coffin.

O'Hara blew out a breath and looked at the container.

"The hand, I assume?"

The young cop had had the misfortune to delve into the rosewood and discovered the contents. He would never forget it.

"The hand," the young cop said, choking back a major league projectile of vomit. "The killer"—he drew a brave breath—"apparently mutilated the corpse by—"

"I can see what he did, Officer," O'Hara said softly. "I've seen this before. Similar case several years back." He shook his head. "Christ Almighty."

Samuelson stood by awkwardly. O'Hara looked back to the torso and somehow knew that this type of scene could only come with a winter blizzard. It always seemed to.

Captain Mallinson appeared again from somewhere, foul-smelling cheroot and all. "Samuelson," he said, mercifully dismissing the younger officer from the room, "get out of here before you barf on my boots."

"Yes, sir," the kid said, gratitude suggested by his tone.

"Now you see why I called you, huh, you dickhead," said Mallinson. "I wanted you to take a good, hard look at the crime scene before the local flatfoots come in to trample the evidence. Before the M.E. goes to work, before our camera guy arrives to take the 'prom photos.'"

"Yeah," O'Hara answered. "I see."

"I want to hear it from your own mellifluous vocal chords," Mallinson said. "Can you do that? Talk to me."

"It's a Gary Ledbetter job all over again," Frank O'Hara said. "Can't mistake it. Is that what you wanted to hear?"

"I didn't wake up this morning wanting to hear that, no. But it's what I thought you'd say," Mallinson said. He pondered the point for a moment. "And Gary Ledbetter sat down in the electric chair in Florida this past summer. I'm right about that?"

"He's dead, Captain. Dead and presumably buried."

"So why do we get a copycat killing all these years later, huh?" Mallinson asked. "You tell me that."

"I can't."

O'Hara continued to stare at the body. He tried to picture what had happened. A ritual slaying, and a brutal one. The victim probably made to crawl and beg for mercy. The killer stood above her with a sword, medieval executioner style. Then when he had the impetus, the sword came swiping down and. . . .

O'Hara looked more closely at the side of the corpse. There were teeth marks on what remained of some of the flesh. Animal teeth marks, O'Hara guessed, probably made by some feral wildlife—a fox, a mink, or one of the eastern coyotes that now roamed the region—sometime within the first two weeks of the slaying. The smell of carrion would have driven any hungry carnivore to break into the old shelter. Plus, O'Hara thought further, the doors and windows had both been broken. It would have been strange if some wild animal *hadn't*. . . .

"I understand you're retiring," Mallinson said, mercifully intruding upon O'Hara's reenactment of what had happened. "Don't want to share your life with us state cop yokels any more?"

"Now that you mention it, no. I don't."

"You fuckhead," Mallinson said. "No one walks away from a fine job like this. Shit. You're being groomed as my successor."

"Screw that."

"Fuck it, Frank," Mallinson said from within a cloud of exhaust from the cheroot. "I'll outlive all you pansy-assed death dicks, anyway. My undertaker hasn't been born yet."

O'Hara's gaze rose from the old bloodstains on the floor and settled into Mallinson's older eyes.

"Word travels fast, doesn't it, Captain? My name just went on the 'sixty day' list this morning."

"And I read the frigging list every day before lunch. I mean, how can a man *not* want to spend his time crawling through the fucking New Hampshire wilderness looking for psychopaths?" The captain paused. "Before you retire," Mallinson said, "close this case."

"What?" O'Hara asked.

"You didn't hear me the first time?"

"Captain, the body's probably been here since summer. The trail's got to be colder than the weather, if there's any trail at all."

"Yeah. So?"

"An investigation like this can take months."

"Want your frigging pension? You want to leave with an honorable retirement? Then kick ass. A retirement present from you to me: Find out who this girl was. Then send me the mutt who did it."

"Captain, you have to be—"

"Kidding? Hey, bullshit, I'm kidding, Frank!"

"How can you throw it at me? There are priorities and jurisdictions. Who was the first detective to arrive?"

Mallinson grinned like a big bear. O'Hara felt the trap close upon him. Reynolds had been sent to speed him up the mountain. The only other cops on the scene were locals and uniformed Staties. The captain had seen to it: O'Hara had been the first detective on the premises.

O'Hara felt his spirits sink.

"Frank, listen to me," Mallinson said. "You're familiar with the Ledbetter case. So you'll bring that much insight to a copycat case. And there's something else, too."

"What's that?"

"Until you retire, Frank, you're still the best on this force. In your sleep you got more smarts than my other zombies. Granted, you got your head scrambled with these neurons or neuroses or whatever you got. And Lord knows, you're probably hitting the Irish penicillin pretty hard in your free time."

O'Hara didn't feel like listening to either the compliments or the misstatements. "I'm off booze almost completely."

"That's what I hear. I called that Jewish girl from Boston you been seeing."

"Dr. Steinberg?"

"That's the one. The psychiatrist."

"She's a psychologist."

"She says you're fit for complete duty. In fact, a big case might help you. That's all I want to hear."

"So I win today, huh?"

"Fly solo on the case if you like," Mallinson said. "Or I'll assign a couple of officers to help you. It's your choice. Wrap it up by Christmas and I'll see that an extra couple of weeks of vacation pay lands in your envelope when you leave."

O'Hara listened, and Mallinson forged ever onward.

"Maybe you can find out fast who the victim was," Mallinson mused. "You know how it works. If she was trash, the case is lower priority than if she's someone's wife or daughter."

The usual crap, O'Hara thought, where the "quality" of the victim became a factor in how many detectives were assigned.

"Thanks, Frank," the captain concluded. "Talk to me when you have something. That's all."

O'Hara watched the big man leave the death chamber. Alone with the cadaver, O'Hara suddenly felt awkward. He supposed it was nerves. Moments later, a police four-wheel jumped to life outside. Mallinson had accomplished everything he'd set out to do at the crime scene. Now the captain was going home.

Not so with O'Hara. He spent the next half hour with his attention turned to the mutilated female corpse, suddenly aware again how brutally cold it was.

He borrowed a notepad from Reynolds, and his better forensic instincts shifted into gear. From long habit, he set aside the notion that the mutilated remains had been someone's daughter—and maybe someone's wife, sister, mother, or lover.

There would be time for those thoughts later, when and if he needed an extra impetus to continue on the case. It was his job now to take the first steps that would lead to the discovery of a murderer. So he trawled for clues, vigilant for perhaps the one mistake that the killer had made, before the backup teams came in and walked all over the evidence. As he worked, visions of Gary Ledbetter tap-danced not so attractively before his eyes.

Why would someone copy a psychopath like Gary? And how would someone have known Gary's modus operandi so well? How, when Ledbetter had appeared to be a typical "lone wolf" killer?

By quarter after six, O'Hara was finished.

It was no more than eighteen degrees in the cabin and, upon O'Hara's conclusion of work at the scene, the ancillary people were ready to come in and mess things up.

A police crime photographer—a fat guy named Leonard without whom no such corpse scene was complete in southern New Hampshire—was first to enter the cabin. The prom photos, Mallinson liked to call them. The photographer took the usual eight-by-ten color glossies, then returned with a camcorder and repeated the procedure. The photographs and the videotape would become reference pieces for the police investigation. They could also serve as evidence in court.

Then the Medical Examiner, Dr. Vincent Paloheima, went to work. Paloheima was a big, hulking, insensitive Finnish-American with white hair, who still spoke in the accent of the old country. He was usually adept but was not above major blunders.

O'Hara hated to watch Paloheima work almost as

much as Paloheima enjoyed fussing with dead people.
Gloved fingers in the eyeholes, coming out with a ge-
latinous substance that defied the temperature. Then
there was some gunk with a minty medicinal odor that
Paloheima rubbed on the flesh of the dead woman's
arms. It smelled like the deodorants that people spray
in public latrines, creating the stench of pine-scented
toilet seats. All this mixed with the residual stink of
Captain Mallinson's cheap cheroot.

The examiner made his way down the cadaver,
working with cotton swabs, taking measurements,
rubbing ointments, and finally using a scalpel to take
a small sample of the remaining flesh. He dipped the
skin in and out of the shadows created by the emergency lamps, then placed it in a plastic bag with no
label. When Paloheima came to where the right wrist
had been severed, O'Hara had seen enough. He turned
and left the room.

There was a loud rumbling noise outside.

At first O'Hara thought it was an engine, maybe a
helicopter arriving. But when he arrived at the broken
cabin door and looked out, he realized that it was the
wind again, howling out of the north with another
great, big, wintery roar.

And again he felt his stomach churn. As O'Hara
had inspected the death scene, the blizzard had only
heightened. How the hell, when the hell, were they
even going to get the body of the dead woman out of
there?

Yet he already knew the answer: after the storm had
subsided. A day from now. Two days, when the roads
reopened. Three days, maybe. The snowfall looked as
if it might never stop. Then O'Hara realized that with
Captain Mallinson's departure, he, O'Hara, was the
ranking officer on the scene. *He* was in charge. And he
knew damned well he couldn't dismiss himself for the
day.

O'Hara stared at the storm and cursed violently to himself. Why couldn't this grisly discovery have waited two months? If the murder had gone undetected by the time the mountain was impacted by snow, well, no one might have found the dead woman until spring. By that time O'Hara would have been gone. Instead, this death had reached out and grabbed him by the lapels.

He wished he had a flask of bourbon. He could have handled one hell of a belt right then. Like half the flask, and Dr. Julie be damned.

Then he caught himself: depression from work and the weather. Professional pressure. The urge to take a drink. Galloping paranoia. These were all the things that he and Dr. Steinberg had worked for the last few months to overcome.

Don't let yourself regress now, he told himself. He and the lady shrink had worked too hard to get his head screwed back on nice and tight. He would *not* regress, he told himself.

O'Hara's gaze drifted back to the damnable snow which fell as mercilessly as it did silently, dropping a heavy white mantle over the assemblage of police vehicles.

Partially to prove that he was not intimidated by it, and also to momentarily escape the death cabin, he stepped out into the snowfall. He walked several paces, inhaling the frigid air, feeling the snow sweep against his face. When he looked up again and surveyed the area, something else caught his eye. Absurdly, young Samuelson was busy with thick yellow tape, marking off the cabin as a crime scene. As if a bunch of Boy Scouts or tourists were going to come tramping through and want to wander in.

Samuelson's actions were so wasteful of police time that O'Hara opened his mouth to tell the young cop not to bother. But then O'Hara remembered that the

kid was simply going by the handbook or acting upon
Captain Mallinson's instructions, whichever had come
first. So O'Hara let it go.

Then his smile changed abruptly to a shiver. Some
unpleasant feeling stirred within him, something that
made him uneasy. He realized what it was. An internal
snapshot from one of those disturbing dreams he had
endured the previous summer had suddenly emerged.

Along with the dream came its soundtrack. Words
and music by an unknown author. Certainly not Sinatra.

Ask yourself, what is your greatest fear?

*What are you truly afraid of? What is it that could
happen that you fear the most?*

O'Hara looked again at the cabin. He stared at it for
several seconds, feeling the storm upon him. He began
to sense an aura around the place, something deeply
disturbing and unnatural.

Something very similar to that night the previous
August when he had awakened and sensed a presence
in his home. He had from time to time in his career felt
similar strong sensations around death scenes.

But never this strong. Never this distasteful and
repugnant. Never quite like this one. And he hadn't
even been drinking.

Chapter 4

At eleven P.M. that same evening a state trooper named Jack McConnell drove O'Hara back down the mountain. O'Hara began to reflect on all that touched upon Gary Ledbetter. One might have thought that the murders would have stopped the previous summer when executioners in Florida finally had their way with Gary.

But even that was proving wrong.

Fatigue hung over O'Hara. The snow had eased off, but only slightly, and no plow had yet touched the rural routes. McConnell drove a state police jeep that followed the tire tracks of the police vehicles that had come and gone earlier that day.

"How much snow did we get today?" O'Hara absently asked his driver. "Anybody hear?"

"Ten, eleven inches," McConnell answered. He glanced from the jeep. "Pretty ain't it?" he offered.

"I hate it."

"Yeah," McConnell said, suddenly agreeing. "A damned pain if you have to go anywhere. To be honest, I hate it, too."

But O'Hara wasn't even listening. He stared out the side window, his eyes heavy. But his mind was far away, rattling skeletons from the past.

Seven years ago? A lucky number for an unlucky

case. But that was how far back O'Hara's involvement in the Ledbetter case had begun. In 1986. Taking a longer view, of course, some might have said that the Ledbetter murder spree might actually have begun a dozen years earlier, closer to 1981 when the first of Ledbetter's purported victims met her demise.

But this was not O'Hara's moment for understanding human behavior, particularly in its depths of homicidal depravity. What sort of bent pathology prompts a man to behave like Ledbetter, he wondered. To murder a woman, decapitate her, then hack off a hand as a coda. And why would . . . ?

Then O'Hara caught himself.

Don't be crazy, he thought. The case in this cabin is fresh. Maybe six weeks or two months old. This slaying echoes the Ledbetter murders but it is in no way associated with them. It *cannot* be! Ledbetter was locked on Death Row for three years before his execution. I helped put him there, O'Hara reminded himself. Gary is dead. We all understand that as well as the finality of death. To think otherwise is preposterous.

Consoled by this argument, O'Hara then moved his thoughts to their next logical plateau. If Ledbetter was dead, what sicko had made such a careful study of him that he could recreate a Ledbetter crime scene with such perfection? Who could have found inspiration in Gary Ledbetter?

Who, indeed? And why?

And, considering how many weeks had evidently passed since the murder, how many thousands of miles away might that killer now be? Is he out there somewhere killing again? Selecting another victim? Or is he very close? Still in New Hampshire. Just biding his time . . . waiting. . . .

In the jeep, O'Hara closed his eyes for a moment and thought about it. . . .

Gary Ledbetter. The case that would never rest. The

lynchpin of Frank O'Hara's twenty-year career. And here it was bubbling up again in O'Hara's final months as a cop.

A few of the facts came back. So did the chronology of O'Hara's life.

Frank O'Hara had always been viewed as a cipher, even to those who knew him. A cipher and sometimes—like Ledbetter—a man who fit nowhere perfectly.

He had grown up in Chicago, the only son of an electrician and a City Hall secretary. As a kid in one of Mayor Daley's favorite wards, he was too open-minded to be a good redneck, race-baiting Irishman, too agnostic to be a good Catholic, and yet too hard-nosed to be considered suspiciously sensitive. His scholastic record was excellent, and he was the best percentage hitter on his high-school baseball squad.

But the universities he liked were into minority recruiting at the time and, unable to get past his name and address, saw him as a blue-collar yahoo. The places that liked him, institutions that specialized in straight-arrow Catholic kids, he perceived as finishing schools for anti-intellectual bigots. In 1965 at age twenty, he found his way into the United States Navy, instead.

There he found that he could both give orders and dish them out, particularly under pressure. His first commanding officers were impressed and bounced O'Hara to San Diego where he emerged as an ensign. Next stop, Vietnam.

He embarked upon a three-year stint—including thirteen genuinely rotten months on Mekong River patrols. He lost count of how much hostile fire he saw or how many shore parties he participated in, ferreting out Vietcong in the jungle underbrush around the riverbanks.

He expected to be killed. During one horrible ship-

to-shore firefight against ARVN regulars south of Ho
Xiem, the man on his left and the man on his right
got whacked within four minutes of each other. But
O'Hara never lost a drop of blood.

He returned home from the war, staying briefly in
Chicago, but anxious to move on. He enrolled on the
G.I. Bill at a university in the northern Midwest, a
university more noted for pigskin than for Rhodes
scholars.

Sentiment about the war was running high from
both the left and the right. O'Hara kept his opinions
to himself, a talent which often led people who were
talking to him into thinking that O'Hara agreed with
them.

But in November of 1971 the students in the Conservative Union, noting his classroom articulation and
aware of his three years as a naval officer, invited him
to speak about the war.

"What do you want me to say?" O'Hara asked.

"Whatever you think."

O'Hara shrugged. "Okay," he said. And so he
spoke, treating his audience to the most scathing in-
dictment of the war and the idiots running it that most
of the students had ever heard, particularly from
someone who had been there.

A couple of thick-shouldered Sigma Chi muscle
boys in the front row got up to leave before O'Hara
was finished. They chipped in some opinions as they
rose. O'Hara, setting aside intellectual arguments,
pushed up his shirt sleeves and challenged them to
come up on stage to duke it out. He would entertain
both of them at once, he offered, and teach them a
little about real combat—not the type theorized by fat
armchair warriors who thought it would be a great
idea if someone else fought. Or else, O'Hara said, they
could sit down and shut the hell up. They sat. O'Hara

was not invited to address the Conservative Union again.

The incident might have made him an idol for the antiwar types on campus, but O'Hara wanted nothing to do with them, either. He considered them a bunch of druggies, wimps, and fools who didn't have any idea what they were talking about, either. So once again, Frank O'Hara was the odd man out.

He lasted one year at the university, acquiring a 3.6 grade point average. But he never felt himself intellectually challenged. So he read heavily on his own. Novels. Histories. Politics. Anything. But he also felt an overwhelming urge to get back out into the real world. There was much to do. He wanted to get out to help people on a one-to-one basis. To many of his generation, that meant VISTA or the Peace Corps. O'Hara said the hell with that.

He learned that certain police departments were making special accommodations for veterans. In particular, Oregon and New Hampshire were seeking state police recruits. One night O'Hara decided to flip a coin. Heads he'd go to Oregon, tails he'd go to New Hampshire.

The coin came up heads. Oregon. But his instincts told him New Hampshire. And how could something like this be decided by a coin flip anyway? He closed out his apartment, bought a second hand Volkswagen and drove to New England. He went on the job in January of 1974.

He spent his first few years on the force being jerked around the state, a lot of time spent on highway surveillance. He hated the red tape of being a cop, but overall much police work really *was* a matter of helping people, or setting things right for people who'd been victimized. And the job, tooling along in a spiffy uniform in one's own car, offered a certain frontier-style independence. A Lone Ranger on wheels, highteched with modern weapons and two-way radio. And at first even the long, bitter New Hampshire winters were a novelty. Almost "Christmas Tree" quaint at forty fucking degrees below zero. It was only much later that he started to hate the deep-freeze season.

Five years into his career, he passed the detective's exam with the highest grade in the state. He began plainclothes duty a few months later, just in time to work on the state protection detail for the parade of presidential candidates who invade the state every four years. Up close he listened to their hollow promises and developed a new and deep contempt for almost all of them.

There was one happy offshoot of the campaigning, however. One night in March of 1980 he stopped a car with New York plates when it slid through a stop sign. It was driven by a woman.

Her name was Barbara Godfrey and she had just hit the New Hampshire "Happy Motoring" trifecta: She didn't have her license or registration or insurance certificate. But O'Hara recognized her from one of the campaign rallies. And she did have beautiful dark eyes and a nice smile, a couple of qualities that could balance out a lot of petty motor vehicle infractions.

O'Hara let her go. He guessed he would see Barbara Godfrey again at her candidate's next campaign stop. He was right. When he did, he asked her out for coffee. She agreed.

It turned out she, too, was Irish-American, was originally from the Midwest, and had left a similar university after two years for many of the same reasons as O'Hara. Her candidate dropped out of the race two months later after igniting only nine percent of the electorate in the California primary. Barbara took the occasion to revisit New Hampshire. She and O'Hara were married eight months later.

For the first several years of their marriage, they

were happy. During non-campaign years, he worked Vice, Grand Larceny, and Narcotics. His job took him from prostitution operations along Hampton Beach during summers, to busting a ring of Alabama-born cracker strongarms who were running hot trucks in and out of the state.

Then there was a memorable evening in Franconia when a guido white powder operation in North Boston made him as an undercover cop in a sting operation. They put a Cuban triggerman on his case. O'Hara stepped out of his car one night and found himself looking at a guy leaning into a firing position with a monster piece of sawed-off technology.

Barely time to think. O'Hara dropped down behind his car and went for his weapon as the shooter blew out all his car windows with the first of two barrels. O'Hara came up from the back end of the car and drilled his would-be assassin with four rounds.

The sting blown, his nerves a wreck, part of the hearing gone in his left ear—the one closest to the shotgun—O'Hara got himself transferred to something more peaceful. Statewide homicide. This was 1979.

He worked with a detective named Carl Reissman. Carl was a world-class cynic, a man who figured someone had died the second he saw a bouquet of fresh flowers, and further figured that the death had probably been unnatural. Reissman was an outstanding cop, even though he was a borderline alcoholic as well as a head case himself.

Reissman took a liking to O'Hara. Jointly they made a couple of high-profile busts within the first month of their partnership. They even circled back into O'Hara's recent unlovely past and hung conspiracy to commit murder raps on the two Boston drug lords who had ordered the hit on O'Hara.

"Homicide is where the big-time action is in a small-time dingbat state," Reissman said. And in a sense, it was . . . without the dirt and corruption that went with narcotics.

"A homicide dick's desk is never completely clean," Reissman liked to say. "There are always names of dead people on the wall. If not, there will be soon."

Reissman had a sense of the macabre, a habit that O'Hara picked up quickly. On major cases, he always kept a small possession of the victim with him: a ring, a money clip, an earring or some other piece of jewelry. It kept him focused. It kept him thinking.

Reissman also wanted to rearrange his wall chart of unsolved murder cases to list them in red marking pen by their most salient features:

Stabbings. Shootings. Strangulation. Suspicious drownings. Suffocation. Fags. Mutilation. Sex. Children.

"A lot of these cases," O'Hara noted in eyeing the chart one day, "fit into three or more categories."

"Fucking awful world, isn't it?" Reissman answered.

"Yeah," O'Hara answered, "but I like your approach."

"You're the only one who does."

District Command complained about the classification system, so Reissman and O'Hara did the next best thing. They put their active open cases on the wall by picture of the victim. Every day the dead would stare out from the wall in Reissman's office. Some smiling. Some forlorn. Each silently asking for resolutions to their cases. Eventually, male and female, all ages, they became a makeshift family.

Staring from another world.

Asking for justice.

Not that O'Hara even needed to look at them. The wall had an eerie feel. For the first time in his life, O'Hara could sense the eyes of the dead upon him.

Sense their presence. They recurred to him like acid flashes at any unpredictable time.

Like when he slept. When he tried to make love to Barbara. When he tried to watch hockey on television during the increasingly miserable New Hampshire winters.

"Working deathwatch is a good way to keep a finger on the pulse of the public," Reissman explained, further elaborating that stabbings increase in tougher financial times, whereas the gun was the sign of boom years.

"This is an era of shameless, obscene greed," Carl Reissman announced in 1982. "Buy stock in Remington, Browning and Colt, vote Republican, wear your bulletproof vest at all times, stand back and wait for a shitload of gun crimes." Statistics would prove him correct. As for Reissman, he was entering into a manic-depressive era of his own.

But O'Hara listened and learned. Working with Carl was better than going to college. From Reissman, O'Hara learned how to sweet-talk confessions out of icepick murderers with vampire complexes, how to toss a crime scene before the locals arrive, how to read black-and-white crime scene photos in a way that revealed more than the glossy color jobs, how to bribe the state pathologist's office (when necessary) to get a warm corpse examined faster and more accurately than the cold dead trash that gets shipped in early Sunday mornings, and how to pass for a nighttime maintenance worker in order to lift institutional records at the state nut houses, at the phone company, or at Social Security. From Reissman, O'Hara even learned how to stay completely clear—or, failing that, at least on the good side of—the button-down, tie-clipped mick assholes at the FBI outpost in Nashua. His mentor also imparted probably two hundred other little subtleties of murder detection not covered by the criminology texts.

Together, Reissman and O'Hara solved several big-time, bad-assed cases together, got their names in the Manchester *Union-Leader* during the old-time, rock-ribbed reign of William Loeb, and drew front-page coverage of the new statewide tabloid, the New Hampshire *American,* published by Wilhelm Negri, a right-wing darling, publishing mogul, and more recently a radio loudmouth with a growing audience of quasi-fascist yahoos. Next to Negri, Rush Limbaugh was squishy soft, and the *American* was quickly supplanting the *Union-Leader* in regional wallop.

Not surprisingly, the Reissman-O'Hara team had already come to the attention of Captain William Mallinson, who considered Reissman and O'Hara his best two men.

"My best two, with no one in third place," Mallinson frequently growled. It remained that way for several years. Up until the advent of Gary Ledbetter.

Gary Ledbetter. A low-rent Lothario. A bluebeard of dirt bike society.

The final atrocity linked to Gary Ledbetter, officially known as "Ledbetter homicide number five," had been discovered in the basement of a garage attached to a white cape-style farmhouse in Antrim, New Hampshire.

The usual.

Head of a young woman severed at the neck. Right hand at the wrist. Deft chopping motion, followed by sawing. The victim's head then placed on a makeshift altar at the front of the chamber. The hand placed in a rosewood box tied neatly with pink ribbon.

Pink ribbon. What a cute touch. Same in all five killings. Pink for the little girls, one shrink noted. Pink for childhood innocence. Pink was a favorite of mass murderers, another pathologist noted. Pink had been

Hitler's favorite color, too, and when Gary was young, an abused kid with a brutal father, there had been this portrait of Hitler in Gary's room. And on and on it went. . . .

The final victim's name had been Karen Stoner, and she had been a waitress at a doughnut joint near the Massachusetts state line. A friendly girl who didn't sleep around and who needed a ride home one night. Pink uniform, by the way.

Reissman and O'Hara drew the investigation. Karen Stoner's picture went up in their gallery of open cases. A color glossy. Right in the middle.

Reissman began by running through violent sex offenders in the area, trying to close the case by sifting through killers. O'Hara focused on Karen and figured the crime was not committed by anyone local who was already known. He scoured the countryside, beat the brush for someone new in the area and came up with some virgin psychos.

Gary Ledbetter was one of them. He was working in a 7-Eleven and someone complained that Gary had shot the neighbor's dog. Sixteen bullets, which even people who didn't like the dead mutt thought was excessive by maybe ten bullets or so.

O'Hara investigated the arf-arf assassination and came away with chills after five minutes with Gary.

"No, sir. I didn't shoot no one's doggie."

"Then why do three witnesses say you did it?" Detective O'Hara inquired.

"Don't know, sir. Guess they don't like me."

"Think this guy's our pigeon?" Reissman asked his partner.

"He gives me the creeps," O'Hara answered.

"That's not what I asked."

"I know what you asked," O'Hara said.

"Let's get a camera."

Reissman took a surveillance photograph of Gary

and mixed it in with photographs of six other Granite State lunatics. He and O'Hara took all seven shots back to the doughnut dive where Karen had worked.

Surprise. A couple of people recognized Gary and picked out his snapshot. They said he'd come in several times, all tidied up, neat and clean with a smile in those cobalt blue eyes. And he had seemed very sweet on Karen.

"Yeah. Real sweet," O'Hara answered.

Then, working backwards, O'Hara and Reissman foraged for some evidence, or, failing that, witnesses. A woman in a notions store in Peterborough volunteered that she thought she had sold Gary some pink ribbon. And two of Karen Stoner's girlfriends said that she had gone out with Gary a couple of times. They had gone to her place where Gary had played the piano for her—old church hymns favored in the South, played with feeling on a ratty old spinet.

But where had Gary been when the murder occurred? O'Hara and Reissman finally asked him after they had hauled him into an interrogation room at the big roundhouse in Nashua.

"I was home watching smut videos."

O'Hara did the questioning. "What were the names of them?"

"Who knows names of beaver movies? I was jacking off. Should try it some time, you fuckhead cops. You'd be in a better mood."

"And maybe we wouldn't be," Reissman answered, interjecting. "Where did you rent the videos?"

"Don't remember. I rent them a lot of places."

O'Hara again: "Name a couple."

"Don't remember."

"If I were you, Gary," O'Hara warned, "I'd start remembering. You're going to take a fall on homicide."

"Bullshit. I got friends in this state, man. Big shot friends."

"Yeah? Name two."

"You'll fucking find out," Ledbetter snarled.

"Why don't you tell me? Save us all some time."

"If I tell I'm dead meat anyway," Ledbetter said. "So what's the fucking difference?"

"On one hand you tell me you have friends, Gary," O'Hara said. "Then you tell me your friends will let you fry. So I'm not following you."

"Good. I don't want you to."

"You're in a lot of trouble. Don't you understand that?"

"Fuck you."

Then Gary clammed up, answering virtually nothing else.

"The empty profane threats of a cornered, delusional psychotic," Reissman complained. "Fuck it. This guy's guilty as sin."

"Think so?"

"Don't you?"

"Where's the evidence?"

"If we can't find any we'll make some."

"Very funny."

"Who's kidding?"

O'Hara visited every video store within thirty miles, flashed Gary's picture and found no place where the suspect had rented anything. For that matter, O'Hara discovered, Gary didn't own a VCR. A case began to build itself around Ledbetter.

Reissman became possessed. So did O'Hara. A year and a half of combat, a dozen years as a cop, and O'Hara had never seen cold-blooded brutality the way he had seen it inflicted upon Karen Stoner. Both detectives worked like demons. They slept in their clothes at the office. Then Reissman came up with a major break. Acting on a tip, he and his partner broke into a storage locker rented to an "S. Clay." In the locker, among some perverse sexual gear, was an ax stained with blood. There was also a shopping bag with some rose-wood boxes.

The blood samples matched Karen Stoner's. Gary's fingerprints were on the ax. His prints were also on the rosewood boxes. And the manager of the storage units, an eighty-IQ sort of guy, had a sharp enough memory to identify Gary as the unit's owner when O'Hara and Reissman returned with a photograph. Not surprisingly, Ledbetter's signature matched the handwriting of "S. Clay" on the storage unit contract.

Within four weeks, the case seemed made, particularly when O'Hara got a call from Delaware where Wilmington cops had been stuck with a similar investigation. And the Wilmington force knew about one in Virginia.

Some fiend, as much of tabloid America knew by this time, had allegedly left a string of four girls up and down the east coast. Decapitated and dismembered by the "Pink Ribbon Chopper." One had been disemboweled. All five had been working-class, and the theory was that the killer had made love to each of them, promised them marriage, then lured them off to isolated spots where he did them in with heavy cutlery after making them crawl. They were all found in the same sorts of places with the same wounds and in the same positions on the ground.

The people who wrote texts about psychopaths had a field day. So did the two-bit four-color tabloids as well as their equally disgraceful television counterparts. Gary had so much of the lowbrow press covering his arrest that he bordered on an environmental hazard: all those trees becoming newsprint just to write about him.

"No, sir. I didn't kill any of them girls." Over and over, such had been Gary's refrain when O'Hara questioned him in Nashua. "I may have romanced them some, but I didn't hurt them none."

"Who did, Gary?" O'Hara had pressed.

"Can't tell you that. Sir."

"You know?"

"Not talking, fuck it." A pause, then again with contempt, "Sir."

Things snowballed. Georgia found a pink ribbon decapitation, too, making it a quintet, counting Florida. Then, working backwards, O'Hara sent around Gary's picture and got a positive ID out of friends of three of the five female victims. Then when the state attorney general, a snotty, little political hack named Ben Ashton, brought the official charges against the suspect, the detectives celebrated by going on a world-class drunk. One of the sergeants had to pull O'Hara out of a snowbank hours later and take him home to his long-suffering wife before he froze to death.

"Crazy bastard," the sergeant had said.

"Me or Carl or Gary?" O'Hara had asked.

"All of you. In your own ways."

The case marked the high point—to date—of O'Hara's career as a detective. It also marked the end of Reissman's. A grand jury indicted Ledbetter for second degree murder. Two days passed. The prisoner failed to make bail. Then Reissman checked out of work one day and—as friends later pieced it together—spent the evening with an eighteen-year-old mistress in Keene whom his best friend O'Hara didn't even know he had. Reissman went to a bar, put down four vodkas, and went home. It was O'Hara who found him the next morning, a bullet through the head from his own revolver and a suicide note pinned to his chest. Sayonara, world. In keeping with the decade of the heater, it appeared that Reissman had shot himself.

It was January 1986. Winter, naturally. O'Hara sat on his partner's doorstep for a half hour. Crying. Feeling the tears freeze on his cheeks before other state police cars could arrive.

Reissman's death hit O'Hara like an express train. Few had noticed, but Reissman had slowly been going crazy on the job. It had all been too much, deeply rooted cynicism combined with daily examples of how the cynicism was justified. There was speculation that something about the Ledbetter case had pushed him over the brink.

"There's an emotional line in police work," Captain Mallinson had said to O'Hara two days after Reissman's death. They sat in the captain's office, just the two of them. "Once a man goes over it, I'll be damned if he ever comes back. Know that?"

"And Carl went across it?" O'Hara said, half question, half statement. "Is that what you're telling me?"

"It's half of what I'm telling you," Mallinson said.

"What's the rest?"

"I'm not letting *you* go across it, also," the captain said. "I'm taking you off Ledbetter and putting you on restricted desk duty. If you start walking around like you got screws loose—like lying out in a frigging snowbank again—I'll take away your gun."

"Captain, you can't—"

"I just did."

"Who's going to guide the Ledbetter case?"

"*I* am," Mallinson answered. "And don't sweat it too much. You're going to see some strange jurisprudence on this case. But Gary's going to get what he deserves in the end. Mark that much, Brother O'Hara."

O'Hara began to drink like a fish. He began to quarrel with his wife who, in turn, suggested that he find another line of work. And it was at this time, too, in reaction to all this, that he walked the straight and narrow at work, kept in his commander's good graces, and buried himself ever more obsessively in New Hampshire homicide.

Then followed the strange form of jurisprudence that Captain Mallinson had augured.

The two statewide newspapers in New Hampshire— particularly the New Hampshire *American,* which became increasingly shrill on the subject—started bellyaching about Ledbetter potentially "getting off" with a life sentence if he went on trial in New Hampshire. Too good for him, the editorials said. The populace agreed and soon the governor started feeling some heat. So New Hampshire cut a deal with Florida, allowing Gary's extradition.

The official excuse was that Florida was the chronological start of Ledbetter's murder spree, so the first trial should be there. The real reason was so that Ledbetter could be executed.

Florida tried him and made damned well sure to convict him. Then they made sure that they could fry him, too.

More than any other crime, more than any other murder, Frank O'Hara could see the Ledbetter case in his sleep. It was the one that had never gone away. The case that had changed him from a man who solved murders to a man obsessed with homicide.

Pretty, innocent Karen Stoner stared down at him off the wall of Carl Reissman's old office, the office O'Hara now occupied, even long after her case was solved and her portrait should have returned to the Closed file. For O'Hara, on some days the entire world was the color of Karen Stoner's eyes. He would have felt better, much better, about it if at least the case could have come to its legal conclusion in New Hampshire—if he could personally have closed out his final questions and suspicions about the case. But the whole mess had been whisked away to Florida. A sense of the incomplete coalesced with O'Hara's obsession with the crime, itself.

Yet not everything that followed was bad.

Upon Reissman's death, O'Hara had twelve years seniority. He had the luxury of picking a new partner or flying solo. He chose the latter. He would miss his old partner, however, and life would have turned out differently had the talented Reissman retained his sanity and lived.

Working by himself, O'Hara quickly had his baptism under fire. On his first day of solo duty he drew the assignment of some backwoods sorehead who shot his best friend one night, then fixed up the body to look like it had belonged to an intruder and a tragic mistake had been made. It didn't take long for the forensic evidence to indicate that the deceased had been shot some fifty yards from where the body had been found, which was a long way for a man to stagger after taking a bullet through the temple. O'Hara had a confession by nightfall.

Then there was Mrs. Hulburt who poisoned her neighbor's cat, then the neighbor's dog as a lead-up to the real thing, poisoning her husband while trying to lay blame on the neighbor. And, to mix low comedy with tragedy, O'Hara also drew the case of a couple of stickup men from New York who blew over a convenience store one night in Peterborough and—for sport—shot the high-school kid on counter duty.

The kid died.

O'Hara put together a license and car description from three partial witnesses, two of whom agreed to be hypnotized. O'Hara had another pair of collars by the end of the week.

But all of this was prosaic stuff. Just basic get-in-touch-with-your-feelings-and-kill-someone jobs. It was never far from O'Hara's mind that homicide was the felony most frequently committed by amateur criminals. Look for the half-wit aspect of most slayings and you can wrap your investigation. Yet in O'Hara's mind, the Ledbetter case had always been one apart: the one that left a bad taste of uncertainty in his mouth and left his partner-mentor dead.

And, oh, yes, it had been snowing hard the day they found Karen Stoner's body in a basement. Just like it was snowing the day O'Hara came around with a couple of local deputies and put handcuffs on Gary. Just like it had been snowing the day in 1990 when Barbara Godfrey O'Hara, with her husband increasingly consumed by alcohol and his work, announced she was leaving him "for a while" to attend law school in Illinois.

"What the hell does 'for a while' mean?" he had asked.

" 'For a while' means until I can file the divorce papers. You love your female victims more than you love your own wife."

A week later, Barbara packed and walked out of his life forever. Thus the further legacy of the Ledbetter case: Shattered lives all around. Collateral damage in every direction. No one normal ever again.

And just like it had been snowing today, in November of 1993.

In a near-dream, another image of Gary reappeared to O'Hara. A quasi-acid flash.

The accused killer sitting in a cell in Nashua, awaiting extradition to Florida. Gary rapping angrily:

I didn't kill no girls, sir. And I know some real big shots in this state. You be careful of me!

Yeah, Gary. Sure, O'Hara thought to himself. A low-rent Lothario, that's all you are. A common killer with a sadistic pink signature.

Not me, man.

Terrific. Would human psychology never cease sinking to new depths? And now, here on a snowy November day in 1993, it was freshly served on O'Hara's plate.

"Yeah, Gary. Sure," O'Hara repeated aloud. "You're dead. So why are you still bothering me?"

Somewhere deep in O'Hara's subconscious, Ledbetter only laughed.

O'Hara's body jumped, as it might in a bad dream.

"You okay?" asked Jack McConnell. He spoke in the front seat of the state police jeep.

"What?" O'Hara answered. His mind was foggy. His eyes fluttered open. He had been miles away and was surprised to find himself in a moving vehicle.

"I said, are you okay?" the driver repeated. McConnell turned his head for a moment and glanced at his passenger.

"Oh, hell," O'Hara answered, snapping back to attention. "What's going on?" He blinked. Their jeep was on a snowy road. O'Hara's mind leaped into a forward gear. Where were they? It looked familiar.

"You haven't said nothing for forty minutes," McConnell explained. "I didn't know whether you was asleep or just dreaming."

O'Hara drew a breath. "Neither. Just thinking," he answered.

McConnell grinned. "Yeah," he said.

O'Hara recognized the location. They were about a quarter mile from Hancock, his hometown. His mind had drifted as McConnell had driven him home. O'Hara knew he had had his eyes closed and had that punchy feeling of having been half asleep. But, as they drove for another few minutes in silence, he wasn't even sure of that.

"Did I doze off?" O'Hara finally asked.

"Think so," the driver said. "Anyways you weren't saying nothing and your head was slumped. Figured that as long as you hadn't had a stroke or somethin' you'd wake up again."

"Yeah. Thanks. I appreciate it."

McConnell grinned.

"Anyways, we're here," McConnell said next.

The jeep turned into a driveway in which there was about a foot of virgin snow. The headlights of the jeep travelled across the blanket of white and then illuminated a house.

It looked alien to O'Hara's tired eyes, an ominous structure rising out of the storm. Then his eyes settled on the building. Its details became more familiar and O'Hara realized that he was home.

Chapter 5

O'Hara entered his house through the garage. He left his boots near an outside door and walked to the kitchen. He was exhausted.

He pulled a bottle of beer from the refrigerator and sat down at the kitchen table. He listened to the silence.

O'Hara was still shaken. What he had seen could not have really happened. Gary Ledbetter all over again.

Not possible.

The ugly details pursued him. How could anyone replicate such a hideous crime? Worse, how had anyone known so many details of the Ledbetter slayings? How could anyone other than Gary Ledbetter, the convicted murderer, have arranged the crime scene perfectly in the Ledbetter style?

O'Hara sipped his beer and sunk into an unsettling line of thought. What had he really seen in that remote cabin? And what had he felt? What was that chilly fearful sense that had been sneaking up on him in that place?

And beyond that, more questions: Who had been this victim? Why had she died? His mind raced back for any women who had turned up missing in the area during the past summer.

There were always reports, but none stood out in his memory. He groaned. If this was his case—and Captain Mallinson had already determined that it was—there would be hundreds of Missing Persons reports to wade through.

And what about the "quality" of the victim? A good girl from a good family and the case would merit more attention than if she were some whore or hophead from Boston or New York.

Then again, did good girls from good families just disappear? Usually not without a Missing Persons report, even though there was not a damned thing illegal—public impression to the contrary—about a citizen going missing of her own free will.

O'Hara's eyes drifted to the window. Snow still falling. November, and it was already winter. He had been right. The snow always brought death.

He pondered the elements. A decomposed body, a ritual slaying. More satanism? Vampirism? Witchcraft? Another fucking repressed New England psychopath enacting executioner fantasies? A would-be Charlie Manson?

Great!

His mind circled back: Why, why, why, the contrived parallel of the Ledbetter slayings? What was this killer trying to say? What was he trying to prove?

And why now?

O'Hara set down the bottle of beer again. He reached for it after several more seconds of thought, lifted it to his lips, and found it empty. So much for the first brew of the day. Why did they always go so quickly?

He went to the refrigerator and found another. He opened it and knocked down half the bottle almost immediately, then remembered that two was his quota.

Two of anything containing alcohol. A promise he

had made to Dr. Steinberg during the summer. A way
of keeping away from throwing a good solid drunk
whenever he got anxious or depressed.

Yeah, Dr. Julie, he thought to himself. I know
you're watching. I'm thinking of you.

Visits to Dr. Steinberg were still scheduled once a
week. There was some at-home follow-up that he was
supposed to do. If he had more than two drinks in the
evening she had asked him to write down a record of
it and present it to her on the next visit. Similarly, if he
spent too much time talking to himself he was supposed to record that, too.

He sat down again and leaned back, half a beer to
go. As the alcohol settled into his system, his eyes
travelled the room. His gaze settled again upon the
kitchen window and the snow that was piling against
it.

He felt himself in some sort of tomb, with snow
blanketing him. He finished the second beer and began
to think about food. His stomach gnawed at him. He
hadn't eaten all day.

Then another thought was abruptly upon him. The
thought that he was not alone in his house. The
thought that somewhere there was some sort of living
presence not far away from him.

Then, as if on cue, there was another one of those
creaks from somewhere off the kitchen. Somewhere on
the ground floor of his house. He felt his own pulse
quicken in response.

O'Hara finished the beer and reached for the automatic pistol on his hip. Quietly he unclipped it from its
holster. He raised it in his hand, aloft, ready to fire if
necessary. A bullet was already chambered, with a full
clip waiting behind the first round.

O'Hara turned slightly where he sat and his eyes
focused upon the doorway beyond the kitchen. Yes.
Someone was upstairs. A bizarre notion was upon

him, in spite of its lack of logic. The intruder was Gary Ledbetter.

The passage to his dining room and living room was dark. O'Hara heard another creak and felt himself start to sweat. There was no way he was imagining this, he told himself.

O'Hara stood. The feeling was unbanishable now. There was someone in the house with him. And sure enough, no sooner had this thought formed than there was another sound, something similar to a footfall on old floorboards.

"Christ Almighty," O'Hara swore softly. He took two cautious steps forward, stopped, and listened again. Nothing. Then came another creak, farther away, closer to the staircase at the front of the house.

O'Hara's stomach had ceased churning, but only because all of his nerves were now in his throat. The palm of his hand was suddenly sweating against the grip of the pistol.

He moved forward again.

"Anyone there?" he called.

No answer.

O'Hara came to the doorway at the rear vestibule. He reached around it to the light switch. The overhead came on and as O'Hara cautiously turned the corner it revealed an empty room.

He stood, hand aloft and ready, weapon pointing upward. He looked toward the living room.

Another creak. No, he wasn't imagining this. This was real. He was really hearing something.

He stepped to the living room, moved his free hand to a wall switch, and turned on another light, still holding his weapon upward.

He scanned. The usual furniture. The sound system. The old piano. Again, he saw nothing unusual.

Outside the snow continued to fall. Occasionally the wind moaned. O'Hara stood motionless and heard yet

two more creaks—or were they two more *footfalls?*—
this time ascending the front steps.

He moved quickly through his living room. He
turned a corner and froze. He stared expectantly at an
empty staircase.

Nothing. No further sound. He pointed his pistol
upward and waited, listening to his heart ripping away
in his chest.

"Hello?" he finally called, his eyes narrow and
squinting, fixed upon the darkness at the height of the
staircase. "Who's there?"

When there was no answer, he called again.

"I know someone's there! Make yourself known!"

Again, nothing.

He cursed mildly. Whatever it was had climbed the
steps. He was sure of that. *Wasn't he?*

He followed, climbing the steps carefully. There
were three upstairs bedrooms, plus a bathroom. He
searched the two unused bedrooms, plus their closets.
He threw on a light in the bathroom and looked in.
Every corner of the room was visible. Then turned to
his own bedroom.

He entered the room very cautiously, every few seconds glancing over his shoulder to cover his back. He
found nothing. He looked in his clothing closets and
even leaned down to glance under his own bed. Nothing at all. Nor did he hear any creak again.

Whatever it was, whatever he thought he had heard,
wasn't there any more. If it had ever been there at all.

O'Hara sighed. His nerves were betraying him
again, he told himself. He sat down on the edge of his
bed and tucked his weapon back into its holster.

Again, the silence of the house surrounded him. His
gaze rose to the window across the room. Then he
walked to it and looked out.

There were outdoor lights on in his neighborhood,
little points of yellow to serve as beacons against the

continuing storm. They formed a pale light through the blizzard. O'Hara stared at the wooded area that surrounded his home.

If he looked very carefully, and let his imagination go, he could see the forest ghosts again, flitting between the trees.

Snow ghosts. What a concept! What loony, old, native medicine man thought that one up? Yet by now, O'Hara practically felt on close terms with these figments of a waking dream.

"Yeah I see you," O'Hara said aloud. "You fucking snow ghosts. I know what you're trying to say. You're telling me that it's time for me to get out of this state. Well, you know what? You're right. It *is* time! And I *am* getting out."

He stared at the figures. The more he stared, the more they moved. That was the irony of them. The paradox. The more he knew they weren't there, the more he saw them. The more certain a man was that they were imaginary, the more real the snow ghosts became. A man could get lost in the dark illogic of it. Get lost and never find one's way back . . . much like the Indians who went out looking for those same spirits, never to return alive.

O'Hara spoke to them again.

"Are you the guys who make my floorboards creak, also?" he demanded. He paused and grinned. "Come on. Don't be scared. Answer me, you supernatural fuckers."

One of the ghosts almost seemed to wave back. It mocked him. That, or his own imagination mocked him.

"Bullshit," he said aloud. "Anyone comes in this house and I'll make a real ghost out of him."

Angrily he patted his gun. "When you're ready to come out in the open, man to man," he said, "let me know."

Angrily, he pulled the curtain shut.

"Bullshit," he said again. He retreated to his bed, lay down on it and tried to relax, blowing out a long sigh.

It had all been too much this day. First the snow, then the blood chilling echo of the Gary Ledbetter case. Events almost meant to strangle him, first physically, then mentally.

He tried to sort out his own baggage. Tried to make sense of the day's events.

He was disturbed by the snow, he told himself. A final winter blizzard that he did not need. That had set his psyche into a vulnerable position. And that had made himself more vulnerable to suggestion.

"How am I doing, Dr. Steinberg?" he asked himself aloud. "Miss Julie?" He laughed and considered another beer. "Not too well, I guess."

One more beer and he'd have to file a report on himself. And he'd already had quite a conversation, both with himself and whatever phantom was floating through his home. The phantom remained unseen, of course, which meant that he had been carrying on a monologue.

So he cut a deal with himself. If he succumbed to no more beer, he'd lie a little about the talking aloud. One more forbidden brewski and he'd report both.

Seemed fair. A carrot and stick approach to home psychological follow-up.

Fortunately, he was dead tired and knew that he would soon sleep. After lying on his bed for a few minutes, he turned on the radio for companionship. A news station in Portsmouth said the storm would last through the night. All schools and offices would be closed, though O'Hara knew that he would end up reporting for another double shift. When the station moved along to an advertisement for Wilhelm Negri's radio show, O'Hara poked the dial. Even a slight mention of the hypocritical right-wing windbag was enough to set him off.

He would have loved some Sinatra right then, but that was too much to pray for from the local airwaves. Instead, O'Hara turned the radio off.

Then he had just enough energy to rise from the bed, go downstairs, and find some cold turkey left over from the previous day. He made himself an atrociously large sandwich and washed it down—There, Miss Julie, see!—with a diet cola.

Then he went back upstairs, showered quickly, set the alarm on his radio, and fell back into bed. His weapon, as always, was kept on the shelf of the nightstand.

As he was drifting off, he heard a final creak for the evening. It was in the room with him, no more than ten feet away.

Then a second creak, sounding for all the world like another footfall, half the distance closer. Five feet away, and indicating that it was approaching.

He opened his eyes. The room was dark. He studied the configuration of chairs and dressers and tables.

One more creak. Right beside his bed. Right there! An arm's length away.

From somewhere: *Hello, Frankie.*

"Go the fuck away," O'Hara muttered sleepily, seeing nothing.

He turned on the light and scanned the room. In the light, as in the dark, nothing was there.

Nothing, that is, that he could see.

He closed his eyes again. If there had been anything in the room, it never came back. And it never harmed him that night, because seconds later O'Hara drifted off. He slept soundly—undisturbed and apparently untouched—for seven hours.

With the light on.

* * *

Meanwhile, in Philadelphia, late autumn remained balmy. Brown leaves swept along the sidewalks, and the universities and music schools were well into their fall terms. The city was bright with life and with young people. Saturdays meant the season's last few Ivy League football games at Franklin Field and Sunday meant the Eagles at The Vet.

The weather was pleasant. It had nowhere approached the deep freeze of the autumn storms in New Hampshire. And Adam Kaminski, seeing so many college kids in love in his buildings, was contemplating the latest mysteries surrounding Carolyn Hart.

Kaminski maintained good relations with other tenants on the street. The Levins, two doors away, knew that Carolyn had indeed moved into 565 South Oswell Street. They recalled hearing some sounds coming out of the building. Nothing to complain about, they quickly added. They just thought that they had heard *something*.

The DeLorenzos, on the other hand, lived three houses in the opposite direction and maintained that no one had ever come and gone from Number 565. It was difficult, Kaminski began to realize, to maintain a daily vigil over a woman when she remained so elusive even to normal sightings.

This prompted him to start thinking further, as well as passing by the house even more frequently. He even used one of his spies with the telephone company to try to find a number for the property. But there was no listed number for Carolyn Hart. She had an unlisted number under another name, a name he did not know.

"How does a person even communicate these days without giving out a phone number?" Kaminski asked a male friend one evening while walking their terriers in Rittenhouse Square. "I mean, a phone is probably the most basic means of communication in the world."

"Maybe she doesn't *want* to communicate," answered his friend. "Some people want to be left alone, you know."

The comment sent Kaminski's mind churning again. His imagination fed upon it until he came up with a new interpretation of the Carolyn Hart affair.

Carolyn, he now theorized, had been involved in some sort of traumatic love affair. She had broken up with her boyfriend and feared possible violence. Hence, she didn't wish to be located, not by anyone—including family—until tempers cooled down. That explained almost everything.

Seeing her in this light made Kaminski feel more protective. Her privacy, and hence her safety, was his responsibility. What choice did he, as a decent man, have other than to serve as her buffer against the outside world?

It was a duty which he took very seriously. He, Adam Kaminski, would serve as the young woman's "chevalier." And from his personal viewpoint, this history of Carolyn's past served perfectly.

He could snoop mercilessly into her personal affairs, he told himself, because he would need to know all about her in order to protect her.

Kaminski, home alone in his own apartment in the second month of Carolyn's tenancy, felt a surge of excitement. He welcomed this new challenge. And, pushing Paula Burns out of his thoughts, there were now some romantic tunes playing in his mind.

Kaminski pictured sultry Marlene Dietrich, husky voice and all, singing to him and his new lady. Adam Kaminski was already looking forward to falling in love again, head over heels as Marlene rhapsodized, if only Carolyn Hart would join him.

And somewhere, way back in the darkest recesses of his mind, there was another sort of music. Funny, he could hear the eerie tinkling of a piano playing a sad, old Southern hymn.

Chapter 6

The next morning in New Hampshire broke clear, sunny, and very cold. Yet most of the state highways remained closed. The secondary roads were impassable. The official snowfall was measured at thirteen inches, a record for so early in the season.

O'Hara arrived at police headquarters in Nashua by ten A.M. Captain Mallinson was still singing the same tune as the previous day, that the case of the Jane Doe found in the Monadnock cabin was to rise immediately to the top of O'Hara's priority list . . . at least until the case could be scoped out.

Preliminary evidence—photographs and material found at the murder scene—had already been brought to O'Hara's office at headquarters for New Hampshire Homicide. The latter was a set of cluttered cubicles located in a single large room on the west side of the new State Police Building. The room had all the charm of a high-school gym.

The corpse of Jane Doe, according to Captain Mallinson, would be retrieved that morning. By helicopter, if need be. A police guard had been left through the night, a single young cop in a jeep amidst a blizzard. State law: A body couldn't be left without a police guard. No stipulation about the weather.

The remains would be at the medical examiner's

office on the other side of Nashua by noon. A preliminary examination would take four hours. Since nothing ever went on schedule, O'Hara planned to go by Dr. Paloheima's office in the evening.

In his office, O'Hara had the plastic bag containing the woman's clothing that had been found in the cabin. O'Hara pondered a point. The clothes had been neatly stacked. Men don't normally stack women's clothing neatly, which suggested that she may have taken them off by herself . . . or at least voluntarily. Another nasty echo of the Gary Ledbetter homicides where the victims, according to the police psychologists, willingly undressed for their executioner.

O'Hara began his first careful examination of the clothing. It would also be his only examination before the police labs got hold of everything.

A light cotton skirt, a blue blouse. No stockings. Bra missing. Maybe she hadn't worn one either. He continued: Two sneakers, laces still tied as if she had pulled them off rather than taking the time to undo them.

What did that tell him? Anything?

There were no socks. No blood or rips on any of the clothing. No sign of a struggle. Panties. Fresh and clean.

Why hadn't the killer kept them? Often psychos collect the panties of women they kill. O'Hara thought back to the Ledbetter slayings and couldn't recall a parallel. He already knew that he was going to have to review the Ledbetter files very carefully.

In his mind's eye, O'Hara saw Gary standing before him. Shaggy blond hair. Those eyes. A dirtball Adonis, all right.

Gary speaking. Bayou tones. In another century, Gary could have been a sergeant in the Confederate infantry.

No, sir. I didn't kill no girls. Gary communicated

from somewhere beyond that room, speaking within O'Hara's mind. O'Hara dismissed the thought.

No, sir. I didn't kill no girls, the voice returned a second time.

"Shut up, Gary," O'Hara said aloud. Gary grinned and disappeared. Then O'Hara continued with the work before him. Another tactile moment with a dead lady's garments.

O'Hara looked at the labels in the clothing. He noticed something that he had not caught the first time. The clothing was upscale stuff. Labels from Boston and New York. Banana Republic sneakers. Ann Taylor blouse and skirt. Undergarment also from a quality department store. Not cheap stuff from the Ames or the Kmart. If this were actually the victim's clothing, then she might be more middle- or even upper-middle-class. Girls in that milieu tended to disappear less frequently. This was also a variance from previous Gary Ledbetter slayings. Gary's girls were solidly blue-collar: two waitresses, a beautician, a secretary, and a doughnut shop clerk.

Then, as he picked through the clothing, O'Hara found something else he hadn't seen. Something moved in the girl's left sneaker. O'Hara tilted the sneaker, and the small object slid again. He reached in and found a delicate chain necklace.

Nothing memorable. Nothing with huge intrinsic value. Just a gold chain with a small turtle charm as its pendant.

O'Hara weighed it in his hand. He guessed that the dead girl had removed it and slid it into her shoe for safekeeping. That, of course, suggested that she didn't expect to be murdered, even when she was undressing. That hinted that she hadn't been raped, either.

But further, why would she have removed it from her neck if she were going to make love? And why would the killer have left it there among her clothing?

While there was nothing special about it, the gold chain had a cash value. O'Hara guessed maybe a hundred fifty to two hundred dollars. The typical low-rent killer takes such things. First, to impede identification of the victim. Second, for cash. Those circumstances underscored O'Hara's notion that the girl had undressed voluntarily and her murder came seemingly out of the blue.

That raised another question. Why had the body been left in the cabin where surely it would someday be found? The shrinks always had a ball with something like that.

O'Hara could hear the psychiatrists arguing:

The killer wanted to impress society. The killer got off as much at having the public read about his grisly event as he did in the commission of the act, itself. The killer wanted to be discovered . . . and caught.

O'Hara sighed. He knew a detective could overthink this aspect of a killer's behavior as well as other motivations. Much in a homicide was chance. Much was careless. Yet this killing, following so closely the Ledbetter pattern, seemed intensely calculated.

O'Hara looked again at the neck chain and its pendant. Somewhere, at some time in the past, some young girl had bought the item. Or some boy had bought it for her. (The killer? O'Hara wondered. He doubted it.) The charm had been part of her persona. Part of her. He pictured the girl as having peaches-and-cream good looks. Light brown hair, pretty, perky. Someone's lover. Someone's daughter. Now she was dead. Whenever O'Hara followed this line of reasoning he became very indignant over death.

Over murder.

"Obsessive, once you get to know your victim," his ex-wife had once told him. "You become like the spurned lover to these girls, the guy who could have set things right. It's not normal and not healthy."

He answered his ex-wife aloud, much the same way he spoke to Gary. "No, Barbara, it's not normal and it's not healthy. It's not even smart. But that's how I am."

"Obsessive," she said again, then faded.

Didn't do it, man. The voice was Gary's again, inside O'Hara's head.

"Get lost!" O'Hara whispered, angrier than the last time he had addressed Gary's memory. Both Gary and Barbara disappeared.

Together. Gary put an arm around Barbara as they faded.

O'Hara cringed. He forced the image from his mind.

Then he tucked the necklace into an evidence envelope and sealed it. He put the envelope in his pocket. His old habit picked up from Carl Reissman: one possession of the victim that he would keep with him till the case was closed.

He returned to the blouse and turned the top of it inside out. He found what he needed: a human hair. It was light brown, the same as the hair that remained on the decomposed head that had been discovered with the body. He removed the hair with a pair of tweezers and placed it in a small waxed envelope.

Then he phoned the state police Central Records Division, located in that same building. He requested the files on the Karen Stoner homicide, plus any other material relating to Gary Ledbetter. All material was to be sent to his office.

With that accomplished, O'Hara cleared his desk. He called in two younger members of the state homicide bureau, Detective Leslie Parks and Detective Lawrence Rossiter. O'Hara turned over to them a trio of current cases.

The usual dirtball New Hampshire stuff:

One, a Hispanic teenager from Holyoke had been shotgunned in a Nashua parking lot the previous Sunday morning, a drug deal gone sour, his brains splattered across the concrete wall of a bar.

Two, an aged couple in Bennington—the husband had Alzheimer's—found dead in their beds at home. Bullet wounds. Double suicide, murder-suicide, or double murder? The assembled evidence pointed in various directions. So which was it? Hint: Their ne'er-do-well forty-year-old son didn't seem much upset and had already embarked on a spending spree.

And three, a chump-change stickup at a convenience store in Wilton. The counterman had been shot dead with a small-caliber handgun. This one had the signature of a couple of inner-city types out to see autumn foliage and looking to score a few bucks along the way. When the counterman produced a deer rifle, things went bad.

It took O'Hara the early part of the afternoon to review the three cases. He went for a sandwich about 4 P.M., but spent part of his lunch hour in the frigid parking lot, letting his Pontiac's engine idle so that it would start later. Then he came back to his office.

On his desk he found a preliminary Missing Persons list of women under the age of fifty. It had eighty-six names on it for New Hampshire, one hundred seventy-six for New Hampshire and Vermont combined, and three hundred eighteen for New England. And none of that included New York. New York victims had a way of landing in New Hampshire.

O'Hara scanned the list, sighed when it gave him no insight, and flipped it back onto his desk. Then he went downstairs to his car, treaded carefully across the ice in the parking lot, and cursed the glacial wind from Canada when it stung his face.

The sun had dropped and the temperature was on its way to the single digits, the territory of frozen fuel lines and dead car batteries. And there probably wasn't a lake or river in the state that couldn't be crossed on foot. Too bad that didn't help.

O'Hara found his Pontiac and forced the old engine to turn over. The Pontiac responded, and O'Hara began his slow drive across the snow-clogged Nashua streets to his next destination, the office of Vincent Paloheima, M.D.

The medical examiner was seated in his workroom finishing dinner when his visitor arrived. The doctor looked up.

"Ah! O'Hara!" Dr. Paloheima said. "Glad to see you. I'm not supposed to go home until I've spoken to you. Captain Mallinson's orders. So you came by just in time."

The room was tomb-like and frigid, much like a butcher's storage room, but less cheerful.

"Just in time for what?" O'Hara asked.

"Just in time so that I didn't get bored," the doctor said. "Time to talk. You and I."

Paloheima was using a steel examination slab as his dinette set, a body sheet for a tablecloth, and God-knew-what for a tray and plate. He set aside a scalpel that he had been using as a knife and rose from his meal. Ham and eggs. He dabbed at a corner of his mouth with a sleeve of his lab coat. Beneath the half open lab coat, the doctor wore a Boston Bruins sweat-shirt.

O'Hara's eyes travelled the room and settled upon Table Five, the main examination table. The center ring of Dr. Paloheima's gory little circus. There lay the remains of Jane Doe, NH:11-20-93 A. O'Hara felt a shiver coming on. He suppressed it. Paloheima's office contributed little to the gaiety of police work in New Hampshire.

O'Hara remembered coming to this same room as a

recruit in the police academy too many years ago and witnessing his first autopsy—that one done by this same Dr. Paloheima. On that distant day, half the recruits had vomited or passed out. O'Hara, who had seen much worse in Southeast Asia, had done neither. He remembered this clearly because he was fighting off such impulses again today. The odor of death was strong, thanks to the advanced state of decomposition of Ms. Doe. There was also the vague distant scent of marijuana in the room. Paloheima occasionally indulged.

"I got some pictures to show you," the M.E. said, moving to a Mr. Coffee on a side table. "Want some coffee first?"

O'Hara declined.

"You sure?"

"Just show me the pictures, okay?" O'Hara said.

The doctor looked at him with mild reproach as he crossed the room. "Lighten up, would you, O'Hara? By the time you're dealing with me, there's not much you can do for your victims. So maybe you ought to do something for yourself. Develop a sense of humor. Ever thought of that?"

The advice was offered in friendship. Paloheima liked O'Hara.

"I'm out of this job in another two months, Doc. And if I can wrap this Jane Doe I might even be able to get out a few weeks early. So let's get moving. Okay?"

Paloheima stopped a few steps short of the coffee maker. He turned. "What? Leaving a great job like yours?" O'Hara didn't answer, unable to tell whether Paloheima's remark was predicated on sarcasm or genuine surprise. Meanwhile, the doctor's eyebrows moved toward the ceiling. Then, after a moment's pause, he continued across the room.

Paloheima moved the way many large fat men do, rocking slightly side to side as he lurched forward.

The doctor also had a prominent forehead and deep-set dark eyes. From time to time, he also had a smile, but it was stark and gaunt, almost frightening—suggestive of a bloated skull that was forcing itself into mirth.

Many years ago, following graduation from a medical school in Honduras, Paloheima had nearly lost his medical license as fast as he had obtained it. He had been practicing at an abortion clinic in Brattleboro, Vermont, helping out college girls at fifty dollars a pop. But one girl had left the clinic with a perforated uterus and another had nearly died of infection. There were some nasty lawsuits.

Insurance money silenced the victims and Paloheima agreed to leave the state on probationary status as a medical practitioner. He looked for employment in neighboring New Hampshire, but the only opening was in the state M.E.'s office. There, it was theorized, he could do no lasting damage to his patients since they were already dead. Plus the only talent Paloheima had ever displayed as a doctor was the ability to cut.

So he was hired as the assistant state M.E. He kept free of any other serious screw-ups and ascended to the main position in the office by 1979. By then his aspirations were no higher than where he already was. In truth, he was lucky that a career in any sort of medical practice had been salvaged. So there he stayed, the Ben Casey of the cadavers, the Marcus Welby of the murdered.

Paloheima arrived at the Mr. Coffee. Steam rose from both the coffee maker and a plastic cup when Paloheima poured.

"Sure you don't want some coffee?" Paloheima asked a second time. "You're going to be up late."

"Why?"

"You're going to be up late *thinking,*" the doc said softly. "What you got here is an impossibility. When I see an impossibility it makes me stop and ponder. So I figure you'll be doing some thinking."

"Just show me what you have."

"Gladly."

The doctor led O'Hara to a wall where he had affixed some X rays and photographs. The doctor had two display screens arranged on the wall. He turned on a light behind a set of photographs.

"First off, Jane Doe was killed ninety to ninety-five days ago," the doctor said. "I can tell from the flesh on the hands and feet. See, when the killer cut the hand off and put it in the box, he kept it clean. It looks like some wildlife messed with the rest of the corpse. Look at this here. Teeth marks around the rib cage. And the rest of the body was exposed to air and elements. Not so with the hand."

"So the time of the murder," O'Hara said thinking back and making mental notes, "was sometime in August. Maybe the tenth to the twenty-fifth?"

"That's how I see it," Dr. Paloheima said. Then he told what else he saw.

Female Caucasian, probably of northern European extraction, aged twenty-four to thirty. Blood type O +, which narrowed things down to half the population of the United States and Canada.

"No other blood types found at the scene," Paloheima said, "even under her fingernails. So I can't give you a lead on your killer that way." The doctor paused. "Some monster spilled every drop of this girl's blood without losing any of his own."

O'Hara nodded. No sign of a struggle anywhere in the cabin. No sign of blood anywhere on the girl's clothing. She had stripped, left a neat pile of her own things, and assumed a position on the floor for her executioner.

Just like the Ledbetter case.

Why, O'Hara kept asking himself. Rough sex? A kinky form of love play? Kneel before me while I hold a sword above you? And then the fiend had gone ahead and snuffed her anyway.

Paloheima's words broke in upon Ledbetter's thoughts.

"It was impossible to tell if the girl had been raped," the doctor said. "The decomposition was much too advanced to tell of any vaginal assault or even the presence of semen."

Jane Doe had not been pregnant. The doctor couldn't find any traces of narcotics anywhere in the body and guessed she wasn't a junkie. He couldn't offer anything further except for the fact that she may have had a poor choice of acquaintances. O'Hara thought of offering his own conclusions that he'd made from looking at the girl's clothing, but didn't bother. No point.

"It looked to me that she was executed there," Paloheima said. "The blood pools on the ground would indicate as much. I guess that's your feeling, too."

"Yeah. It is," O'Hara answered.

"Pretty obvious, huh?"

"Pretty obvious, Doc."

"Get a reading on any fingerprints in that cabin?" Paloheima asked next.

"Forensic went back to do a second dusting," O'Hara said. "They don't know if they've got anything or not."

O'Hara grimaced, usually when the armada of technicians arrived on the scene their first accomplishment was to trample everything in sight.

"What about an ID on the victim?" the doctor asked.

"Not even a lead. What about you? Fingerprints?"

Paloheima said that he had rolled the frozen hand and had obtained a clear set of prints, plus palm impressions. The prints had been sent to the FBI central computer in Virginia. No report back yet. Fed match-ups would take twenty-four hours minimum, and the batting average was low for a potential connection from that source: maybe one time in ten.

Then the conversation turned to the modus operandi of the murder, and once again Dr. Paloheima had some theories.

"This one has strong resemblance to the Ledbetter case, doesn't it?" the M.E. asked.

"Uncanny."

"I did the dice-and-slice on that last Ledbetter victim. Remember?"

"I remember."

"So do I," Paloheima said. Paloheima stepped to the second display screen and flipped on the lights. He turned to O'Hara, his gaunt smile gone. "So since we both remember, what do you think?" he asked, motioning to two sets of autopsy examinations.

O'Hara drew a breath. "What am I looking at?"

The detective's eye drifted back and forth between two sets of photographs, showing the incisions made by the swords. Dr. Paloheima looked at him expectantly. The medical examiner said nothing. He only waited.

"Same thing, right?" O'Hara asked, looking back and forth. "Jane Doe right hand, Jane Doe right hand. No?"

On closer examination, the hands were different from the first screen to the second. Two different right hands.

"Jane Doe, November '93," said the doctor, indicating the first set of prints. "Karen Stoner, December '85," he said, indicating the second.

O'Hara's eye nervously fluttered back and forth. "So?"

"Same killer," said the doctor.

It took a second for it to sink in. "No. Impossible," O'Hara answered.

"Not impossible. Same killer," Paloheima insisted softly.

"It's *made* to look like the same killer," O'Hara said. "Gary Ledbetter was executed."

"Then that's a shame."

"Why?"

"The man who killed Karen Stoner also killed our new Jane Doe. My computer tells me so. Ninety-nine percent certainty. I'd swear to it in court based on this evidence."

"Doc . . . ? *How?* Christ Almighty! What are you talking about?"

It was a question for which Dr. Paloheima had been salivating worse than one of Pavlov's mutts. The M.E. put on his very own slide show.

"Check out these hack marks, Frank," he said, as if to take the younger man into his confidence. "Look at this and don't reject what your eyes tell you."

Hack marks. Sword impressions. Close-in photographs of a nightmare. In his lifetime, O'Hara had seen a lot and forgotten very little. But this was something else: The angle the sword had come down on Karen Stoner was the same as a similar sword had come down on Jane Doe.

"Same force, same angle . . ." Vincent Paloheima said. "I was so struck by it—you'll excuse the pun, right?—that I fed it all into the computer. Same pair of hands."

O'Hara stared at the evidence before him. "Can't be," he insisted again.

"Why?"

"Gary Ledbetter killed Karen Stoner."

"Never convicted of the Stoner murder," the doctor reminded O'Hara. "He was convicted in Florida of a separate and associated crime. Frank, my computer has more integrity than anyone in this state. It doesn't take bribes, it shows up for work every day and it *never* lies," the doctor said. *"Comprenez?"*

Paloheima extinguished the lights that illuminated the display, but O'Hara continued to stare at the photographs. The detective drew a long, confused breath and looked to the doctor. He felt the presence of the mutilated corpse on Table 5.

"You said ninety-nine percent certainty," O'Hara finally said. "What about the other one percent?"

"It's theoretical bullshit."

"Where does it figure in?"

"Statistically, you have to count it. Margin of error, one to two percent. But know what? I been doing pm's here since 1972 and I haven't seen the 'one percent' surface yet. Mr. Computer's got a perfect game going."

The doctor looked at O'Hara, then looked back and forth to the pictures again.

"You can take the X rays with you," Paloheima said. "Take them home. Study 'em. They're yours. I can make more. But they only tell you one thing."

He looked back and forth again from Jane Doe to Karen Stoner. Hand to hand, neck to neck. With the edge of his white coat he dabbed at his lips, a small yellow particle of egg left over from his meal.

"Same killer, Frank," he said. "Bank on it."

Midnight. Frank O'Hara lay on his bed and stared at the ceiling. On the bedside table were the remains of his second shot of bourbon and water.

As the bourbon wrapped its tentacles around him, O'Hara listened. Sinatra sang on the tape deck across the room. Sad Sinatra. Moody, tormented, mid-1960s Sinatra, gripping the blues the way only he could, creating and releasing more tension than a Hitchcock movie.

One of the great things about living alone, possibly the only great thing, was that O'Hara could play Sinatra as much as he wanted, as loud as he wanted and whenever he wanted. And no one would give him any heat about it.

His ex-wife had hated Sinatra. "Isn't that man a gangster?" Barbara used to ask him. Not a prescription for a long and happy marriage.

"People named Frank do things their own way," O'Hara always answered.

Barbara speaking: "Doesn't mean it's the right way."

O'Hara answering: "Doesn't mean it's the wrong way, either."

O'Hara lay back, relaxed, and listened to the more famous Frank. And as Francis Albert crooned, O'Hara sorted through the events of the day, plus their implications:

The same hand that had killed Karen Stoner had killed Jane Doe. The doc was convinced of it. Well, well, well. Where could that possibly have fit into anyone's orthodoxy?

Three scenarios presented themselves. O'Hara liked none of them.

Number one, Gary *had* killed Jane Doe. But the body was much, much older than Dr. Paloheima had attested. Paloheima was off by, say, one thousand percent. This theory had two aspects of it that worked: Paloheima was not beyond making a major error. And second, it accounted for the matching sword strokes.

Number two, Gary had worked with an accomplice.

Strange that this would never have come out after Gary's arrest or during his trial. Would Ledbetter have taken a solo fall to protect a partner? Doubtful, based on what was known of Gary. Ledbetter had seemed like a textbook lone wolf psycho. This theory further disintegrated because none of the five witnesses against Ledbetter in Florida had ever mentioned seeing Ledbetter with anyone other than his victims.

"An ultimate, incorrigible loner," one state shrink in Florida had testified of Gary. "He roams and kills."

Sinatra intruded gloriously. "I've Got You Under My Skin." Perhaps Frank's most perfect recording. The emotional context ranged from a whisper to a primal orgasmic scream. O'Hara stopped thinking about Gary and concentrated on Old Blue Eyes. Funny how well Sinatra went with a good bourbon.

The song ended. Silence now. Empty tape running toward the end of its reel. O'Hara's thoughts returned to Ledbetter.

Then O'Hara checked himself. He caught himself thinking of Gary in the present tense. Wrong to do that, he reminded himself. Gary belonged to the past.

The third theory. Gary had not been guilty in Florida. An innocent man had gone to Florida's hot seat. The Stoner murder resembled the others but wasn't part of the Ledbetter spree. There had been two different killers committing the same brand of murder. Now the other killer was in New Hampshire. Or has been.

O'Hara wasn't in love with this line of reasoning, either. It made sense, but its implications were as horrible as the murder itself. It suggested a mistake, and a bad one, by prosecutors and police. He reached to the glass next to him, finished the sour mash, and felt the booze settle within him.

The Sinatra tape clicked off. "The Chairman of the Board" was gone and O'Hara was alone.

There was a fourth theory, too, he realized, one that tied back into the first. Dr. Paloheima and his computer *were* wrong. Jane Doe's wounds and Karen Stoner's wounds *were* from different hands. O'Hara considered this final notion. He rooted for it.

O'Hara rose from his bed. He walked to the side window of his bedroom. The night was clear. A bright three-quarter moon. Crisp icy air on hard snow. Moonlight through the bare trees from the surrounding woods.

O'Hara stared at the darkness and let his thoughts unravel. Once again, he felt the overwhelming urge to go get that bottle of bourbon and really have a go at it. Now *that* would feel good, particularly under the circumstances.

He went downstairs and gave in to temptation. But only a little. He poured himself one more shot of Old Crow. He looked for some water to mix with it. Finding none, he didn't bother. Down the hatch, his feet not moving from where he poured his drink. He downed the entire shot.

He climbed the stairs again, feeling the comfortable glow of the sour mash. There! He felt much, much better now! A real improvement.

He imagined how much better he'd feel with a fourth shot, just the final measure that he would need to bump him into a state of real relaxation for the evening.

But he fought off that impulse.

Instead, he returned to the window and stared at the woods. He enjoyed the grip of that third bourbon and swore that he was finished drinking for the evening.

His thoughts drifted back to Jane Doe. And Gary. And how seven years ago the case had been pulled away from him on the heels of Carl Reissman's death, pulled away from him before O'Hara could personally convince himself *one hundred percent* that they had the right man.

Before he could really put to rest all those unnerving impulses within him that struck a strange echoing chord whenever Gary sounded that familiar theme:

I'm innocent, man.

"Fuck," O'Hara muttered. "What if he was?"

The thought shot a chill through him. The idea gnawed at him, then gripped him much like the bourbon. It had been years since O'Hara had really let the idea come forth from deep in his subconscious.

Years since he had let it come out where he could really think about it.

Gary. Innocent.

"Like hell, Ledbetter was innocent!" he muttered aloud.

O'Hara knew a killer when he arrested one. Always had, always would. Two fucking decades of police work and he'd never made a mistake. How could he have made such a big one? What about all that evidence? This was crazy to even be thinking about it.

I'm innocent, man.

O'Hara exhaled a long tired breath. "Shut up, Gary!" O'Hara snapped. "And get out of my head!"

Why was he almost fifty years old and still gripped by self-doubt? He was an intelligent professional who had done his job and done it properly.

Why was he nervous?

Anxious?

Scared?

An alcoholic about to fall back off the wagon?

"Fuck," he said aloud.

O'Hara told himself that he would have to talk to Dr. Steinberg again. There was one more cold winter to endure, plus one more big-time murder case. He wanted to graduate from both with his sanity intact, thank you. And he knew he would need Dr. Steinberg's help again.

Well, hell. That's what she was there for, he told himself. No shame in seeking assistance. The shame was in not seeking help when a man needed it. Just keep up with the visits to Dr. Julie, do what she says and everything will be hunky-dory.

Right!

The final shot of booze had now settled comfortably into his blood. Sure as hell, he felt much better. Who said there was anything wrong with two or three shots of liquor to steady a man's nerves?

Whatever floats your boat, pal!

There was a foreign voice inside him, one he couldn't control. It was more than his imagination. It was more than his mind wandering. It kept *addressing* him with slithery suggestions and insinuations. Just like that one. The voice disturbed O'Hara. It had a vaguely mid-Southern inflection, he didn't understand its presence, and worst of all, he couldn't shut it off.

It was one thing, he reasoned, to conjure up an image of Gary and imagine his words. It was quite another to be addressed involuntarily. The voice had a nasty echo of Gary's. O'Hara wished to hell that it would go away.

Ask yourself, Frank. What is your greatest fear? That you made a big-time boo-boo? That you helped send an innocent man to the electric chair?

Insane laughter from somewhere.

Shame, Frank!

O'Hara remained at the window, trying to ignore the voice, willing it to vanish. He forcibly moved his thoughts in other directions, pondering for example whether to put Sinatra back on or maybe play some Louis Armstrong. Meanwhile, his gaze melted into the darkness beyond his house. He stared at the dark, fingery branches and thin trunks of the naked trees.

First, he sensed the snow ghosts. Then he saw them. Illusory figures moving stealthily from tree to tree.

O'Hara grinned ruefully.

Hello, you fucking snow ghosts, he thought. Welcome back. You're bringing out my sorehead, belligerent streak, you know. But tell me, are you having fun out there in the . . . ?

Jesus!

His heart kicked the way a man would kick at an electrocution. A seismic bang inside O'Hara's chest!

Christ Almighty! His mouth went dry and his heart roared like a race car.

This was real! He wasn't imagining what he was now seeing!

The snow ghosts were suddenly gone. Or all but one! A man—the figure of a man—stepped out of the woods. Out of the darkness.

O'Hara stared, his mouth suddenly bone-dry.

Even in the nearly nonexistent light, the pale illumination provided by the moon against the snow, O'Hara could see the features of the intruder.

He was about five feet ten. Handsome in that rough-hewn white trash way. Shaggy blond hair. Eyes that . . . blues eyes that transfixed O'Hara's attention.

And what was worse, the man wasn't dressed for the snow. He wore a white shirt and dark slacks. Oblivious of the frigid temperature. The figure stood on the top of the snow and gazed upward at O'Hara. Then a smile crossed the man's face.

O'Hara felt his palms go wet with terror! He was looking at a dead man! Gary Ledbetter! And Ledbetter, with those calculating cold baby blues, was glaring right back up at him.

"No, no, no!" O'Hara whispered. "I am not seeing you, Gary! These are D.T.'s! I've had too much to drink! You are not there!"

Gary's voice. Unmistakably. Coming from nowhere

and from everywhere. Inside the house; inside O'Hara's head.

I'm here, Gary said.

"You are a dead man. The State of Florida executed you."

I am here, anyway, Frank.

"But why?"

Maybe I'm here to take you with me.

"With you where?"

To the land of the dead, Frank. To the land where you sent me.

"You sent yourself. You were a murderer."

No, no, no. I gone on account of your stupidity. I was innocent.

O'Hara averted his eyes and shook his head. The liquor made his head swim. The glass in his hand fell to the wooden floor and shattered. O'Hara was barely conscious of it. And he refused to look at the specter lurking outside his home.

But it called to him.

Frankie? Frankie? Frankie? Diminutive. Insulting. Taunting.

O'Hara refused to respond.

Look at me, Frank. Answer me, my fine detective friend.

"No!" O'Hara snapped. Very loud. Very firm. His words echoed in the lonely room. "I don't believe in such things!"

Asshole!

O'Hara raised his eyes and stared downward. The specter remained. Gary looked up at him, eyes gleaming. No longer blue. Red like those of a wild animal, frozen in winter headlights. Red like a demon. Hatred, hatred, hatred.

O'Hara screamed.

I was innocent, Frank. Surely you must have always

suspected. Surely you will soon know if you don't already.

O'Hara breathed hard and heavily. He had not moved, but he was out of breath. The terror only built. He wondered if he was on the verge of a fatal heart attack and Gary was there to take him . . . take him . . . to Hell!

Somewhere in his mind, way off in the distance, O'Hara saw himself with the last bout of D.T.'s, the time the red crab crawled down his throat. He saw himself running through his home screaming until he pitched himself down a flight of steps and knocked himself unconscious.

The whole incident flashed before his mind again, on this night when the late Gary Ledbetter stood outside his window, smiling up at him. O'Hara was on the edge of screaming out loud in much the same way. Only this time it wasn't a crab crawling down his throat. It was a dead man crawling back into the world of the living.

Frank? Look at me, Frank. Or don't you dare? Ask yourself. What is your greatest fear?

O'Hara turned from the window, trying to shut out the image.

A very polite Gary. Southern schoolboy now. The kid who tickled the ivories so nice at the church social:

May I come into your home, Detective O'Hara? May I sit in your bedroom and maybe put my hands on your neck?

O'Hara felt a scream in his throat. He bolted from the room and ran down the steps, down to the kitchen utility closet where he knocked over every household tool in his way. He lunged to the object that he kept hidden at the rear of the closet, behind the brooms and the mops.

His twelve-gauge shotgun. Always loaded.

O'Hara grabbed it with both hands.

He whirled, crashed into the closet door, and nearly lost his footing. He ran to the back door of his home and threw on an outside light, one that would illuminate the wooded area where Gary had been standing.

Then he stopped. The door, the door that stood between him and the outside, was rattling. The doorknob almost seemed to shake.

Gary? The vision he had seen outside? Something now trying to enter O'Hara's home.

Yes, Frank. It's me.

O'Hara stood away from the door and raised his weapon.

"Who's there?" he bellowed. "Identify yourself!"

No answer. The door gave a final quiver. Outside the wind howled. Had it been the wind at the door? Or some other force?

Cautiously, O'Hara unlocked the door. He threw it open, his shotgun ready to blast. Frigid air poured in, but nothing else.

Mocking. Taunting. Gary again: *You're not being very friendly. And it's me who has the right to be angry.*

But no one was visible.

O'Hara felt his heart kick again for several seconds. Then, in shirt, pants, and shoes, O'Hara was out in the freezing cold, a shotgun at Order-Arms across his chest. The only sound: the wind, plus one step after another—his own—crunching through the thick snow.

He turned a corner and confronted the strip of land where he had seen Gary.

Nothing. No one.

O'Hara's gaze bored into the woods. Even the snow ghosts had fled. The only sound was a sudden rush of wind. The frozen branches clattered against each other, rattling like ancient bones. Winter's icy spirit in the treetops.

"Come on out!" O'Hara demanded. "Come on fucking out here!"

But again, no Gary. No one.

O'Hara's adrenaline began to subside. And as it did, he realized that he was cold. Very cold. Freezing. He shivered and looked at his breath as it coned in front of him. He felt his bare hands starting to adhere to the metal trigger of the shotgun.

He cursed violently to himself. He approached the spot where Gary had stood. His feet broke the surface of the snow and left tracks. When he got to where Gary had been, he looked down.

No footprints. Nothing. Virgin snow.

O'Hara cursed again. He could feel the aftertaste of the bourbon on his breath.

He wondered: Had nothing been there at all? Or had his visitor been so far out of the ordinary that it had stood on top of the snow and made no impression?

Something supernatural.

What was any man doing out in the New Hampshire snow without a coat? In that sense, the vision had been an impossibility.

Maybe he should have been thankful for that, he told himself. A hyperactive imagination, even with some of the blame laid upon the booze, had lesser implications than if he really had seen something.

Again, O'Hara looked carefully at the untouched snow. Then he turned with his weapon. Sleepily, groggily, angrily, he walked back to the warmth of his home.

He wasn't going crazy, he told himself. He was perfectly sane.

He closed the door behind him. He carefully locked it. He replaced the shotgun in the downstairs closet and covered it again with the implements of housekeeping.

He wasn't drunk, he told himself. And whatever he had seen, he did not wish to see again.

Chapter 7

Julie Steinberg sat across the office from her patient. A single brass lamp was unlit on the corner of her desk, a green glass shade upon it. There was a window but the venetian blinds were drawn.

Ten in the morning. Bright light from outside—sun upon the snow—turning into a softer light within. A feeling the doctor nurtured.

Dr. Steinberg was in her thirties, dark and attractive, but nothing fancy about her. Alert brown eyes, a practicing commercial psychologist for thirteen years. Divorced, no children. She had finally revealed this on their last meeting.

She smiled, putting him at ease. "I hear you've handed in your retirement papers," she said.

O'Hara nodded. He sat in a comfortable leather armchair, facing her. "How did you know?"

"Captain Mallinson and I speak occasionally."

He rolled his eyes. "I might have known."

"And that went successfully?" she asked. "Your application for retirement?"

"That went fine. So far. No problems."

"Then tell me," she said, "what's wrong?"

"I think I need to talk," O'Hara said hesitantly.

"Then you were wise to come," she answered.

Wise and, he might have added, embarrassed. Why

couldn't he handle one more case without psychological support?

"I only have this one case that I'm working on," he said. "And it ties into an older case that has resurfaced." He paused. "You remember the Gary Ledbetter case?"

"Everyone in New England remembers that one," she answered. "Ledbetter was just executed, wasn't he?"

"He was."

"Then how could his case come up again?"

He drew a breath and then explained it to her: the discovery in the cabin and the known parallels between the Stoner murder and this most recent Jane Doe.

Then O'Hara related how this voice that resembled Gary's came to him from somewhere, putting thoughts in his head. He also told her about the snow ghosts, how he had seen them so vividly as he rode up Mount Monadnock to the murder scene a week earlier. And he told Dr. Steinberg about what he had seen the previous evening: the snow ghosts, then the image of Gary Ledbetter, dressed exactly as he had been the day O'Hara had arrested him, stepping out of the woods to communicate.

Dr. Steinberg listened intently, a clipboard before her, a pencil in her hand. Her gaze rarely left her patient's eyes. She made notes without looking down.

O'Hara continued for twenty minutes. When he finished, the psychologist blew out a slight breath.

"So you think you saw a ghost?" she asked, intrigued and frowning slightly.

"I don't believe in ghosts," he said.

"You don't believe in what you saw?"

"No." He drew a breath. "You know I had a bout with the D.T.'s a few years back. Well, I had a few drinks last night. Before I saw this . . ." he searched for the word, " 'hallucination.' "

"How many's a few?"

"One more than the house limit," he confessed. "Three."

She shook her head. Annoyed.

"I don't want to see Gary Ledbetter again," he answered. "I even phoned Florida. Gary's dead and buried. I could not possibly have seen him."

"Anything else?" she asked.

"Yes. I have a current murder case to close. I want to close it without losing my mind."

She raised an eyebrow. "I suppose that's a good start," she said. They exchanged a smile. She waited.

"What were you doing when all this began?" she asked. "Last night, I mean."

He thought back. "Just listening to some music."

"Alone?"

"Yes."

"What kind of music? Moody? Suggestive?"

He laughed. She smiled. "Is that a professional question or a personal one?" he asked.

"Maybe a little of both."

Sinatra, he was thinking to himself. And he felt the eyes upon him of a woman a decade and a half younger.

"If I tell you," O'Hara answered, "you'll be convinced that I'm a hopeless old goat."

"Jazz? Show tunes?" she asked.

"Nope."

"Not classical?" she asked with a doubtful tone.

"Nope."

"What else is there? Let's see, something current. Alternative grunge?"

"I said a hopeless *old* goat, not a punked-out young goat," he answered.

They both laughed. "I'm withdrawing the question," she said.

He shrugged. "Good."

Julie Steinberg put her head down and wrote for several seconds, maybe half a minute. Then she began speaking without looking up.

"Remember, Frank. You have to be honest with me. Right?"

"Right," he answered.

Her brown eyes came up, sharp as thorns. "How long have you been going past the two-drink limit in the evening?"

He sighed. "Last night was the first time."

She waited.

"Honest," he said.

"So it coincides with this current case?"

"Well, yes."

Julie Steinberg smiled. "Doesn't that suggest something right there?" she asked. "You're under pressure. Troubled. A final winter is coming to New Hampshire. You feel comfortable with an extra drink, but if you examine the results, you're making things worse. Not better."

He weighed her words and felt a sinking feeling. He knew where she was leading him.

"Frank, you cannot drink alcohol at all. You think you can handle it, but you can't. The spirits of the dead do *not* just step out of the woods and they do *not* carry on telepathic messages with you."

"How do you know they don't?" he asked after several seconds.

"You just told me you didn't believe in such things," she countered.

"I *don't* believe in such things."

"Then you're contradicting yourself. Try to reason this out."

He shook his head. *"Help* me reason it out."

"Certainly. In the entire history of human civilization," she said, "no one has ever proven the existence of a disembodied human spirit. Not once. Nor is telepathy found in any of the precise sciences."

"Then where does what I saw come from? And where do these messages come from? The ones that I'm hearing."

Dr. Steinberg leaned back in her chair. She tapped a finger to the side of her head, then pointed a red fingernail at her patient. And she smiled, to make it all perfect.

"From your own imagination, Frank. Gary Ledbetter wasn't outside your house, and no one else was, either. That's why there were no footprints in the snow. But combine your final uncertainties about his case with the pressures of ending your career successfully, mix them both with alcohol and . . . boom!"

She clapped her hands once to make the point.

"Sure," he said, "but—"

"Was this the only man you ever arrested who was eventually executed?" she asked.

"Yes."

"It's natural that you should feel some guilt," she said. "But you shouldn't. Doubts are normal concerning an event of that magnitude." She shook her head gently. "You might be having an extreme reaction to this, but not an *abnormal* reaction."

He nodded.

"And you're going to have to drop the booze. Cold turkey."

He settled back in his chair, obviously displeased. "Aw, come on," he finally said.

"I can't give you any other advice, Frank. I'd be a quack if I did."

He studied the carpet. Their eyes met in silence. Then a small wave of relaxation overtook the doctor's office. In the light of day, things that reared up as demons at two A.M. slipped neatly and obediently into place. And maybe, just maybe, O'Hara reasoned, he could get through a few weeks on nonalcoholic beer and Coca-Cola Classic.

The psychologist continued. Softly. Very soothing feminine intonations.

"You have to reject the reality of spirits of the dead and telepathic messages," Julie Steinberg said. "And you have to do that with a clear head. Further, if you can't curtail your drinking by yourself, I'm going to ask Captain Mallinson to send you to the AA or some- where else for treatment of substance abuse. And that will hold up your retirement."

"Oh, hell. Don't do that."

"Then do what I'm asking, Frank," she said. "The decision is in your hands. I'm being tough on you because your life and future are in your hands. Not my hands. *Your* hands."

He sighed again and nodded. Their eyes met.

" 'Tough love,' huh?" he asked.

"Call it what you will." She managed a smile. "You came to me for help. That's what I'm trying to pro- vide. All right?"

For several seconds he thought about it. "All right," he finally agreed.

O'Hara returned to state police headquarters and went to his office. The files on the Karen Stoner case should have been on his desk by now. They weren't. He went downstairs to retrieve them himself.

Central Records was jammed into the basement of the police headquarters building. The official word was that CR was located there for the convenience of the detective bureau. Everyone in the building knew better.

When the new headquarters had been planned in

1986, a location across the street had been designated as the future annex for police records. Files, paperwork, court proceedings, and evidence from all previous investigations. Great location, plenty of logic to the proposal. There was even talk about computerizing everything and giving every homicide dick a desktop terminal. The high-tech, no-shoe-leather approach to case resolution. Real modern for a hick state.

But then came the stock market crash of 1987. Boston Yuppie money stopped moving into the southeastern section of New Hampshire. There went the state tax base. The records annex and the computers were great ideas whose time had already gone.

For nineteen months crates of old records languished in a warehouse in Preston—actually a barely heated converted barn that still smelled of horse dung. Every cop, when he needed a file, had to go over to the barn and pick through the accumulated mess until he found what he wanted. No concise inventory was ever established, few files were ever checked out properly and much was not returned. So in July of 1991 the last seven years of material (or at least what the filing clerks could find of it) was shipped back to Nashua and crammed into the drafty basement at headquarters.

Once there had been a clerk, a short, tubby, genial, puffy-faced spinster named Rose Horvath. Rose had sat in this claustrophobic chamber from nine A.M. to three P.M. five days a week, reading romance novels between the occasional records inquiry. Rose had been playing out a few final years on the state payroll before retiring.

Previously, Rose had worked as a secretary in the governor's office during the inspired reign of John Sununu. Then she had found a situation with the Nashua district attorney after Iron John moved to the cushy federal payroll in Washington. Later in her career, Rose had been a secretary in state police homicide. O'Hara had always been unfailingly courteous to her while others treated her like dirt. He also used to give her a two-pound Whitman Sampler for Christmas, which she usually had finished by the evening of December 26. In return, she told O'Hara anything she had seen, read, overheard, or suspected in any of the offices in which she had worked.

It was a wonderful relationship, O'Hara and his plump Rose. He fed her addiction (chocolates), and she fed his, professional tips and department scuttlebutt. But like most perfect relationships, this one, too, was doomed. The bureaucrats fired her late in 1992, seven months south of her full twenty-year pension, a casualty of the state's economic wreckage. She now lived in the town of Bennington, New Hampshire, with six cats.

So when O'Hara entered Central Records and turned on the light, he was alone, although Rose's desk and chair were unmoved from where she had last occupied them. Even her well-worn posture cushion remained—battered, curved foam rubber, crushed at its center—tied to the chair by brown twine. Less apparent was the background of the Karen Stoner case, which was buried somewhere before him.

O'Hara tried to remember how the room was organized. Then he remembered that it wasn't organized at all. All homicide arrests had been grouped together, convictions together with cases dropped for lack of evidence. Killers rubbing shoulders with the innocent.

O'Hara went immediately to work. There were seventeen cabinets of murder cases from 1985 onward. When he started opening drawers he found decaying, mildewed folders of occurrence reports, trial transcripts, indictments, and countless water-stained mug shots.

Some of the cabinet drawers hadn't been opened for

years. There was a particularly New Hampshire touch
to these files, O'Hara noted. They had been in a filthy
barn which had been stifling, then freezing, trapping
moisture within the folders. Many pages were stuck
together and needed to be pried apart with a sharp
blade. And in each case's records, there was usually a
picture of the victim or victims, sometimes clipped
right to the photo of the convicted perp.

O'Hara growled a low profanity to himself as he
began his search. Within the files themselves, he found
another layer of disorder. The alphabetization had
been in connection to the county where the murder
had occurred, then assigned the number of the homicide for the year. Smaller counties tended to have few
murders. O'Hara remembered that Karen Stoner had
been found in the basement of an abandoned garage in
Antrim. Thus she rested in peace under "Cheshire
County 11-13-86."

O'Hara located her file and pulled it.

Then he pulled the linked file on Gary Ledbetter. He
placed his hands on three thick manila folders and
withdrew them. Then he stopped because he heard
something.

Muffled gunshots. A fusillade of six in quick order.
Then another volley of eight, higher caliber and more
rapid than the first reports.

For a moment, O'Hara felt a flash and stopped
breathing. Then he relaxed. The state police indoor
pistol range was on the other side of this room. There
was seven feet of solid cement between him and the
ass-end of the target range. Nonetheless, when O'Hara
took a space at a table, he chose one around the corner
of the room. Finally, he settled in to contemplate some
of the horrors which earned him a living.

He read carefully.

Ledbetter, Gary, the file began. Born in Metarie,
Louisiana, 02-25-65. Arrested in Peterborough, New

Hampshire, 01-15-87, charged with homicide, degree two, maximum rap under the law.

There were several separate envelopes within Gary's file. Some of the early ones were familiar. O'Hara found his own arrest report. He remembered typing it and signing it. Police officers normally took to typewriters the way fish took to bicycles, but O'Hara's case summaries and arrest reports were not embarrassments of misspellings and abominations of grammar. They were concise and properly detailed.

He took a moment on Envelope Two. The original incident report. O'Hara reread his own summation. Decapitated female torso found in the basement of a converted garage. He remembered the day with a chill. The stench. The obscenity of the discovery. The pink-ribboned box containing the severed hand. The head of Karen Stoner placed on a mock altar before the nude, bloody body.

He cringed anew. He recalled the feeling of his knees involuntarily buckling and how he tried to make like a veteran criminologist so that he wouldn't barf. The hunt for the killer came back. The questioning of Karen's friends. The first time he laid eyes on Gary. Gary's lies. . . .

Not me, man. I didn't hurt no doughnut shop waitress.

"Yeah, Gary," O'Hara whispered. "It's past history. Shut up and let me read."

I was innocent, man. You're starting to suspect so yourself.

"Get out of my head."

Gary fell silent.

The first four envelopes contained evidence which O'Hara had assembled. The next three contained material assembled by one Ben Ashton.

For a moment, O'Hara drew a blank. Then, fuck it, Ashton came back. Too clearly, the way the pain of an abscessed tooth comes back.

Ben Ashton had been the state attorney general in 1987. A little thirty-one-year-old prick with lofty ambitions and a common sense IQ to match his sleeve size. University of New Hampshire Law School, Dartmouth College undergraduate. Gained admission to both places on family suck. O'Hara always wondered who had taken Ashton's law boards for him; probably the same dude who took his SATs. It was inconceivable that he could have scored well on either by himself. The guy was a dolt.

Attorney General Ashton: Tiny events from the past bubbled up in O'Hara's memory almost faster than he could correlate them. There had been something about an anti-Semitic, anti-black, anti-gay letter that Ashton had signed in his Dartmouth days. The letter surfaced during his campaign. Ashton had denied it, then claimed he didn't remember it, then apologized for it, then claimed it was a forgery. Not that it offended more than a few hundred people in the state. Fact was, it solidified his yahoo credentials among certain elements of the electorate.

Now, in 1993, Ashton's name still popped up in some political circles in the state. He was in private law practice, and a darling of the neanderthal wing of the Republican party. Behaved like the Duke of Des Moines, the big fish in the small pond. Back in the gung ho eighties, Ashton had secured his nomination as state Attorney General in return for many political favors done by his daddy. The year he won election, his party won *in spite of* him, not because.

O'Hara had been rid of Ashton since 1990, the year the voters threw a lot of the bastards out of office. But the memories came back. None of them good. Ashton barely knew state law, much less the Bill of Rights, much less how to prosecute. He had a great relationship with Wilhelm Negri, publisher of the New Hampshire *American,* however, who was tight with Ashton's family, so he received friendly press. But despite good PR and his vocal pro-cop public stance, a lot of police didn't like Ashton. He had blown too many big cases through incompetence.

O'Hara opened the files containing evidence assembled by the A.G.'s office in the Ledbetter case. He began to turn pages. How was this for irony? Ashton had assembled little more than O'Hara had already provided. Had Ashton prosecuted, he would have had to call O'Hara as a chief witness. Ashton and O'Hara had locked horns many times. The bad feelings between the two men were mutual.

O'Hara's finger began to drum on the reading table. A constant tapping on the same spot.

Lazy bastard, O'Hara mused. Ashton had never built his own body of evidence. Then a thought reached O'Hara. It was a given that Ashton was a lazy bastard. But had he actually never planned to prosecute the case? If not, why not? He couldn't possibly have expected Gary to cop a guilty plea.

O'Hara followed this line of thought, flipping ahead to more evidence in envelopes. Forensic reports. Fingerprints. Photographs from Leonard the photographer, the Mathew Brady of New Hampshire homicide. A windy discourse on blades from Dr. Paloheima.

But where had the A.G.'s own investigators been? Hell, this was a high-profile murder case. What kind of prosecution had the State intended to build? From what O'Hara saw, the in-state investigation stopped the day O'Hara had been pulled off the case.

Had Ashton not planned to try the case because Florida planned to prosecute it? But how would Ashton have known that so early? O'Hara thought back and recalled the shrill editorials in the the New Hampshire *American,* and the strange jurisprudence which suddenly had the case whisked out of state so that

Gary could face the hot squat instead of twenty-five to life.

Or had Ashton just been his usual incompetent self, started to assemble a flawed case and then been saved when Ledbetter was extradited?

O'Hara reexamined his own thoughts. A *flawed* case? The one against Gary Ledbetter?

Not guilty, man.

What was going on here? O'Hara had never seen any of this before. Seven years earlier, O'Hara had been tuned into the basic "I.A.P.I." of the Stoner case: identification, apprehension, prosecution, and incarceration. Not the backstage bullshit. And he and Carl Reissman had done the I.A.P.I. step by step. Resolutely and by the book.

None of this stuff that he had assembled before him today, O'Hara recalled, had ever been intended for general viewing, much less a private reading by a state cop. What was in this file seemed to be an abridged version of what had been left over in Ben Ashton's briefcase when he dumped the case to Florida.

A flawed case? Flawed where? Flawed how? O'Hara's impression of the state prosecutor plummeted to a new low. And the sloppiness of what was assembled was breathtaking. Envelopes Eleven and Twelve were missing.

O'Hara flipped ahead in the file to see if Eleven and Twelve were out of order. But they weren't. They were gone.

Why? What had been in them?

It would be nice if you knew, man. O'Hara wasn't sure if that was Gary talking or himself. *Real nice.* Silky tone. "Big Easy" accent. Gary all the way.

O'Hara found Envelope Thirteen and saw that it marked a continuation of correspondence surrounding the case.

O'Hara kept opening files. Now what the hell *was*

this? Right after O'Hara had been pulled off the case, some of the big shots in the state started to take a more active interest.

Gary speaking: *See? See? See? I got some friends in important places in New Hampshire, man.*

O'Hara whispered. "What were you talking about, Gary?"

You never believed me, did you, you fuckhead?

"So what were you trying to tell me?" O'Hara paused. "Come on. Tell me now," he said.

Fuck you, pal!

The correspondence in Envelope Thirteen continued from the two missing envelopes. It didn't take a genius to guess that it should have been "lost" with Eleven and Twelve.

"Holy Christ," O'Hara whispered when he saw what was in front of him. Included was a memo about the case from the governor of New Hampshire.

O'Hara read the governor's words to his own A.G.: ". . . hoping that this sordid matter will reach a speedy conviction and conclusion . . ." and ". . . am certain that you understand my ongoing interest in the case. . . ."

The A.G. back to his boss: ". . . proceeding with every priority of this office . . . You will not be disappointed in the final ajudication of the case. . . ."

"Ajudication." [Sic.] Seven years of the best higher education in this state and Benny Boy still couldn't string together the proper letters to master a five-syllable word. Who expected literacy out of high-school kids these days when law-school graduates couldn't spell?

And, returning to the larger issues, what the hell were these letters all about? Since when did the governor set up a private cheering section in a homicide prosecution?

O'Hara waded through more correspondence. An angry memo from the governor about the troublesome opinions of one "JS" in the case and how the opinions of "JS" could be shelved.

O'Hara, piqued, wondered: Who the hell was J.S.?

O'Hara ran the initials through his memory of the case. Prosecutors, legal aide mouthpieces. Cops and family members. Witnesses. No goddam J.S. anywhere in sight.

And where had he seen a stray initial or initials before? He placed it. "S. Clay." The name on the storage unit. A Gary pseudonym?

It's me, man.

"What's you?"

S. Clay. It's me and it's not me. Okay?

O'Hara's voice was a whisper again. "Explain it to me. 'S. Clay'?"

You figure it out. You're the genius.

O'Hara racked his brain. S. Clay receded and J.S. came forth.

Seven years ago. Who was O'Hara forgetting?

Whoever the troublemaker had been, the J.S. who had gotten under Ashton's skin, O'Hara reckoned as he slowly turned over more pages, the snotty, little A.G. seemed to have successfully dealt with him. J.S. had probably been fired by now. A final memo to the governor, marked "HIGHLY CONFIDENTIAL," on Ashton's stationery made matters clear.

". . . opinion of JS has been dismissed and replaced with a more favorable summation of details re Ledbetter," the semi-literate Ashton had written. "JS has been advised that JS opinions show lack of mature judgment, are marked by inexperience and are of no value to the prosecution and conclusion of said case and that their will be reprecussions upon JS's continued employment by the state if JS in any way damages final disposition of the case."

The Attorney General was so pleased with himself that he took the liberty of signing the letter, "Ben," a conspicuous break from previous signatures which included his surname. There was almost an insinuation that he had done the governor some sort of service.

And curiously, at the bottom, was a handwritten postscript from Ashton.

"This is the type of shit," Ashton's note read, "that we get into with affirmative action hiring." The A.G. was so bright that he didn't even know enough *not* to put such thoughts in his own handwriting. O'Hara sighed. He no longer wondered how Ashton had graduated from law school; he wondered how he had successfully completed sixth grade.

Then O'Hara was abruptly jarred back to the present day. There was a series of loud reports beyond the concrete wall of Central Records, followed by a second and third burst. O'Hara's head came up with a snap. His heartbeat accelerated. He was reminded of those naval shore patrols along the Mekong.

Gunfire! Several seconds passed as he placed it. Then he calmed. Slowly.

The sound came from the target range next door. O'Hara listened again. Someone, with great enthusiasm, was blasting away with some new grossly overpowered automatic weapon. New issue. Just testing. Tactical heavy weapons. The rounds had obviously smashed through the regular targets, passed through the bales of hay behind the targets, and were smacking up against the seven feet of concrete. Some of his peers would have been happy with howitzers in every cop car. New Hampshire staties used to spend their time dragging the cars of drunken skiers out of ditches. Now all anyone could think about was how the county roads could turn into miniatures of Medellín, Columbia, or the back streets of the cities could turn into downtown Beirut any week now. Snow wasn't the only white powder that brought death to the state.

O'Hara drew a breath and returned to the present. *Didn't do it, man. Can't you see?*

"I don't see anything yet, Gary," O'Hara said aloud.

Also in Envelope Thirteen was a bio of Gary Ledbetter, an embellishment on the material put together by O'Hara seven years earlier. The bio was in several different sections compiled by various police agencies. Much old stuff. But O'Hara had never seen this.

O'Hara scanned.

Ledbetter: Lower-class white family. Three children. Fundamentalist Christian mother. Abusive alcoholic father, then absentee father. School? Yeah, occasionally Gary dropped by academia from time to time when he felt like it or maybe when he was hiding out from his old man. Never passed a grade after seventh. Family moved several times across the South. Brother died in car accident. Sister left the family. For Gary, Henderson Juvenile Correctional Facility in Charleston, South Carolina, at age sixteen for ten months, a finishing school for tough boys who wanted to be tougher. They were after a few weeks at Henderson.

One Grand Larceny, Auto: Atlanta, 1980. The GLA was hitched to a felonious assault rap, charges dismissed when the owner, a man in his sixties, dropped the charges. Said he'd "given" Gary the keys to his BMW and had asked for some rough stuff while they drove around. Apparently Gary had gotten out of hand and had shoved the old dude out of the car at a traffic light then took off down Peachtree in his new Beemer.

O'Hara's brow furrowed. Now *here* was stuff about Gary that O'Hara had never seen. Reading between the lines, it looked like a fag encounter, an old guy with an expensive ragtop who liked to pick up rough trade. Was that it? That's how it read to O'Hara: An old queen looking for a hard, young bugger. Had the old guy picked up a street punk and things got out of hand?

Two other arrests. Both in 1982. Assaults. Male victims. What the hell? O'Hara thought again. He had never seen any of this stuff. Nor, he reminded himself, would he have had any occasion to. The case had been whisked away from him five weeks after the arrest.

O'Hara kept reading. Gary had done two short stretches in county jails. Six weeks here. Thirty days there. He had finished a high-school correspondence course, joined the Army, and had been booted out of the service almost as fast. June 1983. A three-month enlistment ending in a dishonorable discharge.

Someone had placed a copy of Ledbetter's dishonorable discharge in the file. "Moral turpitude," the document said. Again, what the hell was going on here? The term was normally used for homosexual activity, O'Hara reasoned, and at no time had Gary Ledbetter been identified as gay.

Was he? Or had he just hustled gay men? The latter fit better than the former, based on what O'Hara knew.

Yet as O'Hara prowled through the paperwork on the executed man, such questions began to grab the detective by the lapels.

O'Hara was getting into the mood. He reached for more. Envelope Fourteen was marked "Serial Killers: Psychological Profiles." He grabbed that next.

O'Hara opened it. He found a composite of opinions contrived by various doctors on the state payroll. Outlines of social portraits of one of America's sexually homicidal male citizens. He spent half an hour picking through opinions that were both lurid and clinical.

It all seemed to point in the same direction. Some of the more memorable stuff stood out. O'Hara read carefully.

"Ledbetter is a 'lust killer,' " wrote a psychiatrist named Richard Hawkins, who—judging by the expensive stationery—apparently had a booming private practice in Concord.

Obviously sexual oppression and confusion contributed to Ledbetter's mental state. Most lust killers cannot comprehend the act of sex with a live, functioning woman. A dead body poses no threat. This is coupled with a tremendous rage toward women, a feeling that a certain female is not "female enough" to turn him on.

O'Hara drew a breath and forged ahead. The psychiatrist offered an aside that if you got past the dirtball veneer, Ledbetter resembled Ted Bundy in his psychological profile.

A handsome, intelligent, one-time law student who carried on several successful nonviolent liaisons with women and actually wrote a rape-crisis manual. But even Bundy became a necrophile in the end.

Perfect twenty-twenty hindsight, O'Hara noted. A diagnosis to fit the apparent findings. Thank you Dr. Hawkins for your regurgitation of what's already known and your lack of insight. A few minutes later, O'Hara focused upon the ruminations of Edward Diehl, M.D., writing from his observation post as Chairman Emeritus of the Psychiatry Department at the State of New Hampshire loony bin at Manchester. Dr. Diehl, after all those years in the public nut house, was probably a pretty wild and crazy guy, himself. And naturally he had some opinions.

Once the killer sees that these women will comply with his deviant demands, even forcibly, he concludes that this nice girl is no more than a whore. Less than a human being, she deserves to die. The dismemberment that occurs after the homicide is a mental effort to both commit suicide himself and obliterate the truth of what he himself has done.

O'Hara curled a lip and continued. Dr. Diehl wrote with perhaps too much glee.

Killing, sex, and mutilation are inextricably bound!
Assuredly, Ledbetter nurtured sexually charged homicidal fantasies for years before engaging in his first murder. It can take years before a killer can overcome societal restraints and his own inhibitions to enact his private horror. Killers thus often begin with petty crimes, simple assaults, while keeping up the appearance of a normal life—the very traits that lure unsuspecting female victims.

O'Hara looked for dates when the various doctors had examined the patient. Again, the file was incomplete. He found no references to time or venue of patient interviews. And, maddeningly, the shrink profiles were to be continued in Envelope Fifteen. Reaching for it, he found it was empty. Had someone made off with its contents for private amusement? Or was its absence part of something larger?

Then again, stepping back from the matter at hand, how could the Ledbetter case have been part of anything larger? O'Hara went back to his own discovery of fingerprints. Witness IDs. Gary's refusal to offer anything resembling a coherent alibi.

Not fucking guilty, man. I keep telling you.

O'Hara, speaking aloud in the empty room, another rumble of gunshots behind him: "Then why couldn't you account for your time, Gary? Why were your fingerprints all over those rosewood boxes? Why did witnesses identify you with Karen Stoner? And with the girl in Florida? Tell me that, Gary?"

Lies. All lies.

Even in death, Ledbetter could resemble a broken record. Like O'Hara's nervous finger on the reading table, Gary tediously kept tapping on the same point.

"Sure, Gary."

Hell! You're the detective. You find out!

O'Hara glanced at his watch. He had been in Central Records for more than an hour. Time to take final inventory and wrap up. He glanced for anything he might have missed. He reexamined some of the earlier envelopes, those containing the evidence he had accumulated himself seven years earlier. He looked for anything he might have forgotten.

Then he found something. It was a correspondence on the stationery of a private psychiatric hospital in Concord, addressed to Benjamin Ashton, Attorney General, State of New Hampshire. The letter was misfiled, having been stuck in with documents that O'Hara had turned over to the A.G. He glared at it with surprise, then began to examine it. Clearly, it should have been filed with the shrink reports that were in the higher numbered envelopes. And—more sloppiness on the part of Ashton—it was perhaps this misfiling that had spared the document. Otherwise, O'Hara began to suspect, it probably would have been destroyed.

From the opening line, O'Hara knew he was in the presence of an intellect. And a troublemaker.

This doctor wrote:

I must call your attention to the inaccuracies and misinterpretations contained in previous analyses of patient and NH Dept./Correct. #87-2634. I must equally take issue with almost all of the conclusions previously drawn on patient Ledbetter's case.

O'Hara settled in, leaning back in his chair, and holding the two-page letter in his hand. This doctor had started with an identical background analysis of Ledbetter, but had come away with different conclusions.

Mr. Ledbetter does not fit the profile of a heterosexual serial killer. Nor does he even fit the profile of a heterosexual. Under several hours of questioning, Mr. Ledbetter conveyed great empathy for his alleged victims, even an association with them. . . . Rather than a deep hatred toward females, Ledbetter almost seems afraid of them.

The empathy, O'Hara learned as he continued to read, was in direct contradiction of traditional serial killer psychology. So was the absence of hatred for the victims. Of course, O'Hara reasoned, this doctor's evaluation could have been wrong. But it sounded good, so O'Hara pursued it. The doctor then moved to Gary Ledbetter's overall sexual orientation and saw fit to include a section of a patient interview:

Doctor: *Gary, are you more comfortable with men than women?*

G.L.: *Yeah, you know. Somewhat, I guess.*

Doctor: *Are you gay, Gary?*

G.L.: *I don't know sometimes.*

Doctor: *You must know. What's in your heart?*

G.L.:   *(Doesn't respond.)*

Doctor: *You can tell me, Gary.*

G.L.:   *(mumbles) . . . lot of things in my heart.*

Doctor: *Sadness?*

G.L.:   *Yeah, sadness.*

Doctor: *Over what you've done?*

G.L.:   *No, on account of what I seen. I ain't done nothing bad, me personally.*

Doctor: *Then what have you seen?*

G.L.:   *I seen the real horror of this world, Doc. And if they're going to kill me for doing it, they're wrong, but they're probably going to kill me, anyways. See, I shot me a New Hampshire hound dog one time 'cause it was doing all this here barking when I was trying to sleep. But I didn't kill no girl.*

Doctor: *Do you know who did?*

G.L.:   *(Declines to answer.)*

Doctor: *Do you know who did?*

G.L.:   *What's it matter? I ain't no squealer.*

Doctor: *It's very important.*

G.L.:   *(very angry) I said I ain't no squealer.*

The interview began to resemble O'Hara's own questioning of the suspect, though the doctor noted that Ledbetter was particularly difficult when he did not wish to reveal something intensely personal. One such exchange:

Doctor: *Gary, you become very defensive on certain subjects. Why is that?*

G.L.:   *(exhibits anger) 'Cause you're asking*

> *things that's no business of anyone's but*
> *mine. I'd take my own personal business to*
> *the grave with me, I would, rather than air*
> *it all out in public!*

Doctor: *Wouldn't that be foolish, Gary?*

G.L.:   *(still angry) A man's got his pride. That's*
> *how I am! I got my personal honor even if*
> *you people are fixing to kill me.*

Eventually, the doctor risked another display of anger by returning to Gary's own sexual orientation. The doctor asked again if the patient were gay.

The doctor wrote:

The patient flirted with an admission several times, then withdrew. I didn't push him harder because to evoke his anger again would be counterproductive. I felt he had tacitly admitted his homosexuality. . . .

O'Hara continued to read until he reached the doctor's summary on the third and final page of the memo:

Serial killers of women can gratify their desires only after the women are bound, unconscious, or dead. If this patient is a gay man involved in the serial murder of women, he would be the first such known case in the United States. . . . This is one of the many incongruities between Ledbetter's psychological makeup and the crime of which he is accused. . . . I urge further evaluation to discover if this patient actually possessed the neurotic disorientation that would have led him to participate in the Karen Stoner murder. My interviews to date raise troubling questions. I request more time to evaluate. . . .

The time wasn't forthcoming nor was much else for this doctor other than a firm rebuke. This was Dr. J.S. at the doctor's troublesome, meddlesome worst, throwing a potential damper upon the State's explanation—and prosecution—of Gary. There was no interest from the attorney general in hearing tunes that he hadn't requested, and the governor wasn't buying it, either.

Hence the state police—particularly O'Hara, the arresting officer—weren't even brought into the larger picture: Even though the evidence pointed to Ledbetter as the lone ax murderer, the loony bin profiles on Gary were casting some disturbing shadows over the case.

Hence, the A.G.'s impatience with J.S. Hence, his desire to get this meddlesome doctor out of the picture. And yet Ben Ashton hadn't even been competent enough to cleanse the files of all the communication.

O'Hara stared at the date of the correspondence. March 12, 1987. Then his eyes widened when they hit the finish line, the signature at the bottom of the letter.

The nuisance: J.S.

Dr. Julie Steinberg.

Probably twenty-four years old at the time, fresh out of Boston grad school, and brimming with fresh textbook knowledge and irreverent interpretations of traditional nut cases. Worse, here she had been a young woman about to mess up the State's most high-profile case. Truth was, O'Hara recalled from one of Ashton's references, the State hadn't even wanted to hire her in the first place.

O'Hara wished to hell someone had told him at the time. Failing that, it would have been nice if someone had tipped him over the ensuing eighty months.

He gave it several more second thoughts, then folded the file together. He thought of checking it out, but looked at Rose Horvath's empty desk. And he remembered how things in this room sometimes slipped into black holes, mysteriously and just all of a sudden.

So, angrily, he folded the file under his arm and stole it from Central Records. He climbed the back stairs to his office, freezing because someone had left a window open in the stairwell, probably to disperse the stench of an illicit-in-a-state-building cigarette. But he was also angry.

Angry that no one had painted him a full picture about his only executed arrestee until after the man was dead.

Angry at the governor and that little Ashton twerp.

Angry at Dr. Steinberg for never making reference to her own involvement in the case.

And angry that he had gone to Central Records seeking answers, and had come away instead with even more questions.

As he climbed the stairs, he expected to hear Gary's voice echoing. But he didn't.

Instead, the only message he thought he received came from the gold chain and pendant picked up from Jane Doe's belongings. He continued to carry it with him in his inside jacket pocket. He thought he sensed a cry for help from that. A plea for justice.

Or was he imagining that, too?

In truth, the only sounds he was certain about were those of his footsteps upon the cold concrete steps of the stairwell. And below him, in the distance, there was a new round of gunfire from the boys playing with automatic artillery in the basement.

It sounded like they were having a wonderful time. It was nice that someone was.

Chapter 8

Captain Mallinson's office was on the second floor of the state gendarmerie, a plush corner suite with a big, dark desk, a five-line telephone, a couple of flags, and a wastebasket big enough to pass for an ice cream maker. Behind him there was a wall of awards and photographs and an enormous plate glass window, overlooking the snowy town square. Plate glass of that size and beauty just about screamed out for a brick.

Mallinson spent as much time in this office as possible. O'Hara visited it as rarely as he could. Today, the two time frames intersected.

Mallinson's eyes rose as O'Hara appeared at his door. "Talk to me, Frank. How is Jane Doe doing?"

"The case hasn't moved for two days," O'Hara said. "I've been doing some digging. Missing persons. I have the forensic people working. But nothing of substance yet."

Mallinson nodded very slightly. It was a nod that conveyed both understanding and disappointment.

O'Hara studied his captain. On some days, when a harsh light hit him, Mallinson looked thirty years older than he actually was. His face had acquired an entire road map of wrinkles, lines, and spidery veins over the last few years. This was one of those dreadful days when Mallinson looked like a man terminally tired of life itself, a guy who would—to realize his worst fears—just drop dead on the job some day.

"Any other angles to the case?" Mallinson asked.

"Gary Ledbetter."

"What about him, aside from the fact that he's dead?"

"The two cases are linked," O'Hara said. "Karen Stoner and Jane Doe. Like it or not, they're closely connected."

The captain did not look pleased. He patted down his shirt pockets until he found one of his atrocious cheroots. As he lit it and smoke clouded around him, he said, "You're making me itchy, Frank. What the hell are you talking about?"

"I'm talking about the Ledbetter case. At the time I never knew half of what I know now."

"Like what?"

"There were three shrink profiles, for one thing. Ben Ashton didn't like the first one, so he went out and got two more."

"So what? Fuck the shrink profiles." Mallinson squinted through his own cancerous smoke. "Hey. *You* made the arrest and accumulated the key evidence. What are you complaining about?"

"I never completed the assembly of evidence," O'Hara said. "I was pulled off the case."

"I remember. You think I got amnesia? I pulled you off myself."

"Why? Your decision? Or did someone want me removed from the investigation?"

Mallinson eased back in his swivel chair. For a moment it looked like there was anger on its way. Mallinson was known for such outbursts. But then he relaxed a notch, and when he spoke he sounded as if he were taking O'Hara into his confidence.

"It had nothing to do with you, Frank," Mallinson said. "I was dealing with a bunch of suits in Concord."

"The governor and his midget-mentality attorney general?"

"And all those who play golf with them," the captain said. "The case became political. It shouldn't have, but it did. And we were better off sending it to Florida. Ashton didn't want the pressure of having to try it in court, and thank God for that. He probably would have fucked it up, then blamed us for giving him a faulty case. Next we'd have Gary walking after turning the Stoner girl into hamburger patties."

"The problem is," O'Hara said, "I don't think the case was as perfect as it seemed."

Mallinson took a long drag on his smoke. The light seemed to brighten outside his window. And in the whiteness of it, he continued to look aged, almost sickly.

"Oh, come on," Mallinson finally said.

"That's what I think, Captain."

"No case still smells perfect when it finally heads for a courtroom. You know that. Anything with a judge and a jury and a couple of mouthpieces turns into a crapshoot. Where's the news there?"

O'Hara remained silent and let Mallinson talk.

"Were the charges stronger against Gary Ledbetter in Florida?" Mallinson asked. "Sure. That was another factor in his extradition." Mallinson paused. "But, shit. You know what those assholes are like in Concord. Want to know the inside baseball? The suits took a look at the Ledbetter trial, figured it would put the State out two million bucks and buy us another million dollars worth of bad publicity during tourist season. So they shipped Gary to the 'Sunshine State' where they cook a killer every week. So Gary got fried and the State of New Hampshire speeded it along. So what? Why are we even discussing it?" Mallinson asked.

"Was it ever your impression that Gary Ledbetter was gay?" O'Hara asked.

"What?" Another pause of displeasure. "Frank! Talk to me! Where the hell are you getting this stuff?"

"Never mind. If Gary was gay, he didn't fit the profile of a serial chopper of women. That was observed by one of the shrinks at the time. It's a factor that should have been considered."

"Aahhh," Mallinson growled, giving a dismissive wave of his paw at the same time. "I just told you what I thought of the shrink profiles," Mallinson answered.

"Do you think Gary had a boyfriend?" O'Hara asked.

"Jesus! Why are you asking *that?*"

"Because I don't remember that we ever ran down that angle," O'Hara said.

"That's right. There was no need to."

"It only occurred to me yesterday," O'Hara said. "Key evidence came out of a storage unit. The storage unit was rented to an 'S. Clay.' Who was 'S. Clay'?"

"Maybe it's a pseudonym for 'S. Claus,' " Mallinson suggested. "Maybe you have something there, Frank. S. Claus: *Santa* Claus. I'll bet Gary and Santa spent many joyful winter nights buggering each other. My only question is which one of them used to get on top. My money's on Gary. I always thought Santa looked a little too sensitive."

"This is serious stuff, Captain."

"And you're going off on numbskull tangents, Frank. The 'S. Clay' at the rental units matched Gary's signature, if I recall," Mallinson said. "And the attendant at the storage lockers identified Gary's photograph."

"So we were told," O'Hara said.

" 'Told'? What the hell does that mean?" Mallinson snapped. "You did that part of the investigation."

"Carl Reissman did that part," O'Hara said. "Carl's dead. I can't ask him, so I'm asking you."

Mallinson shrugged. "My memory is no better than yours. Or the official files. Go back and—"

"Certain parts of the official record have also been removed," O'Hara said. "Any idea of what the 'suits in Concord,' as you call them, might have wanted to disappear?"

Mallinson appeared legitimately baffled on that point. "No idea," he said. "I can only remind you what a shambles Central Records is. I doubt if there's a single case down there with files intact. If something's missing, I wouldn't attach much significance to it."

O'Hara tried another angle. "How did Wilhelm Negri filter into the case?" he asked.

The captain's brow knitted into a studious scowl. "Who?"

"The publisher of the *American*."

"None at all. Why would he?"

"He was leading the pack of jackels who wanted Gary tried outside the state," O'Hara reminded. "And he was the governor's buddy, wasn't he?"

"Ah," Mallinson scoffed, dismissing the point. "Sure. But who the fuck reads the editorials in that paper?"

O'Hara proceeded cautiously.

"Vincent Paloheima maintains that the same hand committed both murders," O'Hara said. "Karen Stoner and Jane Doe."

Mallinson stared at him as the notion sank in. "Want to run that past me again?" he asked.

"Whoever killed Karen Stoner killed Jane Doe," O'Hara repeated. "That thought rather overtaxes the imagination, doesn't it?"

Three more seconds. Then a fourth. All were moments of tense silence. Then came the eruption.

"Paloheima's got his frigging head up his ass!"
howled Mallinson. Like many men his age, when he
was inordinately angry, his face turned crimson and a
vein throbbed in his neck. "And not for the first time!
Come on, Frank! What kind of crap is that, Stoner
and Jane frigging Doe killed by the same perp! Ledbetter's frigging dead! Dead people don't kill live people!
Doesn't anyone understand that?"

If volume could resurrect, Mallinson's fury was
loud enough to arouse a few souls by itself.

"Come on!" Mallinson roared. "What are you trying to tell me? That a frigging *ghost* killed Jane Doe?
Or that Gary Ledbetter didn't kill Karen Stoner?"

"Dr. Paloheima showed it to me," O'Hara said
evenly. "Computers. Strokes with a heavy blade. He
makes a solid case."

"Oh, this will be just so much fun in court, won't
it?" Mallinson raged. "Want to arrest Gary Ledbetter
again?"

"I'm not finding this funny, Captain."

More fireworks: "Yeah? Me, neither!" Mallinson
exploded. "A damned riot! That's what it is," he said.
"And you know as well as I do that Vincent Paloheima
is an incompetent drunk! Ignore whatever he says. Go
with your own boot leather, Frank. Ignore the nay-
sayers. Gary Ledbetter was as guilty as Judas Iscariot!
His prosecution was on the square. And when he got
'Old Sparky' in Florida, it was exactly what he deserved!"

O'Hara leaned back in his chair. "I'm glad *you're*
convinced," he said.

"You're not?"

For several seconds, O'Hara did not answer. Then,
finally, "I don't know whether Gary was guilty or not.
He may have been. But there was something wrong
with his case."

Mallinson looked at his subordinate with continuing annoyance. Then he snuffed his cheroot and a little wave of relaxation went across the room. Mallinson changed the subject, having expended his patience on Gary Ledbetter.

"How about the ID on the current Jane Doe?" the captain asked. "Have anything yet?"

"Nothing," O'Hara answered. "I checked with your esteemed cohort Vincent Paloheima just this morning. Nothing from him, nothing yet from forensic."

"If we only knew who Jane Doe was, at least we'd know how much we'd have to kick ass," Mallinson said, calming. "Seems strange that a middle-class girl gets butchered in a cabin and no one misses her."

O'Hara and Mallinson shared one conclusion from that aspect of the slaying. The victim was from out of state. If she was missing, she wasn't missing locally. So now they would have all of the United States and Canada to prowl for Missing Persons Reports. O'Hara had concluded by the woman's clothing that she had been American. Her dental work suggested the same.

Mallinson ran his hand across his eyes.

"You're going to need some luck in this case," the captain concluded. "I hope you're planning to get out there in the frigging snow that you love so much and make some."

"I can't wait," O'Hara answered, standing and matching his superior's sarcasm point for point. He left the meeting with a strong feeling of dissatisfaction.

The rest of the day passed uneventfully. O'Hara spent time prowling through other recent murder cases in the state, as well as recent abductions of women. Again, nothing.

There was only one glimmer of promise. The much maligned Dr. Paloheima had arranged with a forensic sculptor to build a wax model of Jane Doe's head. The model was now complete.

O'Hara thus sent a computer art analyst to Dr. Paloheima's office to create a photo-simulated approximation of what the victim had looked like. This would take only a few hours. A picture which would hopefully resemble Jane Doe could be circulated to newspapers and police departments by the next morning.

After work, O'Hara drove to the town of Marlborough, where he remembered that Gary's storage locker had been located. It was a long shot that the same attendant would be there, much less that he would remember anything. And the long shot failed because the self-store unit had failed, too. It had gone out of business two years earlier, O'Hara discovered from the Marlborough town police. All that stood was a dilapidated brick shell, the aluminum roof partially caved in, and the windows filled in by concrete blocks. When O'Hara tried to trace the ownership, he found only a paper corporation from Boston that had long since faded into bankruptcy.

O'Hara returned home in the evening, his thoughts askew. He made himself dinner, put some Sinatra on the downstairs sound system, and at one point spent more than an hour staring straight ahead, trying to analyze the case before him. Meanwhile, the other Frank went through some Cole Porter.

The house, at those moments of silence between the other Frank's tracks, did its own singing. The usual creaks and moans. Once, O'Hara could have sworn he heard two footsteps upstairs. But he stayed away from alcohol for the evening and rejected the notion that there could be anyone in the house.

He did, however, keep his thirty-eight on his belt. A man never knew when he might want to fire a shot through a closet door.

"Where are you, Gary?" O'Hara finally said aloud sometime past ten P.M. "Here I am wondering whether you were railroaded, after all. And you're not talking to me anymore."

O'Hara waited. No answer.

"What about this 'S. Clay'?" O'Hara asked aloud. "What was it you told me once before? S. Clay was you but it wasn't you?"

No response.

There was a distant creak in an upstairs room several seconds later. But then again, the furnace was on, guzzling oil—and his policeman's modest paycheck—at almost a buck a gallon.

No booze, no Gary, no inspiration.

And no answers to any of the questions confronting him.

Carolyn Hart lay perfectly still in her bedroom, her spirit keenly attuned to her surroundings. Outside her window there was noise curling up from Oswell Street. A conversation of passing children. A woman's loud voice addressing a recalcitrant dog. Then silence. A breeze which almost seemed to bear whispers upon it. A few birds, then distant traffic.

A peaceful universe, at least as far as she could hear.

Carolyn's head moved slightly from where she lay on the bed. Her eyes travelled the room and settled upon its unmatched furnishings. Someone else's surroundings. Someone else's dresser. Someone else's life? Did it matter?

What mattered was what she was doing in this city. In Philadelphia. She reminded herself. There were old scores to settle, accounts to balance.

She rose from the bed. Then she went to the window and peered down to the street. A boy in a blue blazer with a red backpack was walking home after school. It was a chilly afternoon at about four o'clock. Not the time of day when a young woman should be isolated within a musty house. She wanted to get out.

She passed before a mirror. She looked at the pale face that stared back at her. Carolyn had always been seen as a pretty girl, then a pretty young woman. But she had never been content with her own appearance. She had never considered herself pretty even if others had.

And now? Her beauty was gone, she told herself.

Her hands came to her face. She played with the skin on the underside of her chin. Once past twenty-five she had developed a very vain mannerism of constantly massaging the skin beneath her jaw in the desire to reduce it.

But now the focus of her attention wasn't that skin. She stepped away from the mirror. An overwhelming loneliness was upon her. She knew no one in this city and tried to regain her focus upon what she was doing here.

She went down to the first floor of the house and felt the need to get out. She left the house and went out to the street, followed an inclination and walked westward.

There was a small grocery store on the corner at Spruce and Twenty-second Streets. Carolyn went in, looked around, and left without buying anything. Then she went farther west until she came to Fitler Square at Twenty-fourth and Pine.

Fitler was a small but nice public park. A sensible city block, a tiny oasis of quiet. Carolyn took a position on a bench and stayed there for more than an hour, barely moving, saying nothing to anyone passing by.

An hour passed almost invisibly. As the afternoon died a man in a polo shirt and shorts sat down on the other end of the bench from her. He stared ahead of himself for several moments, and Carolyn was convinced that he was going to try to pick her up.

She would have welcomed it. But he didn't speak. He took out a paperback book instead and began to read. Another half hour passed this way until the man placed a bookmark at the end of a chapter, packed up his book again, and walked away. A wave of disappointment overtook Carolyn. Had he even known she was there?

Minutes later, she rose and walked back to the house on Oswell Street.

She was in the second floor of the house when a sensation hit her. It was sort of a vibration or a feeling, the type of thing that had been coming to her for a half-dozen years now but which she didn't completely understand.

She knew what was about to happen. Or what was happening.

Someone was looking for her. Someone had her on his mind.

It was a man, she realized. There was a man looking for her.

She held very still in the house, as if to listen. The sensation, the intuition became even stronger.

She wondered. Gary?

Carolyn drifted to the window before her, the one that looked down onto Oswell Street. She stood behind a curtain and looked downward.

Nothing. For several seconds, nothing.

But the feeling was unbanishable. She hoped so much: Gary? Would it be Gary?

Then a man came into view, stopping before her house.

Who was he? What did he want? She could only see the top of his head. But when he started to look upward, Carolyn retreated so that he couldn't see her.

Then there was a knock on the door.

Silently, Carolyn went down to the first floor. The man knocked persistently a second time. Hard. Firm. A solid rapping.

Carolyn moved for a fleeting second to a downstairs window and glanced out.

But it wasn't Gary. It was Adam Kaminski, the rental agent. What did he want?

She stood her ground and chose not to answer the door. But she kept him in her sights. What could he possibly want?

Kaminski leaned forward and slid something through the mail slot. Carolyn waited. She watched the rental agent turn and leave. Then she went to the envelope that lay on the floor.

It was a note from the rental agent. It said that he had been trying to contact her. If she was encountering any problems, the note continued, she should feel free to contact him.

She moved the note to a table and left it there. Such little details of living bored her. From the second-story window she watched Kaminski disappear down the block.

Carolyn took stock of the situation. So it was all innocent enough. It was Kaminski who had been tracking her. He had been trying to make contact.

That's what logic said.

She sighed and rose again to her bedroom. But she was unconvinced that it had only been Kaminski, that out there somewhere there wasn't someone else.

Someone much more important.

She was, after all, very intuitive about these things. It was an extra sense that she had and she was rarely wrong.

Chapter 9

Bennington, New Hampshire, lay twenty-five miles up the frozen county road from Nashua. The drive there was a trip O'Hara would have wished upon no one.

The chains rattled relentlessly on his blue bomber, but the old Pontiac faithfully held the road. The entire state had been frozen like Siberia for four days now, and O'Hara half expected to encounter a woolly mammoth somewhere along the icy two-lane.

He took one consolation. The detective had finally bailed out on the AM-FM radio in his car and now packed a portable tape deck. So at least Sinatra could accompany him on this pain-in-the-ass drive and fill the rumbling old cop-mobile with a touch of elegance.

The trip took seventy minutes, through two lingering snow squalls and skies the color of steel. Finally O'Hara turned a bend in the highway and sighted the small town. It had seemed more like *seventy hours*.

Bennington was a handful of small stores, one good inn, a white church, and about four hundred residents, none of whom ever seemed to appear. So it took O'Hara only another five minutes to find King Street, an inappropriately named collection of boxy single-family houses of various shades of brown, green, or blue. All were mantled with the cursed snow which actually improved their appearance. On one front lawn there was a retired refrigerator with a rusting washer-drier, also mantled with snow. A Currier and Ives touch on a front lawn junkyard.

Reaching 5 King Street, a dozen doors from his destination, O'Hara pulled the Pontiac as close to a snowbank as was safe, sat for a moment, and took stock. With the car motor off, the raging cold began to penetrate the vehicle within seconds.

Across the narrow street, a muffled figure walked a small, shaggy mongrel with a rope leash. Man or woman? O'Hara couldn't tell. The individual with the mutt was tall but shapeless. It wore an orange wool hunter's cap and a bulky coat. The dog wore some tattered makeshift garment around its middle, looking like a sad miniaturized military horse that long ago should have found its way either out to pasture or to a glue factory.

O'Hara turned his gaze away from the mystery-gender human with the animal. From habit, he studied the street scene before him, trying to read its layout, instinctively trawling for concealed danger. He saw none.

Then the landscape took shape. The snow along the road had an ugly hue, having turned into a frozen grayish-brown stew of dirt and ice and salt. When he could take the view no longer—and the sense of depression and condemnation that came with it—he stepped out of his car.

The wind whipped fiercely. O'Hara pulled his leather fedora close to his head. Yet the incredible coldness made him feel like his head was bare and his heavy sheepskin coat would protect him for only a few minutes. The ice particles in the air were like little industrial chain saws; they would eventually cut through anything.

There were no sidewalks. He walked down the road which had not yet been sanded, hard snow crunching under his boots. In his nostrils was the scent of several dozen fireplaces: burning maple and the odor of creosote.

O'Hara arrived at 17 King Street, a low one-story house with a roof that sagged. Beside the porch was some ragged shrubbery which stood like bizarre sentries, covered with virgin white.

O'Hara had been here a few times previously, including one memorable time for a birthday party, so he knew the layout. He followed a makeshift line of bootsteps that had tracked a path from the driveway to the front door. He noted that there were no tire tracks leading to the garage door and thus guessed that the occupant's car hadn't been out since the snowfall.

O'Hara arrived at the front door. The house paint was peeling. He rang the bell. Immediately, a large dog barked from within. A big-time, throaty, menacing, I'll-rip-you-to-shreds-if-you-don't-mind-your-own-business bark. Seconds later, O'Hara could hear some sort of bull mastiff clawing and snarling at the other side of the door. Only wood, steel, and sash separated O'Hara from one hundred pounds of canine menace.

A stream of thoughts flowed in O'Hara's mind as he listened to the dog: Once, in High Bridge, down by the Massachusetts border, O'Hara had visited a GLA suspect at the chop shop where he reinvented cars. The suspect had set the garage's animal—a big prime-time Rottweiler—at O'Hara with instructions to latch its jaws onto O'Hara's windpipe. It had taken three bullets from a Colt thirty-eight police special to bring the damned mutt down. Then two days later some do-good fuckhead from the ASPCA read the newspaper report, felt that O'Hara had been somehow insensitive, and filed a cruelty-to-animals complaint against the State Police. Ultimately, the complaint had been dismissed by an understanding magistrate in Concord who had himself spent many happy autumn afternoons in a forest, blasting away four-legged critters.

Always a first time in the line of duty, O'Hara thought as he waited. Always the first time to make an arrest, break a murder case, whack out a mutt with a thirty-eight, or chase a ghost.

Then there was the sound of latches falling on the other side. Bolts were being undone. Very methodical. Top to bottom, the locks were coming loose.

"No, Nixon! Down, boy!" O'Hara heard a husky matronly voice proclaim. "Hush, you bad dog until we know who's here. Then maybe you'll get to bite his balls off and maybe you won't."

O'Hara sighed, recognizing both the voice and the attitude. Then the same voice called out, "Yes? Who's there?"

"Rose?" O'Hara called into the frigid air. "It's Frank O'Hara! From the state police in Nashua!"

The dog went silent and so did the woman. But the bottom lock came away immediately.

From within, first the interior door opened while the storm door on the outside remained locked and closed. A large, graying woman with a pinkish porcine face swelled into view, using a meaty left forearm to hold a German Shepherd at bay. The woman wore a deep green sweater and was shaped much like the refrigerator on the lawn down the block.

For a moment, she suspiciously appraised him, her two shrewd eyes glassy and wet like an infant's. Then there was recognition.

"Hoo! Well, I declare!" the woman said happily. "It *is* Frank O'Hara!"

"Hello, Rose," he said softly. "Got a hot cup of coffee for an old friend?"

Rose Horvath's eyes flicked quickly past his shoulder to see who might have accompanied him. Then, finding no one, the fat face of the former doyenne at

Central Records illuminated with a smile. And they could hear each other quite well through the storm door because the top pane was cracked. A shard of glass one-by-six inches was missing, though a covering of clear plastic had been taped upon it.

"You beast, you!" Rose exclaimed. "Dropping in unannounced on an old girlfriend! Not letting me get myself all tarted up! How are you? You, the most unrequited of all my loves."

"I'm well," he said. "Are you going to invite me in or are you going to let me freeze out here?"

"You monster," she said. "I should let you freeze, then thaw you out for the time that would suit me."

She unlocked the storm door and pushed it open before him.

"Thank you," he said.

"If I were in my right mind I wouldn't entertain any state employees. Not after what they did to poor old Rose. But you're the exception, Franklin. You, I think, I still like." She paused. "Right, Nixon?"

Nixon, the dog, sniffed inquisitively as O'Hara stepped into the house. As for the "Franklin," Rose had always called O'Hara that. The reason had always escaped him, although he guessed it had something to do with either Roosevelt or Benjamin.

"I'm grateful, Rose," he said.

She stood before him, like a teacher with a star pupil several years after graduation. He was a head taller than she, but she was a decade older. She grinned foolishly. She let him remove his hat and coat, then gripped him by the shoulders.

It was kissy-kissy time. O'Hara inclined gently and received two such moist proclamations of her affection, one on the left cheek, the other on the right.

"Please sit down," she said. "And I'll make you some coffee. I have hazel nut-peach cappuccino. Got it at Peterborough mall. It's instant. Only a moment in the microwave."

He was in no mood to protest, fruit coffee or not. And Rose had a fire going, though it was burning down. So he sunk into an old armchair by the side of the hearth. As he sat, he felt that the chair was warm and knew that this was where Rose had been sitting when he had arrived. So quietly, as she rattled with spoons, cups, and the microwave oven in the kitchen, he moved to a less comfortable chair that was also beside the fire.

He spent a moment studying the room.

The chamber was dim with no piece of furniture less than a decade old. Like the exterior of the house, paint would have helped. Yet the room's very dreariness accounted for much of its charm. And he also spotted a couple of absurd touches.

The first one: Over the mantel was an eight-by-ten-inch frame containing a picture of her animal, Nixon, and a photo of the world figure of the same name. O'Hara wasn't sure what Rose was suggesting, and he also knew he wasn't going to ask.

Then the second touch: On a table near O'Hara's chair was an assortment of books. Something flashed inside O'Hara when their titles fell into a pattern: *Fifty Famous Hauntings, Unsolved Ghost Stories of New England, Vampirism in Rhode Island.* The latter volume was astonishingly thick. And so on. Spiritualism. Exercises and studies in the paranormal. Someone had been doing some reading recently. O'Hara assumed it was Rose. The books reminded him of what had brought him there in the first place.

O'Hara's toes were just starting to thaw when Rose reappeared with some coffee. Sure enough, she had nuked it, and it had only taken half a minute.

Rose had aged badly since the last time he had seen her. She had gained probably five years' worth of gray in the twelve months of her retirement. Plus maybe twenty pounds. He accepted the coffee and sipped. Rose had put milk in it, plus what tasted like half a cup of sugar. It was sweet enough to blow out his triglyceride count for a week. Rose meanwhile went to the front window and peered out, fussing with a curtain, which was drawn.

"Know what I used to do at this window, Franklin?" she asked. "I used to stand and watch in the first year of my retirement," she said. "I'd stand here and wait, hoping my former coworkers would come see me. None did. You came by a few times, though, didn't you, you noble man. Like the time when I threw my own birthday party. Remember that?"

"I remember," he said. And he remembered that she had thrown it to bring some life into her home in the middle of her first winter alone.

Then her hand, out of long years of habit, went to the curtain and parted it. "What time is it, Franklin?" she asked. "I'd guess it's a little after two."

"It's two fifteen," he answered.

"Afternoons can be so long," she said. "And this is such a dark day. Dark outside, I mean. Overcast."

"It's very gray," he answered.

He wanted to offer the sickening cliché that spring was just around the corner, but it wasn't even winter yet on the calendar, so this lie—convenient though it might have been—wouldn't even form on his lips.

"Would you care to put on a lamp?" she asked.

"Thank you."

He found an old fixture, short and ugly with a single bulb under a deep beige shade. It was a thrift shop special, its style dating from the 1950s, if not the 1940s. The bulb was sixty watts and dim. It cast a depressing yellow glow to all corners of the chamber.

"Maybe you could check my fire for me before we get down to business," she said. "There's supposed to be a high-school boy who comes over and minds my fire for me. Name of Mark; named after the saint, I'm sure," she said with heavy sarcasm. "Comes in around four thirty but half the time he doesn't show. Other half of the time he helps himself to small change around my kitchen. Thinks I don't notice, but I do."

She pondered the further point of petty criminality.

"Probably uses my money to buy drugs over in Hillsboro," she added. "But who knows these days? None of these kids seem to be any good, but their parents weren't, either."

O'Hara addressed her fireplace for her. Two logs were down to their last embers. He found some wood stocked at the corner of the hearth. He kindled the wood, arranged it in a grate, and lit crumpled newspaper beneath it. He excused himself for a moment and went outside to her woodpile and brought in a fresh supply. Returning, he knelt by the fireplace and put on a few larger logs. He would have the hearth blazing in a few minutes.

"Bless you, Franklin," she said, watching approvingly. "And make it a good fire. One which could burn a witch." Rose sat down in her frayed armchair and relished the warmth as it built.

"What on earth makes you use a term like that?" O'Hara asked.

"It's just a figure of speech," she said. "But a good figure of speech at that, isn't it? Wouldn't you like to meet a real witch someday?"

"I notice that you've done some reading on the subject," he said, still toying with the logs in the fireplace. He motioned toward her books on the occult.

"Go ahead. Make fun of it. I've done a lot of reading on the subject," she nodded. "There's a lot that the human mind just doesn't understand yet. But I suppose you now think that Rose is going a little soft in the head during retirement."

"I keep an open mind about everything," O'Hara answered. "Particularly matters of life and death."

"Good for you," she said softly. She had brewed tea for herself. She sipped it. "An open mind. How refreshing. Most people in this neck of the woods just have a hole in the head."

The fire cast a warm glow into the room. The dog even rose from his corner and found himself a more suitable position, at Rose's foot and not far from the fire.

O'Hara, for his part, wiped the wood bits from his hands and returned to his chair. The dog sighed and tried to sleep.

"I thought you had cats," he said. "Six of them."

"I got rid of the kitties," she said.

"Why did you do that, Rose?"

"Gave them to my sister, who lives in Hillsboro."

"To make way for the puppy?" he asked. Nixon, the "puppy," was three quarters the size of a Harley-Davidson.

Rose caught the joke and smiled. "The kitties weren't doing me any good," she said. "A bunch of brat high-school kids used to yell obscenities and throw rocks at my roof. Mark's friends, no doubt. Put a few stones through my bedroom window."

"Why did they do that?"

"They decided they didn't like me."

"Did you call the police?"

"The little punks were always gone by the time the police arrived."

"You should have called me."

She sighed. "Maybe I should have. I know you would have sorted them out. Right?"

"Right, Rose."

"Well, I bought Nixon, instead. The high-school boys came by one more time, and I sent Nixon out to rip their balls off."

"Let me guess," he said, "and the stone throwing stopped?"

"It stopped."

O'Hara nodded and sipped the fruit coffee. His teeth ached from the sugar. In the hearth, flames danced like little yellow spirits around the logs. O'Hara's fire had become a thing of winter beauty.

"I have a roommate now, too," Rose said. "So I'm not here alone."

The roomie, Rose explained, was a woman named Donna. She worked nine till two for the electric company's collection department, badgering deadbeats who had taken too literally the state's "Live Free Or Die" motto. Donna was due home any time. So O'Hara now understood why Rose had gone to the window and why she had asked the time.

One of Rose's two brothers was a doctor, O'Hara remembered. The other brother became a judge in Maine. Her father had been a teacher at the prep school in Concord and had sent all three children to good schools. Rose had been the best student of the trio, probably the smartest. Hiring practices being what they had been for females, many opportunities were closed. So Rose had gone to work for the State of New Hampshire in the 1970s. Nothing better ever came along. Over the years, Rose had forgotten very little, especially the feeling that life had shortchanged her. She felt she had deserved something better than what she now had, and O'Hara would have been the first to agree.

"So what do you want from this old lady?" Rose eventually asked, her spirits up a bit in the glow of good company and a fine fire. "What could I possibly give you other than time, of which I have both too much and too little."

"Your memory, Rose."

"Which part of it?"

"Central Records. Your stint in the governor's office. Things you may have heard over the years."

Her voice acquired an edge. "In reference to what?" she asked.

"The Gary Ledbetter case."

She made a distasteful expression. "Hoo," she said. "Nasty piece of work, that one."

"I know. I arrested him."

"I remember." She sipped her tea. Her gaze found the fire, then returned to her guest. "Why are you rattling old skeletons? Aren't you about to retire?"

"I am."

"Then why not let the dead rest?"

"Sometimes they won't allow it."

"Who won't let it rest? The dead, or the people who sign your paycheck?"

"Both."

"Don't speak in circles to me, young man," she answered sharply, "or Auntie Rose will send you briskly packing."

O'Hara grinned. This was Rose's way of working her way into a point. The sharper her voice grew, the more O'Hara liked her.

"There's another case that's come up. There are parallels," he said.

"Murder?"

"Murder."

"Was it in the papers?" she asked. "I didn't see it."

"You know the newspapers in this state: long on opinion and bad grammar, short on the facts. The death was recorded in the police logs and not one reporter has yet asked a question."

"Of course," she said. "But *you're* asking questions, aren't you, Franklin? Probably a lot of them."

"I tried to check the official record of Gary Ledbetter," he said. "I found material that was never shown to me the first time. Other parts of the file were missing."

"Central Records is a snake pit. What do you expect? If you found a file complete, *that's* when you should be suspicious."

O'Hara thought about it for a moment. "Tell me something, Rose," he said. "There was one hell of a push to make sure Ledbetter looked guilty. And then he was quickly shipped out of state. Why? Did I miss something?"

Rose picked something small and white, a piece of fuzz, not a snowflake, off her formless green sweater and let it fall to the floor.

"I have no idea why there would have been any extra attention to the case," she said. "I assumed that Gary Ledbetter was guilty."

"I did, too," O'Hara answered.

"Someone slaughtered those five girls."

"Someone," O'Hara agreed.

"Hoo!" she said. "The man's dead! And now you think there was someone else?"

"I don't know what I think," O'Hara answered, "other than that the State was in an unhealthy rush to close the case."

"Maybe Gary deserved it," she said.

"What about the governor and the attorney general at the time?" O'Hara asked. "Ben Ashton. You worked in his office, didn't you?"

Rose's face took on a nasty frown. *"That* little runt!" she said. "Typical New Hampshire politician: small stature, physically and mentally. And if you'll excuse my French, Franklin, when the governor ate beans, Ben Ashton farted. Get my picture?"

"He was the governor's lackey," O'Hara said.

"That's not news to you," she said sternly. "Don't play games."

"I'm not," he said. "I'm here to have my memory

refreshed. To let you confirm that I'm on the right track."

Rose's eyes drifted to the front window again, and O'Hara feared for a moment that he might lose her attention. He pressed onward.

"I don't entirely understand the relationship," O'Hara said. "Ashton was young for a political hack, even for this state. Where did the governor find him? Surely there must have been a number of overeager law-school graduates who would have. . . ."

"My God!" she said. "You've been looking at cadavers too long. Check out the living."

"In what way?"

"Benjamin Ashton's father was a college classmate of Wilhelm Negri. Negri is the publisher of—"

"The New Hampshire *American,*" O'Hara said.

"And Negri—" Rose continued, only to be interrupted almost as quickly.

"—was the chief financial backer of the governor in his last campaign."

"Right," said Rose.

"And, of course," O'Hara continued, recalling the frozen January and February of 1987, "the *American* was running those incendiary editorials about life imprisonment being too good for the killer of Karen Stoner."

Rose shrugged again. "So you've answered your own question," Rose said. "Ashton was merely completing the dirty work for his father, his father's chum, and the governor. The incompetent little pipsqueak was anxious to get the job done. In any way possible."

"Apparently he had a psychological profile done on Ledbetter by a Dr. Steinberg. Do you know her?"

"No."

"The profile came out the wrong way. So Ashton went out and got two others. Does that surprise you?"

"Not a bit. Standard operating procedure. They

used to keep going in that office until they got the result they wanted."

"What about evidence?" O'Hara asked.

"What about it?"

"I never knew who Ashton used as investigators. Did he have any? I never saw them."

Rose laughed. "Oh, sure," she said. "He had investigators. Former roommates from the Green Indian college. Country club golf partners."

A beat, as it sunk in. "More hacks, you mean."

"Hoo! 'Hacks' is too kind a word! Two or three of Ashton's Yuppie buddies who fancied themselves sleuths. They barely knew how to trace licenses at Motor Vehicles. I don't think they could have found a lost cat if the cat scratched their ass." More tea, lukewarm now, then, by way of benediction, "If they ever went out and found fresh evidence in a case, I never saw it for as long as I worked there."

"Then where did they get what they needed?"

Another shrug. A dyspeptic grin. "From you people. State police, if they were lucky. Local cops, if they were luckier. Newspapers sometimes, when some cub reporter did a little extra digging. That, or, well . . . use your imagination, Franklin."

"They fabricated evidence?"

"All the time. When they needed it. And sometimes, because they were so stupid, even when they didn't need it."

"They just made stuff up? Witnesses? Documents?"

"You're a big boy, Franklin. You can't be shocked."

"I'm only shocked if they did it in a case like Ledbetter's," he said. "Why bother? There was so much *real* evidence. If they had only—"

"Be shocked," she said. "What is 'real' evidence? A scrap of paper? The word of a witness? Some girl who says she thinks she saw a man with her dead friend? A

fingerprint from God-knows-where? Come on, Franklin. Not too hard to work a little magic in those departments, is it?"

"Not without the help of the police," O'Hara said. "And I know that *I* never—"

"You know that you *what?*" Rose asked. "You were only at the gateway of the Ledbetter case. Had just scratched the surface when Mallinson removed you. Right? You weren't even to ask any more questions about the case, if memory serves me."

"Right," O'Hara said, recalling.

Rose held O'Hara in a tight gaze. "You know, right after the case broke, right after you made the arrest, Mallinson had a couple of deputy inspectors down in Peterborough flashing pictures of Gary. Did you know that?"

"It doesn't ring a bell," O'Hara said. "But there was a lot of confusion. One team of investigators going over the path travelled by another."

"I seem to remember seeing something in Central Records about it," Rose said. "After all, deputy inspectors? Awfully high rank to be playing backwoods Humphrey Bogart."

"If there was anything in Central Records about it, it's gone now," said O'Hara.

"Wouldn't you know it?" Rose said, almost as a refrain. "That Billy Mallinson sure is a busy boy when he wants to be."

O'Hara remembered Rose and the captain had locked their stubborn horns together more than once in the past. One of the great things about Rose was that she had scores to settle with almost everyone.

"So why don't you talk to Mallinson?" Rose asked.

"I already did."

"So what did the great man say?"

"He said no case is perfect," O'Hara said. "He said

he had no impression that there was anything unusual about the case other than its high profile."

"And you believe him?" Rose asked.

She didn't expect a response and didn't get one. And she suddenly looked very tired. Rose set aside her cup and leaned forward. She put two fingers to her eyes, pressing them, and then looked up again.

"Oh, that Bill Mallinson is such a damnable liar," she said. "I suppose you'll tell me next that he became the head of homicide clearly by merit. That he didn't whiz past some equally capable people because of his agility in state politics."

Now it was O'Hara's turn to sigh.

"I never asked questions about how Bill Mallinson got where he is," O'Hara said guardedly. "Sure, I've heard stories. But even if the path was dirty as sin, that still doesn't mean that evidence was fabricated in the Ledbetter case."

"Franklin," she said, "look at it from their point of view. You want this case to fly quickly. So you pull it away from this honest Irishman named O'Hara. And then, well, why *wouldn't* you put the fix in? You assume Ledbetter's guilty. You assume you got the right man. Why take chances? Why let the facts compromise a good case? You have methods that have worked for years, rainy days and sunny. So you damned well use them. Come on. It's just so much easier that way, Franklin. Cleaner. Faster." She paused. "If you'll excuse the expression, they got away with murder in the Ashton years. They would have done whatever was expedient. And you know it."

"But now, Rose," he told her, "I know it better than I ever did before."

"Does it make you feel better?"

"No."

"Then I don't know why you bother. Take your retirement, move to someplace sunny, and find yourself a girl. You start messing with past histories of old murder cases, Franklin, and you'll find yourself in a bottomless cesspool. Don't just take Rose's memory, dearie. Take her advice, too. Please?"

"Ever know of anyone named Clay?"

"Only Cassius."

"I need someone with the first initial 'S.' "

She pondered it for a moment. There was a loud crackle in the fire, so loud that they both were startled. An ember shot from a log and died on the bricks before the hearth.

"I'm drawing a blank on the name," Rose said. "Sorry. What's it mean? Who's 'S. Clay'?"

"I wish I knew, Rose," he answered. "And if I find out, I'll tell you."

There were other points of business which O'Hara wished to address. Specifically what had Rose known about William Mallinson's ascent to authority. Exactly what other cases in which there had been a certain creativity with respect to evidence. And then there had been that collection of books on the paranormal. Certainly after his own experiences, a few questions might be permitted to a man.

But time ran out. There was first the rumble of an automobile outside, then voices. Female voices, one bidding adieu to the other. Then there were the sounds of someone banging snow off a pair of boots on the kitchen doorstep, followed seconds later by the sound of a door opening.

Rose looked toward the kitchen. Her entire face illuminated with a smile. Suddenly, she looked five years younger.

"Donna?" she called.

"Hello, honey," a female voice returned.

Rose looked to O'Hara and shared a smile. "My roommate," Rose said. As if O'Hara couldn't have guessed. "We got company, doll!" Rose called back.

Donna appeared a few moments later, a lean woman in a short black skirt, black tights, and a mean red sweater. Red hair, close-cropped. She was about thirty years old, freckle-faced and pretty, but in a way that wasn't quite out of *Family Circle*.

"Shit. What a day," Donna said. She smiled to O'Hara and gave him a tepid hello. Then she came to the older woman, leaned over, and, as the two women exchanged a squeeze of the hands, Donna kissed Rose full on the lips.

Then Rose handled a formal introduction. "This here is my friend Donna Salinger," Rose said. "Donna, this is Frank O'Hara from Nashua. Old friend from when I worked for the State."

Donna offered a limp handshake. O'Hara accepted it and said the right words of greeting.

Donna had little else to say. She fumbled into her pocket. She produced a hash pipe and prepared to get it fired up.

"Donna, Mr. O'Hara is a detective with the state police," Rose continued.

"Shit," Donna said again, now fumbling to get rid of the pipe as quickly as she had found it.

"Fortunately," Rose said, "my friend Frank has very poor eyesight today."

"Very poor," O'Hara confirmed.

"I'm going up to the girls' room," Donna said. "I'll see you all later."

O'Hara told her it was nice to have met her, however brief it had been.

"Yeah," Donna answered. "Me, too. Real good."

Rose looked at him in mild befuddlement. "What in God's name were we just talking about?" she asked. "Where were we?"

O'Hara shook his head. He knew he had lost Rose. Or at least he had lost her attention. And she had attested to quite enough as it was.

Several minutes later, O'Hara was out the door. But not before passing by a bookcase in Rose's den. The books on the end table about those on the paranormal were just the tip of Rose's iceberg on the subject. Mixed in with volumes on the movies and on women's studies, must have been a hundred more volumes on the occult.

If there were people in the state with a larger collection on the subject, O'Hara mused as he walked to his car, he didn't really want to meet them. Fact was, Rose was falling into focus as an expert on many useful subjects. Some obvious; others not so obvious.

As O'Hara walked back to his car, the wind whipped little ice crystals off the surface of the snow, up against his coat, hat, and bare face. He struggled against it.

One of winter's wonderful little pleasures: The lock on his car door had already frozen shut. He worked it with his key for several seconds, but it wouldn't budge. Then he pulled from his pocket a butane lighter. He coaxed up a flame and held the fire against the lock of the car door, thawing the metal. As he repeated the process, he singed his finger—fire and ice at the same time. But with another jiggle of the key, the car door opened.

Then he stopped. As the wind pounded him, as the arctic freeze gripped him, O'Hara sensed, or thought he sensed, a presence close by. Another moment and he was sure it was Gary.

He whirled, his heart starting to kick as violently as it had the previous August when he thought he had felt a hand on his shoulder in a dark bedroom.

His eyes swept the snowscape. He was certain of the presence, but saw nothing. And he felt nothing, other than the notion that Gary's presence was as large and imposing as the winter snowscape, itself.

"You're not going to go away, are you?" O'Hara

said aloud. "You're going to pursue me until this is settled. Aren't you?"

No psychic message this time. No sharp crackle in the fire or creak on a floorboard. Just an overall sense, a menace as huge and cold as the New Hampshire winter.

That . . . or he was nuts.

O'Hara quickly sidled into his car. He wanted to be out of there before the lock froze again.

The reliable old engine cranked over obediently. O'Hara found a plowed driveway and turned his car back toward Nashua, alternately cursing the winter, trying to sort out everything Rose had told him in general, and specifically wondering how the falsification of evidence could have occurred—if it occurred at all—in the Ledbetter case.

He further tried to figure how it could have helped send an innocent man to the electric chair. If in fact, Gary was innocent. And if he had really gone to the chair.

Chapter 10

Three miles from home. Just three miles. And now this.

Stacey Dissette stood by the side of her stranded automobile and felt like crying. This was something out of a nightmare.

Stacey had tried to take the short route from her job at the bank in Nashua to her home in New Preston. The hilly, winding back road through Devil's Glen. She had lived in the state for four winters. So she should have known better. But the unseasonable earliness of the storm, plus its intensity, had ambushed a lot of people.

The snowdrifts on the county road were as high as two and a half feet in certain spots, and the undercarriage of her Ford Fiesta, when it came down a steep hill in Devil's Glen, had gotten stuck. The vehicle was mired in the snow, and there was no way to move it. It wouldn't budge six inches now, either in forward or in reverse.

It was 6:10 P.M. on a Thursday, five days after the massive November storm. Daylight was long gone, and few other cars travelled this route, particularly after dark. And she would soon be out of gas if she kept the car's engine running. Out of gas meant out of warmth from the car's heater. Stacey was in deep trou-

ble with the fifteen-degree weather predicted overnight.

She was alone and terrified. This was a great way to
freeze to death.

"Don't panic," she told herself. "Think. Think. Do
the smart thing. . . ."

She stood by her car, feeling the frigid air of the
New England night close in on her. She rallied her
spirits and tried to remain calm. But she knew she had
to make a decision. Soon.

She could set out on foot and hope to make it
through a mile of snowy, unpopulated highway—no
house anywhere in sight. Or she could stay with the car
and pray that another vehicle happened through the
same road.

It was one hell of a decision to make. She cursed her
own foolishness for having tried to cut through Devil's
Glen. Never, never, *ever* again in the winter, she promised herself. This had been just plain idiotic.

Game plan: She would wait for fifteen minutes and
pray that another car came by, someone who would
help her. After fifteen minutes, she would start out on
foot, walking back in the way she had come, toward
the main road that led back to Nashua. More likely to
find help in that direction.

She waited. Her car idled. She kept the radio on low
and tried to imagine a better plan. There wasn't one.
Her eye drifted to the gas gauge. The needle was on
one quarter.

Then she nearly jumped out of her skin when there
was a knock on her side window.

She whirled and almost screamed. A man! Where
had he come from? He smiled at her.

"Hello!" he said. "You okay? You stuck? You need
help?"

Her heart fluttered, then settled. Had God sent her
an angel?

She stepped from the car and almost cried in gratitude. But she withheld the tears.

"Oh, I'm so glad to see you!" she said. "I'm stuck!" She motioned at the car. "I don't know whether if you gave me a push I'd be able to move or what."

He glanced down at the vehicle. Snow up to the bumper. He shook his head. He was dressed in a heavy parka with boots and gloves, but the hood of the parka was pulled back. His hair was shaggy and dirty blond. He was slightly unshaven, but Stacey wasn't complaining.

"Impossible to push," he said, quickly assessing her predicament. "You'd just get stuck again." He thought about it for a moment longer. "You're going to have to get a flatbed tow truck in here after the road's clear."

"Well, then . . . ?" she asked.

He offered her a hand, which she didn't take. He smiled again. His face was now kind. Reassuring.

"Walk back this way with me," he said. He motioned in the direction in which she had planned to walk, back toward Nashua.

Then she looked for his vehicle. None. She looked for his bootprints in the snow.

For some reason, a flash of suspicion seized her. Then fear.

"Where did you come from?" she asked.

He motioned to the endless darkness behind him.

"I have a four-wheel over the other side of the hill," he explained, indicating the high crest that she had just crossed and slid down. "I had just decided to turn back when I saw your lights up ahead. I came down to see what was going on."

"I never saw your lights," she said.

"They were there. But I cut them on the other side of the hill."

"Why didn't you drive down here?"

"No place to turn around. Hey, there's only so much magic you can do with a four-wheel, you know. They can get stuck, too. They're not snowmobiles. You want us *both* to be stuck?"

"No," she said.

But what really bothered her was the stranger's fresh tracks in the snow. It was as if he had just *appeared* from amidst the dark trees.

He seemed to read her mind. And he could tell that she was afraid of him.

"I didn't fly down here like Peter Pan," he said. "I walked in your tire tracks, okay? I'm not some sort of Abominable Snowman." He paused. His blue eyes twinkled.

"What's your name?" he asked. His voice was soft now, engaging.

"Stacey."

"Stacey, honey," he reassured her. "I have a Jeep Cherokee over that ridge. Chains and four-wheel drive. I got a CB in my vehicle, okay? You can call your husband or your family or whoever you want and tell them where you are. And I can get you to safety in twenty minutes. Sound like a good deal? Or do you want to stay out here in the snow?"

He smiled. A most engaging smile.

She exhaled a long breath. "I'm sorry. Yes," she nodded. "I didn't mean to. . . . Yes, it sure does sound like a good deal."

"Good girl," he said. "That's more like it."

He looked at her disabled vehicle.

"Lock your car. Leave your flashers on," he advised. "In case anyone else is crazy enough to drive through here tonight, the flashers will help them see. Maybe your car will avoid being hit. Okay?"

"Okay," she said.

"Don't leave anything valuable in the car. You never know."

She agreed. He waited as she retrieved her purse and a flashlight from the glove compartment. She locked her car. She was already freezing. She glanced at her savior, however, and the cold didn't even seem to be touching him. Not at all.

Then she was ready to walk. She joined him in the tire tracks, an easier path than clumping through the unpacked snow.

"This will all be over before you know it," he promised her. When she struggled with her footing, he turned and offered her a hand.

He had beautiful eyes, and by now she trusted him. So she accepted his hand. It steadied her for the climb up for the hill.

"I never got your name," she finally said.

"I didn't give it," he said. "But, you can call me 'Gary.' "

Chapter 11

The next day began when it was still black as tar outside. Six A.M. The phone was ringing like a fire bell in the darkness.

O'Hara: a sleepy hello from his empty bedroom. He had caught the call on what he thought was the third ring.

On the other end was a male voice, crackling with belligerence. Familiar. Captain Mallinson.

O'Hara struggled to become alert. But nothing is fast before a frozen dawn. "What's going on?"

"We got an ID on Jane Doe."

"Jesus. . . ." Sleepily, coming awake, O'Hara: "What can you tell me—?"

"Nothing on the frigging phone, Frank. Get over here."

"Right," O'Hara was already rising from his warm bed into the cold room. The phone was in his hand. "Where? Headquarters?"

"Paloheima's chop shop," Mallinson said, which again told O'Hara that this wasn't the ordinary. The captain continued. "The roads still stink with ice. Should I send a jeep?"

"No. I'll get there."

"Now, Frank."

Mallinson hung up. O'Hara climbed into his clothes

from the previous day. He stumbled downstairs, the wooden steps moaning under his feet, his own soul moaning under his breath.

He found his way to the kitchen. In the microwave, he nuked a cup of water and juiced it with a double shot of instant coffee crystals. Anything for a quick caffeine fix. He cut the brew with a half cup of milk, tasted it, and winced. Success: It tasted so bad that it had shocked him slightly more awake.

A few minutes later he was in his garage, swigging bitter, ersatz coffee from an open thermos.

The latch on the garage door had frozen. Not unusual. The temperature was about twelve Fahrenheit. He picked up an ax and butt-ended the latch from within. He heard a tinkle of frozen chips falling on the other side. Winter music: shattered ice cascading onto more ice. The latch gave, the door lifted and, along with darkness, a blast of cold air swatted him in the kisser.

He climbed into his car, backed up, and felt the crunch of his tires on the jagged chunks of ice in his driveway. He tried to use the electronic switch in his car to close the garage door, but that, too, had frozen to death.

Out onto the road. Car lights on. A brutal morning. He joined the rural two-lane which would meet the highway to Nashua. No other car in sight. Who else was insane enough to be out?

"Fuck it," he growled. He had forgotten the tape deck. Couldn't even play Sinatra.

"Fuck it," he said again. All he could get was programmed drivel on the car radio, a half-wit early morning shock-jock from New York. There was also a Jesus-blaster, a Christian station from Vermont which was even worse, plus some incomprehensible French crap from Quebec. His fingers worked the dial.

He found All-News from New York: the gory account of a murder at an ATM in Queens.

Then, a white knuckler of a drive. Black ice all the way—the thin, invisible sheet of the fucking stuff on top of the asphalt. An engraved invitation to land in a ditch.

Seat belts, he thought, occasionally sipping coffee. He buckled up: If he were going to skid off the highway somewhere, he'd just as soon not stick his skull through the windshield.

Halfway to Nashua he caught up to an oil truck. In his mind, Captain Mallinson was already barking at him for the time it would take to get to the chop doc's office. So O'Hara steered the Pontiac into the wrong lane and passed the oiler, looking up to see if the truck driver happened to be awake. A surprising number of six A.M. vehicle operators weren't. This one was. . . . Wide.

One good fishtail gave O'Hara a sweet reminder of his own mortality. He hooked the Pontiac into the truck's lane, too close in front of the oiler. The trucker gave him a self-righteous blast of twin air horns.

Then the truck tailgated him. Fifty miles an hour, bumper to fucking bumper, on black ice. An up-all-night sorehead trucker.

O'Hara had an impulse. He would slam on his brakes and then hit the fuckhead truck driver with his state police shield as soon as the indignant asshole jumped out of his cab.

But instead, O'Hara pulled up a beacon that he kept down low beneath the radio. He plopped it on the dashboard and flipped it on, filling his entire world with pulsating blue. The trucker took the hint and dropped the bumper-to-bumper crap.

"There you go, buddy," O'Hara mumbled. "Good morning, get off my ass and fuck you, too." O'Hara flipped the man a finger and pulled away toward Nashua.

There were three cars in the M.E.'s end of the parking lot when O'Hara pulled in, all cozily nestled together.

The first was Paloheima's Buick. As nondescript as the man itself. Dull brown. Like an old hockey glove or an ice skate.

The second car was Mallinson's bad-weather car, the one with the illegal studded tires. It was a big, purple, 1984 Colony Park station wagon. It featured a 402-cubic megadeath engine which could do 120 m.p.h., a number which Mallinson claimed to have hit from time to time on the Massachusetts Turnpike west of Springfield. On the license plate there was bolted a medallion proclaiming, "Captain–New Hampshire State Police." Meaning: Don't go pulling this old white dude over. Professional courtesy.

The station wagon was purple, but had two replacement doors that were black. A purple-and-black Colony Park. A great New Hampshire vehicle, O'Hara concluded: A car the color of a bruise.

Then there was the third car. A big blue Mercedes-Benz, as fancy a set of wheels as existed since the death of the Deusenberg. It was a Benz from the 500 series: a land yacht. The Benz was brand-new and must have borne sticker numbers which looked like triple O'-Hara's annual pay stub.

O'Hara could tell instantly: the Benz spelled trouble. Big, expensive, fancy wheels were always a pain in conjunction with a homicide: They meant someone had money and thus influence. A few moments later, by the time O'Hara was in the building, in the quiet corridor leading to Paloheima's ice box room, these observations were still washing around inside him. What he didn't know was that it would get even worse.

Then everyone and everything converged at once.

Vincent Paloheima, M.D., stood in the anteroom before his examination chamber. His buttoned white lab coat hanging like a tent over his belly, a Styrofoam cup of coffee in his hand. O'Hara spotted him at almost the same instant as the faint but evident stench of pickling fluid accosted O'Hara's nose.

Paloheima turned toward the detective as O'Hara approached. Paloheima looked as if he was about to warn O'Hara about something, but Mallinson emerged from a doorway.

"Here's the detective now," O'Hara heard Mallinson say to someone still inside a conference room. "Best man on our force. We'll give him whatever he needs."

If there was a response from someone, O'Hara never heard it. Paloheima stopped in his tracks. The only warning he could give was a wary look. Then Mallinson was in the hall between them, motioning, indicating that O'Hara should join him.

O'Hara did. Wordlessly. Seconds later, O'Hara was in the conference chamber. A man in a deep navy suit, much too fine for the weather, sat at a table. The man was thick, jowly, and dark. A little pear-shaped. O'Hara knew him somehow. Nasty face: the type that pulled over your toes in that big road locomotive of a Benz and hogged a handicapped parking place. But O'Hara's mind was not yet churning fast enough. Tough to peg strange, hostile faces so early in the A.M.

O'Hara, though, knew the obvious. The man was related to the Mercedes-Benz by ownership, and he was related to the victim by either blood or lust.

The man's gaze rose and assessed O'Hara. Reproachful gaze, mixed with a lethal combination of anger, indignation, and bereavement. And coldness. Big-time chill.

"Frank," Mallinson said in funereal tones, "this is

Mr. Wilhelm Negri. As I'm sure you know, Mr. Negri is the publisher of the New Hampshire *American.*"

Simultaneous to Mallinson's introduction, O'Hara had pegged the face and uttered another strong profanity, a good hearty, "Oh, fuck it." But only in his mind.

O'Hara extended a hand. Negri's half-reluctant handshake matched the weather. So was the look he gave by way of greeting.

O'Hara said, "Pleased to meet you, sir."

Negri said nothing. It passed through O'Hara's mind—as strange thoughts do at such moments—that silence was an ominous commodity from a man who had five right-wing gabfests a week on syndicated radio, and whose vocal delivery ranged between Ronald Reagan fake-homespun to Times Square crackpot.

O'Hara waited for the shoe to drop. It dropped quickly. And hard.

"Frank," Mallinson continued in overly formal tones that he hauled out only for such occasions, "we've identified the woman found last week in the cabin on Monadnock. The victim was Abigail Negri. Abigail was Mr. Negri's wife."

There was a silence in the room. O'Hara used it to find his textbook voice.

"Oh, God," he then said. "I'm deeply sorry, Mr. Negri."

O'Hara's words were automatic. He had developed the art of using one part of his mind to process the events that unrolled before him, while a separate part sought their historical connection. He already knew that something was even further off-kilter about this case than he could have possibly imagined.

"Detective O'Hara is in charge of the investigation," Mallinson explained in his most unctuous voice.

Negri's gaze rose to the captain, his voice following. "I thought *you* were in charge."

"Detective O'Hara is directly under my command."

After a split beat, during which Negri's overall dissatisfaction registered, Mallinson saw fit to add a convenient lie. "We confer every day. I oversee every action Detective O'Hara makes," Mallinson said.

"I don't want any half-wit cop on this case," Negri said.

"O'Hara is our best man," Mallinson said.

Negri's attention snapped back to O'Hara. "How are you doing, Officer? What are your leads? Have anything yet?"

O'Hara floundered for something positive. "The case is already on the top of the department's priority list. It's my only case," he said.

"No leads, in other words."

"Leads, but nothing I can share with you."

"Bullshit," said Negri. "You have no idea who killed my wife. Is that what you're saying?"

Mallinson gave a look toward the ceiling, as if searching for some divine intervention. O'Hara answered. "We've had the investigation for less than a week."

"What the fuck does that mean, Officer?" Negri continued. "My wife's been murdered and. . . ."

At this point of any homicide investigation, it was O'Hara's custom to ask the questions, not duck the accusations. Custom and proper procedure. Part of him told him to shut up. Another part of him told him to counterattack.

O'Hara's first thought: Why was Abigail Negri lying out in an abandoned cabin for two months? Where was the Missing Persons Report? And how about the May-October aspect of this: Did the eye deceive, or didn't Wilhelm Negri look two dozen years older than his dead bride?

Had this been a factor? An element? And where did Gary Ledbetter filter into *this?* O'Hara's instincts began to surge forward, like a hound catching a scent.

O'Hara was poised for a counterattack, seconds away from launching it, when the divine intervention arrived.

"Wilhelm! Oh, Wilhelm, I'm so sorry."

Through the open door came a navy blue wave of police brass. The State Commissioner, Paul Vogelman, rarely wore his uniform but had dusted it off for this occasion. With him were a couple of night-shift harness bulls in bulky parkas, slinging sidearms the size of short rifles. With them was a deputy inspector whose name O'Hara recognized from some commendation he had once been awarded. Someone, either Mallinson or the governor, had launched an armada of brass to baby-sit for Negri.

The publisher never finished his sentence. The commissioner took him under arm and ushered him out of the room. Negri never gave O'Hara another look or even another word. O'Hara was left with his captain, with whom he exchanged glances of exasperation.

"Thanks for keeping your mouth shut," Mallinson finally said when Negri was safely down the hall.

"I couldn't have slipped a word in edgewise once that guy got going."

"Thanks for not even trying," Mallinson said.

"I'm going to have to talk to him eventually," O'Hara said. "Can't avoid that."

"Yeah, I know." Mallinson found one of his damnable cheroots. He lit it. "Just wait for the right time and place. Give him a few days to settle down."

"Was he estranged from his wife?" O'Hara asked. "Or did she just have this habit of disappearing for months at a time?"

Mallinson gave him a hunch of the shoulder to indicate how the hell should he know.

Dr. Paloheima appeared at the door, his coffee cup

replaced by photographs, a stack of forensic gore shots.

Mallinson eyed him with irritation. "What's going on, Doc?" Mallinson asked. "Run out of big toes to tag?"

"No, I was just wondering if you guys needed any souvenir body parts," Paloheima asked. "I've got some extras. I mean, with Christmas coming and everything. . . ."

"Very frigging funny," Mallinson answered.

"Actually, I'm going for breakfast," the medical examiner said. "Anyone want to join me?"

"Yeah, I'm in," O'Hara said. "As long as you're not eating off one of your steel stretchers again."

"Hey, what do you think I am? A barbarian? We're talking about across the street over there in 'Heartburn Heaven.' "

Predictably, with all the upper brass from the department on the premises, Mallinson declined.

O'Hara and Paloheima walked to the Sunrise Coffee Shop situated adjacent to the M.E.'s office in the shadow of two taller buildings. The Sunrise had never seen a sunrise in its existence.

O'Hara had put down many quick meals there following autopsies, though not as many as Paloheima. As they sat down, O'Hara's instincts were already churning on the case before him.

Jane Doe had turned into Abigail Negri. A case which could have gone no-profile or low-profile was now the highest in the state. Paloheima explained that the ID had come from dental records, a long shot that followed an anonymous telephone tip a few weeks earlier that Mrs. Negri had gone missing the previous summer.

Paloheima also had the gossip:

Officially, the young Mrs. N. had taken leave of her husband to visit parents out West. But the rumor mill had it better. The couple was estranged, and the high-priced divorce lawyers from New York were already wheeling the artillery into place.

An estrangement explained how Abigail could have vanished with no Missing Persons for all those weeks. But estrangement also posed a lot more questions, particularly the unpleasant ones that had to do with motivation.

"Why did the marriage split?" O'Hara asked. "Anyone have any spin on that?"

"There's one story around that says that Mrs. N. had some nasty personal stuff to snitch on her husband," Paloheima said. The doctor hunched his shoulders. "Who the fuck knows? Abigail was only married to him for a few years and then looked to be going for a million-dollar payout. So how does *she* look, even if we learn that he likes to be spanked?"

O'Hara pondered it. "Any truth to the rumors?"

Another shrug. "About the spanking? No. I made it up."

"About the nasty personal stuff," O'Hara said.

"Why does any marriage split when the husband's a couple of decades older than the wife?" the M.E. asked. "Maybe she figured she'd banged him long enough to nail the big divorce settlement. And she was tired of feeling old age creeping up on her every night."

"You got a cheerful way of looking at everything, Doc," O'Hara said.

"Hey, I'm in a cheerful line of work, Frank. Same as you. I see what people do to other people. It'd drive me nuts if I couldn't understand why they done it."

"Same as me," O'Hara agreed.

But Paloheima always was a man with an example that needed to be given. This morning's was a hooker snuff from a by-the-hour motel in Hampton Beach. A mocha-skinned Hispanic girl, probably about twenty, had been strangled with an electrical cord *after* she had been shot six times.

"Why strangle a girl after you've shot her? Why kill someone twice? Frank, to me that connotes a very warped psyche. That or extreme vengeance, know what I mean?"

O'Hara knew. And the stack of forensic gore shots—prom photos by Leonard, natch—that Paloheima had under his arm were from this case, which had broken two days earlier.

But O'Hara began to tune it out. Over bad coffee, as a cold dawn finally broke behind the grayness of downtown Nashua, O'Hara felt a headache coming on as Paloheima rambled forward on life and death and the implications of the later. O'Hara's headache intensified as he ate. And yet, the worst of the day's events had still not presented itself.

O'Hara did, however, run four-square into those events as he sat in his office an hour later. Mallinson arrived in the office on foot, and, by the look on the captain's face, O'Hara knew instantly that they were ready to travel again.

A car was waiting. A big state cop four-wheel with a driver. Mallinson sat in the front seat and stewed while O'Hara assumed a safer position in the rear.

"So what's this?" O'Hara asked.

"More of the above," was all Mallinson would say.

They drove out to Devil's Glen at a mad speed, considering the ice. And O'Hara, had he not guessed what he was about to be shown, surely would have known from the encampment of police vehicles along the highway. And farther down the road, down at the bottom of a gully in Devil's Glen, there was a single green Ford Fiesta, flanked by another pair of cop cars.

Mallinson's four-wheel stopped by the road, its large wheels crunching onto a shoulder of snow. The captain jumped out of the car and led O'Hara fifty

yards into the woods. They advanced on a position
that was swarming with state bulls in blue parkas.

And swarming with obscenity.

There, under a low gray sky, O'Hara stopped short.
The cold was so sharp that it felt as if it were slicing his
face with little razor blades.

"I found this," a local patrolman told O'Hara.

The cop showed O'Hara the contents of a woman's
purse, notably her driver's license and other identification.

O'Hara looked at what the officer held. Then his
eyes travelled to the carnage.

There was a large clump under a canvas in a clearing
between some trees. It wasn't enough that this woman
had been murdered. But the same rules of the game
seemed to have applied as in the Abigail Negri killing,
formerly known as Jane Doe.

There was a frozen river of blood on the snow.
There was also the rosewood box with the pink ribbon. O'Hara didn't have to ask about a decapitation
because he already knew. There was another canvas
about ten yards farther on from the first one. And
something much smaller than a body beneath it.

Something about the size of a human head.

"Oh, Holy Christ," O'Hara said.

He braced himself. A uniformed officer lifted the
first canvas and showed O'Hara the mutilated remains
of Stacey Dissette. The officer, in his blue cloak, reminded O'Hara of a U.S. cavalry man, alleging an
atrocity to the Indians on the snowy plains of the
upper Midwest.

But then O'Hara's thoughts hurtled back to the
present. He was sorry he had bothered with breakfast.
He suppressed the urge to vomit. He felt Captain Mallinson's eyes upon him.

"Holy Christ," O'Hara said again.

The uniformed officer gently let the canvas settle

again, covering the remains of the torso, saying nothing.

It was not yet ten o'clock in the morning. So much had already happened. None of it good.

O'Hara stared at what was before him. He tried to correlate it back to Abigail Negri, but failed—aside from the fact that in searching for the killer of one, he was now searching for the killer of both.

Then, as the wind whipped into him, and as other officers huddled in their parkas, O'Hara was beset with an image of his late partner, Carl Reissman, a suicide years earlier. He imagined Carl standing right there, taking this all in. O'Hara wondered how Reissman would have attacked the case.

He knew that nothing would stop this fiend from striking again. And he wondered how all this—all these brutal deaths in this frozen Hell—circled back to Gary Ledbetter.

Gary Ledbetter. A dead man, who was his chief suspect. Try telling the captain that a guy who had taken the hot seat in Florida was the numero uno suspect in a pair of New Hampshire homicides. Try feeding that one to the state's attorney. Why not tell them that he'd *seen* Gary, too?

Why not advertise that he, O'Hara, was going *completely* nuts, losing his mind like Carl Reissman had?

The police parkas moved methodically around him; big, bulky, humanoid, blue bears making clumsy tracks in the snow. Not talking to him. Not disturbing him. Their words hibernating along with their thoughts. The harness bulls were waiting for him to come up with answers. So was everyone else.

But O'Hara had no answers. Only questions that grew more complicated and paradoxical each day. And to top it all off, as he stood looking at Stacey Dissette's blood in the snow, he felt himself not just losing his mind. He was freezing, also.

Sure, he thought again. He was freezing to death. The image was fully upon him.

The cold in this state and the relentless pursuit of homicide would finally drive him nuts and kill him. Just as it had disposed of Carl Reissman. Drove his former partner so crazy that he'd pulled the trigger on himself.

Or, he wondered, was insanity a perfectly logical response to the boundless inhumanity inflicted by some human beings upon others?

He blew out a breath, losing his focus upon the other cops around him.

Oh, this slide into looniness wouldn't be complete today, O'Hara knew. Or tomorrow. Or even the next day. But it was down the road waiting for him, like a black beast in a dark tunnel where he would inevitably have to travel. O'Hara was certain that he was embarking upon his final journey to a frozen, lonely death. And these murders, inspired by a dead man, were the first steps of a descent into insanity and destruction.

Steps? Call it a push. Like a shove out of a top-story window, complete with a concrete kiss onto the sidewalk.

What else could it be? The feeling was clearly upon him. And O'Hara knew that he was helpless to stop it.

Not far away, someone was talking. The words were distant and didn't register. After several seconds, the same phrases came again. "You all right? You all right?"

O'Hara turned. "What?" he asked.

Captain Mallinson, standing only a few feet away from O'Hara, addressed him. "Talk to me. I asked if you were all right," Mallinson said.

"Why wouldn't I be?" O'Hara heard his own voice as if it were being played back to him.

" 'Cause I'm standing here frigging talking to you

and you're not answering me," the captain said. "What planet are you on?"

"Sorry," O'Hara said. "I was trying to assess this."

"Yeah, well assess fast, okay? I'm freezing my nuts off." Then there was the stench of a freshly lit cheroot, one of the real cheap stinkers made in Guatemala. Smelled like horse hair on fire. Then, "Got to call Forensic, Frank," the captain said, his tone relenting slightly. "No point all of us standing out here freezing again. Got to get to work."

"Yeah," O'Hara said. "I'll make the calls. Got to get to work."

Chapter 12

In the house on Oswell Street, Carolyn Hart lay in the silence of her bedroom. She tried to make some sense out of her thoughts. She knew that it was time to fulfill her mission.

It was early on a Sunday morning. Her house was very still. So was the city that surrounded it. The stillness allowed her to follow her own patterns of thought, her own stream of ideas.

Crazy ideas. That's what some people said. That's how certain people had thought of Carolyn. Maybe they were right, she pondered. And maybe they weren't. Maybe she alone knew what was best for her.

Carolyn did know that she wanted to feel alive again. She felt distanced from the world around her and had felt that way too long.

She drew a breath. She could hardly feel herself breathing she was so silent. Well, it was time to break that spell, she told herself. Time to return to. . . .

To what?

She thought of her parents, who were deceased, and wondered where exactly she would find their spirits.

She thought of her brother. . . .

She cringed. In the comfortable bed where she lay, a wave of extreme sadness washed over her.

She spoke aloud, but very softly. Like a whisper on the wind, subverting the silence in the room.

"Yes, definitely," she said. "Now is the time."

Nutty talk from a lonely woman with no one to listen? The restlessness of a human spirit? Or dedication to one's beliefs.

More than anything else, she wanted to return again to the real world. She also knew what else she wanted to do.

She wanted to make love with a man. It had been a long time since she had done so. Too long. Making love would make her feel alive again. She was sure.

Her right hand slipped under her nightgown. Gently, as a sexual intensity grew within her, she found the spot between her legs. The spot that her strict mother had always told her never to touch, but which brought her such pleasure when she touched it. Or when a lover toyed with it.

If only she had a lover, Carolyn thought.

She considered Adam Kaminski. The rental agent had been watching her from a distance. Did he think she was so foolish that she did not notice?

She knew he had feelings for her, and in a way she was flattered. Maybe she would give Kaminski his opportunity. She could flit in and out of his life, and neither would be the worse for it. But she couldn't picture herself in bed with him. Adam wasn't a man with whom she could feel comfortable.

Saddened, Carolyn sighed. Then she relaxed and escaped into a fantasy. In her mind, she was a seventeen-year-old girl again. She was in the South on a warm summer evening and taking a handsome stranger as a lover. . . .

She drifted with her thoughts. Her hands focused upon giving herself pleasure. Without much difficulty, she brought herself to an orgasm. Then afterward, for as many moments as she could, she continued to go with that feeling of satisfaction. She drifted sleepily until she could hold the fantasy no longer.

But then she was left instead with the unhappy reality: What she really wanted was a real man to do these things for her. To love her—both spiritually and physically. To give himself to her so that she might do the same for him.

She rose from her bed. She stared out of her window, looking down upon the street. The street was quiet as a tomb. And for that matter, so was her entire existence.

"Yes, very *very* definitely," she said aloud. Time to return to the real world.

She turned. Where was that name? The name of the man she had never met but whom she wished to see?

She had it written down somewhere. But instead, she searched her memory. He was a policeman in New Hampshire. She recalled his name. Frank O'Hara. He was still a detective with the state police last time she had inquired.

If she could contact him, if she could see him and if he could see her, maybe Carolyn could set things right. If she could draw him to Philadelphia and set him on the proper course of investigation. . . .

Carolyn smiled. She heard the sound of small voices not far away. Children's voices.

She gazed out the window again. Two young boys, aged maybe seven and five, had come out to the empty narrow street to play with a large red ball. Their father was with them.

Carolyn smiled again. The city was waking. So was she. She would find this man she had never met, this Detective Frank O'Hara. Through him she would be able to get on with her life.

*   *   *

O'Hara arrived home that night angry enough to smash furniture.

He hadn't eaten since morning, in the hours before the discovery of Stacey Dissette's body. So he brought home a pizza from Raimondo's in Nashua. The usual selection: one of Ray's mega-cholesterol specials with extra sausage and cheese. Eight slices: six for dinner, two for breakfast the next day. The pie was cold by the time O'Hara arrived home. So was he.

He reheated the pizza, then brought it to the living room. Dr. Steinberg be damned: After the events of this day, O'Hara was going to quaff some brew with this pie.

He opened the first bottle when he put the pie in the oven. He was on his second by the time the pizza was hot again. And by half past eight, as O'Hara settled onto the sofa before the television in his living room, the beer and the pizza were in a tie: three slices, three bottles.

A fourth bottle brought a comforting glow. A fifth, as he worked clockwise around the pie, went down very easily. By quarter to ten, O'Hara was feeling better than he had all day.

A morose feeling came upon him: Poor Stacey Dissette. And for that matter, poor Abigail Negri. What a privilege it was to find one's natural death at a comfortable time and place. Not traumatized by a sadistic killer. Not crushed or incinerated in some horrible accident. Not shot down in wartime, not slowly expiring from disease or starvation.

O'Hara was drunk. And he brooded upon the great fortune of any individual who could die peacefully in his sleep.

He held that thought.

Then somewhere upstairs there was a creak. O'Hara made every effort to ignore it. But how could a man fully ignore something when he knows it's there?

Then came another creak.

"Fuck it," he grumbled drunkenly.

He took another swig of beer, attempted to set down the bottle and instead knocked it over. The contents—about a third of a brew—spilled. O'Hara attempted to mop it up with a handful of napkins from Raimondo's. But he never rose from where he sat.

A nice beery rumination: He wondered if there were a *Good Housekeeping* award for mopping up beer with pizzeria napkins.

Another creak upstairs.

"Fuck you!" O'Hara shouted to the creak. Then he laughed. Yeah! That was telling them . . . whoever they were. Don't go creaking around in *my* upstairs!

He laughed, pleased with himself until there was a loud, violent bang above him. Whatever had made the creaks had answered him.

His whole body went very cold with fear. Cold with impending terror. Worse, he knew he was drunk. He knew his reactions were slowed and his logic muddled.

A *bang*. What had banged? What could have fallen over on the floor above him? Or who was there?

Then there was another bang in a different room. It sounded like furniture moving.

He muttered angrily. He looked to his ankles, half expecting one of those red crabs to appear, booze-generated D.T.'s, a good creepy-crawly spectacular working its way up his body.

"Fuck it," he cursed. He used the flat of his hand to slap his cheeks, trying to sober himself. He reached for the remote control of the television and turned off the set.

He sat very still and listened. Another soft creak.

Frank O'Hara's hand went slowly to his hip. He drew his pistol. Several seconds passed. Then there was a creak in the floorboards directly in back of him . . . as if whatever had been upstairs had glided downward through the floor to settle behind him in the center of his living room.

I'm here, Frank.

O'Hara, barely breathing: "Who's here?"

Bayou inflection: *It's me, man.*

"Who's 'me'?"

A horny, urgent whisper: *It's me, man. It's Gary.*

"You're dead."

I'm here. Laughter. Gary's laughter.

O'Hara, aloud, starting to sweat: "You're dead, Gary! You're not there! Christ knows, you're not there!"

Then why are you talking to me?

Silence followed. Then near-silence. O'Hara could hear something thumping. After several seconds, he placed it: the thunder of his own heart.

O'Hara spoke again, his hand soaking wet against the service revolver in his hand.

"You're an illusion," he intoned softly, trying to build his own confidence. "An hallucination. The product of too much beer and too much stress. A function of my imagination, the outgrowth of my own loose grip on my own sanity."

Think so?

"I know so."

Then why don't you turn around, Frank? Afraid to look a dead man in the eye?

O'Hara could feel the sweat all over his body. He tried to rally the courage to turn, terrified of what he would see.

Then there was another creak in the floorboards behind him, only an arm's length away. For a split second, O'Hara thought he could feel something very close by. . . .

He bolted from the sofa and pitched forward, turning as he sprung to his feet. Instinctively, as years of training kicked in, his arm extended with his weapon.

He stared, wide-eyed behind the sofa. Nothing. No one. No Gary.

No laughter. No voice from some other dimension. Just another maddening creak somewhere beyond the living room. Another innocent old house creak from the heat? From expanding wood in the floorboards? Or an invisible footfall?

The sound only made O'Hara angrier, more drunkenly furious. He swigged on the most recent beer bottle.

"Come out here, Gary!" O'Hara demanded. "If you're here, come out! Let's see you!"

No answer. None until a floorboard creaked near the staircase. O'Hara turned and pointed his pistol.

"I'm warning you!" he yelled.

A creak near the steps. Or so he thought.

"God *damn!*" he yelled. Wildly, he waved the gun in the direction of the noise. Then he squeezed the trigger.

The pistol erupted with a powerful blast, followed instantly by the sound of a bullet smashing into the hard wood of his stairs.

O'Hara staggered, both from the sound of the pistol and from the alcohol.

Then the creaks led upstairs. Like a line of a man walking. Yes! It was unmistakable now! There were footsteps in his house. Intruding footsteps.

O'Hara lurched to the bottom of the stairs, saw nothing at their summit and followed. He leaned on the banister as he staggered upward, his gun hand hanging at his side. He arrived at the upper floor of his home and weaved toward his extra bedroom.

He threw on a light and stood in the doorway. A sturdy table had inexplicably turned over. It lay askew in the center of the room, as if it had been pitched there by a strong, angry man.

O'Hara's heart raced ever faster. Heart attack terri-

tory! Stroke territory! DT territory: Derangement Tonight.

Who had done this?

"Gary!" he screamed. "Come on out, Gary! I know
you're here somewhere!"

No answer. But the door on the closet seemed to
move just slightly. Just enough.

A breeze? A little imbalance?

A ghost?

Gary alive? Gary dead?

Who cared? O'Hara pointed his pistol at the closet
door.

"I'm warning you, Gary!" he shouted. The cocksure
certainty of an inebriated man. "That's enough!"

O'Hara steadied the gun. The trigger was easier to
pull the second time. He blasted. A massive hole
ripped into the closet door. O'Hara felt greatly satis-
fied until he heard the sound of steps behind him,
moving toward the master bedroom.

"Fuck it," he yelled.

He turned and lurched through the dark hall. His
hand found the light switch in his bedroom. His eyes
froze. A chair had been turned over.

Something *was* there! O'Hara might have been
drunk and losing his mind. But he was *right!* An intruder was present!

O'Hara scanned the room angrily. Under the bed?

He fired a shot into the darkness under where he
slept.

In his clothes closet? O'Hara moved to it, steadied
himself and aimed his gun again.

"Ledbetter!" he roared.

No answer again.

So, hell! He fired another bullet. Another hole
ripped its way into the woodwork. Shards of wood
flew in all directions. The hole left behind was gaping,
as if a musketball had tumbled through.

O'Hara raised his gun and weaved forward. He knew he was disgustingly drunk. Sickeningly drunk. Better-See-Dr.-Julie-real-soon sort of drunk.

He pulled the closet door open. Darkness, coming quickly to lightness. He looked at the path of the bullet, where it had gone through some old suits.

"Oh, man, am I soused!" he heard himself say.

But no Ledbetter. And no more creaks to the floor.

He sighed. He braced himself. He leaned against the door frame, his pistol hand hanging at his side.

"Christ Almighty," he mumbled. There he was. A crazy drunk staggering around his home firing bullets. A mentally disturbed cop. A menace to his world. Chasing his own private demon, a spirit that only he could see.

"Where the fuck are you, Gary?" he asked.

"Oh, Gary's here, Frank," came the response. "But you better be real careful!"

"What the—?" O'Hara answered.

The voice he had just heard had not been Gary's. It had a strange hollow echo. Something unworldly. But it had been a familiar voice and not an unfriendly one.

O'Hara turned, raised his head, and jumped as if hit with a thousand amps.

Carl Reissman stood in the corner of the room. Smiling Carl. His partner dead for almost seven years.

"Hello, Frank," Carl said.

"Carl . . . ?" O'Hara rasped. But his jaw locked. He was unable to speak. Like a nightmare, except a man knows he is going to wake up from a nightmare. There was no way to awake from this.

Before O'Hara's eyes, smiling Carl aged ten years in two seconds. He became grim, disturbed Carl, the ace homicide dick who put a bullet through his brain in a motel room one night after one final round of fornication with his mistress, a girl who majored in both Classics and fellatio at Keene State College.

Carl answered. Nice of him, since he still bore the head wound that had gotten him buried. Part of his upper right cranium was now gone, but who cared? He was there and talking, anyway.

"Gary's here," Carl's ghost explained. "Here to see you."

"Why can't I see him?"

"You will. He's close by."

"Show me. . . ."

"In time," Carl answered.

"Now! I want him *now!*"

"You always were an impatient fuck," Reissman said, turning chip-on-the-shoulder belligerent and smiling like a barracuda.

"Now!" O'Hara demanded drunkenly.

"No can do right now, pal. You can't rush me, because time doesn't exist any more for me."

O'Hara raised the hand that held the pistol.

Carl Reissman laughed. "Going to shoot your own partner? Shame, Frankie!"

"Fuck you, Carl!"

"I'm already dead, Frankie. Don't bother."

O'Hara pulled the trigger. Once, then twice. The pistol exploded. O'Hara thought he saw the bullets crash through Carl Reissman, then hit the wall of the bedroom. Big, nasty holes again. The ghost smiled, waved, and was gone.

O'Hara blew out a long breath. He holstered his gun. He was so drunk that he could fall down at any time.

He staggered downstairs. He paused. Now he was sure he had heard a rumble somewhere within the house.

Then he realized: The heat! He had jammed on the thermostat. No wonder there were creaks. The heat was making the wood expand.

Perfectly logical. Of course!

So much for Gary Ledbetter. And so much for the hallucination of Carl Reissman upstairs.

And what about the overturned furniture, my cop friend? an internal voice asked. *Don't you understand? I did that.*

"Go away, Gary," O'Hara pleaded. His voice was reduced to something between a whisper and a croak.

O'Hara weaved back into his living room. The room was dark, and he was sure he hadn't left it that way.

O'Hara staggered into the room and reached for a lamp on a table. Then he jumped in cold, stupefying terror. What his hand landed upon wasn't the cord of the lamp, but an icy human hand . . . which arrived simultaneously under the shade of the lamp. A hand intent on keeping this room in darkness.

O'Hara bellowed in fear. He recoiled, backing into a corner. The lamp flew from the table and rolled to the wall.

Then O'Hara screamed again. In the center of the room, another human form became visible.

It was a silhouette, much like those snow ghosts that flitted silently from tree to tree in a winter storm. The figure made no noise. But O'Hara knew he saw a man.

Thin, wispy hair. Blondish. Muscular. About five feet ten. Blue eyes gleaming.

A smile took shape, much like that of the Cheshire cat, as it seemed to be fixed in the air and floated in some unnatural defiance of any law of God.

Then features came into perspective, and the figure spoke.

Hello, Frank.

O'Hara bellowed in terror again. This wasn't real! This couldn't be! Gary Ledbetter! But he *was* there! Either real or the man's god-awful cursed spirit.

Oh, praise God, O'Hara said to himself. Don't let this be! This cannot be reality! This cannot be happening!

O'Hara sank against the wall, cowering into a corner, his pistol in his hand again, wavering.

I'm here, Frank, the voice spoke. *Now you can see me, can't you?*

Gary's voice. Calm. Insinuating. Slithery. The voice of those taped interrogations that O'Hara had replayed more times than he could count. The voice of a man who had died in the electric chair.

Or should have died! The man's physical being was surely dead. But the spirit was here, confronting its one-time accuser, a few feet away from O'Hara's piano.

"No! No! No!" O'Hara said.

Don't believe in me, Frank?

"No! You're not real!"

Then why am I here, Frank? If you don't believe in me none, why are we speaking?

"We're *not* speaking! And you're not—!"

Not here? Oh, yes I am. Ledbetter's expression turned into one of sheer malice.

O'Hara raised his pistol. At point-blank range, he pulled the trigger twice. The sound filled the house. Gary Ledbetter stood in place. Both bullets smashed violently into the brick and plaster of O'Hara's fireplace.

O'Hara turned away. Gary misted into the gunsmoke. The gunfire resonated within O'Hara's head, joined a few seconds later by a maniacal laughter which came from Ledbetter.

O'Hara pulled the trigger a third time and felt the impotent click of an empty weapon.

A terror unlike any that had ever come before engulfed the policeman, a terror so monumental that he had to steady himself to keep from quaking against the wall.

It was a terror as great as the outdoors because it combined imminent threat with a fear of a supernatural being, an entity that was now right in front of him.

And it was coming closer all the time.

The room was cold. Yet O'Hara's whole body was rolling with sweat. And he was certain he wasn't hallucinating. Not this time.

He was next aware of another sensation. A scent. A heavy, repugnant smell. He recognized it from the previous summer when he had come downstairs in the middle of the night and had seen the rocking chair gently moving.

And then suddenly O'Hara identified the scent of burning flesh. Human flesh. The odor of mortality that follows an electrocution. And it had turned up in his home, he now realized, at the very hour that past summer that Ledbetter had been put to death.

And in that moment, O'Hara was faced with the realization: He was indeed visited by—haunted by!—a dead man.

Gary glided a little closer. No sound now. No footfall.

Frank. I'm here. It's time to talk.

Gary approached. The presence had a field of its own. It was preceded by a drop in the surrounding air pressure. There was also a coldness—a winter deadliness—to its aura.

Frank? Speak to me, Frank.

O'Hara's heart thundered. His eyes were accustomed to the darkness. The figure was five feet away from him. Dark, hands dropped at its side. Shaggy hair. Stocky build. And the odor of burning flesh— Gary's odor—was so pungent that it seemed as if it would suffocate the detective.

"Please go away," O'Hara breathed through his drunkenness. "By everything that is holy, please go away."

The presence laughed. *Nothing is holy. There is no*

God. There are only spirits. And I will not go away until there is justice.

The voice. Soft. Silky. Slithery. Unmistakable.

The figure knelt down, settling in a sitting position on the floor in front of O'Hara.

"If I turn the light on," O'Hara tried desperately, "I will wake to find that I am only in the midst of a vivid nightmare. You will be gone, and I will be alone in this room."

Try it.

"You will be gone."

I'm here, man. Wishing will not get rid of me.

O'Hara sat up. The figure remained before him. O'Hara threw out an arm, fumbled with the switch on the lamp, and then found the ON button.

His hands, wet. His throat, frozen in terror. His nostrils clogged by the acrid aroma of execution. His heart, kicking as if it would explode in his chest.

He pressed the button.

The lamp came on. Light filled the room. Strange, angular light. Very bright beam. Very dark, jagged shadows.

Gary Ledbetter didn't go away.

Ledbetter—more intense and hyper-real than in actual life—remained an arm's length in front of O'Hara, grinning wickedly, blue eyes alive, burning like pilot lights as they bore into O'Hara's soul.

O'Hara felt himself gasp, his heart continuing to kick, and he felt a scream forming in his throat. There was no imagining this.

"You're alive!"

I'm dead.

"You're real!"

I'm a ghost.

"You can't be!"

Want to shoot at me again?

O'Hara, screaming: "You cannot be!"

I am!

"Why?"

I'm innocent, man. I didn't kill no girls.

"Gary . . . !"

There's a lady gonna come see you, Frank. Or maybe you'll find her. Go with your instincts, man. Go with what you know is right.

O'Hara was unable to speak. He was paralyzed into his position against the wall, facing a man whom he knew to be dead.

Facing death itself.

I'm innocent, man! I didn't kill no girls!

O'Hara summoned up every bit of courage that he owned. He leaned forward, then desperately lunged, extending one arm directly at the specter.

O'Hara watched his hand. It entered Gary the way an arm would enter a beam of light. It entered and passed through him. Gary was there. His spirit was there, but only in form.

And O'Hara was aware, as his arm passed through the ghost, that it had entered a field that was cold beyond imagination, a coldness that only could be duplicated by sticking one's arm directly into a frozen lake or a bathtub of ice water. And leaving it there for an hour.

Words caught in O'Hara's throat. A scream did not. He lunged with his left arm, and that limb, too, passed through Gary. Again O'Hara felt that deathly cold.

All this time Gary spoke of a woman who was coming to find O'Hara. All this time Gary's laughter continued.

O'Hara sprang backward against the wall, and now his entire home was filled with Gary's maniacal laughter. Laughter that was soon joined by a cry of terror and horror unlike one ever heard by the living.

O'Hara screamed long and hard, hid his eyes, looked back, and Gary was still there.

Standing now.

Leering.

Defying him.

Glaring downward and terrifying him.

O'Hara slumped into the corner where the wall met the floor. The moment, like the rest of the world, seemed frozen.

O'Hara screamed and screamed and screamed. And the last two visions the detective had, before losing consciousness, was first one of Gary grinning and turning away, this small part of his mission accomplished.

And an illusion quickly followed of a big red crab climbing up O'Hara's feet. And the crab began that long, horrifying march—all claws and pincers—across his legs, across his knees, across his genitals and chest until O'Hara was looking at it eye-to-eye, hard-shelled claw to teeth. There it remained for several minutes, O'Hara screaming the entire time, until the crab, which was about the size of a football, crawled into the drunken man's open, imploring mouth; choked him in a beery, boozy vomit of fear; and—as O'Hara bordered upon losing his mind—brought him into a night where the cold and the blackness were absolutely total.

Chapter 13

"You may be my patient," Julie Steinberg said the next evening, "but I don't usually make house calls."

"You don't normally have a patient like me," O'Hara answered, holding open the front door to his home. "So come in."

"Thank you," she said.

He closed the door after Dr. Julie had entered. She stood uneasily in the front hall, surveying everything before her. He took her coat. Somehow O'Hara had limped through a day of work, despite the memory of the previous night.

Shortly after noon of that day, he had phoned her and asked if she could come by that evening.

"Frank," she had asked, "is this a professional request or a social one?"

"Professional," he had assured her. "Purely."

"I don't see people socially whom I see professionally," she said. "I want you to know that."

"I guessed that before I called," he assured her. "And this is sort of an emergency."

"Why can't you come to my office?"

"I want to tell you what happened. And I want you to have a sense of *where* it happened."

"Six o'clock. On my way home," she said.

"Done."

The day had moved slowly. No progress on the dual homicides before him. He scheduled an interview with newspaper publisher Wilhelm Negri for the next morning. He spent the afternoon readying himself for that interview, but thinking ahead of his appointment with the psychologist that evening.

He invited her in and sat her in the living room before a fire. He poured her a cup of coffee. Then, with the earnestness of a man mixing confession with controlled hysteria, he ran through the events of the last twenty-four hours.

Julie Steinberg listened patiently, sipping coffee as she absorbed what O'Hara had to say.

She found herself wanting to make notes on paper, and at first made them only mentally. Eventually though, she halted him for a moment and brought a notepad out of her purse. He did not object. Nor did he waver from his account of the previous night.

When he made reference to having seen a ghost in that very room, her eyes found the specific place. Yet the spot seemed so mundane and pedestrian now. Harmless. Empty as a broken promise. But it was clear to her that *something,* something rather terrifying, had transpired, whether it had a basis in reality or not. The bullet holes in the wall attested to that much.

His recounting of the evening, from the first suspicious creak, to the red crab, to the final unconsciousness, took about twenty minutes. During his explanation he led her upstairs. There she saw where he had fired bullets into the wall and the closet when confronted first by the image of Carl Reissman and then by a companion vision of Gary Ledbetter, both of them returned—maybe—from God knew where.

Dr. Steinberg said nothing, merely listening. Nor did he ask her for comments. Eventually, he led her back to the living room where they sat down again.

Then finally, when he was finished, the house gave

a strange creak, as if to add a punctuation mark to the end of his story. The creak sounded much like a distant footfall, which was how his whole tale had started. The detective and the psychologist both lifted their eyes to the spot in the ceiling below the sound. The timing might have amused them, had the previous evening not transpired. Each saw the apprehension in the other's eyes. Then the moment passed.

"You have a wonderful fire burning," Julie Steinberg said after a moment, a glance to the fireplace. "Fires warm old houses very nicely. And as we both know, the warmth causes the walls and floorboards to expand, causing them to creak."

He recognized her attempt at reason.

"And yet sometimes recently," he added, "the creaks come on cold nights when the heat is not a factor. Or when the fire has been on and the temperature has reached an equilibrium. There are still creaks then, just as there were last night, as a prelude to everything else."

"What are you trying to say?" she asked. "That you believe something supernatural occurred?"

He shrugged. "I invited you here to get a feel of the place," he said. "I wanted you to have a sense of me, where I live, and what could have happened."

She set aside her coffee cup.

"Frank," she said. "I don't believe in ghosts. And you'd be better off if you didn't, either."

He drew a breath and let it go slowly.

"I'm not saying I do," he said. "I'd be much better off if I hadn't had the experience of last night, either. But I had it. And it was very real."

"No," she said. "It *seemed* very real. There's a difference. A movie can seem very real and scare you, leading you into its own reality much the same way."

"You're comparing what I saw to a movie?"

"If you want me to, I will," she said. "It's not a bad

analogy. Voluntary suspension of disbelief. Seduction of the viewer into an imaginary world that creates its own reality. A world into which the viewer *wants* to go, I might add."

"I'm not so sure that I imagined anything," he said, shaking his head. "Nor did I want to see Gary Ledbetter again. Or Carl Reissman." Suddenly he was quite adamant. "Jesus, let the dead stay dead, all right? And yet what I saw looked and acted as if it had come from another . . . another. . . ."

He fumbled for an accurate terminology. "Another world," he tried. "Another dimension."

She looked at him very seriously.

"Gary Ledbetter. And your ex-partner, Carl Reissman. They were both here? That's what you believe you saw?"

O'Hara drew a very deep breath. "I know it sounds, what, 'crazy'? Is that the word I should use?"

"That's one term for it," she said. " 'Dementia' is another. So is 'Falling-down drunk.' Which do you prefer?"

"Are you here to lecture me or help me?" he asked.

"Both if it's necessary," she said. "It's not enough for you to relate to me what happened. You have to understand it yourself."

"And if I don't?"

"Then it will happen again. Only worse."

She set aside her coffee. She walked to the living room and stood two feet away from where a slug from a thirty-eight had formed a crater in the woodwork. She stared at it and turned.

"If I didn't think I'd be courting trouble," she said, "I'd ask Captain Mallinson to take your weapon away from you."

"Why? For shooting the wall?"

"For going crazy in here with a gun," she answered. "You could have killed yourself. Or someone else."

She glanced through the nearest window, her eyes settling upon the home of the closest neighbor. "What kind of weapon are you using?"

"Standard service piece, old-fashioned variety. Colt thirty-eight-caliber revolver."

"At what distance does a round remain lethal?"

It was a question from the firing range, one for new recruits, or for old boys such as himself who needed reminding.

"Maybe seven hundred meters," he answered.

"How far is the nearest house?"

He sighed. "I get your point."

"Then say it out loud."

"Less than seven hundred meters."

"I'm worried about you, Frank," she said, turning back to him. "I'm worried about you on a professional level, and I'm worried about you on a personal level. Crashing around your own house in a D.T.-stupor is not exactly symptomatic of emotional stability. Nor is it a prescription for a long and happy life."

She paused and he knew what was coming next. "And, of course, you weren't supposed to drink."

"I know," he sighed. "But what about what I saw?"

"What do you think?" she answered. "Do you think the red crab was there?"

"No," O'Hara answered.

"Then why do you think Gary Ledbetter was here? Or Carl Reissman?"

"Because that seemed different," he said.

"Listen to yourself. *'Seemed'* different," she stressed. "Even *you* are subconsciously admitting that you know that they couldn't have been here."

"Yes, sure. But—"

"Frank, examine this," she said. "Gary Ledbetter. Carl Reissman. What have you told me about both of these men?"

He blanked on the connection. So she led him to it.

"Both might be considered major tragedies," she said. "Would I be correct about that? Traumas. Unresolved emotions on your part: a respected partner who committed suicide; a man whom you arrested who went to the electric chair. Frank, I'm not trying to put words in your mouth, so tell me whether or not you agree."

He answered after a moment. "I agree," he said.

"Don't you think," she said, "given too much alcohol, given a suggestive mood, given too much stress, given cause to think about both too much, that you might see things that aren't really there?"

He pondered that one long and hard.

"Might I have?" he answered. "Maybe. *Did* I? That's another question. So I don't know."

"Frank," Dr. Steinberg said, "The dead do not walk among us. We've had this conversation already."

"Maybe they do sometimes, Doctor," he answered.

"You are seeing things that cannot be there," she insisted. "Never in the history of humanity has it ever been proven that someone living interacted with someone dead."

"And the opposite hasn't been disproved, either," O'Hara replied. "Inexplicable events happen all the time. Like the ones that have happened to me. It's just that they defy proof of a traditional sort."

"Then you *do* think the dead walk among us?" she challenged.

"I used to think they didn't," he said. "I used to laugh at those silly Indian legends and those optical illusions in the trees. Now? Who knows? I only know what I saw."

"It's not possible, Frank. Should I have you visit the grave of both Reissman and Ledbetter? Should I have copies of the death certificates obtained to give you a good dose of reality? You have to look at all this in the cold light of day. And you have to understand it for yourself. Just to have me tell you this is ludicrous. It won't work that way."

He said nothing.

Gently, she moved to a conclusion.

"As long as you entertain thoughts like this, Frank," she said, "you're flirting with a real emotional disaster. I don't want to see that happen. Do you understand?"

"I understand that," he said. "I just wish you'd been here to see what I saw."

"If I had been here," she said firmly, "I would have taken away the liquor and cut you off from your weapon. Then neither of us would have seen anything. And you wouldn't have bullet holes in your wall, either."

His expression fell a bit, and he momentarily felt his emotions sag. He wondered why he had even called her to his home since her reaction, that of an enlightened rationalist, a scientist, was so damnably predictable. And what the hell? To make matters worse, she was probably right.

A wave of relaxation crossed the room. "All right," he said. "More coffee?"

"That would be nice," she said. "Then I have to leave."

"Where's your home?" he inquired. "I don't know much about you personally."

"Dublin," she said. "About a half hour from here."

"A bad drive?"

"I could do without the ice. But it hasn't been too bad for the last two days." She smiled at his expression of concern. "I'll be fine," she assured him.

"Tell me one other thing," he said.

She waited.

"Seven years ago you did the State's first psychological profile on Gary Ledbetter. Why didn't you ever tell me?"

He thought he had her off guard. Instead, she was ready for the question. She had eventually expected it.

"Professional ethics," she said. "If you don't ask, I can't tell. And even then, I shouldn't."

"Still bound by those same standards? Gary's dead, after all."

A log shifted in the fireplace. Their eyes went to it, then returned to each other.

She considered her response. "How did you find out?" she asked.

"I read what remains of Gary's file in Central Records. Your interview was one of the things that wasn't removed."

"I'm surprised," she said. "They didn't like my conclusions. So they hired someone else right away. Got the conclusions they wanted on the next two tries."

"I know. I read those, too," he said. It was his turn to smile. "I'm sure you appreciate the irony. You and I were both reassigned from the same suspect. Leads me to think that they didn't like what I was doing, either."

She sipped some coffee. "A valid point," she allowed.

"Or maybe they didn't like what I would eventually have done."

"And what was that?"

"Continue a fair investigation," he said. "Instead of just making sure we obtained a conviction on the most obvious initial suspect."

"Another valid point."

"Did you think Gary was guilty?" he asked.

"Everyone did."

He paused. "Did you think Gary was gay?"

"My interview was a long time ago. I was young and not as experienced as I am now."

"Your interview pointed in that direction," he reminded her.

"It's one of the things I wanted to pursue," she said. "I asked for more time to evaluate. That's when they cut me off. As soon as I went to work on that angle. Ben Ashton. The Attorney General. He wanted to hear nothing of it."

"I remember," he said. He paused. "But you didn't answer my question," he said. "Did you think Gary was gay?"

She finished her coffee. "It was many years ago. I didn't have the opportunity to pursue that point as well as I should have. And I'd only be guessing now," she said.

"So guess."

"My hunch is that, yes, he was."

The logs shifted again, and for a moment the flame merrily danced on a fresh section of wood.

"Why is it still important?" she asked.

"Same reason it was then," he said. "If he was gay it pulls the underpinnings away from the State's case. It's hard to theorize that a man was a sex killer of women if he wasn't interested in women sexually."

"Too late for Gary," she said.

"Yeah," he said thoughtfully. "Maybe." He waited, then asked, "What about an 'S. Clay'? Some of the worst evidence against Gary was found in a storage locker leased to an 'S. Clay.' Do you remember that name ever coming up?"

She shook her head.

"It wasn't in your transcript, either," he said. "But Gary had someone who knew his ways pretty well. Either that or he's back as a ghost committing more murder." Several seconds passed. "Or," O'Hara mused further, "Gary was never guilty at all. And the real killer remains among us."

The logs hissed.

"Gary's dead," she said.

"Yeah," he agreed. "Gary's dead. That's the one

thing everyone agrees on. And know what? That's
what troubles me the most."

"How do you reconcile all of that?" she asked after
several more seconds.

He threw up his hands, as if to end all serious discussion. "I have no idea," he said. "And if you think of
something, please tell me."

"I promise," she said. Again, she smiled. And he
liked her all the more for it.

He stood and gathered the cups and saucers. There
was a silence in the house as she remained in the living
room, the glow of the fire keeping her company. It
occurred to him that a woman's presence in the house
was something that he sorely missed.

For a moment in the kitchen, as he poured out the
remainder of the coffee, he thought of putting on some
music, as their professional encounter had apparently
run its course.

But naturally, O'Hara would have preferred Sinatra. Maybe one of the tapes from the mid-1950s when
Francis Albert's voice was as powerful and smoothly
polished as a new Caddy V-8, the epitome of brash,
romantic, snap-brimmed cool. Maybe some hard-core
sexy stuff like that would loosen Julie Steinberg even
more.

He would like that if it happened, O'Hara decided.
And yet, he couldn't bear one more defensive discussion of the other Frank.

So he let the moment pass. No Sinatra for his guest.
Damned thirty-something psychologist from Boston,
he reasoned. She was probably into Aerosmith.

Their final cups of coffee were consumed peaceably.
No mysterious creaks upstairs, no visitations from a
netherworld. The fire remained constant, and Julie
Steinberg was gone by seven P.M. O'Hara laid off any
booze, and the rest of the evening passed less eventfully than the previous one.

* * *

O'Hara's feelings toward Wilhelm Negri were purely professional. He knew before he went into Negri's office at the newspaper in Nashua the next morning that they would have to be.

Negri broadcast his daily radio show out of the newspaper's executive suites. A small broadcast chamber had been constructed adjacent to the publisher's office, and he took to the airwaves at eleven thirty each morning, filling his half hour with conservative opinions, liberal-bashing accusations and, when it was convenient, the assorted half truth. The targets were familiar and easy, and his growing audience loved it.

In New England, many stations had once used Wilhelm Negri as a cheaper, watered-down version of Rush Limbaugh. This had so mortified Negri that he had asked his writers to intensify all his attacks. He moved as far right as a man could on the radio and not be termed crackpot, then edged even a little farther.

Ratings soared. He became the Dracula of far-right radio commentators. And in the last few years, he had gone national.

Wilhelm Negri's grandfather, Benjamin Negri, had owned a papermill in the early part of the century. After World War One, Grandpa Negri had had two commodities in abundance: a lot of nasty opinions and a lot of cheap paper. In 1920, he combined the two, founding the New Hampshire *American,* and staying in business by covering hunting accidents, sticking up for the timber industry, selling advertisements for local hardware stores, and printing jingoistic editorials.

Through some select Jew-baiting, Red-bashing, and FDR-hissing, Benjamin Negri became a regional celebrity in the 1930s. He had mined all these topics very profitably and mixed them with some Olympic-caliber flag-waving up until the 1940s when he went to jail for income tax evasion.

The next Negri, Wilhelm's father Peter, had been sent to school at Exeter and Princeton. Somehow sanity prevailed. Peter Negri ran a temperate middlebrow local rag that served the community and let the Manchester *Union-Leader* do the editorial screaming. This changed in the 1980s, however, when Wilhelm Negri at age thirty-five took over from the old man, who retired.

Wilhelm Negri turned the *American* into a tabloid, launching screaming editorials, and backing redneck causes—such as finding ways to execute every convicted killer in America. He turned the journal into a pulpit and a power base. Apparently in the Negri family, the wacko stuff tended to skip generations.

On the morning of the interview, O'Hara was met in the lobby by one of Negri's lackeys, a fortyish man named Howard Chambers. Chambers was thin and wore a dark suit. He was half butler and half bodyguard.

Chambers led O'Hara first to a third-floor waiting room outside the publisher's office. The meeting was scheduled for nine thirty. O'Hara was kept waiting till ten.

But as O'Hara waited, he had already come to a few decisions. He would treat Negri as he would the bereaved in any other murder investigation. He swore that to himself and simultaneously knew that he would not be able to. On account of who Negri was. On account of what he did, the paper he published, and the opinions he put forth on the radio.

O'Hara reflected back to the thought that he had had outside the medical examiner's office: Whenever a $60,000 car was parked near a murder case, there were always complications. It never had failed. He knew it wouldn't fail here, either.

Finally, at a few minutes after ten A.M., Chambers admitted O'Hara to Negri's office. O'Hara was given a seat before a long, wide, mahogany desk.

The publisher was preparing for his radio show, he said, but certainly wished to spend a few minutes with the chief investigator in Abigail's death. He received the detective cordially but with coolness. O'Hara was hard-pressed to understand whether the chill had an edge of hostility to it or whether Negri was a man whose emotions had been drained by the death of his wife.

The question was only amplified by the short conversation that ensued. Early in the previous summer, Abigail Negri had asked for a divorce, the publisher said, leaning back in a thousand-dollar leather swivel chair behind a five-thousand-dollar desk. He had never completely understood her reasons, Negri pouted, much less come to grips with them.

"She said things about not wanting to be a celebrity's wife, that she was disappointed with our life together," Negri told O'Hara. "But I'm hard-pressed to see how our life together was any different than what she should have expected."

O'Hara allowed that it was unfortunate when two people fell into avenues of misunderstanding. And that the marriage couldn't have been saved. As he listened, he tried to get a fix on the publisher. Negri stood after a few more minutes and, continuing to talk, went to a clothing closet and began to change his shirt. He also pulled out a sports jacket and tie. He dressed sharper on the radio, he explained.

At forty-seven, Negri remained a relatively young man, even if slightly porky. He had a dark jowl that looked as if it had been knocked off-center and then repaired, as if from an accident or some unseemly fracas. As associations free-floated through O'Hara's mind, the very invocation of anything off-kilter summoned an image of Gary Ledbetter, and O'Hara wondered if Gary was peering over his shoulder right then.

"How long were you married, sir?" O'Hara asked.

"Two years. A little longer."

"When did things start to go wrong?" O'Hara asked.

The publisher turned on him. "What sort of question is that?" he asked.

"I'd call it 'background,' " O'Hara explained.

"I think things were okay for about a year," Negri said. "You know, it's not as if I didn't have a lot of love for Abby. I'm sorry things didn't work out. She was quite a woman." He spoke without affection, rejecting one piece of neckwear from the closet as he spoke. When he found the tie he wanted, he looked up. "Execution is too good for whoever killed her. Do you know what I'm saying?"

O'Hara said he knew. He was even able to say that he agreed.

"New Hampshire has a death penalty," Negri continued, "and it hasn't been used since pre-Gary Gilmore."

"I'm familiar with that fact, sir."

"You're a policeman. Why do we have laws that aren't used? Maybe you could tell me that?"

"I couldn't possibly, sir. And if you'll permit, I came here to ask you questions. Not answer yours."

Negri gave him a look, but backed off.

O'Hara moved quickly past the moment of tension.

"Enemies?" O'Hara asked. "I'm sure you have a few. Any who would do something like this to Abby? Perhaps to get at you?"

"Enemies," Negri repeated. "I probably have millions. Liberal left. The usual hate groups. Homosexuals. Abortionists. Book and film riffraff. Teachers. A lot of schoolteachers really hate me. Many enemies

among them. It was a schoolteacher who shot Huey
Long, you know. Were you aware of that?"

"Can you be more specific about your enemies?"

"I couldn't possibly be."

"Hate mail?" O'Hara asked. "How much do you
get?"

"A bag each week. Couple of hundred letters. Most
with New York postmarks." Negri seemed proud of
this, as if it somehow made him more butch.

"Any specific threats in it?"

"How would I know? I don't read it."

"Could I examine it?"

"Ha!" Negri snorted. "You can *have* it, man. You
don't think I *want* it, do you?"

Someone else, it seemed, sorted through the day's
post. The stuff of pure adulation was passed along to
"The Great One." Questions were answered by staff.
The sicko stuff—most of it unsigned—was piled in a
corner and burned once a month.

O'Hara listened to this without taking issue, just
letting Negri talk. He had been a detective long
enough to know a fraud when he saw one. He thought
he saw a world-class one right here.

"How did you first meet Abigail?" O'Hara asked.

"We met at a social function in Boston," Negri said.
"But I don't see how that ties into whatever you're
investigating."

"I'm investigating her death, sir," said O'Hara with
endless patience. "So I'm trying to understand her
life."

Negri seemed to take this under advisement. He
thought about it as he massaged a wrinkle on the
necktie he had chosen for his radio appearance.

"Yes, I suppose you are," Negri said, a tiny air of
boredom overtaking him. Or maybe it was growing
annoyance. O'Hara couldn't properly tell.

Negri followed all this with several well structured

anecdotes on the nature of his marriage, little stories which reflected favorably upon him and not-so-well upon Abigail. All this while readying himself for air time.

At ten forty, Howard Chambers reentered the room to give Negri his twenty minutes until broadcast notice. This doubled as a hint that their interview time was winding down.

O'Hara frowned. "I thought you were on at eleven thirty."

"Oh?" Negri asked, his interest perking. "You know my time slot? You're a listener?"

"I've heard the show. And when you're on the air you say you're on 'live.' "

Chambers smiled like a cobra. "The tape is 'live' when we make it. Then we do a thirty-minute delayed feed."

"Nothing's on the radio live any more," Negri explained. "But keep listening. I'll put in a good word for the New Hampshire State Police."

"My superiors will be thrilled," O'Hara said, consciously not saying that he would be equally impressed.

Negri looked him in the eye and caught the distinction.

"So what's the deal?" the publisher finally asked.

"Deal?"

"Have a suspect in Abby's murder? A theory? A way to solve the case? That's what I'm asking."

"There really isn't a 'deal,' " O'Hara explained. "We track down every lead, we explore every possibility, we turn every clue inside out. When that's exhausted, we do it over and over again and we hope to get lucky."

"I'd love to see a quick arrest."

"With all due respect, sir, I'd prefer an accurate arrest."

Negri turned away and grunted. "Let me ask you something, Officer," he said. "What percentage of homicides in this state get solved?"

"It's about the same as the national average. We close about fifty percent of our homicide investigations."

Negri nodded. "That's about what I expected," he said. "Some kind of country, isn't it? A murderer can walk away from the scene of his crime knowing that his odds of getting off scot-free are about fifty-fifty. You can't tell me that the Supreme Court of the 1960s isn't responsible for a situation like that."

O'Hara said nothing.

"Pretty disgusting," Negri repeated, angling for a response from O'Hara. O'Hara wasn't in the mood to give him one.

Then Negri was before a full-length mirror on the inside of the closet door, tying an eighty-five-dollar strip of silk Nicole Miller neckwear into a Windsor knot. Nice and tight. The knot, not the interview. As far as the latter was concerned, Negri was signing off. Just like his show: He had said what he wished to in the time he had allotted. Now the performance was over.

Negri must have felt O'Hara's eyes on his back, because the knot came out less than perfect. He pulled the tie apart, the room still in silence, and tried again. Then he turned with his tie in mid-flip.

"Is there anything else, Officer?" Negri asked.

O'Hara closed his notepad. Chambers was waiting and watching, arms folded.

"Nothing else," O'Hara answered.

"Then, thank you for your time," Negri said. "I'd like to proceed with my program. If you don't mind."

"Not at all," said O'Hara.

He rose and thanked his hosts. As he departed he caught a snippet of conversation from the two men, concerning the day's radio script, which apparently Negri had not yet read.

Later, O'Hara put Negri's show on the car radio. The topic for the day was divorce and the alarming number of Americans who no longer were trying to hold their families together.

And your estranged wife was murdered, and it comes as a relief to you, O'Hara thought but didn't say. Fact is, it's damned convenient. Maybe you could someday detail for me all the ways in which it made your life easier.

The gold chain and pendant, which O'Hara should have turned over to the victim's estranged husband, remained in his pocket. He felt it was better off there.

But how any of this might have tied back into Gary Ledbetter and the Ledbetter style of homicide was still something that eluded Frank O'Hara. And it eluded him completely.

Chapter 14

O'Hara arrived at the door to the captain's office at ten the next morning. Mallinson, standing behind his desk, never raised his eyes. His head was inclined downward and he was studying the contents of a fresh file upon his desk as O'Hara entered. The captain finally looked up when he finished reading and as O'Hara shifted his weight before him.

"Talk to me," Mallinson said.

"What are you looking at?"

"Sometimes I don't believe the nickel-and-dime crap we get," the captain said.

"So what's that?" O'Hara asked.

"A bunch of mutts held up a Sainsbury truck outside of Hillsboro," Captain Mallinson said.

Sainsbury was a food and liquor retailer with a string of cut-rate stores across New Hampshire. Low prices, quality that matched. Cheap imitations of name brands. The truck's cargo had been seventy-six cases of house-label booze—vodka with fake Russian names, gin milled in Puerto Rico that called itself Buckingham Palace, and medicinal-tasting Scotch with a McSomething label—the stuff that gives a guy a good quick drunk, but the next morning he feels like a horse kicked him in the head.

"White guys? Black guys?" O'Hara asked.

"White," Mallinson said cautiously. "The truck driver was a colored guy. Vernon Frealy. Got popped in the teeth by one of the robbers. Here. Look at the report."

Mallinson presented O'Hara with a manila folder. Photographs of the stickup scene. Reports from the first uniformed man who had arrived, plus the first two detectives.

There had been three big, sturdy white guys, Frealy had said. They ambushed him when he stopped his eighteen-wheeler outside a late-hour burger joint. The entire stickup team had been masked with heavy headgear. They pulled Frealy behind a building, took his keys, and went to work moving his cargo into a follow-up truck of their own. Meanwhile the backup truck driver, a big, strapping guy, held Frealy at bay with a baseball bat. Sixteen degrees Fahrenheit while all this was going on. Naturally, no witnesses.

In the course of the robbery, however, one of the hold-up men lost his headgear. He was completely bald. Shaved head bald.

That was one of the queer details. Then, as O'Hara kept reading, there was another. During the heist, Frealy—touched with some sort of insanity or indignation—had resisted giving up the company's goods. When his guard glanced away for a moment, Frealy took a heavyweight kick at his captor's *cojones*.

He missed the main target, but did enough damage to flee through a closed gas station and a department store parking lot. No outside phones in New Hampshire. They'd all either freeze or get vandalized. So Frealy found a phone in a bar and called the cops. The locals were home in bed, so the Staties responded. By the time everyone got back to the burger joint, the heist team was gone and so were twenty-eight of the seventy-six cases of booze.

Frealy told everything to the cops. And he had some great details.

The driver of the getaway truck, the guy whose jewels Frealy had tried to wreck, was bald, also. His hat had dislodged in the struggle. Frealy had seen half a bare scalp. He was as bald as his accomplice.

The driver, who wore glasses, had also had something wrong with his eyes. One eye was a floater. It wouldn't focus on whatever the other was watching, which—if anyone gave it much thought—made him a strange choice as a driver and guard.

O'Hara looked up at Captain Mallinson. Thoughtfully, he flipped the file shut.

"Cute, huh?" Mallinson grunted. "Got any insight?"

"Don't know," O'Hara answered. "Who's investigating?"

Mallinson named a team of state police Grand Larceny dicks from Cheshire county: Ed Schwine and Herbert Dreher. O'Hara knew them. A couple of quasi-incompetents who would have done better being assigned to school guard crossings.

"So why don't you just toss this directly into the Old & Open case file?" O'Hara asked. "Schwine and Dreher never close anything."

"What the hell, O'Hara," Mallinson growled. "This ain't what you'd call hi-pro. The bald mutts only got two dozen cases of booze, it's covered by out-of-state insurance, and Frealy didn't even take medical after being popped in the snout."

O'Hara made a noise that conveyed he couldn't have cared less.

"So what are you here for?" Mallinson finally asked.

"I wanted to ask you a few questions on the Gary Ledbetter case," O'Hara announced at last, finding a chair.

"Jesus. This again?"

"If you don't mind."

"I don't know why you keep asking me. You made the frigging arrest."

"But you handled the political end. Dealing with the press. The attorney general. And you helped wrap Ledbetter up so that he could be shipped South."

Mallinson shrugged, irritated. He opened the top drawer of his desk and fished for something to smoke.

"Do I take credit or blame on that, Frank?" he asked. "And by the way, it was many years ago, so what's your point?"

"What went on in that case? Was everything on the level with evidence?"

"Why wouldn't it have been?"

"Damned if I know," said O'Hara.

Mallinson grimaced. "Frank, Gary Ledbetter was as guilty as Judas Iscariot. Florida had no difficulty convicting Ledbetter."

"That's not what I'm asking."

"What *are* you asking?" Mallinson snapped back. "You had witnesses," Mallinson reminded him. "People who made identifications of Ledbetter. Right?"

"I want to know if any monkey business went on. Was it different than any other case?"

"It was more high-profile. We had newspapers and citizens barking at us from the word go."

"That's still not what I'm asking."

Mallinson shrouded himself in smoke from a cheroot. His eyes looked tired. "Frank, what's this all about?" Mallinson asked.

"Every time I take a step forward on this case it looks like Gary Ledbetter has killed two more women. Logically, you and I both know that can't be. But by another field of logic, it's the only answer."

"Frank," Mallinson said dismissively, a pained expression crossing his face. He shook his head. " 'Field

of logic' . . . 'Gary Ledbetter' . . . Ah, come off it.
You're telling me that Gary Ledbetter, as in the *late*
Gary Ledbetter who was executed by Florida, is your
chief suspect?"

O'Hara silently replied, And it's even worse than
that. I've *seen* him. But instead, O'Hara struggled with
words and answered, "Look, every time I examine this
case—"

"What am I hearing from you? We got an evil spirit
loose?" "Was the evidence rigged in Ledbetter's arrest?" O'Hara demanded.

"How can you ask that?"

"I just did. What's the answer?"

"The answer is, No! Of course not!"

"Now tell me that you're telling me the truth. Why,
for example, were there a couple of deputy inspectors
in Peterborough circulating Gary's picture *before* I got
there? That strikes me as real odd, Captain."

"Where'd you learn about that?"

"Detectives have their sources, Captain."

For a moment there was fury in Mallinson's eyes.
But then he eased slightly.

"Bullshit, Frank," Mallinson said. "You been listening to your moody-assed Sinatra tapes too long.
Your brain's turned into cream cheese."

"Would you answer my question?"

For a moment, war remained imminent. But then
Mallinson's tired face softened. He looked at the
younger man with a mixture of impatience and understanding.

"You're going nuts, aren't you, Frank?" Mallinson
asked. "Pressure, pressure, pressure. One final big
murder case, and a hacker of ladies, at that. One more
big investigation, and it's breaking your balls. That's
what's going on, isn't it? That, combined with some
guilt for a guy you arrested going to the hot seat.
Think I can't tell when a man is cracking up?"

"There's nothing wrong with me," said O'Hara. "I'm following a case the best I can."

"Yeah. And I'm the Queen of Sheba."

Mallinson took a long cancerous pull on his tobacco and eyed O'Hara. O'Hara was about to respond, the same tired defensive litany about being fully in control of his faculties and trying to solve a sicko murder case.

But Mallinson kept talking.

"Working as a state cop in this state is a killer, Frank. There's ten months of winter and two months of bad skiing. The state animal is the skunk, the state bird is the black fly, the state citizen is the deadbeat, and the state sport is petty larceny. That's going to drive any sane man nuts. And know what? Us here in the cop department get it even worse than everyone else. Some days, the only people we see are other cops who've already gone crazy and Looney Tune people with criminal records."

Outside the building there was the screech of a car skidding on the ice. This was followed by the sound of impact. Crunching metal. Agitated voices ensued. Mallinson never glanced out his window. O'Hara, who could assess such things without looking after all these years, figured some jerk had taken the corner too fast and had taken out a parking meter.

Mallinson marched forward.

"Eventually, everybody looks like they should be run in for armed robbery, Frank. You do too much, you see too much, and you think too much. You try to make sense out of this job and you can't because human behavior doesn't make any sense. And you go a little crazier every day. Don't you, Frank?"

Mallinson was touching a nerve, and O'Hara wouldn't admit it.

"There are pressures, yeah. But—"

"Frank! Stop it! Some of us are getting damned worried about you. If you keep chasing a frigging ghost, I swear I'm going to put you on psychiatric sick leave. Do you understand me?"

A long pause. Then, "Yeah, I understand."

"Do you want sick leave?"

"All I want is a killer. There's a guy out there who chops women."

"Then find him in this world. Not in another one," Mallinson said. "Okay? For all of us? Cut out this Gary Ledbetter shit and find us a flesh and blood chopper. Okay?"

"Who was 'S. Clay'?" O'Hara asked.

"I give up. What's this 'S. Clay'?"

" 'S. Clay' was the name on Ledbetter's storage unit. There was material missing from Gary's file at Central Records. I was wondering if. . . ."

"To all intents and purposes, Frank," Mallinson answered, thoroughly peeved but equally in control, " 'S. Clay' was Gary Ledbetter. One and the same. You think a psycho killer is going to use his real name where he stores his tools of war? Come on, Frank. Wake up. Stop seeing things that aren't there."

Several moments passed while neither man moved. O'Hara waited for Gary's voice to interject. He realized that he was almost *hoping* to hear from Gary right there. But, naturally, nothing. No messages bouncing through time and space.

O'Hara sighed, then looked at his commander. Through a veil of smoke, Mallinson bore a distant, unflattering resemblance to an old children's woodcut that O'Hara had seen years ago: the centipede on the toadstool smoking a hookah, all one hundred legs of him below an indulgent porcine face.

A nutty disoriented impulse was upon O'Hara: At the end of the captain's lecture, O'Hara felt like laughing. He even had to fight off a weird smile.

"Frank," Mallinson finally concluded, "Gary Ledbetter may not have been treated perfectly in this state.

But he was treated fairly. He was a homicidal maniac. Does that register? Florida gave him what he deserved and which we couldn't have served up. Isn't that enough?"

"Not really. But I suppose it will have to do. Won't it?"

"It will, Frank. That's all," Mallinson said. He leaned back from the desk, dismissing O'Hara. He hacked a cough. "Thank you, Frank. I appreciate your coming by."

Several hours later, Frank O'Hara sat at the desk in his office, watching the day die outside his window. The bitter afternoon had faded into a glacial evening. It wasn't five o'clock yet and already it was dark outside.

It was a moody, quiet hour in police headquarters, the type of time when a man's imagination can seduce him. And darker than the advancing night were O'Hara's thoughts.

No one would believe him: But there was something terribly *wrong* about this case. The murder of Abigail Negri. And the murder of Stacey Dissette. O'Hara had reviewed his notes on the interview with Wilhelm Negri and had covered every known angle in the Dissette case. He had spent the afternoon in a further review of all the material he had accumulated on the killing of Karen Stoner in 1987.

He had even gone through old telephone directories that afternoon, looking for an S. Clay, or any Clay whom he could link to the Ledbetter case. He continued to come up empty.

He began making some initial phone calls to reassemble old evidence from the Ledbetter case: the name of the waitress at the doughnut shop in New Hampshire, the woman who had identified Gary from a photograph. He wondered if anyone would still be around from the storage unit who could recall anything about the case. What about video store clerks who might have given Gary an alibi, but didn't?

He was unable to be optimistic. People drifted from one low-end job like this to another. They drifted and disappeared.

Like ghosts? Yeah, Frank. Exactly.

Yet this was exactly the material which he needed. And it was among the material that was missing from the Ledbetter file. It was almost as if—no, it *was exactly* as if—someone, somewhere, with access to the files wanted to make sure that this path of evidence was never travelled again.

He wondered where his own logbook was from the case. With a sinking feeling, he realized that this, too, would have gone to Central Records, in accordance with official procedure.

And every time he asked himself a question, he failed to find a satisfying answer. And each unsatisfying answer posed a couple more insoluble questions.

What had the relationship really been between Wilhelm Negri and his wife? Was there a motive for murder there? Or was what O'Hara had seen simply the messy aftermath of a failed marriage, one that touched on murder by coincidence?

And yet what connection could the Negri murder have to the Stacey Dissette slaying? Was there a link between victims? A similarity? Or had they been victims of opportunity, unlucky women who crossed the path of a killer at the wrong time?

Then there was the biggest question of all? Where did it all hook back to Gary Ledbetter? How? And why?

And who the fuck was S. Clay?

If one believed the autopsy reports, the cases had to have a link. But if Gary Ledbetter had murdered

Karen Stoner, and if he had acted alone, the homicides could not possibly have been related.

There was almost a whisper in the room. *Not guilty, man. I didn't kill no girls.*

O'Hara sat up quickly. "Then who did, Gary?" O'Hara demanded aloud. "Who? Tell me who!"

O'Hara's fatigued eyes searched the lonely office. No sign of anything.

"Was it 'S. Clay'?" O'Hara questioned. "Tell me, Gary! Was it?"

But there was no answer. A key issue like this . . . and no answer. This time, he concluded that he had imagined Gary's voice.

But the thoughts of Gary kept recurring, as did the images that had been upon him three nights earlier when the red crab crawled down his throat.

O'Hara had seen his former partner. He had seen Gary. The dead had stood before him. Conversing with him. Right there and—in Gary's case—able to be reached and touched in all his icy mortality.

Or could it be called, *immortality?*

It had all seemed too real. Dr. Julie Steinberg be damned. O'Hara was not fully convinced that the most memorable events of that evening—with the exception of the red crab—hadn't really happened. And yet Dr. Julie insisted that as long as he clung to the thought that Carl Reissman and Gary Ledbetter might actually have been there, he wasn't fully in control of his faculties.

Dr. Steinberg: "The dead do not walk among us."

"Maybe they do sometimes, Doctor," he said aloud.

Dr. Steinberg again: "Never in the history of humanity has it ever been proven that someone living interacted with someone dead."

"And the opposite hasn't been disproved, either," O'Hara now said aloud in his office. "Inexplicable events happen all the time. Like the ones that have happened to me. It's just that they defy proof of a traditional sort."

Before him, in the well controlled eye of his mind, was Dr. Steinberg, a patient but reproachful smile across her face, shaking her head.

Or was she right there in his office with him? The vision was very, very clear.

"No, Frank," she said. "Listen to what you're saying. Listen to *logic*. It simply doesn't make sense. What you're saying simply is not *rational.*"

" 'Logic' . . . 'doesn't make sense' . . . 'not rational' . . ." O'Hara repeated aloud.

Logic? Nothing made much sense these days. Nothing was rational any more.

Julie Steinberg disappeared in a snap. O'Hara blinked. *Had* she been there?

A ripple of goose bumps overtook him. The sound of his own voice, as it echoed in his office, had had a funny ring to it.

Ghostly.

Yes, that was the adjective. Why had it popped into his head above all others. Another thought tiptoed upon him. These thoughts, these feelings that kept coming over him. . . . Was that what a haunting was all about?

Hello, Frankie.

Who was speaking to him?

"Anyone there?" he asked.

He waited several seconds for an answer, feeling his pulse starting to pump faster. No answer. Not a sound in the room.

Was Gary playing games? Another weird sequence of thoughts: O'Hara wondered if he, O'Hara, was alive. Could anyone see *him?* Did he know for sure? Maybe he had died that afternoon and didn't know it yet.

Maybe that's what death was like.

O'Hara rose from his desk and walked to the door to his office. He stood in it, looking down the corridor in each direction. A melange of impressions: Stale cigarette smoke. Peeling green paint. A ragged stretch of carpeting. A sense of isolation.

His last thought repeated on him: Maybe that's what death was like. If so, was it as awful as everyone thought? Well, if I'm dead, he reasoned, all I have to do is find the two dead women and ask them who their killer was. How tough could that be?

"Fuck," he muttered to himself. "Got to get a grip on things. I'm going nuts."

O'Hara turned and went back to his desk. Somewhere down the hall another cop walked from one office to another. Heavy foot-fall, deep off-key basso profundo voice making an unintentional mockery of the old Elvis ditty.

"Blue Hawaii."

Yeah, sure, O'Hara thought, distracted for the moment. Fucking Hawaii while they're all shin-splint deep in fresh white snow and the fresh corpses that normally accompany it. Blue fucking Hawaii and I've got a couple of women out there who have been decapitated, then their hands hacked off for sport, and I, Frank O'Hara, don't know where the killer will hit next or even from what world the fuckhead is coming from.

Blue fucking Hawaii, indeed. Hey, Elvis? After you died, you jowly old hog, which place did you wake up in? I can't see you in wings, man, so I'm betting on the hot one.

There was a pencil in O'Hara's hand. On a piece of notepaper, the point found a surface. Almost like a Ouija board, where a hand is supposedly guided by an unseen force, O'Hara began to write.

"A ghost?" he wrote. "A *real* ghost? Gary?"

He was surprised that he had actually written it

down. Sure he was thinking about it. Yeah, Mallinson had given voice to the thought. But to accept *this* as reality?

How could he?

Never mind the old Bowery Boys film routines with guys in sheets over their heads jumping out of closets. O'Hara began to examine what he had seen from a new stone-cold sober perspective. He wondered if what he was undergoing with Gary Ledbetter was, in fact, a spiritual haunting. Some sort of mental thing that was happening with a restless, troubled spirit.

As a cop he was trained to look for evidence. Or events out of the ordinary.

There was the way Gary kept appearing to him, after all.

And there was the way Gary's words, his phantom whispers, kept sneaking in and out of O'Hara's thoughts. . . .

"I'm alive and Gary's dead," he told himself. "That much I know. That much I cling to."

O'Hara leaned back in his chair, deeply troubled. What in hell else *did* he believe?

He knew he was an anomaly as a policeman. Most cops were Sunday morning religious.

"When you're out there with only a badge and a pistol, you don't like to feel that you're alone," one fellow officer had remarked to him years earlier. O'Hara had always wanted to believe in the Almighty the way all the grunt-and-grind harness bulls did. But even as a fourteen-year-old he had fallen away from the Catholicism in which he had been raised.

Atheism was his religion, if he had one at all. And the only thing good about it was that it gave him an extra free morning each week.

For most of his adult life, dating back to the time he was a soldier in Southeast Asia, O'Hara had believed that death was the end. Or at the very least, since there was this troubling ten percent of agnosticism mixed in with his beliefs, death was the end of one's earthly existence.

He had stood over mortally wounded soldiers on battlefields as life slipped away, men he had loved like brothers. Never once had he heard or sensed anything from them again after their passing. Nor, in two cases when men died in his arms, had he ever felt the rush of a soul from a body to . . . to . . . wherever souls might go.

Not that he expected a shocking postcard from San Diego or anything. But might not *one* of these lost loved ones have somehow contacted him, if there were a way to communicate from the other side of life? Might not *one* of these departed souls have sensed O'Hara's lack of belief and sought to ease his life by reassuring him?

But none ever had. So O'Hara was unable to be a believer in the Judeo-Christian sense. And if there were an afterlife, it was not something that he felt he needed to worry about, and it was not something that could in any way intersect with his job as a policeman or his life here on Earth.

Until now.

Now, when there was starting to be a faint skein of logic within the supernatural interpretation of things.

Now, when . . . well . . . O'Hara seemed to be haunted.

The detective grimaced. Way back in his days at the police academy, when O'Hara had taken all the usual courses in crime detection, there had been a much overused instruction: Get inside the criminal's head. Get inside his mind.

O'Hara winced at the irony. In this case, had the criminal seeped into O'Hara's mind. If so, he wondered with a shudder, how long before Gary took him over completely?

And where was Gary in the meantime?

"Spending some time in Hell?" O'Hara asked aloud. "Or just kind of drifting through time and space?"

I'm nearby. I'm very close.

O'Hara cringed. Jesus! Maybe he *was* going nuts! That voice sounded so near, so close, so *real,* that he broke a sweat. He looked around again, then pretended he hadn't. He made a valiant effort to convince himself that he hadn't heard the voice.

Moments later, O'Hara shook his head, as if coming out of a trance. He was unaware of how long he had been sitting in his office staring straight ahead, occasionally whispering to—and being answered by—an audience that remained unseen.

He looked at his watch. Time to go home. He had been sitting there apparently for almost forty minutes, mulling things over at too great a length, searching for answers and clues where none were forthcoming.

He drove home, but the situation did not much improve. What he couldn't shake was an overall impression that something was wrong with the case. Off-kilter. Off-kilter in the same way that Gary had been handsome.

He had dinner. He watched television: hockey from Boston. But he couldn't concentrate on the game.

Late in the evening, a glass of mineral water in his hand, he moved to a window of his home and gazed out. His eye travelled to the thickness of the woods behind his house, the stalwart clumps of trees that stood like soldiers in the winter darkness.

He let his eye grow accustomed to the night. He let his vision dart in and out from between those trees.

"Come on, snow ghosts," he whispered. "Or 'forest ghosts.' Whoever you are. Where are you? Hiding from me tonight? Come on out. Don't you understand? I *want* to see you now."

For a moment he thought he saw something. The

movement of something between some shadows. Or maybe it was just some shadows themselves, the product of the fingery overhead branches clattering in the icy wind.

"Come on out," he said again. "I dare you."

But there was nothing there. No movement. No ghosts. No spirits.

No stuff of Indian legend and, above all, no Gary. The cruelest part of it all was that in his mind there was a link forming. It seemed to him, he reasoned, that the only time he ever saw those things were when he had helped things along by going on a binge with the bottle.

He simmered at the notion. He only saw such things when he was drunk. Was that it?

He held that thought for several seconds.

And yet, he hadn't been drinking the day that he had ridden up to Mount Monadnock in Reynolds's truck, he reminded himself. Not a drop of booze that day and he thought he had seen the snow ghosts then.

He sighed.

No booze, no ghosts. What kind of deal was that? The legends of the Indians were not there this evening. And neither was Gary.

A philosophical point overtook him. Were they *gone?* Or had they never been there? If they were gone, where had they gone to? And if they had never been there, why had he seen them?

He thought back. . . .

The night that he reached out his arm and plunged it through Gary Ledbetter's ghost. The sight of it, the touch of it, the very barbecued-flesh smell of it had been as real as a cut across the cheek with a straight razor.

Nothing artificial about it at all. Nothing imaginary. Nothing illusory.

God damn it! He was stone-cold sober and he knew

that he had seen something that night which was *there!*

What did he have to do? Get drunk again, do another waltz with the red crab that liked to crawl down his throat, in order to ring up Gary on the spiritual walkie-talkie?

"Fuck it, Gary!" he roared. "Get out here! We need to talk!"

He waited.

But the only answer was the echo of his own voice in the house. For a moment, he thought he heard a creak, but then decided he hadn't.

So he turned away from the window and sighed again, a middle-aged cop fighting off insanity, shouting at unseen presences in an empty house.

For a moment his eye caught something outside as he was turning. His heart jumped and he looked back. But the movement was only that of some fresh snow beginning to fall. A nice, gentle coating on top of everything that was already down.

Just what he needed: another image of winter and death.

He turned away from the window.

With tremendous effort, he attempted to guide his thoughts in another direction.

First, his mind went to Rose Horvath, former doyenne of the official records at headquarters in Nashua. O'Hara pondered her collection of books on the occult and supernatural. He wondered if Rose's library contained any answers. Or were all of her volumes pulp for those who *wanted* to believe?

And second, and more immediately, O'Hara thought of the file that had been in Captain Mallinson's office that morning, the one on a couple of bald guys ripping off a liquor truck over the weekend. A couple of things there were starting to fall into place. Maybe.

As he further pondered the point, a few thoughts

came together. It occurred to him that if he spent an hour driving the next morning, and played a hunch properly, a botched stickup in Hillsboro might shed some light upon a hacker of ladies and a killer who seemed to drift across the state with all the characteristics of a phantom.

Another spacey thought: Funny how things sometimes connect.

Chapter 15

The overnight snowfall was less than an inch. By late the following morning the state highways were in good condition.

O'Hara took a two-hour drive northwest from Nashua. The sky finally cleared while O'Hara drove, and the sun raised the temperature to the high twenties for the first time in days. A mini heat wave. The wind, however, remained sharp.

O'Hara's destination was a residence on Route 12-A in Alstead Center, up a hill and not far from a crumbling Grange hall. In the summer, this particular house was a depressing free-standing, one-story structure. Two twin chimney pipes from wood-burning stoves poked through its roof. It had a front yard littered with broken axles, car parts, drive shafts, and cinderblocks. At one point there had also been a dead washing machine and the undercarriage of a pickup truck. But the washer and the undercarriage had disappeared the previous summer when the price for scrap metal hit eight cents a pound. And around back, behind the house, right near a smoldering outside incinerator, sat a ten-foot satellite dish, pointed at the northwest horizon. Two large stumps marked the spot where the aerial path to the horizon had been cleared.

But with the snowfall, the resident—whose name of

P. LaValliere was proclaimed on a dented red mailbox in front—became a fan of Christmas.

A huge fan.

Twinkly multicolored lights were now strung across every conceivable nook, branch, cinder block, and upright axle in the yard. With the mantle of snow, the car parts lay buried, and string after string of Christmas lights, strung with no attempt at order, twinkled nonstop, giving the place the look of an ersatz fairyland.

Here was a winter wonderland, a shrine to St. Nick. Whether the old fat guy wanted it or not.

The official lighting for this year had come on November 14, so O'Hara, when he saw the place as he came up onto the crest of the hill of Route 12-A, was seeing the annual show shortly after its official opening.

O'Hara grimaced when confronted by the day-and-night light show. And when he pulled closer, he could also see the plastic Santa with four fake reindeer, up on the roof like a gang of burglars. Ho ho ho. A Styrofoam Frosty the Snowman, the jolly, happy soul himself, stood sentry on the front lawn, and a couple of plaster elves were conspicuously hiding near a snow covered tire rim, like a couple of diminutive car thieves waiting to pounce.

O'Hara pulled into the plowed driveway and stopped. He stared at the decorations for several seconds. Then he tapped the Pontiac's horn, a little courtesy to the Santa Claus fan. He scanned for any unfamiliar vehicles, anything not belonging to the resident. He saw nothing, which was good because it suggested that P. LaValliere might be home alone.

Somewhere, as O'Hara slowly stepped out of his car, a dog inside the house went nuts. It sounded like a big, major-league mutt, and in fact, as O'Hara remembered, it was. O'Hara pinned his badge to his overcoat. Then he walked to the front door.

No path had been shoveled. O'Hara's pants cuffs and ankles were immersed in shin-high snow, the kind that seeped into the socks and shoes. The detective found the front doorbell and leaned on it, gloved thumb to a brown button.

Two rings. A rasping, grinding bell. It sounded distantly like a couple of short blasts from a dentist's drill.

The dog went nuttier inside the house, and O'Hara, despite a heavy front door, could hear the Santa junkie cursing violently. Next he next heard the dog yelp in pain and fall silent.

O'Hara drew a breath. He knew that the dog had just been the unlucky recipient of a kick in ribs or the haunches and was now being locked into the kitchen. O'Hara had his timing down perfectly, measuring the seconds it would take for LaValliere to ramble from the kitchen to the front door.

Then a very gangly, very tall man—six foot five had been recorded on his most recent arrest sheet—answered the door in a flannel shirt and bib overalls.

Peter LaValliere, the master of the domain, glared at his visitor. LaValliere had a bald head—not natural, shaved—and a short black beard so neat and precise that it looked like it had been shaped with a T square. Also, thick glasses with heavy black rims.

Bad eyes behind the specs. One eye (the right one) was particularly awful. It was akin to something out of a bad-taste Halloween kit. A wild waller with no focus. It floated mercilessly while the left eye fought to settle on the visitor.

Then, recognizing O'Hara, the man with all the holiday cheer spoke.

"What the fuck do *you* want?" LaValliere asked.

"Jesus Christ, Pete," O'Hara said, casting a sidelong glance at the twinkly, sparkly lights. "It's only November, you're not even a Puerto Rican, and still you do this crap with the Christmas lights every year."

"Eat me, O'Hara, you mick bastard. I got me some holiday spirit even if you don't."

"Yeah, right. And probably eight cases of hot whiskey out of the Sainsbury truck to help you celebrate the season."

"I don't know what you're talking about."

"Don't lie to me."

For several seconds, LaValliere did nothing but breathe heavily through his mouth (some sort of sausage was on his breath), blocking the doorway. He looked as if some internal fuse were burning down.

O'Hara didn't give him an inch.

"You're here to arrest me?" LaValliere finally asked.

"I'm here for some talk, Pete. Are you going to invite me in or do I get a warrant and invite myself, in which case I *would* want to make an arrest just to cover my trouble for having to make two trips to this technicolor rat hole."

LaValliere kept silent. An ominous sign. He was thinking it over, or trying to, meaning there might have been something to consider.

"Or would you like a few minutes to put away any embarrassing products that might be scattered around the house?" O'Hara suggested. It was a peace offering: "I can go back to the car, and drive around for ten minutes. How's that sound?"

LaValliere's one good peeper peered over O'Hara's right shoulder, quickly ascertaining that the cop was alone. The other eye, or at least its line of vision, slammed harmlessly into the door frame.

"I am fucking freezing out here, LaValliere," O'Hara said. "Would you make your decision before evening?"

"Sure. Invite yourself in if you like," LaValliere finally grumbled. "You're going to come in anyway."

"You got that part right, Pete."

LaValliere stepped away from the door, and allowed O'Hara to enter. He closed the door with a thud, chopping off the cold.

The dog in the kitchen started barking again, then went berserk, sounding like he was tearing up the place. LaValliere excused himself for a moment to disappear through the kitchen door. O'Hara heard only the sound of a strap repeatedly hitting dog hide, a quick series of plaintive squeals from the animal mixed with a half-snarl, and then a cowering, heavy silence. The big mutt had been flailed into submission.

The house was overheated; two wood stoves were burning, one at each end of a raggedly furnished living room. O'Hara took the opportunity to reach under his overcoat and place a cautious hand on his weapon, in case LaValliere was planning to return with a sawed-off or some other monster piece.

As he waited, O'Hara kept his eyes tight on the kitchen door.

O'Hara knew LaValliere. He knew his arrest record and had used him as a stool pigeon in the past. O'Hara even knew the big guy's mutt, a snarly, barrel-chested, heavy-jowled enforcer that LaValliere always kept hungry. The dog had solid Teutonic lineage: It was half Shepherd, half Doberman, and was named Rudolph after Hess, not the fancy pants reindeer with the incarnadine snout.

LaValliere also knew O'Hara. Their interests had intersected on two previous occasions, meaning the former had been arrested twice by the latter. The Frenchman also knew that O'Hara had once used the business end of his thirty-eight to sing sayonara to a Rottweiler at a Midnight Auto establishment in High Bridge. So he kept his puppy quiet in the kitchen, a prudent and healthy decision for everyone, doggie included.

LaValliere reappeared. Alone, with his hands visible and empty. The gesture of cooperation allowed O'Hara to relax slightly.

The detective pulled his grip off his weapon and moved his own gaze around the living room. Real *House and Garden* horrible. Dead meat male decorating in white trash decrepit-modern: a badly worn carpet, vintage 1970 Woolworth. The rug should have been thrown away by someone ten years ago and probably had been. A spindly pair of tables and a couple of metal chairs looked like they had been swiped from a high-school gym or a place that puts on wrestling exhibitions. The type of chairs used to hit other guys over the head when a race riot follows a roundball game.

The "Elegant Life-style" centerpieces: a frayed, overstuffed sofa and a mismatching chair that made the room look like the employees' lounge at a Billy Carter gas station, complete with soil marks on the misshaped arms of both the sofa and the chair. In front of the sofa was a new Sony TV—probably stolen, O'Hara guessed—with a sparkling thirty-five-inch screen, the only thing in the room less than five years old. The antenna wires were exposed, coiled and running out of the room toward the satellite dish behind the house. And by the side of the sofa was LaValliere's "girlfriend," who must have taken over when there was nothing good on the tube: a stack of badly thumbed hetero skin mags, the crude, Sally Fivefingers, bottom-of-the-line ones sold at bad convenience stores.

Then, as if this wasn't enough, something in the adjacent dining room caught O'Hara's eye. It was big and flat and on the wall. Red and white like a Coca-Cola billboard or a Santa Claus outfit, but O'Hara knew it was neither. Removing his overcoat, O'Hara walked over to give it a glance. LaValliere followed him closely, standing about six inches taller than his visitor.

O'Hara stopped in the doorway. Tacked to the dining-room wall was five feet by seven feet of solid working-class hatred. Red background, white field, and big pitch-black swastika smack in the center. *Seig Heil:* a flag of the Third Reich, a recent product of an industrious local mill. O'Hara didn't see many of these but he saw more than a few, and one was more than enough. He wondered: a little early wave of post-immigration Twenty-first Century America? A little suggestion of the world of tomorrow?

But he really didn't have too much time to think about it.

"Just as I feared, Pete," O'Hara said. "You've taken up an interest in national politics."

"That's my own business."

"Sure. You and all your moronic new buddies. Clean as fairy whistles, all of you. Strong as bulls and almost as smart."

"Fuck you, O'Hara! Somebody got to look out for the white man."

"Yeah. And who better than you and your skinhead friends? Or may I use the word, 'knuckleheaded'? It's more appropriate."

LaValliere breathed anger at O'Hara, but intimidated easily. He didn't dare follow his displeasure with anything physical. Nor did he say anything. Through a dining-room window, O'Hara caught a glimpse of a tree in LaValliere's backyard. From it hung a deer carcass, partially butchered, its stomach slit open and one haunch removed. Now frozen and coated with snow. Another mutilated corpse, of which this case had an overabundance.

O'Hara turned back to the living room, looking for a seat. He selected one of the metal chairs, figuring there was a reduced chance of lice.

"Listen, O'Hara," LaValliere said, following. "I'm clean and I ain't done nothing. I got this job as a Yard Jockey at the dairy in Stonington."

"Yeah? That's great. The kids get milk and ice cream from a neo-Nazi. Does the owner of the dairy know he's got a fascist in his parking lot, dispatching his trucks to the schools?"

"I can't be fired for political beliefs. White men got Constitutional rights, too."

"Yeah, I know. You're a legal scholar these days, aren't you?" LaValliere took the insult as a compliment. "Sit down," O'Hara said. "Let's brood over it, instead."

LaValliere settled into the seedy armchair, which gave sort of a wheezing hiss when he landed in it.

O'Hara studied his host.

LaValliere was some piece of work. For the past few years, LaValliere had played Santa at the Christmas party for the county middle school. Thick glasses, black hair, a white beard clipped on top of a black one, lean with a sofa cushion tucked under his Santa suit, and with those eyes. A walleyed Santa, the floater staring off into opposite directions from the kids on his lap. Presumably Santa was keeping an eye—literally— on the fantasy reindeer.

Santa like no one had ever seen him before. Only the very brightest kids gave a thought to the similarity between Santa's eyes and those of low-rent Mr. LaValliere, the ex-con warehouse man who lived up the hill past the Grange hall. O'Hara was gambling that Vernon Frealy, the truck driver whose nose got rearranged during the botched hijacking in Hillsboro, might be more perceptive than the next generation of citizens.

O'Hara, leaning back, finally answered. "So you're pushing delivery trucks around a parking lot. Big deal."

"It's an honest job, and I'm clean."

"Yeah? You're still on parole, aren't you, Pete?"

"Yeah, I'm on parole."

"You'd be on your way back to the can if you got rearrested, wouldn't you?"

A pause, then, "So? What of it?"

"Someone knocked off a booze wagon in Hillsboro over the weekend. Truck belonged to the Sainsbury Stores."

Again, "So?"

"The dopes who did it were so dumb that we already have a suspect."

LaValliere was set to bluff. At least initially.

"How 'bout that?" LaValliere asked. "Well, I hope you sewer-crawler cops didn't hurt yourself finding the other two."

"I never said there were three, Pete. How did you guess? And thank you for your concern."

Then O'Hara waited. Finally, LaValliere hunched his shoulders. "So what the fuck's that mean to me?"

"The truck driver had a set-to with the guy in charge of driving the heist away. They went cheek to jowl, Pete. Close enough for the honest guy to smell the liverwurst on the geeky guy's breath."

"So?"

"Our prime suspect is a big, tall asshole with thick glasses and a floater on the right side. Now, Pete, damned if I didn't think of you right away. Then I come here for a pleasant talk, to assure myself that you couldn't possibly have been stupid enough to go back to prison thanks to a chump change booze heist, and I see that this year you're mixing Adolph Hitler with Santa Claus. Which explains your association with the bald guys. And how you knew there were three of them."

After a nervous pause, "Doesn't mean nothing," LaValliere answered. "Three was a guess. And there's a lot of bald guys. And there's a lot of guys with bad eyes. You know why? The goddamned Red Russians were putting stuff in America's water supply in the 1950s, and so a lot of us got born with bad eyes."

"Yeah. But there's maybe only one of you around who's six five with a black beard and hangs out with the local Bund. And I say that's the fuckhead who helped pull the Sainsbury heist."

Some wood crackled in one of the potbellied stoves. The wind huffed outside, and a billow of smoke backed down the chimney and seeped into the living room. The timing punctuated the necessary pause that O'Hara wanted before plunging in the knife.

"Care to drive over to Hillsboro?" O'Hara asked. "The truck driver said he'd recognize the thug who punched him out. Or I can just let your parole officer check it out."

The neo-Nazi was downcast, his sad eyes begged. "Come on, O'Hara. . . ."

"No. I mean it. Who's your parole buddy?"

A reluctant admission: "A woman named Deborah Meyner." LaValliere was reporting to a skirt to keep his freedom every month and obviously hating every second of it.

"Deborah's a by-the-book hard-ass, isn't she, Pete?"

"She's a Jew bitch."

"I happen to like Deborah," O'Hara said. "I think she's an intelligent woman. She does her job very thoroughly. But I'd bet she's going to be unsympathetic to your problems. She's going to march you over to Hillsboro herself when she sees that jackboot Kraut flag in there."

"She ain't going to see it."

"Maybe she'll hear about it."

"What do you want, O'Hara?"

"Cooperation. If I get it, I might forget to bring you

by the truck depot where Vernon Frealy might get overanxious and identify you as one of the thugs who hoisted his truck. I might forget to offer the two dicks over in Hillsboro any insights I might have into this case. You got lucky on one thing, Pete. You and your skinhead pals drew a couple of real local lugs to gumshoe this case. They might not be capable of finding you."

"Very funny."

"It's not meant to be."

"What kind of cooperation are we talking about?"

"I'm looking for a murderer, Pete," O'Hara said. "A real bluebeard sicko who likes to carve up ladies." He paused. "Since you're the nosiest son of a bitch in this state, as well as a first-class snitch, I naturally thought you might want to help."

LaValliere thought about it.

"This sicko," LaValliere asked, "does he fuck the girls before he ices them?"

"Does it matter?"

"Just asking."

"Don't know. Can't tell yet. But I'll ask when I catch him. Just so I can let you know."

Somewhere in LaValliere's mind there was a directory of New Hampshire lowlife. It was probably as dimly lit as everything else in his head, but it was a working directory, nonetheless. He consulted it.

"Don't know no one like that," LaValliere said. "The only killers I know are pro. Drug niggers from New York and pizza boys from North Boston. I don't mess with them."

"The guy I'm looking for has a similar MO to Gary Ledbetter."

A moment passed as LaValliere placed the name. Then he asked, "The dude they fried in Florida last summer?"

"The one and only."

LaValliere pondered it. "Don't ring no bell," he said.

"You ever hear anything about Gary working with someone?" Did he have a partner?"

"Why would I know that?"

"What about an 'S. Clay'? That name mean anything?"

"Should it?"

"I'm asking the questions, Pete. I'm looking for someone with the same MO completely. Everything matches," said O'Hara.

"So maybe fucking Gary's fucking back as a fucking ghost," the Frenchman said.

"Why do you suggest that?"

"It's a joke."

"It's not a very funny joke. I'm extremely upset, Pete. I got a case that doesn't make any sense: two recently decapitated women and my best suspect was executed five months ago."

"What are you crying to me for? Maybe you pigs fried the wrong guy."

"Not funny, either."

"What other kind of explanation you got?"

"I don't know. This is where you come in."

"Where?" LaValliere asked uneasily. "How?"

"Peter, you're one of the most singularly disreputable people I know. And you've got no loyalty other than to yourself."

"So?"

"I want to know who might have been involved in a pair of copycat murders. I wouldn't mind knowing the how and why, also."

"You expect *me* to find out?" As the Frenchman growled, one eye burned at O'Hara, the other rolled in its socket, trying to find a mark in outer space.

"I expect you to find some leads for me, LaValliere. Otherwise I whisper to your parole officer. About your stolen booze. And about your repulsive Adolph Hitler flag. You got a week to find something, Pete, or I talk to Debbie Meyner."

A pause as it sank in. Then, "You're a fucking top drawer bastard, O'Hara."

O'Hara rose from the metal chair. "Good. I'm glad you finally understand," he said. He glanced at the kitchen door. "You can release your mutt, but keep him away. If he nuzzles me in the ass or tries to hump my leg, I'll blast him."

But Rudolph was out like a kayoed middleweight. LaValliere had fixed the animal a canine cocktail to keep him mellow while there was a badge-and-pistol present: a Seconal wrapped in beer baloney. Rudolph would be cutting doggy Zs until midnight, then would be lurching around bumping into all the classy furniture until dawn. Tomorrow would be a woozy day, too.

A moment or two later, O'Hara found the door. He didn't have the heart to bust the dog for substance abuse. And as he walked back to his car, as the cold wind clawed at his face like fingernails on an invisible hand, O'Hara thought back on how easily LaValliere had first become an informer.

It had been Carl Reissman who had first flipped Pete into a professional snitch six years earlier. And O'Hara never forgot how easily Reissman had turned the trick.

It had been a love-at-first-sight thing, Reissman marking LaValliere immediately as a low-intellect, backwoods goon, susceptible to the crudest sort of head games. So while LaValliere was freshly arrived in the state cage on an armed robbery charge, Reissman had sent a pair of cops each day to take Pete from his cell for interrogation.

Nothing much had happened. But on the fourth day, Reissman had asked if LaValliere was willing to

inform on any of his compatriots. LaValliere answered
with an unimaginative torrent of obscenities. Reissman smiled graciously and rewarded the Frenchman
with better jail conditions.

Two days later, Reissman summoned him again,
again asked him if he wanted to inform. Same tough-
guy response. Reissman reciprocated by removing
LaValliere's cell mate, giving the wannabe Nazi a single cell. Two days later, Reissman gave LaValliere his
own television in the clink.

Rewards for noncooperation continued for ten
days. LaValliere, thanks to his improved jail conditions, was eventually marked as an informer. So there
he was, a hateful, tough-as-nails Aryan hard-ass afraid
to leave his cell. Somewhere out there in the general
population of the slammer, Pete knew, there was a shiv
with his name on it.

After a few more days, Reissman gave him a choice.
Return to the general population with five black cell
mates, all violent long-termers. Or start talking.

LaValliere warbled like a six-foot-five, walleyed
wren. He'd been singing ever since, beating small-time
misdemeanors with each concert.

O'Hara struggled with the lock on his car door. It
had partially frozen. Then the lock gave. As O'Hara
stepped into his car, he caught the reflection of the
twinkling Christmas lights in the rearview mirror. The
lights and the Styrofoam snowman.

He smiled.

LaValliere had been singing ever since Carl Reissman had first turned him. And not Christmas carols.
And it further intrigued O'Hara, as he slammed the
door and gunned the engine, how the late Carl Reissman was emerging as a minor player in this case,
haunting it only a bit more distantly than Gary.

* * *

Driving home that evening, O'Hara stopped again in Bennington, presenting himself for the second time in as many weeks at the door of Rose Horvath.

Rose was entertaining. Several small, banged-up, compact cars, the type women drive, were banked in the snow on Rose's street. The epicenter of the cars was Rose's doorstep.

It was a cat show. Or a perverse variation on one.

Rose, her special friend Donna, and four very masculine female friends had all brought their kitties over for the evening. The ladies called it "Cats Night Out," a distant cousin of human transvestism. Rose's dog Nixon had been dispatched to the kennel for the evening, and even the Nixon pictures on the mantel had been turned toward the wall.

There was a supply of doll clothing, to which all the girls had contributed. Rose and her guests took turns dressing up their cats in anything from little evening dresses for the female kitties to suits and ties and—in one case that didn't last too long—a top hat for one of the two neutered males. The fashion show was in progress when O'Hara arrived.

"I want to borrow something," he explained in a whisper. "Don't let me disturb anyone."

"Wouldn't dream of it, Franklin," Rose answered, looking particularly butch in black jeans and a Franconia College sweatshirt. "And borrow anything you want except a kitty."

O'Hara didn't want a kitty.

Instead he led Rose to her bookshelves. He stood before them. On the top were Women's Studies and on the bottom a selection on beekeeping. Rose, he recalled, put up dozens of pints of honey every autumn and used to sell them for a dollar a pint at work. That had lasted a couple of years until some prick from the state department of taxation sent her a summons alleging two hundred sixty dollars of undeclared income.

But then O'Hara knelt down and explored what he wanted: Rose's collection on the occult and supernatural.

"Seen a ghost, Franklin?" Rose asked, watching him.

"Maybe, Rose. Who knows?"

"Want to get in touch with someone who's departed?" she teased next.

"Maybe again, Rose," he said, making three or four selections. "Who knows? I sure don't."

"Is this a case you're working on?"

"Uh huh." O'Hara read the titles on the spines of Rose's books, his head turned at an angle.

"Donna knows," Rose said.

O'Hara had five books on hauntings balanced on his right arm. He looked at his hostess. "What?" he asked.

"My roommie. My Donna," Rose said. "Donna knows, that's who knows. She's a psychic. She can also be a medium."

O'Hara blinked. Then his eyes shifted past Rose and found Donna in the next room, surrounded by cats dressed up for their evening meal. Donna looked up, making eye contact with O'Hara.

"Donna can get in touch with the dead for you, Franklin, if that's what you want. She's done it for me."

As if on cue, Donna came over. Completing the lamb-and-wolf motif, Donna wore a dainty, little yellow party dress to complement Rose's sweatshirt and jeans.

"I contacted Rose's mother once," Donna said. "She died in 1984. I'd be happy to try anyone you want. Just ask me."

"Not now."

"Franklin's a skeptic," Rose teased. "Typical male

mentality: won't accept anything he doesn't understand."

"Give me a break, Rose," O'Hara said.

"Just trying to help. You got anything that belongs to your victim? Let Donna catch the karma. Does that cost you anything, Franklin? You said yourself that you're stumped on this case."

"I want to do some background reading first," O'Hara said, standing. "Then I'll let you know what I need."

"Any item," said Donna sweetly.

O'Hara was about to dismiss the idea again. He turned to the young girl, prepared to answer with another polite refusal. His eyes settled into hers. Up close, she was very, very pretty. Dark eyes. A younger Dana Delany. Her smile implored him.

"Whatever you want," Donna said.

On an impulse, he reached in his inside pocket. He found the evidence envelope that he had been carrying. Abigail Negri's gold necklace.

"Try it," O'Hara urged.

Donna opened the envelope as Rose stood guard. The chain and turtle pendant slid into her hand. Donna made a production of letting it settle in her palm, then gently closing both hands around it.

She also closed her eyes and held the moment, seeming to communicate with God knows what, God knows where. Then she opened her palm, gave O'Hara a cute lift of the eyebrows, and returned the jewelry to him.

"Yeah?" O'Hara asked. "Any messages?"

"Donna took a psychic imprint," Rose said.

"It takes a few days," Donna explained. "Eventually I'll feel something. Then I'll let you know."

"Uh huh," O'Hara said. He looked from Rose to Donna and back and forth again. He was waiting for them to burst out laughing.

Big joke.

But there was no joke. The ladies were in deadly earnest.

"I'm only letting you borrow my girlfriend because I love you, Franklin," Rose giggled. Close-in, there was a blast of cheap perfume about her. Evening in Concord. O'Hara also had the impression that she had had a belt or two of sherry with the rest of the girls.

"May I take these?" He indicated five books on his arm.

"They're yours for however long you need them."

"Thanks, Rose."

He gave her a kiss on the cheek. Rose's friends made cooing sounds when they saw it. Then he was out the door as the party continued.

In an hour, after a lousy drive across some slick roads, he stopped back at his office in Nashua. There he looked through his list of phone calls. He'd missed about ten. Included among them was one from a woman named Carolyn Hart. From the two-one-five area code of the number she had left, O'Hara knew she had called from southeastern Pennsylvania.

Yet he didn't recognize the name and she hadn't divulged why she was calling. So he kept the number on his list of things for the following day.

Then he went home, made himself dinner, and spent a nonalcoholic evening prowling through the take-outs from Rose Horvath's library. With the fire glowing in his living room, for the first time in his life, he gave some intelligent thought to the prospects of a life after this one, and visitations from those who had passed on to wherever that life might exist. He did this until he was completely exhausted. Then he slept peacefully and without interruption.

The next morning, he made a call to Florida and spoke to administrative personnel of the prison where Gary Ledbetter had been executed. From the assistant warden, O'Hara obtained the name and number of the one individual to have visited Ledbetter regularly, a local priest, Father Robert Trintino.

Later in the day, O'Hara reached Carolyn Hart. When she spoke knowledgeably about Gary Ledbetter and his past, O'Hara made a decision. He wished to interview her in person. And for that matter, O'Hara further brooded, a visit to Florida and an audience with the final custodian of Gary's earthly fate might pay dividends as well.

"The State of New Frigging Hampshire," growled Captain Mallinson when faced with O'Hara's request for travel expenses, "is not keen on financing Florida vacations for homicide dicks who are about to be let out to pasture. And I assure you that I'm not either."

Mallinson followed this assertion with such a violent hacking cough that O'Hara worried about his commander's health. Fact was, these first winter days Mallinson looked like death warmed over. And pressure from the Negri case wasn't doing much good for anyone's respiratory system.

"Just three days, Captain," O'Hara said, "and I'll be back."

"See that you are," Mallinson said, fixing his spidery signature to a travel permit. "And see that you bring back results."

O'Hara called Carolyn a second time and rang Father Trintino for an initial talk. He set times and places for meeting both. One of the civilian employees of the New Hampshire State Police booked a pair of flights. O'Hara actually began to look forward to the trip.

It was only three days and it *was* official business. But it would get him out of the New Hampshire deep freeze, and all that came with it, for seventy-two hours. It was only that night, in the quiet of his home as he packed, that he recalled a promise that Ledbetter had made on the night of Gary's most recent appearance.

As he packed, his hands froze for a moment, for the words seemed to tiptoe back to him. Something that he had forgotten came to the fore.

There's a lady gonna come see you, Frank. Or maybe you'll find her. Go with your instincts, man. Go with what you know is right.

"Who is she, Gary?" he asked aloud.

Predictably, a harsh, intimidating silence settled upon him in response. Several seconds later, far up in the attic of his home, there came one more of those damnable creaks on the floorboards.

Chapter 16

O'Hara flew to Philadelphia the next afternoon. He rented a car at the airport and drove into the center city. Carolyn Hart had designated the northeast corner of Rittenhouse Square as the place to meet. O'Hara found the location easily.

He settled onto a park bench. It was just past three o'clock. He waited for several minutes, watching traffic move westward on Walnut Street. They had agreed upon three thirty as a time to meet.

Then, ten minutes early, he felt a presence near him. He began to wonder whether he was developing some sort of instinct about such things.

He turned. Standing nearby was a pretty woman in her late twenties. Dark-haired, very pale skin, dressed in heavy sweater and jeans. She smiled very slightly.

"Hello," she said. "Is this seat taken?"

"I saved it," O'Hara said. "For you, I'd guess." He moved to give her more room. Already, he sensed that there was something out of the ordinary about her. A distant voice of warning was screaming at him, telling him that, like Gary, there was something off-kilter about her.

She sat. He returned the woman's gaze, then stared straight ahead. He waited.

"Getting colder," she said.

"Guess it is," he said. "But you know what? For me, after twenty years in New Hampshire, this is a trip to the tropics."

"New Hampshire," she said, turning over the words that identified him. "New Hampshire." She thought it over some more. "You came all the way to see me?"

"I did."

"I'm flattered."

"I was hoping you'd make it worth my while."

She smiled again. "I promise to," she said. "In as many ways as I can."

He offered his hand. "Detective Frank O'Hara," he said. "New Hampshire State Police."

She accepted his handshake. Her touch was tentative, a little chilly. There was something wrong with that, too.

"You're not from New Hampshire, are you?" she said. "Not originally."

"Illinois," he answered.

"I can tell," she said.

"How?"

"I just can."

"I'm complimented, I think," he said.

"And you're a policeman," she said next.

He nodded. "But you *knew* that."

"I could tell, also," she said.

"You're very perceptive."

"I've had bad experiences with policemen," she said.

"I'm sure this won't be one," he said. "And after all, you chose to contact me."

She smiled. And there was something wrong with the smile, too, he finally decided. Something a little off about her in every way. O'Hara's initial overall impression was that she might be wacko.

"Why did you contact me?" he asked.

"I had my reasons," she answered.

"Could you share them with me?"

"No. Not entirely."

He waited a moment.

"Then your name would be a good starting point," he said.

"I'm Carolyn Hart," she answered. "I told you that on the phone."

"That's your real name?"

"It's the name I use now."

"What's your real name?"

"Carolyn Hart."

"We're starting to spin our wheels a little, aren't we?"

"Not too much too quickly," she said softly. "Okay? I have my reasons for everything."

He held her in his gaze for several seconds. In the world of homicide investigations, some material witnesses needed gardeners. Some needed weed-whackers. The key to success was guessing which was which. There was something fragile about her spirit, something which told him that if he went too quickly, she would clam up. Or disappear. So he decided that if she wanted to be brought along slowly, he would have to honor her wish.

"And what do you and I have to talk about, Carolyn?" O'Hara asked.

"Gary Ledbetter."

"What about him?"

"He's still around, you know."

"Gary's dead," he answered, almost out of instinct. Certainly he did not answer out of what he had seen and felt over the last weeks.

"Oh, I know that," she replied. "The State of Florida executed him. For something he didn't do. But Gary is still around." She said this in a plaintive voice, but very matter-of-factly, as if commenting on the previous day's weather: 'Twas cool and milder yesterday, with some sunshine, and, by the way, the dead walk among us if you're drunk enough.

Sure.

He could almost hear her saying it. And so, involuntarily, he felt himself fighting off a chill. Not from the weather, which was in the low forties and tolerable, but from the thought that finally he had found someone else who might have shared his same demented vision of a dead man walking the mortal Earth.

"You see him?" O'Hara asked. "You see Gary?"

"Sometimes."

"And he speaks to you?"

"Sometimes."

"What does he say?"

"He asked me to contact you," Carolyn said. "Gary didn't kill any girls, you know. Gary wouldn't do that. He was afraid of females." Her intonation, her accent, had a trace of the bayou. Like Gary's, but not as prominent.

"You're a female. Was he afraid of you?" O'Hara asked.

"With me it was different."

"How was it different?"

"It just was."

"Did Gary love you?" O'Hara asked.

"We loved each other."

"You were his girlfriend?"

"No. It wasn't like that. We just loved each other."

"Soul mates?"

"Call it what you will, Mr. O'Hara."

The detective again felt the conversation spinning around in circles.

"Then why me?" he asked. "Can you tell me that? Why did Gary ask you to contact me?"

"'Cause you're Gary's last hope," she said to him. "You were the only one who ever thought Gary might not be guilty. See, they all ganged up and killed Gary for something he never did. But he still wants to be vindicated. And you're his last good hope." She gave it a long pause. "Otherwise. . . ."

"Otherwise what?"

"Otherwise his spirit is just going to keep roaming the world. Can't get settled in his grave. How would you like that for your soul? Not being able to settle into your grave?"

The traffic backed up on Walnut Street. O'Hara watched it for a few moments as he let the enormity of what he was hearing settle in. Then he decided to try another angle.

"Look, Carolyn," he said. "The last thing I'd want in my line of work is to think I'd helped convict an innocent man. So I went through all sorts of evidence with Gary. Everything at the time pointed to his guilt. Everyone else thought so, too. And the courts agreed. Perhaps unfortunately."

"You had your own suspicions. You know that."

"But how do *you* know that?"

She glanced away, almost demurely. "I *know* that."

"But how?"

"From him."

He took a stab. "From Gary?"

Carolyn nodded.

O'Hara felt a chill. "Gary told you?"

"Yes."

"When?"

"Many times. He's been telling me that for years. He says that Detective O'Hara is the only man who had even the slightest suspicion that he was innocent. Gary told me that when I visited him in prison."

The assertion grabbed O'Hara by surprise. "You visited him in prison?"

"Three times. When he first went on Death Row."

"And when did you speak to him last?"

"The other day."

"Come on, Carolyn. I don't believe in ghosts."

She smiled. A strange, enigmatic smile now, one that gripped him. Brought him into her. "Sure you do," she said.

A tingle in his blood again. "How would you know?" he asked.

"You believe in ghosts because you know you've seen Gary."

O'Hara felt as if he were going to break a sweat. How had she so quickly pulled the rug out from under him?

"Even the last time Gary and I spoke," she continued, "he said the same thing. Frank O'Hara is the man. He's the man who will prove I was innocent."

"And when was that, Carolyn?"

"A few days ago."

"So even though he's dead, he still talks to you?"

"He talks to you, too, doesn't he?" she asked.

"How would you know that?" O'Hara asked.

"Gary told me that, too. He comes to you in your home. In your bedroom. In your living room. See, in your home in New Hampshire, Mr. O'Hara, there is always a room for the dead as long as Gary's spirit is walking. That's where Gary's going to live until you do something. Do you understand? It's really very simple."

He blew out a breath. He was developing a headache. His brain felt as if his skull had been whacked with a hammer. And he knew why. Carolyn, and for that matter Gary, too, were slipping into his head.

"I wish he'd stop killing women," O'Hara protested. "Whether he's dead or alive."

"But Gary is innocent," she said. "That's why I'm here. To help you prove it."

He had to leap back into reality, before she pushed him over an unseen brink.

"I have two murder cases to close, Carolyn," he

said, almost running out of patience. "The cases are located in this world. The very real world of cars and taxes and city streets. That's where I have to close these cases, not in the realm of spirits. Are you going to help me do that?"

"That's why I'm here."

She smiled. To make everything worse, he felt himself drawn to Carolyn, drawn against his better instincts. As if she had some surreal lure that she was employing toward him.

He knew he could fall in love with a smile like that.

So O'Hara looked away again, watching the time and temperature flicker alternately on the side of an office building, as he steadied himself and gathered his thoughts. He turned back to her in a mixture of confusion and anger.

"Did anyone ever suggest to you that you're crazy?" the detective asked. "That you see things that aren't there? And that you'd be better off under psychiatric supervision?"

"All the time," she said. "I know I don't live in the real world."

"Then what world do you live in?"

She shrugged. "Something midway between," Carolyn said.

He worked up considerable courage to pose the next question. Courage, because it was a real question, not a facetious one. He wanted to know the answer.

"So are you a ghost, too?" he asked. "Like Gary?"

"Now it's *you* who are talking crazy," Carolyn said. "I'm real."

"Let's just see," he said. "Let's find out if you're real or if I'm imagining you."

He reached for her. She did not move. And although they had exchanged a handshake minutes earlier, he half expected his wrist to pass through her plane. Ice-cold, like the time he had reached into Gary.

So very gently, he placed his hand on her shoulder. To his relief, the feel of humanity was definitely there. Firm. Tactile.

A woman's body.

Something went through him that he didn't recognize. He had not touched a woman for so long. He moved his hand to her wrist and held it until he found a pulse.

"See?" she said. "I wouldn't lie to you. I can't tell you the whole truth, because I don't know the whole truth. But I can point you in the right direction."

"The right direction for what?"

"For Gary," she said. "To prove he was innocent."

Always winter, he thought to himself. Always these insane things happened in the winter.

"I can only steer you in the right direction," she continued. "I can't take you directly to the answers."

"Why not? Wouldn't that make everything easier?"

"Just can't," she answered.

He wanted to ask her why, but instinct told him not to press. "So steer me," he said.

"Got a car?"

"Yes."

"I'll show you where," Carolyn said.

They walked to his car which was parked in a metered spot within sight of Walnut Street. She gave the directions and O'Hara drove, straight ahead to West Philadelphia. The day remained clear and cool. Her presence in his car seemed strange to him, alien in a way he could not place, and again he wondered if he were sensing something.

Off-kilter.

He drove past the campus of the University of Pennsylvania and up onto Baltimore Avenue until the university city neighborhood fell off into racially mixed working-class neighborhoods and those in turn gave way to urban disintegration and slums.

"You sure you know where you're going?" he asked.

"I'm sure," she answered.

His only reassurance was that he still carried his service weapon. The neighborhood went from bad to worse.

But apparently, she did know her directions. They turned a corner in a section of Southwest Philadelphia, and O'Hara felt a chill upon him. Not because of the climate or the cold or the fact that the sun was coming down. Rather, she had directed him to the front gates of an aging cemetery. Brick and iron, the bricks crumbling and the iron rusting.

"Here," she said. "Stop here."

He eased his car to the midpoint of the block. He liked to think that he could read an urban street as well as any cop. This one didn't give a very pleasant reading.

Four cars were parked on the entire block, two were mere chassis, having been abandoned. Doors gone, axles up on cinderblocks. Stripped like carcasses by the vultures of too many unpoliced midnights.

"We'll only be a minute," she said.

"That's the best news I've heard all day."

He stepped out of the car, and so did she. His instinct reminded him again of the weapon on his left hip. Idly he thought that no matter what the depths were of some cases, some others were even worse.

He eyed the crumbling row houses across the street from the cemetery. He shuddered. One looked like a crack house, another as if it were occupied by squatters. Occasionally a curious face appeared at a window, stared for a moment, then disappeared just as unpredictably.

"Come on," Carolyn said. She seemed oblivious of her surroundings, as if she had no fear of physical harm.

He turned. She had already pushed the gate open a little farther. "There's just enough daylight left," she said.

She went through the gate, and he followed.

He might have known that this investigation would see him crawling among tombs, tiptoeing among the dead and half dead. The thoughts he kept to himself contained torrents of profanity and a multitude of suspicion and fears.

The graveyard was deeply in disrepair. The grass, which was tall and brown from the cold, was overgrown. It had declined along with the neighborhood that surrounded it, and those interred here were now, in a sense, dying a second death. Even the shrubbery had grown out of control. Small trees edged up through long forgotten family plots, their naked branches reaching like spidery arms across gravesites.

They walked through a collection of broken old stones, markers worn by weather and overturned by vandals. Then, as daylight was dying, they were in a newer section of the yard, and for a moment Carolyn didn't quite seem like she knew where she was going.

She stopped for a moment to get her bearings, and O'Hara took the occasion to glance back toward the gate through which they had passed. He could no longer see it. Nor could he see his car and he marked the chances as fifty-fifty that the vehicle would be broken into by the time he returned. Then, as if operating on some bizarre form of radar or instinct, Carolyn corrected herself again and went toward a fringe of the yard.

Of course, a fringe, O'Hara thought to himself. This whole damned case was about people on the fringe. Or a few steps beyond it.

But he followed her. A few moments later, they had descended into a small hollow near the periphery of the cemetery, a stretch of lower ground which seemed almost rural, considering it was well within the city.

On one side, the area was boxed in by a high brick wall. The wall had been graffitied from within, and many of the bricks were crumbling, same as the stones within the yard. Across the top of the wall, there was a strand of old, rusting, concertina barbed wire which didn't appear to keep anything out any more.

They stood among a tangle of unkempt trees. They were out of sight of any building, far from any sounds of the city. The whole place immediately struck O'Hara as very strange, almost as if they had stepped into a little pocket that existed outside the normal world.

She finally stopped.

"Are we wherever we need to be?" he asked. "I sure hope so."

Inside him, warning lights and signals were flashing. He couldn't take his eyes off her. He almost wanted to touch her a third time to see if she was real.

Almost.

"Yes. We're here," she said.

She held him in her gaze, then looked down. Her fingers touched the top of a tombstone. O'Hara immediately registered that despite this location, despite the unkempt nature of the yard, despite the veritable "oldness" of this area of graves, this stone was relatively fresh.

"So what's this?" O'Hara asked.

"The key to your puzzle," she said.

"What key? What puzzle?" he asked.

"Do you expect me to do your work for you?"

"Look, Carolyn," he began gently. "I'd appreciate it if you'd tell me whatever you know. I'm here on serious business and I don't care much for games."

"I didn't even have to contact you," she said. "I

don't have to tell you anything. I'm doing you a favor just by being here. Remember?"

He heaved a dispirited sigh. He would still have to play by her rules. "So what the hell is this?" he asked.

She looked downward. Her gaze told him to follow hers.

There was a name on the stone, and he could just make it out in the fading light of the afternoon.

Travis Jones. R.I.P. And there were dates. January 23, 1957–July 8, 1987.

"Whoever he was, he died very young," O'Hara said, making the statement almost sound like a question.

"He was murdered."

"Doesn't anyone die a natural death any more?"

"Maybe not."

O'Hara knelt down by the grave marker. He placed his hand upon it, almost as if to see if he could pick up any vibrations. But there were none. The only other inscription implored a forgiving God to have mercy.

"So what about this Travis Jones?" he asked.

"You have a badge. You must have contacts," Carolyn said. "I don't have the answers," she said. "I only know how to put you on the right path. So that you can find them."

He stood. "You'll forgive me if I complain a little," he said, "but you're not making it any easier."

"I *am* making things easier," she insisted. "You just can't see it yet."

"I wish I could."

"I'm helping you as much as I can."

Darkness was falling. She looked around and pulled her sweater closer to protect her against the cold. "We're finished here," she said. "Will you take me home?"

"Gladly," he answered. Again out of instinct, he reached to take her hand, to direct her back toward his car. They walked in silence for several seconds until she spoke again.

"What are you doing next?" Carolyn asked. "After checking out this murder?"

"I'm going to Florida," he said. "I want to look at the prison records," he said.

"There was a priest," she said, "a man who came to see Gary when he was on Death Row. You might talk to him, too."

"Father Robert Trintino," he said.

Carolyn nodded.

"You know a lot, don't you?" he asked.

She smiled shyly at him, as if she didn't know whether to construe his words as a compliment or a complaint. He might have given her some indication if only he had known himself.

They reached his car. It was still intact. The unknowing rental company would have been grateful.

He opened the door on the passenger side of the front seat and she slid in. Moments later he joined her from the driver's side and she gave him her address.

The trip back downtown took twenty minutes. Darkness had fallen by the time they arrived at Oswell Street. Despite her protestations, he guided his car down the narrow pavement that ran before her house.

She thanked him and stepped from the car.

Silently, he watched her enter her home. At least he knew where she lived, he thought to himself. At least he could find her again. Yet something about her was deeply unsettling. He had been around witnesses enough to know who was playing straight, who was lying, and who was telling only part of the truth. Distinctly, he felt, Carolyn Hart fell in this last category.

That evening, O'Hara visited the big police round-house on Benjamin Franklin Parkway, the cop HQ for

the city of beastly brothers. After picking through
some sleazy, unsolved back files, he caught the full
impact of what Carolyn had shown him.

Travis Jones had been a bartender in an after-hours
gay bar on Thirteenth Street. Travis had apparently
gone home one night with some Street Meet, a rough
boy from out of town. The detectives who had covered
the case at the time had noted that the visitor had
a Dixie accent, which made it perfectly logical to
O'Hara that he might have been Gary.

A picture of Travis Jones peered out of the file. A
good-looking kid with dark hair. Pretty boy good
looks which led him to a murder victim's grave at age
thirty.

O'Hara's heart jumped as he scanned the file. His
disgust was nice and fresh because he hadn't had to
think about human mutilation for a full twenty-four
hours up till this instant.

The victim, Travis Jones, had been decapitated.
And one hand had been chopped off at the wrist as
well.

Gary's alleged MO, plain and simple. Only this time
the victim had been a gay man, not a woman. Jesus!
What kind of spin was that putting on the case?

The local homicide dicks had done a halfhearted
investigation at the time and had come up with nothing. So they had chalked up the Jones homicide as one
of those things that was just going to happen now and
then in a big, evil American city.

O'Hara managed to find Detective Russell Cummings at the Roundhouse that night. Cummings was
working late in his own office.

Cummings had been one of the two investigating
officers. His partner from that time had retired. The
city detective was a brawny, balding man with a
drooping gray-black mustache. He recalled the Jones
case.

"Yeah. I remember it real good. It was a psycho fag job. You know what I'm talkin' about? The type of case that you can never clear. These gays are out there snuffin' each other all the time. Hey, it was low priority after three weeks. And the same MO never happened here again."

"There were other decaps up and down the east coast at the time," O'Hara said. "Women."

"Yeah?" Cummings answered, vaguely intrigued. He sipped a Diet Sprite and picked casually through his memory. "I don't remember knowing about them." He pursed his lips. "Could have been unrelated, too."

"Maybe. Maybe not."

Cummings paused, lowering his voice. "Let's face it, a queer snuff in a city isn't the most unusual thing we see. Know what I mean?"

"Even with a head and hand mutilation?"

Cummings shrugged. "No offense, Detective," Cummings said. "I mean, you been working up in New Hampshire among a bunch of straight white people, so I don't know how much activity you get. But down here in 'Philthydelphia,' I mean, we ain't as bad as Baltimore or New York or Washington, but do you know how often we find body parts in car trunks or trash bags? Couple of times a week. Don't even make the news most of the time."

"I can imagine," O'Hara said. "But tell me something else. Why did Jones get buried out in some rundown cemetery? Any significance to that?"

"None. Burial space is at a premium. There are a couple of old lots with space. Doesn't cost the city anything. No one claimed Jones's body. So. . . ."

"I get it."

"Can I get you a soda?" Cummings asked, standing. "We got Pepsi, if you don't like Sprite."

"I'm okay, thank you."

O'Hara studied the date of the Jones murder. The killing preceded the alleged Gary-wave in the Northeast by a year. (O'Hara wondered: Preceded it or served as a precursor to it?) So when ladies started turning up without their heads a year later, no one made the connection to Travis Jones. No one tossed it back to a quickly forgotten psycho hack job in Philly because the Philly victim had been gay.

O'Hara ordered copies of the investigation of the Jones case and the postmortem on the victim. Detective Cummings said a day would be necessary.

"I'm going to Florida tomorrow," O'Hara said. "I'm stopping in Philadelphia on my way back, though."

"I'll have everything ready for you," Cummings said.

O'Hara then closed the books on the day. He figured it was safe to take a drink—just one drink—with the other cops at Bertha's Hot House, the harness bull bar across the street on Spring Garden.

The one drink was safe, probably because O'Hara was thinking ahead, thinking about interviewing a priest in Florida, rather than looking back over his shoulder or watching out for Gary in the mirror.

Late in the evening, Cummings sauntered over and joined O'Hara's table.

"I thought of a couple of things about the guy we were looking for," Cummings offered, sitting down.

"Go ahead," O'Hara answered.

"He was a fringe player around the gay bars. A Southern guy. Then he disappeared real quickly," Cummings said. "Know what we nicknamed him, on account of the way he disappeared so fast?"

"No," O'Hara answered. "I would have no idea. What?"

"He was here one day and completely disappeared the next," Cummings said. "So we called him 'The

Spook.' " The detective thought it was funny and gave it a good laugh. O'Hara was unable to join him.

That same evening, Carolyn stepped through the door to her bedroom shortly after eleven P.M. She stood very still and listened to the silence. A moment later, she was before her mirror, looking at her own reflection.

She searched her eyes and tried to find madness in them. She saw none, even if others did. She placed a finger to her wrist and felt for a pulse to assure herself that she was still alive. Just as the policeman had done.

She found the beat of her heart. Her eyes came back up at the mirror again. She found her skin so white that it repelled her. She felt that she wanted some sunlight. Some color. But it had been so long since she could do something like sit in the sun, read a book.

She was a prisoner of her own existence, her own world. She stared at her own face for several seconds more. Far beyond the room, there was noise from the city. Very distantly, she could hear a train on the Amtrak rails that passed close to the river.

Trains made her think of faraway places. How far she had come to this point. How far she would have to go. She certainly didn't want to go back to the place she had been before Adam Kaminski let her move in.

Not there. Above all, not *there!*

She closed her eyes, as if to seek solace in a dream. Her eyes were tired. They burned. She rubbed them and held them closed for several seconds.

Then she felt a presence. And she knew.

Gary.

Her eyes opened.

They moved only a fraction of an inch from where they stared in the mirror. But instead of looking at her own face, she now looked at a male figure taking shape behind her.

First the shape was misty, like steam rising from dry ice. Like some phantasmagoric stage effect in some eerie theatrical production.

But this was real.

The image took shape before her eyes. From what world did it come, she did not know. She only knew it was there.

Gary.

"Hello," she said. Her voice was almost toneless.

She felt his eyes upon her back. And she watched him in the mirror. It was as if he were flesh and blood. He was no longer shimmering and fantastic. He was solid.

And real.

Hello, Gary answered.

"I love you, Gary," she said.

She spoke to him without turning, as if looking directly upon the dead man might destroy the moment. As if being face-to-face with him would be either too intense to bear or might drive him away.

Yeah, Gary answered. *Love. It's great, huh?*

"Do you love me, Gary?"

Of course, I do.

"I love you, Gary. I miss you."

Her eyes were on him diligently, like needles of a compass pointing north. Carolyn's gaze followed him even as he moved.

Love got me killed, Gary said.

He drifted to a point just behind her, close enough to extend an arm and touch. But he didn't touch. In the mirror, his face was directly next to her, and she felt the coldness of the grave close to her.

"I told the policeman what you wanted, Gary," she said to the ghost. "I told him just what you asked me to."

Gary conveyed no specific words. But somehow Carolyn knew he was pleased. Finally, words came.

That's good, Gary said.

"I wish I could be with you," she volunteered.

Someday soon you will be.

Gary moved behind her. He was closer now. He moved with grace and delicacy, unlike the trudging, awkward way he had moved in life. He glided more than he walked. Or maybe he just appeared in one place after being in another.

She looked at him.

"The policeman said that there are two more ladies who are dead," Carolyn told him. A silence hung in the room. The silence accused Gary.

I didn't kill no girls.

"Of course not," she answered without expression.

"I took the policeman to the grave," she said. "I did exactly what you asked me to do."

For a moment, Carolyn again closed her eyes. She closed them very tightly and let her own imagination sail away. She let her thoughts transport her to a far-away place, a place in the American South where she had grown up. It was like a little nova of a dream, flashing quickly, taking her to a warm, comfortable feeling of security, of being with her parents, of being with Gary when he was much younger.

Before all the trouble. . . .

Before all the insanity. . . .

Before the whole world had turned against them. . . .

Before murder had blotted both their lives. . . .

She held the fantasy moment, almost clinging to it in a tactile way. She wanted to ride it like a river of consciousness to see where it took her.

But she was unable to.

Her eyes remained closed. There was the feeling of fingers on her shoulders. Hands. Very cold. Cold as the tomb of an innocent man on a New England January morning. But the feeling imparted love, not hatred. Comfort, not fear.

Gary's hands.

She opened her eyes and in the mirror saw only her own reflection. Gary's touch lifted from her shoulders at the same instant.

She turned abruptly.

The vision was gone. No Gary.

It was as if he had never been there.

Fact was, the room was so empty that she wondered whether she was even there herself. But then again, Carolyn was crazy like that.

Chapter 17

Father Robert Trintino sat in his office, a small enclosure in the rear of a Spanish-style church in a middle-class neighborhood of Tallahassee. Trintino was in a swivel chair behind a desk, the stub of a Roi-Tan in an ashtray near a telephone. There was a notebook open in front of him. He was handwriting the sermon that he would deliver the following Sunday. His thoughts were deeply submerged in the Gospel of John when the visitor rapped gently at the door frame to the priest's office.

"Father Trintino?" O'Hara asked.

Trintino's eyes rose and found the detective. "Yes?"

"I phoned earlier."

"Ah. You're Detective O'Hara."

"I am."

"Please come in and sit down."

O'Hara came forward into the office and extended a hand in greeting. The young priest stood, accepted the hand, and shook firmly. Trintino smiled tightly. O'Hara sensed that the young clergyman was on guard—either about something or about everything.

O'Hara found a worn Naugahyde chair. Both he and the priest settled down at the same time.

"You've travelled quite a way," Trintino said amiably. "Did my secretary take the call properly? You've travelled all the way from New Hampshire?"

"That's correct."

"Not just for the sunshine, I hope," Trintino said, trying to make a joke of it. "Although the sunshine is here for the enjoying."

"At the taxpayers' expense, I wouldn't dare," O'Hara answered. "I'm on business."

There were a few minutes of small talk. Then, "How can I help you?" the priest finally asked.

"I understand that you're a chaplain at some of the state prisons," O'Hara said.

At the statement, Trintino's expression fell slightly, as if some of his worst fears over this visit had been immediately confirmed.

"I am," he answered.

"You called upon a condemned man named Gary Ledbetter several times, I'm told."

The priest hesitated. "That's correct, also."

"This doesn't appear to be a welcome subject," O'Hara said.

"It's not," the priest explained. "I found that visiting a young condemned man was emotionally exhausting. Whether he had killed or not barely entered into it."

"You felt for him?"

More hesitation. "In what way?"

"Sympathy?"

"Sympathy? Yes. I *tried* to feel sympathy for Gary Ledbetter," Father Trintino said. "And I think I managed to. The same as I would minister to anyone looking for God's love and grace. It wasn't always easy, but that's part of a priest's challenge."

"Did you feel you had gotten through to Gary?" O'Hara asked.

"I'm not certain I understand the question."

"Did he accept the reason you were there?"

Trintino glanced away, then his gaze returned. "Perhaps not," he said. "Any man likes to think that he has succeeded with whatever he set out to do. In this case . . . I don't know whether I did or not."

"What did you and Gary talk about?"

Trintino opened his palms in a plaintive gesture, then joined his hands again. "A great number of things," he answered. "Not all of which I could ethically discuss with you."

O'Hara nodded.

"I'm sure Gary insisted upon his innocence," O'Hara said.

"I think that would be a safe guess."

The priest's answers were noncommittal, flatly intoned, and cautious. So O'Hara waited, hoping for more.

"The talks were confidential by nature," Trintino finally said. "You're waiting for me to divulge more. And I'm afraid I can't."

O'Hara nodded, trying to understand the priest's position. Clearly though, Father Trintino was unprepared for the next line of questioning.

"How did you feel about Gary's guilt?" O'Hara asked.

"What about it?"

"Well, you visited him. You heard him insist upon his innocence. I was wondering if you drew any conclusions."

The priest's eyes wandered to the window and beyond, to his garden at the rear of the parish house. The eyes stayed there for several seconds, for what seemed like a long time to Frank O'Hara. O'Hara tried to read his mind, but couldn't. When Father Trintino's gaze returned, his expression was much darker.

"My guess is that Gary Ledbetter was guilty as charged," he said. "But I must say I also had doubts."

"Doubts in what way?"

"It was just a feeling. I sensed a great deal of evil in the man, I'm afraid. But I also saw him as something of a victim."

"Did you think Gary was gay?"

The priest seemed taken aback by the question. "Why do you ask me that?"

"You were among the last people to deal with Gary one-on-one," O'Hara said. "I thought you might have had an impression."

"What does that have to do with anything?" the priest answered.

"It has to do with a lot," O'Hara said. "I'm trying to close some cases in which Gary may or may not have been involved," O'Hara said. "It would help to have as accurate a portrait of Gary as is possible. Warts and all."

"There were plenty of warts," Trintino answered after a moment.

"I know that," O'Hara said. "But do you mind answering the specifics?"

Again Father Trintino tried to avoid the question. "It's not something that I was thinking about."

"What was your impression?"

"He might have been," Trintino allowed. "It wasn't my role to make such a decision or observation. All I tried to do was bring comfort to a man and help him prepare to meet God."

"Do you think he did?"

"Did what?"

"Meet God."

An ironic smile from Trintino. "That's what my faith would suggest," he said. "It's hard to tell. I pray that God's judgment was merciful."

"Did he ever mention any friends?" O'Hara asked. "Did the name of 'S. Clay' ever come up, for example?"

Trintino thought about it. "If that name was ever mentioned, I don't remember it," he said. "Certainly not as anyone who visited him. I was the only regular visitor he had. Me and, for a while, that woman who—"

"What woman?" O'Hara asked, thinking immediately of Carolyn.

"I don't know," Trintino said. "Gary spoke of it once very early on in his imprisonment. But he didn't tell me anything about it. Who she was or anything."

"And you didn't ask?"

"It was clear he wouldn't talk about it. So we discussed other things. When he would discuss anything at all. I never pursued it, but the prison records might help you. I'm sure they have a list of visitors."

"Did Gary give the impression that she was a lady friend? You know, in the romantic sense, Father?"

The priest shrugged to indicate, no.

"And you never met her?"

"I'm afraid I didn't. And she stopped coming. About three years ago."

"That seems strange. Any idea why?"

"No."

"Did he have any pictures in his cell?" O'Hara asked. "Of women. Any link like that?"

"Not that I saw."

"Who took his personal effects after his death? Who arranged for the burial?"

"Personal effects? I don't know. And I believe the State handled the funeral arrangements."

"Family?"

"Either disappeared or disowned him long ago. Unhappily."

"I see," O'Hara said. "So you were confused. You thought he might be gay, but he seemed to have a lady friend. Is that what you're saying?"

"You're putting words in my mouth."

"Would they be inaccurate?"

The priest grimaced. He appeared to be running low on patience. "Detective, forgive me. But am I under suspicion here for something? You came to ask me a few questions, yet this is beginning to sound like an interrogation."

O'Hara eased back. "My apologies, Father. It's just that I also find myself grasping for meaning in this case. You see, I brought Gary into the legal system. You saw him through to the end of it. I thought if we compared notes, we both might learn something."

The priest nodded. "Yes. Of course. I understand."

"Any final thoughts?" O'Hara asked. "After all, I flew all the way down here for a short conversation. Anything you can tell me would be of infinite help."

"Yes. Of course," the priest said. There was a contemplative look in his eye, joined by something far away. The priest sighed and his eyes, his gaze, came back to O'Hara. And with his gaze came his thoughts.

"I suppose there is one other thing," Father Trintino said.

"What's that?"

"I hallucinated one time. Shortly after the execution. I was out in the garden behind the parish. It was a very hot day. And I thought. . . ."

The priest's brow was moist as he spoke. His eyes went away from O'Hara again, then returned.

"I felt some eyes upon me," Trintino said. "You know how you just feel that you're being watched. Then you discover that you are?"

O'Hara admitted that he knew exactly what the priest was talking about.

"I looked up. It was midway through a hot afternoon. I thought I saw Gary. Watching me." He paused. He motioned to the window. "Right over there," he said, indicating a place past a hyacinth tree.

Plain as day on a sunny afternoon. Then I looked away, looked back, and he was gone."

"Uh huh," said O'Hara, suppressing a chill.

"I was hallucinating," the priest said.

"Why do you think that?"

Trintino seemed almost as shocked by the question as by Gary's appearance in the first place. "Well, come on," he said patiently. "Those things don't happen, do they?"

"It's been a long time since I was part of the church," O'Hara said. "But isn't that part of your orthodoxy?" O'Hara asked. "If we believe in spirits, believe in the soul . . . ?" He let the question pose itself.

"It's not part of the Catholic faith to accept spiritualism here in this world," the priest said. "With the exception of angels or part of the divinity." A slight pause, and he added, "I don't think Gary was either."

"Or the dark angel," O'Hara suggested. "Satan's presence on Earth. Right?"

The priest sighed again.

"I'm trying to be very rational about this," the young clergyman said. "For the sake of theological argument, you have a point. But on the other hand, we're not in the 1690s. We're in the 1990s. Many educated priests don't believe in the Devil any more. As a metaphor for bad or evil, perhaps, but not as a person. And in any case, as it pertains to a vision of Gary. . . ." His voice trailed off for a moment. "I was hallucinating," he repeated.

"What would you say, Father," O'Hara said, "if I told you that two other people had had a similar hallucination."

The priest thought about it for a long moment, then, "I would say that you just expressed the situation perfectly," he said. "Gary Ledbetter was a very disturbing individual. Had a way of playing upon another individual's mind. Made people think of many things that were not right. So, given those circumstances, it should not be surprising that out of the thousands of people Gary met in his life, as few as three would have a funny hallucination after his death. Nothing more, nothing less, Detective O'Hara. A simple hallucination."

O'Hara opened his mouth to pursue the point. But the young priest was having none of it.

"Good day, sir," Father Trintino said. "I hope I've helped a little. I must be getting back to my work."

"But—?"

"Good day," the priest repeated.

Father Trintino saw O'Hara to the door.

When O'Hara arrived at his car a few moments later, his back was to the church. On the bright, clear afternoon, O'Hara scanned the backyard of the rectory. The garden and the shade trees. His eyes found the spot where the priest said Gary had appeared. Overhead, an airplane drowned out the sounds of birds and a breeze.

"Where are you? Somewhere nearby, Gary?" O'Hara asked. "If I'm going to clear you, I need your help now, too. But damned if you don't seem to have been a murderer whether you were dead *or* alive."

For several seconds, O'Hara's eyes scanned the landscape in silence. Nothing. Only humidity and a little gust of wind.

"Damn," he said to himself.

He slid the key into the lock of the car door, turned the lock, then jumped in shock when a firm hand come down on his shoulder, much as it once had in his sleep.

O'Hara whirled reflexively, his heart skipping. The figure of a man in black came into view right behind him.

"I'm sorry. Did I startle you? I called after you, but you didn't hear. The airplane."

Father Trintino stood close to him. Almost too

close, and in the priest's eyes, in his mannerisms, O'Hara caught a suggestion of something that Gary, too, probably had sensed.

"Yes. The airplane," O'Hara said. His fluttering heart tried to settle.

Trintino withdrew his hand.

"I did startle you," the priest said. "I apologize."

"I'm fine, Father," O'Hara said. He waited. "Was there something else?"

"Gary was gay," the priest said. "I'm certain of it."

"Thank you."

"Does that make him more of a criminal?" Trintino asked.

"It possibly makes him less of one."

The priest nodded. Then his eyes ventured over to the scary area near the big hyacinth tree.

"I haven't been over there since the day I saw Gary," Trintino said. "I don't know if I could ever walk over there again without thinking of him. In my mind, that's sort of his place, though rationally I shouldn't believe in such things."

The priest paused.

"This is between us, isn't it? Our conversation. It's not to be repeated?" Trintino asked.

"Strictly between us," O'Hara said.

The priest looked back to O'Hara. "The truth is, Detective O'Hara, I have no explanation for what happened. The vision of Gary. It didn't seem much like a hallucination at all. It seemed very real. Almost hyperreal. Ever experience anything remotely like that? A man was standing there, and it happened to be a dead man."

"I'm one of the other two who saw him," said O'Hara.

"Ah." Trintino nodded. "I'm not surprised. I sensed that was the case." In the priest's eyes was an extreme edginess. "Something in the universe is somehow out of whack," he said. "Is that too colloquial an explanation? In terms of accepted theology, I can't interpret events like this. They make no sense. Nor is there anyone I can speak to."

"If it makes you feel better," O'Hara said, "I understand. And perhaps there are things you have to accept, not question."

The priest shrugged. "Sounds like the advice I try to give myself," he said. "Well, I always thought that priests and policemen had a lot in common."

O'Hara nodded.

"Something else disturbs me, too," Trintino said. "And I didn't discover it until long after the execution. Several weeks after 'seeing' Gary in the garden, if that's what I could call it. I was making some notes on the case."

"And?" O'Hara pressed.

"Well, it did occur to me that Gary was executed on the stroke of the sixth hour of the sixth day of the sixth month."

For a moment, O'Hara's brow furrowed without recognition. Then a lesson from Catholic school kicked in from four and a half decades earlier.

"God in heaven!" O'Hara exclaimed abruptly. And the priest's eyes were mildly downcast from the profanity. "Six six six," O'Hara said. Several ribbons of goose bumps crept across his flesh.

"Revelation 13:18," the priest affirmed. "Six six six. 'The Devil's number.' But I suppose that would just be coincidence. Wouldn't it?"

In the late afternoon, O'Hara visited the Florida State Correctional Facility at Tallahassee. The assistant warden to whom he had spoken by telephone allowed him access to prison records. From the log of visitors, dating back to 1988 and 1989, O'Hara answered one question, but found himself posed with several more.

Gary had had a female visitor. She had signed in as Heidi White of Marshall, Texas. The name rang no bell for O'Hara. Nor was Heidi White the same name as Carolyn Hart.

O'Hara stared at the records. He searched through them further looking for Carolyn's name. He didn't find it.

Was Carolyn the same person as Heidi White? If so, why was she using a pseudonym? O'Hara found that she had used a Social Security number and a Texas driver's license as identification. O'Hara recorded both numbers.

Another question posed itself. The visits from Heidi White stopped short in 1990. Why? There were any number of explanations, depending on who the elusive Ms. White had been.

O'Hara went to a telephone and called his office in New Hampshire. A computer check was run on Heidi White, Texas license and Social Security number. An hour later, a phone call for O'Hara came back to the prison. O'Hara was summoned from the archives to the phone room. Here was the answer to his inquiry.

Not only had Heidi White disappeared from the prison visitor's log three years ago, but she had also disappeared from the map of America. Her license and credit cards had lapsed. No income had been reported. No address. No employment.

No nothing. Just missing.

Ominous suspicions, the handiwork of a paranoid mind: Dead? O'Hara wondered. Murdered? A suicide?

He thought of Carolyn Hart in Philadelphia. He was glad he had taken her pulse to see if she was alive. But even then, he wasn't so sure.

He returned to the archives and sat down at the reading table where the visitors' logs remained open.

But O'Hara was finished reading. Now he was thinking.

Nutty thoughts again.

He drew a breath. He felt like going off for some booze but decided to lay off. He shook his head. There he went again with these crazy notions of dead people interacting with the living. Utter nonsense, he kept trying to convince himself. The problem was, if it were utter nonsense, why did it seem like the only explanation that made any sense?

A half-baked thought gripped him: Where was Gary right now? Kicking around O'Hara's home in New Hampshire? O'Hara could picture it. Did that make O'Hara crazy? Did it become a reality because O'Hara could picture it? Or, flipping the idea inside out, was the only reason that O'Hara could picture it was because the thought already *was* reality?

Sometimes O'Hara envisioned himself in a room in which all the walls, plus the ceiling and floor, were mirrors, and he was stuck trying to figure out where reality began and ended.

Then, as he chased away that image, he was beset with another one. Back home in New Hampshire. He could hear the musty off-key tinkling of the aged piano in the living room of his home.

He never touched the piano, himself. But he heard an old New Orleans hymn being played. In O'Hara's mind's eye, the player turned around and the music became louder.

More poignant. More vibrant.

It was Gary Ledbetter playing, of course, invading O'Hara's home, O'Hara's life. Another image emerged of Gary lying in bed with Barbara, O'Hara's ex-wife. Gary had his clothes on, but he had completely undressed Barbara, who was white-hot with passion, sweating with desire.

Just waiting for Gary. . . .

Where did these goddamned images come from? They were metaphors for what? Subconscious wishes for what? Julie Steinberg would have a field day if O'Hara were ever uninhibited enough to reveal them.

O'Hara closed his eyes to dismiss them but the most recent one only intensified. Now Gary was naked on top of Barbara. He was between her legs, bringing her to a fast, successful, and noisily enthusiastic orgasm.

Your woman left you. Now I claim her, Gary said to him. *You wreck my life and I'll wreck yours!*

He wondered if that's what was going on somewhere. Gary was out there bedding O'Hara's ex-wife. *Finally giving her what she wants, man!*

O'Hara sprang to his feet quickly, growling and chasing away all these images. "Fuck it!" he snapped aloud. "Go away."

Gary laughed and faded.

Simultaneously, the prison librarian looked up sharply. O'Hara was reduced to returning the log-books with an apologetic shit-eating smile.

O'Hara went back to his hotel in Tallahassee and stared at the wall. He turned on the television and watched, but nothing made any sense. His mind was deeply inside another dimension: that of Gary Ledbetter. A killer who killed even after death. A serial killer who wasn't.

Within his mind, a damn burst, and with it came a torrent of profanities.

Something inside him shut down his common sense. Some voice inside him—not Gary's!—told him that he could operate now on instinct and instinct alone.

Instinct.

Nothing else made much sense.

He picked up the telephone and dialed Philadelphia. On the other end of the line, after several rings, Carolyn Hart came on the phone.

"I talked to the priest," he said.

"And?"

"And I want to talk to you again," he said.

"Here I am," she offered. "Talk."

"No," he said. "What I mean is this: I'm stopping in Philadelphia on my way back to New Hampshire. I'd like to talk in person. I'll take you out to dinner."

There was a long pause on the phone, one that strongly suggested that he had overstepped. That the invitation was somehow inappropriate.

So he was about to alter it. Or amend it. Or even start speaking there on the phone.

"That would be wonderful," she finally said. "I'll tell you the perfect place."

Chapter 18

O'Hara met Carolyn Hart at a small restaurant on Locust Street, a neighborhood place not far from where Carolyn lived. Carolyn had given him the address over the telephone, and O'Hara, with twenty years as a backwoods gumshoe, had found the location easily.

She was already seated at a corner table when he entered. She smiled sweetly when she saw him. She looked slightly different from the last time he had spoken with her, and O'Hara attributed the change to that of the light.

She looked different at night than in the day. This thought occurred to him, and it seemed quite natural. Quite sensible.

"So?" she asked as he sat. "You had a good trip? A successful one?" she asked.

"I think so," he said.

"What did you learn?" she asked.

"Not an awful lot that makes much sense," he said. "Father Trintino has seen Gary, too. What do you make of that?"

"I'm not surprised," she said. "He's there to be seen. If you know how to look."

They ordered food as she elaborated on the concept.

"It occurred to me," O'Hara said, "that Trintino

had some reservations about Gary's guilt, too. That's what unifies all of us who believe to have seen him. We all had a sense that an injustice of some sort may have been done."

She leaned forward. Increasingly, in her blue eyes, he found something that simultaneously drew him toward her and terrified him.

"You told me you loved Gary," he said to her. "How?"

She opened her hands. "I loved him as an individual," she said. "As a human being. Not as a man to woman. It wasn't a physical thing between me and Gary."

"Some woman visited him in prison," he said. "Then stopped suddenly."

"Me," she said.

"Why?"

"Why wouldn't I? I loved him. I told you."

Again, the conversation was elliptical, if not circular.

"What are you?" he asked. "Friend? Family? Your accent is Southern. Same as Gary."

"Am I on trial?" she asked.

"No."

"Then spare me the interrogation. I'm keeping you on track, aren't I? I'm sending you in the right direction, aren't I?"

"So far. Maybe."

"Believe it," she said, "I am. Then don't break what's working for you."

From here he sensed a delicacy and fragility of feeling that he had never noticed in any other woman he had ever met. She had shades and colors that he couldn't explain, and guessed he didn't know how to explore. Being with her was always like being before an unopened door, like being on the edge of some unworldly experience.

Another strange image came before him: There was a warm sunlit path before him that would lead him out of a perpetual winter. All he had to do was take the right steps at the right time.

In the right direction.

Instinct again, he told himself. He needed to go with it rather than fight it. His confidence was growing that it would lead him in that proper direction.

"Do you know anything about Gary's lover?" he asked.

"Wish I did," she answered.

"And it wasn't you? His lover."

"No," she said.

"Was his lover a man or a woman?"

"It depends what you mean by 'lover,'" she answered.

"Carolyn, please. No games, okay?"

Sweetly, almost teasingly, she raised an eyebrow. In the soft, flattering light of the restaurant, she seemed ageless, almost timeless. And yet now, at the same time, O'Hara sensed something sinister about her. But then he blinked and that latter impulse was gone, replaced by the more positive impressions.

He drew out a breath. A waiter arrived with their order. They ate in near silence. Then, after the meal, over coffee, he began to question her again.

"Let me ask you something, Carolyn," he said. "Let me ask you something and tell you something. If you visited Gary in prison, you used the name Heidi White. If you didn't use that name," he said, "then you didn't visit him."

This one she thought about long and hard.

"I visited him in prison," she said.

"As Heidi White?"

"It's as you say," she said.

"Jesus," he said. "At last an answer. At last a small

piece of something that makes a little sense. You were Heidi White."

She nodded.

"Why the pseudonym?"

"Are you kidding me?" she asked. "With the tabloids all over. With the media? You think any sane person would visit Gary and use her real name?"

"Why did you visit him?"

"I cared about him."

"Why did you stop going?"

"I didn't have a choice."

"Why?"

She wouldn't answer.

"Better yet," he continued, "three years ago you chose to disappear. You shed your old identity and presumably slipped into a new one. Why?"

"Why not?" she asked. "It's the type of thing I do. Okay? Why not?"

"Are you sure you're alive?" he asked. "Are you sure you're real?"

"What about you, Detective? I could ask you the same. If I'm dead and Gary's dead, what about you? Are you dead, too? Is that why you see us? Or are you caught somewhere in between, waiting to go one way or the other? Give it some thought."

What she said disturbed him. Again, he chose not to press her, particularly when she shifted the tone of the evening by taking the conversation in an unexpected direction.

"Now, let me ask *you* something," Carolyn said. "Would you like to see where I live?"

"Why do you ask me that?"

"Because I know what you're thinking," she said. "And I know what you'd like."

"I'm not sure what you mean," O'Hara insisted. "What am I thinking? What do I want?"

"Come over and you'll find out," she said. "Even if

you don't consciously know, you'll find out when you get there."

Within him, danger signals chimed. In spite of them, or maybe because of them, he plunged straight ahead.

Her house was a short walk from the restaurant. They walked through the square and past a busy area of shops and restaurants on a block of Twentieth Street. Then they turned to a darker block of large town houses, some of which had once been very grand indeed. To O'Hara's trained eyes, these former mansions featured many nameplates and many doorbells, signifying their breakup—noble old buildings buzzsawed into small one-bedroom apartments.

Oswell Street was even darker. One of the street lamps at the foot of the block had burned out. O'Hara saw the block as any trained policeman might: a shadowy stretch of cityscape that might harbor heaven knew what in the shadows. But he perceived the neighborhood as not being particuarly dangerous, and proceeded, intrigued and beguiled by his hostess. All this time, she kept him amused, taking him into her confidence about little things in her past—her girlhood, art school, a secretarial job she had once held. Yet each detail she gave seemed to stand independently, and served not at all to illuminate any larger portrait.

Finally he asked again, very gently this time, about the last three years.

"The last couple of years I don't much want to speak of," she said to him. "Not since 1990. June. I don't talk about anything after June of 1990."

"Something bad happen then?"

"Something very bad."

"Life has to go on," he said.

"If you say life has to go on, then it has to go on. You're a very convincing man." There was amusement in her voice, and a quick sense of glancing relief.

"Thank you," he answered.

"I've been in places I don't want to be," she said. "Unpleasant places that I don't wish to go back to. All right? May we let it go at that?"

"For now," he said.

"Thank you."

They reached her building. He followed her through the front door.

She lived alone, he discovered, but he had guessed that already. There was a streak of loneliness to her, something that seemed very lost. Or maybe something very feminine that he sensed needed protection. Again, he didn't know.

The living room was long and sparse, and she quickly explained away the furnishings as having belonged to a previous tenant who never returned for them. The landlord had let her use them, which to O'Hara sounded unusual yet plausible. It also barely mattered.

She went to the kitchen and poured some brandy, accomplishing it very quickly and returning with it in a pair of mismatching snifters, also holdovers from the previous tenancy. Nor had she asked if he wanted alcohol. She had just assumed that he might. She had assumed correctly, though he accepted it with a moment's hesitation.

"I don't entertain that much," she said. "If I start entertaining maybe I'll get some new glassware. I don't know."

"Maybe you'll find a husband and he'll come equipped with a complete bar," O'Hara jested. It wasn't a serious suggestion. It was an attempt to flush her out more, to get her to talk more on a personal level. It partially succeeded.

"I'll never marry," she said.

"Why's that?"

"Just won't," she said.

"On account of something that happened?"

"Uh huh."

"Let me guess. Something that happened in 1990. June of that year."

"You catch on quickly."

"I've paid my dues. Twenty years as a backwoods cop."

"You don't strike me as a backwoods cop."

"You don't strike me as a woman who would never marry."

"Then we're even," she said. "Cheers."

She raised her brandy and sipped. Then she set aside the glass.

She sat on the sofa right next to him, her knees drawn up. She was strongly sexual and thoroughly innocent all at once, as if there were something fresh and unspoiled about her. There was also something unnatural, a quality that kept throwing O'Hara off, an essence that he did not recognize from any other woman he had known. It was at this moment, as she sipped brandy and sat beside him, and as he watched her when she took her eyes off him, that the desire to sleep with her intensified profoundly.

And he wondered, or thought he knew, where this evening was leading. Not so much in the short term, but in the long term, too.

They spent another half hour talking, all the while O'Hara's sense of fascination and mystery was growing. Finally, finishing the brandy, she set aside the snifter.

"You don't want to go back to your hotel, do you?" she asked.

"No," he answered.

"Then you can stay with me. Would you like that?"

"Of course I'd like that," he said.

"Well, then we'll do it," she said with a half smile. "Tell me, if I do things you like for you, will you do things I want for me?"

"I'm not sure what that means," he answered.

"You will," she said. "You will. Come along."

She took his hand and led him to the stairs.

They went up the steps quickly and into her bedroom. O'Hara noticed that this chamber was furnished sparsely, much as the rest of the house. More of the previous girl's furnishings, she said, though she had added a few small things, curtains on the window and an antique table. Upon the table was a bowl of fruit, and she paused to look at it as she began to undress. Then Carolyn killed the room's only light. And she killed it very quickly.

To O'Hara, going to bed together seemed like the only logical thing to do. She pulled away the sheets and covers.

Then they moved to each other as if they had known each other's moves from another lifetime. They coupled into each other's grasp, arms and legs intertwining as if each were the perfect biological partner of the other.

We fit together, O'Hara found himself thinking, so nicely.

After a few initial moments, she was very passive. And he, starved for the physical act of lovemaking, was as aggressive as he had ever been with any woman.

She brought this out of him even more by whispering in his ear. "I'll do anything you want," she said. "I will be the lover you have always dreamed about, the woman who will please you exactly as you instruct."

He could barely speak in response. His physical passion was releasing itself with an urgency that shocked even him, like a fast spring thaw after a frozen winter of cold, dead emotions.

She was passive, yes. But she had effortless orgasms, first in the minuet stage of their lovemaking, then bigger, more powerful ones during the hell-for-leather stage.

Throughout, he could not shake the feeling that he had had early on: that he fit upon her and within her perfectly, as if she had been custom-designed for him at some formidable laboratory. And she swore without being asked that she felt the same way.

She clung almost violently to his neck as he was upon her, her arms tightly around the muscles of his shoulders, occasionally gripping his hair in her fists. Her legs strained against him and wrapped themselves tightly around him as he pushed himself inside her.

Each time she surrendered to an orgasm, she said, "Oh, my God, I love you!" and repeated much the same each time she felt him having one inside her. The funny thing was, she sounded as if she meant it.

Afterward, when he felt himself sated from physical desire, she cuddled against him, moving her body within the wrap of his arms. Her flesh was against him, but it felt as light as the voice of an angel. He could feel his own heart in a rhythm with hers, and understood again—for the first time in years—what it could be like to be cut off at the knees by the emotion of love.

And yet, he had never found an emotional intensity like this. He had never felt what he now saw himself on the verge of.

As his heart settled, he felt sleep coming over him like an opium high, something resembling a warm, reassuring serpent which slowly coils and gathers a man within its grip and surrounds him with a euphoria unlike any other. His happiness—his physical and emotional satisfaction—was this great moments after going to bed with Carolyn for the first time. And as he dozed, he also knew in advance that by morning his infatuation with her would be total.

Sometime past three A.M., when it was very still in the city, Carolyn rolled out of bed. Her movement awakened O'Hara who, in turn, kept his eyes closed and did not budge.

She was naked. She walked across the cool bedroom to the window that looked down on Oswell Street. There were curtains but they were not closed. O'Hara watched her, wondering what she might be looking at, then wondering if she were sleepwalking.

Then another pair of impressions was upon him. First, he was reminded of the night at his home in New Hampshire four months earlier, the night he had arisen with an overpowering fear in his throat and his heart, the night that had eventually driven him to Julie Steinberg, the police psychologist.

Then a second thought was upon him, one that scared him. Looking at her in the dim light, her skin seemed unnaturally fair. White as cold marble. Lifeless, which played upon the worst fears that he had about her.

He wondered: Was he imagining all of this? Was he really here? Was Carolyn really there?

He reached beside him in the bed. The space was still warm where she had been. He reached to his own groin and knew, as he had remembered it, that he had made love to a woman.

And yet her back, her skin, her flesh, her entire body, looked so very *horribly* pale and white. The longer he looked at it in the dark, the more opaque it even seemed to become, much the way a dim light fades when one looks at it in the darkness. Much, he was reminded also, as those ghosts among the trees in the New Hampshire snowscape, the ones that disappeared when he looked directly at them.

Why was he consorting with the dead? he wondered. Was he on his way to joining them, as she had obliquely suggested over dinner?

Was it something else? Something worse?

The vision of Carolyn and the unsettling ideas that

came with it nagged at him. It caused him to sit up in bed to view her better.

He stared at the whiteness of her shoulders, her back, and her buttocks. She was like something out of an art book, one of those perfectly shaped women who model for artists. Long lovely legs, perfectly rounded buttocks and trim waist, the brown hair disheveled and flowing down to her shoulders. Not a blemish. Not a scar. Not an imperfection or flaw. Granted, the room light was dim, but she was something out of a dream.

"Do you stand there all night or do you eventually come back to bed?" he asked.

She turned and again he had the sense of seeing her face very clearly in the darkness. Particularly the eyes. She smiled as if she had known all along that he was watching her.

"Lover?" she asked.

"What?"

"What's wrong?"

"Nothing's wrong."

"Something is or you wouldn't have sat up."

"I heard you get up," he said, his own voice soft as the rustle of a curtain in the cool room. His words echoed differently from hers.

"I do this often," she said. "I wake up. I don't really sleep much, so I watch out the window. I find it very dreamy. Very comforting, watching a quiet night. It soothes me, and I go back to bed."

"To sleep?"

"To wish I could fall in love," she said.

"I thought you loved Gary," he said.

"Not in that way," she said. "Not in the way I could love you."

"I consider myself honored," he said.

"I'm glad," she answered.

She turned fully. From the table near the window

she picked out a piece of fruit. She stood in the dim light, in all the beauty of her nakedness, and examined it. After a few seconds, O'Hara could tell that she had an orange because she began to peel it with her long fingers, placing part of the peel on the table.

Then she walked to him, continuing to remove the skin of the fruit. His eyes travelled up and down her body, from her toes to her hair as she moved silently across the carpet, a gentle glide to her walk. He felt himself falling for her so hard that it hurt. Never before had a naked woman crossing the room seemed more sensual to him.

She came to the bed and sat down on the edge of it.

"Will you promise me that I won't have to go back?" she asked.

"Back where?"

"I've been in a place that I don't like. Don't make me return."

"Carolyn . . . I can't promise anything if I don't know what you're talking about."

"Just promise that you'll help me stay," she said. "Please?"

"I'll do everything I can to help you," he said. "How's that? I'll do everything I can."

He placed a hand on her leg, midway between a perfect knee and her pubic hair. As he was doing so, he had the impression that he was trying to reassure himself. Yes, she was real. No, this was not a dream. Her body was warm and sensual, and the memory of lovemaking from a few hours earlier was not illusory.

She smiled to him, then leaned over and kissed him, as if to share something. A moment. A feeling. A sense of love. Then her gaze lowered to the orange. The skin was removed. She took sections from it. Without asking, she fed one to him, then another. She took two herself. Without speaking further, they split and devoured the orange. When she leaned over and kissed him again, their mouths were as one, their breaths, faintly tinged with the suggestion of a grove of tropical fruit in a warm, comfortable place.

He wondered if she had done this as a further suggestion of closeness. And he found himself wondering next if she did this with many different lovers, and that was what this getting up and moving about in the middle of the night was all about.

But if he had uncertainties, he didn't voice them. Instead, she did.

"I've never found love the way I wanted to find it," she said.

He held her in a long gaze. "Why did you tell me that?" he asked.

"Because it's true. And I feel something for you. Something the way I've always wanted to feel."

It wrenched his emotions to make the admission. "I've always felt the same way," he said. "The same love that was missing."

She smiled, leaned toward him, and kissed him. He wondered, during the kiss, if he had lost the final part of his sanity.

She drew her head back. A strange reflection from the light outside cut slashing crisscrossing shadows on her breasts, which were naked and perfect in front of him.

"Do you believe in ghosts?" she asked softly.

"What if I do? What if I don't?" he asked in response.

"I think you do," she said.

He felt sweat on his palms. "Are you a ghost?" he asked. "I want to know."

"Could you accept it if I am?" Carolyn asked.

"I think I could."

"Do you want me to be one?"

"No."

She smiled enigmatically. She took both his hands

and pressed them gently to her breasts. Then she guided his right hand to her thighs and pushed it between her legs. She left it there, allowing him to decide when to pull it away.

"Do I have the touch of a woman who's dead?" she asked.

"No." He withdrew his hand.

"Then there's your answer. And you may remain my lover forever," she said.

He laughed. So did she. They kissed again.

He moved his head back slightly, withdrawing from the touch of her finger, which was still scented with orange.

"I believe in *you*," O'Hara said. "How's that?"

"That's perfect," she answered.

Then she motioned him backward onto the bed. He reclined and she moved on top, straddling him. She brought herself downward, and their bodies joined as their lips met again. And that strange feeling came over him again, unlike any that he'd ever had with any other woman.

More passionate. More intense.

He felt, when he was inside her, that he had become one with her, that their spirits were somehow linked much the way their bodies were. It was a euphoric feeling, though vaguely terrifying for reasons that he couldn't exactly explain. He only knew that he had become one with her in some way that he had never imagined before.

Afterward, they lay together for several moments, his arm around her. Her breathing was very slight. And he found himself consciously listening for her heartbeat.

Hoping to hear one. Hoping to reassure himself that if she had a heartbeat, she had to be alive.

He heard one, and was content as he drifted back to sleep.

It was past four A.M. when he awakened again, and he knew Gary was in the room. He knew without looking because he sensed it. And then, as if on cue, that terrible stench was in his nostrils.

The odor of seared flesh. From Gary's execution. And yet inexplicably there was something faintly sweet about the smell, as if it were mingled with something else, far more pleasant.

And then O'Hara realized. It was the scent of Carolyn's perfume and the residue of the orange consumed earlier that evening.

O'Hara's eyes were open. He was gazing at the large part of the room, and he felt Carolyn sleeping behind him, her body gently going up and down with each breath.

Then an incredible thing happened. In the dim room, Gary's face took shape directly before O'Hara's.

If he had reached out to touch it, the face would have been an arm's length away. It was white, but transparent. White like the beam from a spotlight.

O'Hara knew exactly what he was looking at. He knew he was seeing a ghost. His heart thundered, but he kept calm. Somehow, he also managed to remain motionless.

Gary Ledbetter was looking right into his eyes. Or right into his soul. Ledbetter's expression was impassive, as if the dead man could no longer stand to pass judgment upon events in the world of the living.

At first an extra tremor took hold of O'Hara as he suspected—despite the protestations Carolyn had made—that he was lying with Gary's ex-wife. Or ex-girl. Or maybe a woman he had killed.

And then another feeling was upon him, almost as if Gary was answering. Something told O'Hara that for some reason it was all right for him to be with this woman, to be her lover. And it occurred to him what he had suspected all along. That she was some sort of conduit, some sort of agent in his life, bringing him something—from the world of the dead?—or taking him somewhere to impart information to him. To give him knowledge that would set things right in a demented universe.

Perhaps he was reassured by Carolyn behind him. He had an idea.

Slowly O'Hara rose up on his elbows. The specter faded. And then from somewhere a thought came into O'Hara's head.

Please turn, Frank.

O'Hara obeyed. Gary's ghost was fully before him, standing not far from the bed, head to horrible toe. The odor of death still following him.

I was innocent, Frank.

"I'm trying to believe you, Gary," O'Hara whispered. "I know more now, Gary."

You never believed me. You could have saved me.

"I wish I had been able to."

Railroaded. That's what happened to me.

"You could have saved yourself," O'Hara muttered. "Couldn't you have named the real killer?"

Something unspeakable surged forward in the room. An extreme drop in the pressure of the atmosphere combined with the rotting, fetid smell of decomposing flesh.

O'Hara felt sickened, but stayed his ground. He held tightly to his courage and his wits.

The ghost moved closer. Gary's hands came up. The stench intensified. Something violent pulled at the sheet and blanket that covered O'Hara. But O'Hara kept hold of it and snapped it back.

Gary laughed.

"Who killed those girls?" O'Hara whispered.

If Gary wanted to answer, he didn't. Or couldn't. He started to fade. And O'Hara was aware of a pattern of behavior. The spirit withdrew when it was uneasy with a particular subject. Or if it were challenged. Gary had reacted that way before.

The spirit vanished.

And just as suddenly, it was back!

O'Hara felt the weight of a human body seat itself on the edge of his mattress. Gary materialized all at once, inches away, almost face-to-face.

The killer? For you to discover! Gary answered.

"But why can't you lead me? Why won't you tell me?"

There! Among the living! the ghost insisted. *It is for you to make the discovery, Frankie. Not me. It was your job last time, it's your job this time.*

O'Hara, his heart in his throat, entertained the very real urge to run screaming from this haunted place. Instead, he asked, "The killer is among the living?"

For now.

O'Hara pondered the ghost's answer and was chilled by it.

"Where will I find the answers?" O'Hara asked.

In my world. Among the dead.

"Who's 'S. Clay'?" O'Hara asked. "Is 'S. Clay' the killer?"

Gary laughed and leaned forward. He kissed O'Hara on the lips. An open mouth. O'Hara's lips stayed closed. He cringed, sickened again. And the kiss was clammy cold.

"Then who? Who was the killer?" O'Hara asked.

Gary laughed and drew back.

O'Hara felt rivers of sweat rolling off him. He wiped his hand across his mouth where Gary had touched him. O'Hara blinked, and Gary flashed into nothing before his eyes.

O'Hara searched the room. The ghost was gone.

The horrible odor and the intense air pressure went with him.

Carolyn rolled over. Her hand went to him. In the dim light, O'Hara saw her eyes open.

He looked at her for what seemed like several minutes. In truth, it was probably no more than a few seconds.

"Gary was here," O'Hara finally said.

"I'm not surprised," she answered sleepily.

"He's a ghost," O'Hara said. "And you are, too."

"Don't be crazy," she whispered. "I'm very alive. Otherwise I couldn't have been your lover."

"That's what you want me to believe," he said.

"That's what I am," Carolyn answered.

In the blackest watches of the night, this exchange made perfect sense. O'Hara lay back on the pillow. He felt many things.

Thrilled. Exuberant. Terrified. Violated. All of the above.

He felt both sane and crazy at the same time, accepting as reality something that he had always felt was impossible.

He cursed softly to himself, his words a murmur in the room.

"A penny for your thoughts, lover," Carolyn whispered back.

"I just gave them to you," he answered. "My thoughts. All of them. As many as I dare to have." He paused and thought of it. He thought she was sleeping.

"Gary's a ghost, and you are, too," he repeated.

Softly, she laughed.

Was she making fun of him? Toying with him? He didn't know.

"What we both are is crazy," she said. "Everyone can see that. We see things that others can't. The psychiatrists lock up people like us," she said.

She said this so routinely that it seemed acceptable

as a fact, as logical as falling off a log. Moments later, her easy, steady breathing told him that she was asleep again.

His eyes travelled the room.

Then a whole explanation was upon him: She and Gary were one; different aspects of the same personality. And they existed not at all, other than in his dementia, and he had lost control of his mind completely.

He went to sleep with that thought. When he woke up the next morning and she was still there, downstairs making some breakfast, he knew that this line of reasoning was as flawed as several others.

Chapter 19

Here was what made Kaminski most nervous. The stranger standing in front of him, the man he had never seen before who was in his real estate office, had produced a badge.

Police! And damn it all, out-of-state police once again! What was it about his business that kept drawing out-of-state law enforcement?

This time, New Hampshire. And this time, State Police.

Kaminski was sitting down but was weak at the knees. His stomach felt like heaving.

O'Hara folded away his ID case and smiled to reassure Carolyn Hart's landlord.

"If a crime was committed, it has nothing to do with you," O'Hara said. "This is really some very basic background questioning. Do you mind helping?"

Kaminski broke a sweat. "I don't know what I might know that could help you," he said. His voice broke, too.

"One of your tenants," O'Hara said. "A Carolyn Hart. Lives in a residence on—"

"Oswell Street," Kaminski said. Two tenants in a row, cop problems from Oswell Street.

"You know her?"

"I know her," Kaminski answered. His unrequited love, he might have said. But didn't.

"Do you happen to know if Carolyn Hart is her real name?"

Kaminski puffed himself up a bit. "Why wouldn't it be?"

"There are a few things about Carolyn that don't quite follow," O'Hara said.

"Like?"

"Her identity."

Kaminski brooded over it. "Look, she's a very exemplary individual," he said, rising to the defense of the woman he coveted. "She lives quietly. Causes no trouble. Not involved in anything funny that I know about. Why should I bring *tsuris* to her?"

"You shouldn't."

"Well, then . . . ?" Kaminski opened his hands as if the solution were self-evident: Just go away and ignore the whole thing, Mr. Irish Policeman.

"But you shouldn't bring any to me, either," O'Hara said. "And if I can't get answers, I have to involve the local police. Maybe even the FBI. That would involve you, and. . . ."

Kaminski, with a sinking feeling, responded, "I get the hint." He shuddered, sweating as badly as an innocent man could. "What do you want from me?"

"Maybe you could give me an unofficial peek at her application to rent," O'Hara suggested. "I won't tell her you did this. I'd just like to take a glance at the bank references. And any personal ones."

"The references are very sketchy."

"I don't care."

"Some are out-of-date."

"Makes no difference."

Kaminski summoned up all the courage and will-power he owned. "Look," he said. "I, uh, I don't know how to tell you this, but Carolyn and I are, uh, how would you say it . . . ?"

O'Hara frowned in surprise. "What? Romantically involved?"

"Well, yes."

O'Hara held the moment tenaciously. "Does *she* know?" he asked.

A long pause. "Well, no." A longer pause. Then the landlord added, "Not exactly."

"So you have a crush on her. From a distance."

"Sort of."

"Well, good luck with it."

"Thank you." Kaminski felt proud of himself, having at last proclaimed his love and stood up to a tough cop at the same time.

"Now could I see the application?" O'Hara asked firmly. "Or do I need to come back with a summons?"

Kaminski's world crashed. O'Hara sat before him without moving, intransigent in his demand. Moments later, Kaminski found himself at his file, turning over to a policeman he had never seen before—and hoped never to see again—every bit of information he had on the woman he loved.

Late the next afternoon, O'Hara sat outside Dr. Paloheima's examination chamber and waited. As always, the foul scent of death was in the air. The M.E.'s office was busy. A nice spurt of business in the three days that O'Hara had been away from the state.

A man of twenty had been found dead in a new Honda that had crashed off a highway and onto the rocky banks of Lake Hawthorne near Antrim. Problem was, the man had what appeared to be a deep, narrow, and very suspicious wound to the left side of the cranium.

Murder? Or death by auto accident?

Similarly, the body of a hunter had been found frozen in a forest south of Swanzey. The man had been missing for two months. Much deterioration of the corpse. But what about the two bullet wounds to the upper back?

Stray bullets from a low-caliber hunting rifle? (Second degree manslaughter at best.) Or well-aimed bullets from a handgun? (Murder one.) Fortunately for O'Hara, neither were on his desk.

Paloheima emerged from the office shortly after five P.M. He carried with him the Travis Jones pm that O'Hara had brought from Philadelphia.

O'Hara looked up expectantly. "What have you got?" asked O'Hara, folding away a book.

The doctor was faintly redolent of marijuana smoke in addition to chemicals and gore. A cloud of some sort always seemed to follow him.

"I got a man who apparently drove off a cliff after pushing an ice pick into the side of his head, and I got a hunter dead when a deer presumably pulled a pistol and nailed him in self-defense," Paloheima said. "How's that for starters? Then I got some bad news for you."

"What's that?"

"Want to see the charts you brought me from Philadelphia?"

"I've seen the charts. I just want your opinion."

"Same dude, once again," the M.E. said. "Whoever killed Karen Stoner killed Abigail Negri, and whoever killed both of them killed Travis Jones."

His suspicions confirmed, O'Hara heaved a sigh. He gazed off to the middle distance for a moment. Then his eyes came back to the doctor.

"You're sure?" O'Hara asked.

"No. I'm making this up. Do the birds crap in the woods, Frank? Of course, I'm sure."

O'Hara stood. He gathered his parka and gloves. "Thanks," he said.

"Does that make things easier or more difficult?" Paloheima asked. "It's not like I need to know or anything. But I'm curious."

"I'm not sure what it proves either, Doc. I just know that it makes it more complicated."

The doctor nodded. O'Hara turned toward the exit to the ice-encrusted parking lot. Paloheima's voice stopped him as he was at the door.

"Hey, Frank?"

O'Hara turned.

"You don't think that a deer really could have pulled a heater on a hunter, do you? You know? Plugged him before the hunter could get off a round?"

"A deer wouldn't have shot him in the back, Vinnie," said O'Hara. "That one's like extortion and auto theft. More of a human trait. Very low number of instances among animals."

"Thought so. But I wanted to run it past a detective. Have a good one."

There was a bar across the street, and O'Hara stopped there. He had been drinking again since he had gone to bed with Carolyn Hart. He wasn't even sure why. He just knew that he craved the booze, and it seemed to settle his nerves.

He stood at the bar and stared out the window. More snow coming down. Snow on top of the ice which was on top of the snow. No one knew any more what was under that, because no one had seen it for weeks.

He put a first beer down easily. The bartender, a burly, red-haired man named Matt, drew a second one for him.

Then the thought was upon Frank O'Hara. Death was under the snow and ice. As it had been in the case of the hunter who had been murdered by someone off in the tall woods. Murder was under the ice that had covered the new Honda that had plunged off the highway toward Lake Hawthorne. Scratch the surface of anything, O'Hara thought to himself, and you found murder. Human cruelty to other humans. It never failed.

"Know something, Matt?" O'Hara asked the bartender out of the blue. "If a damned deer actually plugged a hunter, I'd give the animal a medal. What do you think?"

"What are you talking about, Frank?" the bartender answered.

"Paloheima's got a case over there," he said, draining a brewski. "A guy got whacked in the woods over in Cheshire County. Small-caliber. Think a deer was packing some artillery?"

Matt assessed him coldly. "You know, your wife always told you that your job would drive you nuts. Remember that?"

O'Hara thought about it. The bartender took the glass and started to fill it again.

"Yeah. Barbara did mention that from time to time," O'Hara answered. He asked for a third beer.

"Make this the last one."

"I was going to anyway."

With a slight pause, O'Hara drained his glass. Then he was on his way.

He drove across Nashua in the snow, stopping at the police parking lot. A plow was busy already, sanding and salting. O'Hara stepped out of his Pontiac, cursed the elements, and walked indoors. He went straight to the second floor, and moments later stood at the door to Captain Mallinson's office.

He knocked. Then he saw that the captain was not alone. His wife was with him. Virginia Mallinson.

Both Mallinsons looked up. O'Hara knew immediately that he had intruded.

"Don't talk to me," the captain said without looking.

Virginia recognized him. She had always liked and respected O'Hara while holding a lesser opinion of many other men on the force. She was a gracious, little lady in her mid-fifties. For thirty-two years her entire life had revolved around her husband and her children.

"Come in, Frank," she said softly.

O'Hara approached cautiously. The captain looked like hell. "Is there a problem?" O'Hara asked.

"No frigging problem!" Mallinson snapped. "Sorry, Virginia," he said, dismissing the profanity. "I'm fine. Why won't anyone leave me alone?"

O'Hara looked back and forth from one to the other and knew there was a problem. The captain's face was even more lined and drawn than it had been a few days earlier. And it was gray. Gray like a man's hair is gray. Gray like a clump of ice on a frozen sidewalk is gray. Worse, Mallinson was breathing funny.

"I'm all right," the captain said again. "Virginia, it's all right. You can leave." He looked at his desk. "I've got so *damned* much work to do."

Officer McConnell, the captain's frequent driver, arrived at the door.

"Chest pains. Short of breath," McConnell explained to O'Hara.

"I was walking back from a late lunch and I felt a little funny," Mallinson said. "That's all. It's nothing."

"Chest pains. Short of breath. Pain on the left side," McConnell warned. "The captain had difficulty walking up the front steps."

O'Hara knew a mild heart attack when he saw one. Or when he preferred not to see one.

"I phoned Mrs. Mallinson, and she insisted we call an ambulance. It should be here momentarily."

"Ah, frig it," the captain said.

His wife tried to calm him, but the chief of homicide was having none of it. Or very little. Virginia Mallinson had to beg her husband to sit. He only obeyed when he tried to stand. Apparently he was too weak and couldn't.

There were tears in the woman's eyes, as if this were a moment she always knew was coming. "Bill," she said repeatedly, "Bill, I'm begging you."

"No hospital," he said. "They'll kill me in the frigging hospital. The doctors in this state. They're all like Paloheima. All they know how to do is cut you. A bunch of pot-puffing abortionists."

"We'll find a good one for you, Captain," O'Hara said firmly. "But you're going to have to listen to your wife."

"You're all against me. All of you. Trying to get me out of here. Why don't you all admit it?"

But with those words, Mallinson relaxed slightly. He sunk back into the chair and, breathing hard, seemed to concede that he was about to spend the night among physicians, nurses, bedpans, and heart monitors. His wife loosened his collar and removed his tie.

"Look at that," he growled. "She's taking my frigging cravat so I can't hang myself in my cell."

Even O'Hara and McConnell had to smile.

"Frank," Mallinson said. "What are you doing here? Did you need to see me?"

"It can wait."

"No, it can't. They might have me locked up for the rest of my life. Talk to me now or forever shut the hell up. You got a suspect in the Negri murder yet? I get phone calls, you know."

"Still the same suspect."

"What are you talking about?"

"I'm talking about Gary Ledbetter."

Mallinson made a moaning sound. He pressed his fingers to his eyes as if O'Hara's response had brought a special kind of pain. And apparently it had.

"My top death dick," Mallinson complained to anyone whose eye he could catch, "and he's got a ghost for a suspect."

"That's my reading of the case."

"Frig it," said Mallinson. He put a hand to his chest as he spoke, apparently experiencing something wrong inside. Simultaneously, McConnell eased past O'Hara and set a series of papers on the captain's desk. "So you think Gary Ledbetter's back from the dead to kill some more women? Is that it?"

"I'm not saying I can prove that's what happened, Captain," O'Hara said. "I'm only telling you where things are pointing."

Mallinson made another low growl.

"Frank, I'm glad you came by right now. Your timing couldn't be better. I need you to do something."

At first O'Hara thought his commander was being facetious. But he wasn't. From somewhere came the word that the ambulance had arrived. McConnell left to meet the orderlies, and Mrs. Mallinson went to get her husband's coat.

"I don't know what's going on in my chest, Frank," Mallinson said, "but it's not going to keep me out of this office more than overnight. I'll swear that to you right now."

"I'm certain, sir."

"But I need you to do something," Mallinson said.

O'Hara waited. Mallinson produced the papers that McConnell had provided. "I need your signature," Mallinson said. "Do this as a favor to me."

Initially, O'Hara thought the form had something to do with his retirement, extending his time of service perhaps, because he saw his name printed at the top.

But it didn't. The document appointed O'Hara to assume the captain's duties as head of New Hampshire homicide if Mallinson should become incapacitated.

Or die.

"What do you want me to sign this for?" O'Hara asked.

"The State requires that someone be ready to act in my place in the event of prolonged hospitalization. Normally there's an acting assistant to my office, but the state budget couldn't provide it." Mallinson sighed. "Who knows?" he added sullenly. "I might have to have a frigging operation. Or be in the hospital for a week. Talk to me, Frank. Do me a favor. Sign this piece of crap. You're the most logical successor I have, so just be ready to be my stand-in this week. All right? It'll be a few bucks more in your paycheck, which will also show up in your pension."

The captain grimaced hard from some pain that he could feel, but O'Hara could not see.

"But the real thing," Mallinson continued in a low groan, "is that if you don't sign I have to get some incompetent asshole like Dreher or Schwine. Now do you understand?"

The invocation of those two names was enough to guide O'Hara's hand to a pen.

"I know you don't want this job, Frank," Mallinson said. "God forbid that you ever frigging get it. So I know you're doing me a favor. I owe you one, big time. Okay?"

"I'm not keeping score, Bill."

"You're a good man. Best I have. Always thought so. Just don't lose your grip like everybody else who walks through these doors."

O'Hara signed.

McConnell returned with the orderlies and a wheelchair. Mrs. Mallinson came back with her husband's coat.

"I'm not going to kick the bucket on you, Frank," Mallinson said. "I'm too damned busy."

"That's the spirit," O'Hara agreed.

Mallinson's eyes rose to the ambulance crew. "No wheelchair," the captain said. "I walked into this building, I'll frigging walk out."

The captain's hand, shaking and feeling very old, touched O'Hara's shoulder as he stood to walk. Partially to thank O'Hara. Partially to steady himself. But Mallinson's whole arm spasmed, and O'Hara suddenly was very frightened for him. Mallinson had always been a big, belligerent, bear-like man. Today an irregular heart had reduced him to a patty.

He took two steps and hesitated as if he would fall. Mrs. Mallinson was at his side, as was McConnell. But O'Hara beat them both, caught the big man with both arms and eased him into the chair.

"Aaah," Mallinson groaned. "I feel like Raymond Burr in this thing. But why walk when you can ride, anyway? I've waited a long time for a free ride in this state. Might as well take it."

"Hang in there, Captain," O'Hara said. Strangely, it occurred to O'Hara that he had never liked Mallinson more than he did at this moment.

The orderlies positioned the commander properly in the chair. They pushed him out the door. An audience of his subordinates stood in the hallway. From their grim faces came calls of encouragement as his wheelchair passed. O'Hara watched from the door to the captain's office.

A few moments later, the state records clerk entered and retrieved the succession agreement that O'Hara had signed. Mallinson had left it neatly—and conveniently—on his desk, right next to an unfinished pack of cheroots.

Then O'Hara watched the clerk disappear down the hall with it to place it on file. And it occurred to

O'Hara that more than the dead could come back to haunt a man.

What did he know?

Inventory time. An opportunity to take stock.

Late that evening, O'Hara sat in the downstairs of his home. A fire burned in the hearth and Sinatra sang softly on the sound system: a bootleg tape of rare, old 78s. The big band era. The 1940s.

O'Hara had a clipboard on his lap with a single sheet of paper. He wrote upon it. Outside, the wind was active but came up short of howling. Inside, he had to admit that the house was cozy.

He wasn't drinking. Not since the three beers in the bar earlier in the day. Upon the clipboard he tried to assemble an outline of the case before him.

The question repeated itself. What did he know?

He knew he had a murderer loose, one who would continue to kill until stopped. A killer who signaled, through the mutilation of his victims, that he was laughing at the police. A killer who was perhaps insane, as insane as he was trying to drive O'Hara.

But who?

Why did the most logical suspect remain a dead man? Why was the totally irrational—the contention that a killer had returned from the grave—the most logical explanation?

There was something wrong with the evidence, O'Hara theorized. There was some fault in the original case made against Ledbetter: He *wasn't* a loner. He *wasn't* a heterosexual psycho killer of women. The witnesses against him *weren't* positive with their identifications. Already he had found cracks in the case assembled six years earlier. How many more would he find?

Who was S. Clay? Was S. Clay anyone? Or was S.

Clay a name that Gary had thought up on the spur of the moment when he rented a storage space. S. Clay.

What was it, O'Hara wondered, that Gary had said to him when the notion of S. Clay first arose? He recalled in Gary's slithery, rasping voice. *It's me but it's not me.* Well, what the hell did that mean? What the hell did Gary intend with that?

Then O'Hara caught himself. Be logical, he insisted. Did he believe that Gary actually communicated with him? Did he *really* believe that? Because if he did, he told himself, then it was rational to believe that Gary could interact with other humans.

And could return to kill.

It was only if he didn't believe in Gary that he had to find a worldly killer. And yet paradoxically, a worldly killer was what Gary was asking him to find.

Not guilty, man.

"Is that you, Gary?" O'Hara asked aloud. "Or is that my memory recalling you?"

He waited for a response. None came. There was a distant creak in the house. But there were always distant creaks in the house.

Carolyn Hart.

He missed her. Who was she? he wondered. He hoped her landlord might be able to tell him more. But who knew whether that little twerp would cooperate at all? Kaminski hadn't seemed very happy to see a cop. Adam probably had had negative experiences with police, O'Hara reasoned. That seemed to be most people's reaction. Maybe Adam got beat up once, O'Hara speculated. He grinned. Maybe Kaminski had deserved it.

Carolyn Hart.

The larger question. Was she dead or alive? O'Hara was feeling very rational this evening. So how could he really accept that he had made love with a spirit? A dead woman.

Something about that idea suddenly repelled him. And yet O'Hara had decided to go with his instincts on this case. And his instincts told him how he felt. Whether Carolyn was a ghost or not, there was something about her that gripped him, that hooked him emotionally unlike any woman he had ever known.

Oh, man, he told himself. The alarm signals were going off all over the place when it came to Carolyn. He wished she could come to New Hampshire to be with him. He wished he could talk to her whenever he wanted.

In a way that he couldn't explain, she was exactly what was missing from his life.

The fire crackled. O'Hara got to his feet. The creaking under the floorboards that he now heard were from his own feet. He took a poker from the side of his hearth and spread the embers around the fireplace so that they would die out. He waited a final minute for the Sinatra tape to end.

It did, with a tune from the Tommy Dorsey days. The tape clicked off.

O'Hara had the urge to take a drink to help him sleep, but resisted it. He climbed the stairs, feeling very alone in the house.

Again, he wished Carolyn could be with him. How much brighter that would make life, no matter what she was. Absently, he wondered about the place she had been in and to which she didn't wish to return.

Jail? A graveyard? The dentist's office? He smiled. A half-dozen absurd notions were upon him. And he didn't like any of them.

Well, he knew one thing. If she would come and stay with him, he would always have a room for her. For as long as she wanted. It had taken a lifetime for him to feel that he could fall so hard in love with a particular woman. Damned if he was going to let her get away!

He went to his bedroom, and walked to his dresser. Upon it, in the evidence envelope, was the turtle pendant that had belonged to Abigail Negri.

O'Hara slid it out into his hand. He hefted it a little, feeling its weight. Its essence. Its vibrations. He wanted it to tell him something.

But it was mute. It refused to divulge its secrets. He put it away.

Then he walked to the window. A bright moon on the freshly fallen snow. Christmas weather. And it was indeed getting near Christmas. Tomorrow was the first day of December.

He whistled a little tune of loneliness. "Jingle Bells, Jingle Bells, Murder All the Way. . . ."

What on earth had steered his mind in that direction?

He gazed out toward the woods. Then he cursed himself. He had meant to call the hospital to see how the captain was doing. He glanced at his watch. Too late to call now and, he reassured himself, if anything terrible had happened, someone would have called him.

No news was good news.

He looked at the woods in the moonlight and shook his head.

Here he was stone sober and those damned forest ghosts were darting back and forth among the trees again. One of them. Two of them. Three. Four. Five.

Then ten of them, going from tree trunk to tree trunk. He lost count. There was a whole colony of them, darting in different directions.

An optical illusion? Yeah, sure. A window on a new, different reality? Why not? He wasn't the first individual to see them. To believe that something could be there.

All of which made his case.

If he believed in the forest ghosts, then he believed that Gary's spirit could walk on Earth.

If Gary's spirit could walk on Earth, then it could kill. That meant Gary, or Gary's ghost at least, was still his numero uno suspect.

It also meant Carolyn was real, no matter what she was. And if she was real, he could fall in love with her.

Was that crazy? Not to O'Hara. It made perfect sense.

Chapter 20

The cat-transvestite party was long since over and Nixon, the dog, had been back home for several days. Even the animal's picture on Rose Horvath's mantel had been turned forward again.

It was eight o'clock on a frozen Thursday evening. Rose stood at the door and allowed O'Hara into her Bennington home. A kerosene heater hummed in her living room as the temperature outside had plunged to the single digits.

"I came as soon as I could, Rose," O'Hara said, unbuttoning a massive sheepskin coat. "What's going on?"

"It's Donna," Rose said. "She's terrified."

"What's the problem?"

"It's that pendant you let her feel," Rose said, leading the detective into her living room. "Very bad vibrations coming from that. Rose had a dark vision."

O'Hara blinked, following. Rose led O'Hara past the kerosene heater and into a small den. Looking ahead, he could see that the room was strewn with knitting and quiltmaking projects and that Rose's live-in lover Donna was draped on an overstuffed sofa. In the same room, a Christmas tree had materialized. The tree reminded O'Hara of Peter LaValliere, rather than joy to the world. It occurred to O'Hara that life had taken an evil spin when a Christmas tree called to mind a neo-Nazi with a floating walleye.

"Did you bring the pendant with you?" Rose asked. "Donna needs a clearer view to help you."

Somehow all the psychic stuff seemed wacko out of context.

"Let me ask you something, Rose," O'Hara said. "Did I drive on ice all the way over here from Nashua because your girlfriend had a vision?"

Rose was already in the den with her roommate. She turned, a touch of petulance upon her. "Frank O'Hara!" she snapped, her voice like the clapper of a new bell. "Did you have anything more important to do this evening? We are about to present you with your dark future in this dismaying murder case. And for your trouble, you laugh at us."

"Believe me, Rose. I'm not laughing at anything these days."

A beat. O'Hara eyed the two women, first one, then the other. Donna raised a faint hand from the sofa and Rose held it. Reassurance.

O'Hara had long ago learned that in any such situation the wisest course of action was to play along.

"So what do you have for me?" he asked.

"Do you have the turtle pendant with you?"

"What if I didn't?"

"I'd tell you to take that jalopy you drive around in and skid all the way back to Nashua to fetch it."

"As it happens," O'Hara said, "I carry it."

He reached to an inside pocket and pulled out the pendant in its envelope. Donna's hand left Rose's and reached forward. O'Hara carefully handed the envelope to her.

"Now," pronounced Rose. "We're in business."

Donna stood. She led Rose and their guest to a small sitting room in the rear of the house, a chamber with many windows that served as a solarium in the summer. In the winter, a set of worn sheets served as makeshift curtains to cut the many drafts. They did not serve efficiently.

O'Hara sat down at a round table that was covered with an antique linen cloth. Donna sat, also. Without asking, Rose produced a bottle of beer for O'Hara. In keeping with elegant winter life-styles so prevalent in their milieu in New Hampshire, she also produced a clean beer stein, one bearing the logo of a nearby bed-and-breakfast.

O'Hara accepted the drink with thanks.

Rose knocked the lights low in the room and Donna lay the pendant in the middle of the table. For several seconds Donna stared at it. Then she looked at Rose, her eyes asking a question.

Rose Horvath looked at O'Hara. "Oh, uh, Frank," she said. "I know you're still on the job. I know you're always on duty. But can you be a little flexible tonight?"

"What are you talking about?"

"Rose needs something to help her get up a little," she said. "Know what I mean?"

O'Hara sighed. He knew what she meant. "It's okay," he said. "Just get on with it."

Donna eagerly produced her beloved hash pipe, stoked it with a sticky little brown cube and lit it. Donna took a puff also to get the cannabis fire going. The women giggled and gave each other a playful push under the watchful eye of the top detective of the New Hampshire State Police. Within a few moments, Donna was sailing.

She hefted the pendant in her hand again. While it didn't speak to anyone else, it seemed to be shouting to her.

"I see deep trouble," she said. "I see a police funeral," she said.

"Whose?" O'Hara asked. He thought of Mallinson. "A commander?"

Donna was looking right at him. "You are going to be drawn out in the snow to a rendezvous with death. I see . . . I see you meeting with the figure of a man. In a heavy snow squall. A man whom you have sought, but whom you do not know."

Donna shook her head. If this were an act, it was a good one. She looked as if she believed what she was saying.

"A big man?" O'Hara tried. "A handsome man? Dark? Light?"

She shook her head again.

"Can you visualize a name?" O'Hara pressed. "Can you describe a face?"

Abruptly, Donna pushed the pendant back to O'Hara. She jumped as if a raw nerve had been buzzed. O'Hara took the pendant in his palm and closed his hand. Donna wrapped her hands around O'Hara's. Her hands were trembling. O'Hara guessed that she hadn't even arrived at the worst part of her vision.

"You try, too," Donna said to him.

He closed his eyes. The only face that would come to him was Gary's. Or a close approximation of it. Then, for some reason, another image flashed into his mind. He saw his own house at night, illuminated with a bluish light from a Devil's moon. The sole light in the house was the one in his upstairs bedroom. There in the bedroom, the vision told him, he held court with a ghost. And at the same time, as O'Hara sat with Rose and Donna at their round table, Gary's face appeared to him in a huge close-up, as big as a winter night, as if O'Hara were looking through Gary's face to see his own home.

It was as if O'Hara's own home were now part of Gary.

"Your home is haunted," Donna said. "Has been for a while. Will be for a long time."

O'Hara felt a chill.

"The pendant's telling you all that?" O'Hara asked.

"The pendant and your hand," Donna said. She held a long pause. A puff on the hash pipe, followed by a long smoky exhalation, seemed to help. "The charm came from a woman who was murdered. Very violently. Very horrible murder."

"Can you see the killer?"

"Same man as in the snow," Donna said. "Same killer." Donna spoke slowly, adding things, amplifying details. "He's a psychopath. Enjoys killing. Killed men *and* women. . . ."

O'Hara's ears perked.

"He won't stop . . ." Donna continued, "he won't stop until his spirit can rest."

O'Hara, with his free hand, took a long draw on his beer. One part of his mind told him that he had to be imagining all of this. The other part knew that he wasn't.

"And I'll meet him in the snow?" O'Hara asked.

"Soon."

"Rose," O'Hara said, "this whole damned state is under a blanket of snow right now."

But Donna was on to greater, more disturbing material.

Donna's gaze had settled on their hands where they formed a union. Now her eyes lifted. They came up with a very frightened cast to them. She stopped short.

"Detective O'Hara is a big boy," Rose said to her girlfriend. "Go ahead. Give him the worst part of it."

"I see the funeral as being yours," Donna said. "I can't be certain, but I do see you prominent in it." She paused. "I think you're going to die soon," she said. "I think you're going to be lured out into the snow by forces you can't control. Maybe by a woman. And I don't see you coming back alive."

Her hands separated, leaving O'Hara holding the pendant. The silence in the room was so palpable that O'Hara felt as if he could whack it with a hammer. He would have liked to.

Both women were staring at him. There was little he could say in return.

"Thanks," he finally said. "I can't tell you how you've made my evening."

But the evening worsened.

O'Hara stayed for a final drink. It was nearly ten P.M. when he departed from Rose's house and slid into his car. But even in the deep freeze, the old Pontiac surged to life when O'Hara cranked the ignition. He fastened his seat belt and let the engine idle for a moment. Then he was ready to face the one-hour drive across the state roads to his home in Hancock.

Snow was rare with single digit temperatures. Meteorologists would explain that it was "too cold" for the atmosphere to produce precipitation. But the early winter was upon the state with a vengeance, and the snow itself didn't know it couldn't happen.

The snowfall became heavy about fifteen minutes away from Bennington. O'Hara had arctic wiper blades on his car and he watched semi-mesmerized as the blades, on the fastest speed, flung the damnable white stuff off his windshield as fast as it could fall. But as fast as it fell, nature replaced it. O'Hara wasn't sure where this snowfall was coming from, because it hadn't been predicted. But it was there, anyway.

He punched a button on his radio. Rock music from Boston. No Sinatra anywhere. A sign of the complete boondocks. Couldn't even hear "Strangers In The Night." He grinned, trying to rally his spirits. Truth

was, Frank—the other Frank, Mr. Sinatra—hated
that song.

The snow was insistent. O'Hara was reminded of
the day when the Negri case had begun, when he was
drawn up Mount Monadnock in a similar blizzard.

He watched the white stuff pour onto his windshield
like so much cotton candy. This, he knew, was a prescription for death on the state roads. An unforeseen
storm. Black ice on the roads. Freezing temperatures.
No sanders or plows out yet. In his rearview mirror, he
watched the snow close the road as he passed, meta-
phorically sealing his way back. This storm was arriving so hard and fast that signposts and reflectors at the
sides of the road were quickly coated.

There was no way to get one's bearings. He cut his
speed to a crawl and knew that the one-hour trip could
now take three if he arrived at all. He navigated by
instinct. Lucky he knew the roads. Another twenty
minutes and he was practically in a whiteout.

Impossible to see fifteen feet in front of the car. He
dropped his speed to ten miles an hour and readied
himself to slide into a ditch. He had chains on his tires,
but already the wheels were slipping and failing to
hold. Several minutes later, he felt a bang on one of his
tires and knew that one chain had broken. When its
jangle disappeared, he knew that he had lost it in the
snow. He had never before lost a chain. Moments
later, the other one broke, and it, too, was lost. Under
his heavy coat, O'Hara broke a huge sweat. He was
miles from nowhere now. And he was afraid to stop
the car. If he stopped, the snow could impact his tires
within minutes. The car would be stuck. He would
have to continue on foot. The eight-degree weather
would close in on him, and he could freeze to death.

He exploded in rage. A torrent of profanities cas-
caded from his mouth. And he contemplated his own
death so clearly that he could visualize it.

Ask yourself: What is your greatest fear?
Lured out into the snow . . . !
He would freeze to death.
A policeman's funeral. Yours . . . !

He could already hear what people would say: Poor old Frank O'Hara! Turned into an icicle at the tender age of forty-nine. Dumb fucking bastard! What was he doing riding around the back roads on a night like that, anyway? Must have been drinking again! Should have known better.

He wondered if Wilhelm Negri would give him an inch of obit space in his disreputable tabloid. He wondered if he would even want it.

On the Pontiac, his rear tires danced. A cute little fishtail on the snow. Bad news. That meant that the snow was already at least six inches deep. Donna's prognostication already had him by the throat, and it was barely two hours old.

He came to a break in the road and realized that he would have to take a terrible chance. The roads were so bad that the good ones were as slow to travel as the habitually poor ones.

Only one thing could save him, he reasoned. He would cut through Devil's Glen. That would take ten miles off his trip. He made the turn and was half a mile into the isolated rural route when he realized how crazy it had been to even try.

That route had been Stacey Dissette's fatal mistake on a similar night. And without chains—he was so rattled that he momentarily had forgotten that his chains were gone—such a route was akin to suicide.

He slid twenty feet down one of the first hills. He must have slid thirty down the second hill. He was amazed that the old Pontiac had had enough gumption to hold the road. The car, too, must have had its own instincts. He blessed the old heap and prayed that they would live to see another morning.

Then, up ahead in the road, he saw something that told him for all the world that another dawn was something that he might never view.

There was a man in the road. Or the figure of a man. A surreal, supernatural vision right out of anyone's worst nightmare. Especially his.

Gary!

O'Hara's eyes widened like saucers and his heart kicked. There was Gary Ledbetter, solid as granite, standing in front of him. Gary was wearing jeans and a flannel shirt, much the same as the night he had stepped out of the woods near O'Hara's home.

Any living man would have frozen to death. But Gary had already died. So he couldn't freeze. Instead, Gary's bare hands were outstretched toward O'Hara, palms down amidst thick, tumbling snowflakes.

Instinctively, O'Hara hit his brake. The car swerved but again held the road. It continued forward until it went right into Gary. Gary's outreaching hands firmly arrested the old hood and stopped the car cold.

Then Gary's grip remained upon the car, holding it in place. And his eyes glared at O'Hara who was at the wheel and trying desperately to get some traction out of his tires.

Ledbetter's eyes gleamed. Cobalt craziness. Big, blue, psycho peepers.

Get out, the ghost demanded.

O'Hara shouted back. "No!"

You will!

Gary's eyes burned. The engine of the dependable old Pontiac stuttered. Madly O'Hara pumped the accelerator and gunned the wheels. The wheels spun impotently in place. O'Hara hit the gas again. The car shook and stalled. O'Hara was as stuck as he had ever been in his life.

He lunged for the car phone beneath his dashboard. He would have to have help. And he'd have to have it fast, though he could only vaguely figure out where he was. The snow was so thick that no landmarks were visible. All the road signs were buried. All he knew was that he was somewhere in the glen.

His hand found the telephone. Then something like fluid ice invaded the car and landed on his hand, pinning his arm down, preventing him from drawing up the phone.

O'Hara looked down, then followed his horrified line of vision up into the seat next to him. Gary was gone from the front of the car. Ledbetter was *inside* the car now. And it was his deathly hand that had settled upon O'Hara's.

O'Hara screamed like an animal in a slaughterhouse. His back slammed against his car door. The ragged seat belt came loose, and the car door opened. O'Hara fell from the car, as if propelled by a violent force or pulled by strong, unseen arms. He landed hard on the snow and slipped trying to stand. The car door slammed in front of him, as if kicked shut.

He put his hand on the door handle, trying to open the car again. But it was useless. The door was as tight and unyielding as if it had been bolted. Or frozen in place. A second scream of terror escaped his throat. Then he turned and Gary was there again in the roadway.

No winter clothing. Grinning. Untouched by the snow.

"You're not really there," O'Hara insisted. "This isn't happening. When it comes down to it, I don't believe in you, Gary."

Too late. I'm in your head. You can't get rid of me!

"You are NOT real!"

I'm real. You know it.

"You're . . . !"

I'm angry, man! I'm real angry!

"Angry how?" The snow flew in O'Hara's face. The

bitter winter air was already seeping through his heavy sheepskin coat.

You've got it all wrong, man. You think I'm still killing!

Gary's voice was a holy terror. Like a primal scream, but not without a plaintive edge to it. Like a wounded angel.

"You *are* still killing!"

No, no, no! I'm innocent, man!

"How can you be?"

Very easily!

"Then lead me to the truth!"

The truth? Gary's voice was nearly a cry now. More like a man condemned. The ghost whacked his arm against the hood of the stalled Pontiac. Snow from the hood flew up into O'Hara's face.

The truth! Gary howled again. His voice rode upon the wind. Near them, a bare black tree buckled under too much ice and snow. O'Hara heard a snap in the bough. An unpleasant snap like a broken bone in a human body. Gary raged, moving through the snow on the road. *Here comes the fucking truth!*

O'Hara's mouth opened to answer. The wind and snow continued to blast him in the face. But then, within the wind, he heard another noise. And he saw a yellow light roll across the road in front of him.

He turned and not too distantly behind him were a pair of huge yellow eyes, coming ever closer, with a motor chugging at their rear.

The eyes narrowed into beams within the snow. Headlights from a four-wheel. The vehicle put on its red flashers and stopped a cautious twenty feet behind O'Hara.

O'Hara stared into the beams.

Then the door of the four-wheel opened.

O'Hara stared at the door, fighting the brightness of the headlamps.

A man stepped out of the four-wheel. He was the same size as Gary and had a similar gait. He moved toward O'Hara. He was a very handsome man in a heavy, hooded, green parka, the hood pulled up against the weather.

"Stuck?" he asked. He carried with him a sharp, hoe-like instrument. For chipping away ice, among other purposes.

O'Hara was so surprised that he could only answer with a single word. "Yeah," he said.

"You got to be nuts driving through here," the man said. "It's one hell of a night."

"Roads are bad everywhere," O'Hara said. "I tried to cut through here." He shrugged. The man was looking at O'Hara's car, his line of vision upon the tires.

"You should use chains if you're trying this road. Otherwise, it's suicide." The man's gaze found O'Hara's. There was something in the man's grayish-blue eyes that O'Hara instantly disliked. "As if the weather wasn't bad enough, there was a woman killed not too far from here. You hear about that?"

"I heard," O'Hara answered.

The snow was relentless, but it was coming down without a wind now. Like big, puffy feathers from overhead.

O'Hara turned to look for Gary. With a start, he saw that Gary had vanished. O'Hara searched in every direction. No sign. No trace. O'Hara looked toward the trees by the roadside.

He scanned. He saw a forest ghost here and there. Just a quick movement at the edge of his vision. Nothing more. Nothing less. Nothing blatant.

Frank?

O'Hara whirled. There was no Gary, anywhere. Except for his voice.

"What?" asked O'Hara.

Very careful, Frankie.

"I didn't say anything," the man said. "You hearing things?"

"Must be the wind," O'Hara said.

"How deep are your tires stuck?" the man asked. "If you're in ice, maybe I can chip you out."

Confused, O'Hara looked at the tires. He couldn't see them well, so he began to crouch.

Don't do it, Frankie.

O'Hara never went completely to his knees. Gary's voice stopped him. And he sensed danger as the man moved closer. So O'Hara stood quickly, surprising the man. The man now had the bladed instrument up high. He could have been readying to use it. Or else he was steadying it on his shoulder.

Shoot him, Frankie, Gary chirped. *Shoot the fucker dead, man.*

Shaken, O'Hara eyed the man cautiously. "Who are you, anyway?" O'Hara asked.

"I'm just passing through."

O'Hara looked to the man's four-wheel. It looked like a blue jeep, but in the snow and the glare, O'Hara couldn't be sure. "With a New Hampshire license?"

"It's borrowed."

"Staying nearby?"

"Yeah. Just up the road a notch."

"I can't imagine where," O'Hara said. "There's nothing habitable through this road. I'm a cop. I know the area."

The man backed off slightly. "You must be new," the man said. "There are places."

O'Hara played along again. "Yeah. I'm real new. Why are you even out?"

"I like the snow. Beautiful, ain't it?" He paused. "Hey, what gives? I stopped to help, and you're grilling me like a criminal."

"Sorry." O'Hara took a mental picture of him. And he memorized the license plate: VPY-643T.

"Why don't you see if your tires will dig in," the man suggested. "We can exchange information at the top of the road if you want. But the snow's only getting worse while we stand here. Okay?"

"Yeah," O'Hara said again. He was still trying to correlate events. "Just one minute. Let me check the front of my car."

"What's the matter with it?"

"I might have hit something. I don't know."

The man stepped back several paces, retreating into the beams of his headlights. No longer could O'Hara see him very well. What O'Hara could see, however, was that there were no footsteps in the snow where Gary had stood. And, looking carefully in the other direction, there were plenty where the man from the four-wheel had walked.

O'Hara slid back into his car. He took inventory on his service revolver in case he needed it. Next to his body, it remained warm. Then he prayed the car engine would turn over again. The Pontiac cranked properly on the first try, and the motor churned to life. Then, very cautiously, O'Hara tried the accelerator.

The wheels started to spin.

Easy, Frankie.

Something hit the car in the back, but the man and the four-wheel remained ten yards away. O'Hara had the sense of being pushed. The Pontiac started to grip the road. As if invisible hands were assisting him, the Pontiac moved forward.

O'Hara kept it in its lowest gear. He was too cautious to stop again in the glen. His vehicle climbed the next hill, then eased down the one following. The path repeated itself more times than he could count. And the yellow beams followed O'Hara for three miles until the road that had cost Stacey Dissette her life came out upon a wider highway.

Miraculously, a sand truck had just come through.

The path to Hancock would be nowhere nearly as bad.

O'Hara eased his car to as slow a speed as he could muster without getting into more trouble. He waited for the yellow beams of the four-wheel to come up out of the glen.

But, to O'Hara's shock, they never did.

It seemed like an eternity passed when O'Hara pulled his car into the driveway of his home. He cut the engine and sat at the wheel for a moment. The electronic door opener had frozen again. He had to raise the garage door manually, park, and then close the door again by hand.

He accomplished this as if in a trance from the events of the evening. And he did all this with the notion somewhere in his head that he had not yet seen the last of Gary for the night.

He entered his kitchen. He tossed his coat on a chair. The snow upon it turned to water and dripped to the floor. He stood for several seconds at his kitchen window, gazing out. He found a beer, then a second one, in the refrigerator and returned to the window. He began to settle his nerves with some good solid drinking.

He tried to put in order the events on the snowy highway.

The way his car had stopped.

The stranger he had seen.

The vision of Gary.

The near fulfillment of Donna's dark prophesy.

He shut his eyes tightly, trying to figure it out. He wasn't certain how long he held them closed, but he knew why he opened them again.

He was listening to music. Piano music was emanating from his living room. No one had touched the old upright for years, but someone was damned well tickling the yellowing ivories right now.

Soft music. Soulful.

Slithery.

He opened the kitchen door that led to the dining room. The piano music was louder.

His normal instinct was to draw his pistol. Yet, even though his hand went to his weapon, he knew the act was useless. How could he protect himself against a man who is already dead? The very touch on the piano told him who was playing.

Silky and seductive. A touch not quite human. A phantom's fingers upon the keys. An old hymn from a Southern church, a mournful Baptist elegy to those who suffered or those who were departed.

A familiar voice hummed the tune as the pianist played.

O'Hara moved through his dining area. There was a figure at the piano. Solid, not shimmering. As solid as if it were a man alive. For a few seconds, O'Hara thought it could have been the man he saw out on the road, the man who had appeared after Gary.

But then, in all the warped logic of the case, he knew that it couldn't be. He knew that the pianist was not a living man, but a dead one.

Come in. It's your home after all.

"Thank you, Gary."

For some reason, O'Hara was no longer frightened. Maybe his fear had receded because now, finally, he was beginning to see his way through to the end of this.

Maybe.

Any requests?

Gary communicated without turning. O'Hara slowly approached the piano from the rear.

"No requests, Gary," O'Hara said.

Not even a little of this?

O'Hara was a few feet from the piano now. He could see Gary's fingers, as nimble as they had been in life, as they danced across the keys. The same fingers that were said to have killed. The same fingers that had held swords and axes to women's necks.

Ah, ah, ah, Gary said. *I know your thoughts. I'm innocent, man. Remember?*

O'Hara had never turned a light on, but the room seemed to have its own soft glow.

From the moon outside, reflected upon the two feet of ice and snow. From Gary. From wherever.

No requests at all? Gary teased. *Not even a little of this? I know you like this.*

Gary's hands changed style and tempo on the keys. A few bars of Sinatra. "My Way." "Young At Heart." And, most ominously, "From Here To Eternity."

Gary turned toward O'Hara. Oh, that face! That beautiful, disreputable, murderously seductive face. And those cobalt eyes. They glowed like a pair of piercing blue pilot lights marking a passage to a dangerous, dangerous soul. Gary's eyes lulled him and soothed him and made him tremble, all at the same time.

I thought a little Sinatra would do you good, Gary said.

"Don't do me any favors."

I'm innocent, man.

"I'm still not convinced."

The statement angered Gary.

The foul, stale smell of putrefaction and death, plus the odor of an executed man, walloped O'Hara so hard that he thought he had been physically struck. He recoiled from it. Gary banged angrily on the keys to the piano, switching instantly from Sinatra, to something with a violent, threatening crescendo. Then he segued quickly into a low dirge.

Gary grinned like a gargoyle. He pulled his hands

away from the keys and turned to O'Hara. O'Hara shuddered. Gary was showing off. Power. He could do things that living people couldn't: Gary played with his mind. The piano continued to play even without Gary's fingers.

And then a second stream of goose bumps and a surge of terror came upon O'Hara. Gary could play not just the music from his own youth, but he could play from O'Hara's, as well. He could see into the detective's soul as easily as he could look into his own.

Gary with his hands at his side. Gary staring at O'Hara while the piano continued: a *"Dies Irae."* Gregorian. It wrapped itself around O'Hara like a snake. Over and over that sad musical elegy. O'Hara broke a sweat: The church organ had played that same damned *"Dies Irae"* at every fucking mick funeral he had ever attended as a boy in Chicago. The tune had haunted him in Vietnam and had seeped into his consciousness whenever he had seen death on a battlefield.

And Gary had pulled it out of his bag of tricks.

Better get ready to sit at a wake, Gary said. *Big cop shindig. Plenty of beer and bullets. Fucking cops! Funeral's a-coming!*

"Whose?"

Everyone's, eventually.

"Whose is next?"

Yours maybe. Gonna come live in my world, Frankie? Gary laughed. *Might as well. You can't even keep me out of your home. Can't keep me out of your woman, either.*

O'Hara's fear gave way to rage. He swiped one arm at the solid figure before him. His arm passed through Gary's body. A glacial flash upon his arm, like being blasted with dry ice. So cold that it burned.

Gary laughed again. He vanished from the piano bench. He materialized across the room.

"What do you want?" O'Hara demanded.

My soul to keep.

"To keep what?"

So I can lay me down to sleep.

Gary laughed, vanished from the hearth, and reappeared directly behind O'Hara. So close and so foul with the smell of death that he backed up O'Hara several paces till the detective had cornered himself against the piano.

O'Hara had an inkling. "You want your soul to rest? Is that it?"

Wouldn't you?

"Who was the man out there on the highway?" O'Hara asked.

Did you think he was pretty?

"You led me there on purpose, didn't you?" O'Hara demanded. "You wanted me to see him?"

Gary faded before his eyes, then misted into a human shape near the window. *Smarter than the average dumb policeman,* the ghost drawled. *Congratulations.*

"And you kept me alive, Gary," O'Hara said. "That must mean there's something you want me to do here on Earth. Something you *need* me to do."

I want justice, Frankie.

"What do I get if I get you justice?" O'Hara asked. "I would allow your soul to rest. But what do *I* get if I close your case again?"

Gary came nearer, faster than any measurement in time. *My eternal gratitude.*

"I want more than that."

You'll never see me again.

"More," O'Hara insisted.

You don't dictate the terms this time. I do!

"I have something you want. You can influence something I want," O'Hara answered. "So we make a trade."

No!

"Then you can wander the universe forever," O'Hara said. "Kill me now and your soul will never sleep."

Gary thundered in anger. An unseen hand swept the keys of the piano, bass to soprano, then back again. O'Hara jumped at the crashing abruptness of the sound, as well as the proximity of it.

"And you *know* what I want," O'Hara insisted.

Gary's voice whooped. A shrill, bayou-rebel taunt. *Carolyn,* Gary said.

O'Hara waited.

Gary, taunting again. *My soul for hers? Is that the deal?*

"She doesn't want to go back."

Back where?

"I can't even comprehend where," O'Hara answered. "But I want to know something else. Who was that man out there? In the snow? Who was he?"

Should have shot him, my sweet one.

"Tell me who he is. He's alive, isn't he? Did you know him?"

Gary wailed unpleasantly.

"Was he your friend?" O'Hara asked.

Gary screamed at him.

"I'm right, aren't I, Gary? He was your—?"

Then Gary did something which O'Hara would never understand. The house vibrated fiercely, as if hit with a tremendous, angry blow from somewhere else in time and space. It was somewhere between a clap of thunder and an earthquake.

O'Hara's home rocked so violently from the impact that lamps and vases and magazines and books flew from tables.

The clap knocked O'Hara off his feet. Gary disappeared from his sight.

O'Hara had no way of knowing how long it took

him to recover. But then he found himself on the floor by the piano, blinking open his eyes in fear.

There was no music in the room as he stood up. No Gary. Not even the eerie light that had dimly illuminated their volatile conversation. But lamps and items from the tables remained on the floor. And the strange sound was still ringing in O'Hara's ears.

O'Hara reached for one lamp that had fallen and set it upright again. He turned on a second light and studied the room.

The chamber looked as normal as any that he had ever seen, except that it was a mess. All the material that had fallen on the floor gave it a distinctive look. It appeared as it might have if a drunk had stumbled through, knocking things over.

Gary was nowhere to be heard. And by O'Hara's feet was the bottle from his final beer of the evening. He didn't even remember carrying it from the kitchen, though he was sure he probably had.

He glanced at his watch. He was stunned. It was four A.M., and he couldn't figure where the time had gone.

The next morning in Philadelphia, Kaminski was stuck with the realization that he had been flummoxed.

The policeman from New Hampshire had piqued his curiosity, but had also raised Adam's defensive instincts. How dare an out-of-state man with a badge come around his office and try to pry information out of him! Not only would Kaminski beat O'Hara to the information, he decided, but he wouldn't turn it over. Not to the police. He would present it to Carolyn. He would warn her that trouble was stalking her. And she would love him for it.

Kaminski used every real estate source file in the

city. Landlords' credit reports. Rental applications, cross-referenced with local employment listings. She had to have been somewhere. If it were anywhere nearby, he would find her.

Kaminski struck pay dirt in an unlikely spot. Mental health records. But there it was. Carolyn Hart. February 1990. Attempted to rent a small apartment in Bryn Mawr. Application withdrawn when Carolyn was honest about her previous address. 4437 Germantown Pike in Drexel Hill. Someone at the landlord's address had called to check the reference. 4437 Germantown Pike was the address of the Northeastern Pennsylvania State Pyschiatric Hospital. Carolyn had been a patient there until walking away in February.

Kaminski didn't wish to proceed any further on the telephone. Instead, on a dreary December morning, he drove up to the hospital to make his further inquiry in person. Eventually, he found himself seated in the office of Dr. Herbert Raymond, Assistant Director of Northeastern Pennsylvania State Psychiatric.

"Carolyn was here, yes," Dr. Raymond said. "Been gone for a few years now. I really shouldn't tell you too much more."

"Was she healthy when she was discharged?" Kaminski asked.

"She wasn't healthy," the doctor answered. "I can tell you that categorically."

Kaminski waited for more. And he knew it wasn't going to be pleasant. The doctor spoke from memory and off the record.

"Carolyn suffered a complete psychotic break with reality," Dr. Raymond said. "Hart was a name she adopted. Her brother was a convicted murderer. Name of Ledbetter. I think his first name was Jerry. Or Gary. Know the case?"

Kaminski had never heard of it. It wasn't his habit to follow such things.

"Carolyn couldn't accept her brother's guilt, even though the guilt seemed quite clear to everyone else. She had some wild story about her brother being hooked up with some professional killer. Her brother was eventually sentenced to die for one or more of the murders, if I remember. But no partner ever was arrested. Who knows whether one ever existed? Maybe she made it up. I don't know. I suppose it had some borderline credibility. But believe me, we hear some strange stories in our line of work."

"I'm sure," said Kaminski. "Would she have used such a story as a defense against having to accept her brother's guilt?"

The doctor didn't wish to speculate, though his own thoughts were in the same territory.

"Carolyn said that the partner was up in New England and would continue to kill. So she kept promising to leave Pennsylvania to find this man and settle the scores." The doctor opened his palms and shrugged. "Not really our department, law enforcement. But it was the opinion here that Carolyn Ledbetter was a pretty sick girl."

"So if she was mentally ill, why was she released?" Kaminski asked.

"She wasn't," Dr. Raymond said. "She first came to us in February of 1989, I think it was. Walked away a few months later. When she tried to lease an apartment on her own, we found her. Naturally, we brought her back. This is not a maximum security institution, so unfortunately she walked out a second time."

"Recently?" Kaminski guessed.

"No, no. Not at all. In June of that next year. 1990. I assume in her warped sense of things, she probably went off to New England to find this man she was looking for. My guess is that she's institutionalized under another name somewhere. I hope so, because otherwise harm will come to her."

"Have you tried to find her?"

"Budget cuts," the doctor said unpleasantly. "We don't have money to do searches. And frankly, the politics of the situation in Harrisburg is such that anything that unloads a long-term care patient is looked upon favorably. So there wasn't much we could do. Unless," he said with a pause, "someone came to us and told us where she was."

Kaminski sat perfectly still and attempted to correlate all that the doctor had told him. One line of thought, however, was in the forefront of his mind.

If Carolyn were returned here, the institution would have to watch her more carefully. And if no one on the outside was interested in her case, he, Adam Kaminski, could easily be her protector. He could visit her and help her back to health. She could be both his lover and his reclamation project. In any case, she would be safe.

And nearby.

"Mr. Kaminski?" Dr. Raymond asked. "I've told you what I can. Maybe you can share your knowledge with me. This hospital remains Carolyn Ledbetter's guardian until notified otherwise."

Kaminski rallied his courage and prepared to speak.

"Doctor," he said, "I think I can be of help to everyone."

Chapter 21

December 12. The twelfth day of the twelfth month. Frank Sinatra's birthday and here was the other Frank, O'Hara, sitting at a booth in a pool hall in the factory town of Tocomset. O'Hara was waiting for his meeting with the local Bund while in his mind Old Blue Eyes sang, "My Way."

O'Hara looked out a dirty plate glass window and saw a mill down the street. Tocomset was a hard-edged, white, working-class town. Low-rent Irish, Poles, and French-Canadians. O'Hara guessed that the mill at the end of the block was the one that turned out the Third Reich flags for the local, inbred yahoos.

Someday, he would have to investigate. Someday, but not this day, because as he entertained that thought he spotted his connection: Pete LaValliere, who had called him and requested this summit conference in this benighted place.

LaValliere thumped into the hall from the outdoors. He held the door to the outside open too long and evoked the wrath of a couple of porky-looking guys who had their bellies hanging over a pool table. But then LaValliere saw O'Hara. He let the door slam shut and sauntered to the detective's table.

No handshake. No greeting. He just sat down and started.

"I been doing some thinking, O'Hara," LaValliere began.

"That's great, Pete. I hope you didn't hurt yourself."

"Now that's a hell of a fucking attitude to start with," LaValliere snapped. "Here I come to try to help you and you give me gas right from the top. What am I supposed to think about that?"

"You're supposed to remember that I'm in charge, Pete," O'Hara said. "And you didn't come to help me, you came to cut yourself a deal. And you're damned lucky I'm offering you one. Now I'm already ashamed of myself for even being in this pigsty talking to you, so what do you have?"

"Secrets," LaValliere said, his voice lowered and properly humbled. "Secrets that you want to know. See, I been asking around a bit. Turns out I knew some friends who'd like 'in' on whatever you're giving out. Do we have something, you and me? An agreement?"

"I'm listening to you, Pete," O'Hara said.

"Do we agree to agree?"

"Just talk, would you? Before I call your parole officer."

"It's about the girl who got her head cut off last summer," LaValliere said. "You know, I got to thank you. I never would have paid no attention to that case if you hadn't come to me. Now I get to cut myself a whale of a deal."

"What makes you think that?"

"Because I got *all* the answers for you, Frank O'Hara," the neo-Nazi said. "Old answers and new answers. I been asking around. And aren't you the acting head of homicide in this state right now?"

"Word travels fast."

"That makes you an acting captain. So you can cut me some slack."

"Talk, Pete. I won't screw you. But first I need to hear what you have."

Given the nature of such things, LaValliere took O'Hara at his word.

He turned and signalled to another table. Two men who had been watching the conversation lurched to their feet and trudged to O'Hara's booth. Two of LaValliere's Gestapo-wannabe friends sat down without introduction. Leather bike jackets. When they removed their respective caps, both were bald. Shaved head, skinhead bald. One guy smelled like a stale barn and O'Hara couldn't tell which.

"Who's this?" O'Hara asked. "Boorman and Himmler?"

"These are my business associates."

"From the Sainsbury truck, I assume."

"I don't like this, Pete," the bigger one of the baldies chimed in. But Pete, the ersatz Santa, held up a hand, dirty fingernails and all, to silence him. "I dealt with Frank O'Hara before. He'll shoot straight. Particularly today." As he voiced his confidence, Pete's wall-eye spun a loop toward the door.

And the two leather guys remained unconvinced. O'Hara decided that they needed a nudge.

"If I like what I hear, and if it's true, the Sainsbury heist is history," O'Hara said. "How's that?" And with Dreher and Schwine on the case, chasing each other's ass all over Hillsborough County rather than doing anything productive, O'Hara knew he was giving away virtually nothing.

"That's good," said one of them. "That's real good."

"Maybe Mr. O'Hara will toss us a freebee in the future, too," said LaValliere.

"Don't press your luck, Pete," O'Hara answered. "You got to remember that I don't like you very much. And I asked you to talk."

LaValliere looked O'Hara squarely in the eye. "Mikalski here," the Frenchman said, motioning to the smaller and uglier of the two baldies. "Mo Mikalski here used to work in a video store in Peterborough. Mo's got something to tell you *now* that he was never gonna tell you *before.*"

O'Hara looked at LaValliere's accomplice. Mikalski was a wiry man of about five feet eight. Thick mustache. A lot of gray hair in the whiskers and a prematurely aged, lined face. O'Hara guessed he was about thirty-five. Another peewee-intellect, backwoods jerk-off. In the local Bund meetings, sewer water obviously found its own low level. The other guy, the bigger one, was thick-browed and sullen. Didn't have much to say at all, and O'Hara guessed he had an IQ to match the speed limit on the interstate.

But Mikalski had taken singing lessons from LaValliere. He placed himself at a video shop in Peterborough seven years earlier, during the unlovely winter of 1986-87. Or, more specifically, at the time when Karen Stoner was murdered and mutilated.

"I remember it was about a week after the killing," Mikalski said, "that I knew they were trying to set a guy up for a fall on this murder. We had a couple of big shot cops come up. Inspector level, state pigs. Flashed us a picture of a guy. Ledbetter."

A disappointed sigh from O'Hara. "Look, I knew there was a separate inspectors' team that made some inquiries right after the Stoner murder," he said. "So what?"

"So you don't know how we answered," Mikalski replied. "We said, yeah, we'd seen him. Gary rented porno films from us. They told us, no, we *hadn't* seen him. They stood there and made us remove Gary's account records from the store computer. They were trying to make Gary Ledbetter available to be arrested."

"I know they fucked around with evidence," O'Hara said. "You're still not telling me anything new."

"Yeah, well try this: See the rumor was that Gary had done some of the seducing. He'd helped kill the girl. But it was his buddy who was the chopper and hacker."

"What buddy?" O'Hara asked.

"A man named Sandor Clay. Or that's the name he went by. Looked a lot like Gary Ledbetter. A pretty boy, too. But his thing was just killing people. Did it for sport at first. Then started doing it for money."

Slowly coming out of a surge of excitement, O'Hara asked, "How can I believe any of that?"

"Don't it fit what you already know?" Mikalski asked.

O'Hara answered guardedly. "Maybe."

"The state pigs ran down to a doughnut shop down near the Mass border. Big shot plainclothes guys. Heavy hitters from Concord. Street talk was that they had something to do with the governor's office. Found Karen Stoner's friends. Showed pictures of Gary to all the local skirts. Told them that Gary must have been the guy who skewered the Stoner girl. Then they said they'd send another team of state cops to ask the official questions. They were to identify the right picture if they knew what was good for them. Close up all the angles, make things official. Shit, the girls just thought they was doing the right thing, putting away a bad-ass. I'd of done the same, myself."

And O'Hara remembered very well how quickly the girls had identified his mug shots of Gary. He had waltzed through an elaborate charade arranged by the state government and, guided through it by his partner, had never picked up on the sham of it.

"So who was this Sandor Clay?" O'Hara asked.

"Gary's buddy? Gary's lover? Gary's partner in crime?"

"All of those," said Mikalski. "All of those and a little more. See, Sandor had done some dirty work for the political people in Concord. Strongarm stuff. Intimidation. People were scared of him. I'd even heard that he'd done some snuff jobs around the Northeast and down South. If he got busted, then he'd sing to the newspapers. So the people who run this state saw to it that he never got busted. See? What he'd done was his life insurance policy."

"And Gary was unaware?" O'Hara asked.

"That's what I been told. Hell, Gary was a queer and got off on a handsome butch act like Sandor Clay. Loved the guy real bad. Hell, he fried for him."

"Though Gary couldn't confess to anything," O'Hara said, filling in the blanks, "without implicating himself."

"So he would have fried, anyway," LaValliere said.

And Gary must have known that his friend had some connections in the state, O'Hara thought to himself. He must have been waiting to get sprung, almost up to the last minute. But the call never came, the deal was never made. And Gary had probably never loved anyone like he loved Clay. So he was ready to take the fall for this guy. To O'Hara it began to fit neatly and grossly into position.

LaValliere's fascist pal expressed the same thought differently.

"How's that for ultimate, macho, butch, fag love?" Mikalski asked. "Gary Ledbetter sat in Old Sparky in Florida on behalf of two guys. And he never gave his buddy away."

The monstrosity of all of this, settling in upon him in a smoky pool hall in a dirtball town, reached O'Hara through a thickening wall of spiritual exhaustion. It left him almost speechless. He was aware, in fact, that he had fallen very quiet.

"Gary got the hot seat and Sandor Clay is out hacking away," LaValliere said with amusement. "I bet Gary's spinning in his fucking grave right now."

"Want to know something, guys? He's doing even more than that."

Five dim-witted eyes focused on O'Hara, seeking an explanation where one eluded them. O'Hara ducked giving out any answers, though. He told them they had a deal, details to be arranged later. Then he set out across the icy roads for confirmation of what he had heard.

It was the afternoon of the same day when O'Hara arrived at the hospital in Nashua.

Captain Mallinson was in a private room on a long green corridor. When O'Hara arrived, the captain was seated in a low chair. He wore a newly purchased maroon robe, just perfect for hospital use. The fingerprints of a caring wife were upon the garment. In the room, the television was on. But O'Hara could tell that the tube was only providing background companionship. The captain wasn't watching. O'Hara knew Mallinson had shot a television set once, but he had never known the captain to watch one unless he thought he was going to be on the news.

"Hello, Frank," the captain said as O'Hara knocked gently on the door frame that led to the room. "Come in. Talk to me. More than ever, talk to me. Everybody else on this frigging floor is senile. Probably I am, too, but I'm too far-gone to realize it yet."

O'Hara came into the room. He sat on the edge of the captain's bed.

"How are things going?" O'Hara asked. "You're

sitting up. You're talking. You sound pissed off. That's good. You look like you might even be your old nasty self."

"If you're all unlucky I'll be back at work within a week," Mallinson growled. "I talked to the docs. I got conjuctive corallery something."

"Congestive coronary failure," O'Hara said.

"That's it. They tell you?"

"Your wife did. And so did the nurse at the main desk."

"Yeah. Bless her. Well, it's supposedly not as bad as it sounds," he said. "Blood's not pumping right through the old ticker. Anyway, they don't have to cut me open yet. I have to take some medicines that do something to my blood."

"Something to thin the blood," O'Hara said. "Makes it easier for the heart to operate."

"Yeah, yeah," said Mallinson, almost sounding mildly heroic. "I just have to take it easy. And I got to stop smoking. If I promise to do that and take my medicine they said they'd let me out of this frigging place. So naturally I promised."

O'Hara nodded. "Good for you," he said.

The captain gave a plaintive gesture with his hands. "Two things that I'm going to have a real easy time of doing," the captain said with an easy sarcasm. "Taking it easy and quitting tobacco. You bet."

"You owe it to yourself, Cap," O'Hara said. "You've busted your butt for years on this job. There's no use overdoing it now."

"Yeah. Right," Mallinson said, sounding one hundred percent unconvinced. He looked back to his visitor. "You know I've said for years that this job will either kill you or drive you crazy. Looks like with me it'll be the former if I'm not careful. So, frig it, Frank. I'm planning to be careful."

O'Hara nodded again.

"How are things going? Keeping my chair warm?" Mallinson asked. "Or did you chop it up for fire-wood?"

"Your chair will be waiting for you next week."

"That's good news. How's the Negri thing coming along? Do you know that the asshole, the one who's on the radio, called me to see what he could find out? Spent one minute asking about my health and another ten asking about the investigation."

"Is he pushing for an arrest?"

"He seemed to be more interested in knowing what was happening in the case more than having it closed. Funny reaction. He kept wanting to know if we had a suspect. Wanted real bad to know. I guess I could have told him to call you."

"I wouldn't have told him."

"Why not?"

"No use giving our hand away." O'Hara sought to make a joke of it. "Negri makes his living by talking," O'Hara said. "Let him talk about something else."

"No complaint from me," the captain said. "But what's going on? You got a break in the case or what?"

"Possible. But I need some background."

"Yeah? From who?"

"From you."

"I don't know what I got on Negri."

"It's Ledbetter I'm asking about."

"Ah, frig it, Frank! You're not beating that drum again, are you?"

"I still need to know things about the case."

"You know everything."

"No, I don't."

"What don't you know?"

"Captain, remember when I signed the succession paper last week? You said I was doing you a big favor. You said you owed me a big one."

"Yeah. So?"

"So I'm calling in the IOU right now. I want to know about the evidence in the Ledbetter case. Was it clean or not?"

"Someone saying it's not?"

"I got a source that says a heavy fix was in seven years ago."

"Who's telling you that?"

O'Hara didn't say a word.

Mallinson looked at O'Hara, started to speak, then shook his head as if he just couldn't. He started with the same old protestations.

O'Hara interrupted.

"This is a big-time request, Captain," O'Hara said. "This is the IOU I want the full answer now."

Mallinson looked down and found the need for a sip of water. He fiddled with a drinking glass that was half full. Then his eyes locked on the younger man.

"You found Ledbetter, Frank," the captain said. "You were the one who went out and did the spade work and came up with him as a suspect in January of 1987. The thing is, we had other detectives on it, too. And no one was finding any hard evidence. Yet we knew we had a guilty man."

"How could you have known that?"

"It came through the state capital, Frank. I don't even know the source of the information any more. I just know that we had it from intelligence in other states: Ledbetter was part of a two-man hit team. Killed for thrill, killed for money. A couple of sickos. Arresting the other guy was off-limits. But Gary was a guy we could grab. If we had the evidence. If we had some murder tools with fingerprints. If we had a girl-friend of a victim who would say the right thing. And if we had, say, a store clerk or two who could make an identification."

"But you didn't have those things."

"And Carl Reissman knew it. So I put Carl on the

spot. I told him, 'This is coming down from on high. So take the gloves off. Build your case against Gary. You'll get help from Concord. Talk to your potential witnesses and we'll cover the inducements. Make sure the witnesses remember.' "

"Feed them information?" O'Hara asked. "Let them know what we wanted to hear?"

Mallinson nodded. "Pretty soon people were standing in line to be witnesses. It's an imperfect world, Frank. You know that. Sometimes you have to construct your own case. Otherwise a killer walks away. We've seen that too many times, haven't we?"

"What about Gary's partner?"

"What about him?"

"A big loose end in the case like that? And we let it hang? Sandor Clay. Who the hell is he?"

Mallinson looked distinctly uneasy with this line of discovery. "Like I said, Frank. We were getting pressure from Concord. Heavy pressure. They wanted a clean wrap in this case. I was under orders to give them one. I was taking orders, not answering questions. Have to do that sometimes to stay in this job."

"Who the hell was Sandor Clay?"

"He had big-time friends in this state, Frank," Mallinson said softly. "The whole government mafia. I'll even take it one step further. I wouldn't be surprised if Negri hired him to have his ex-wife hit before she cleaned him out. That whole connection fits. But I'll tell you this: That case is never going to fly. The whole state government is Negri-friendly. No prosecutor is going to try it, and no judge is going to listen to it. You're after Sandor Clay, Frank? If you are, it's frontier-style justice or it's no justice at all."

"Are you telling me that's what happened? That Negri hired this guy to kill Abigail? And that's why he's back in the state? And that Stacey Dissette was just collateral damage? A little sport on the side, the way some men go deer hunting?"

"I always thought you were too fucking bright to be a cop, Frank. And you just proved it. Frig it, Frank. Do what you want. I'll support you if I live long enough."

O'Hara's eyes found the floor. He leaned back. "I can see why poor old Carl finally drilled a bullet into his head. A career as a good cop going into the trash barrel. Fucking with evidence. Watching homicidal maniacs walk while they fix the case on an accomplice."

Mallinson shrugged.

"Why didn't I know about any of this at the time?" O'Hara asked.

"Carl Reissman was afraid of you," Mallinson said.

"What?"

"Afraid of your sense of ethics," Mallinson said. "He figured that you were in your twenties and wouldn't quite see things his way. Wouldn't quite want to short-cut the system like that."

O'Hara thought about it.

"He was right," O'Hara said. "I would have screamed."

Mallinson nodded. "We all knew that."

"And Carl might have been alive today."

Mallinson gave O'Hara a grieved expression. "In Carl's case, this whole thing was particularly sad. He was no virgin on this. I'd say Carl had been to the trash barrel several dozen times. I guess it weighed heavier on him than anyone knew." Mallinson shook his head. "Poor, poor bastard. I liked him. And he should have known a long time ago that this was how the backwoods homicide business is conducted."

"So all of this," O'Hara asked, hearkening back to the case at hand, "was at Gary's expense?"

"You could draw that conclusion."

"And that's also why the file was robbed at Central Records?"

"Could be. I don't know." Some primal sense of indignation sparked inside of Mallinson and he angered. "Look. Ledbetter was no good!" he snapped. "No question that he killed. The only question was how many. He took a fall, maybe even for something that he didn't completely do, but something which he had plenty to do with. Did we stack a case on him? Yes. But we *got* him. And he was guilty."

"That's not what he says," O'Hara said, slipping.

"What?" scoffed the captain. "You been in touch recently?"

"That's what Gary used to say, is what I mean," O'Hara said, recovering. " 'Not guilty, man.' And he wasn't, in the way he was being accused."

"I hasten to remind you, Frank," Mallinson continued, "that as far as we're concerned, it's all a bullshit point, anyway. We never had to use what we had assembled. Florida took him off our hands."

Mallinson interrupted his own lesson in frontier criminology with a long cancerous cough, one that went on for several seconds. O'Hara was on the verge of calling a nurse when the hacking ceased.

"That leads me to the end of what I wanted to know, Captain," O'Hara said. "You pawned him off on Florida. Did they have a solid case? Or were they cleaning out their desks same as we were?"

"Frank, look at the larger picture," Mallinson said. "Gary was involved. Up and down the east coast. Five women. How many more where the bodies were never found? How many men? How many for money? The fact is, we got him. New Hampshire helped *get* him. Otherwise he'd still be out there."

"Maybe he still is."

"Don't talk nonsense, Frank. There's a psychiatric wing to this hospital, too."

"You ducked my big question."

"Which one was that?"

"Did Florida have a case?"

Mallinson leaned back in his chair. He fidgeted with the sash of his robe, then tightened it.

"Florida looked at us," Mallinson said, "and thought we were doing one fine job of clearing a major case. They *admired* us. What's the old saying. 'Imitation is the sincerest form of flattery'? They imitated."

O'Hara blew out a long breath. Finally, he stood. He shook hands with his commander.

"See you next week," O'Hara said. "I'll let you know what happens."

Chapter 22

O'Hara parked in the lot closest to the tarmac at the heliport in Concord. It was another frigid day, December 13, twelve days before Christmas. O'Hara still wasn't able to think about gift shopping. His mind was still locked on homicide. And on this day, he was taking to the air.

The helicopter pilot was Sgt. Al Hamburger, the top chopper pilot on the state police. Hamburger was a dark-haired, burly, shrewd-eyed man in his late forties, an Atlantan who'd done some college, done some Naval ROTC, and been around the world a bit. One of his longer stops had been in Brussels which was where Hamburger had first developed the unnerving habit of sipping bottled beer as he flew. Not just any bottled beer. Stella Artois, the Belgian brewski. Hamburger had served in Belgium with NATO or something, and had picked up an appetite for anything Belgian, waffles to suds. What was hard now, however, was just finding Stella in the wilds of a New England winter. On this day, however, when O'Hara needed to take to the sky, Hamburger had one.

Fortunately, flying the chopper required two hands, so the alcohol intake was minimal.

They took off at ten A.M., and were over the Monadnock region within a few minutes. Hamburger deftly

ducked the treacherous air currents which shot between the mountains and above the forests. Flying a
chopper in frozen weather was a rough assignment.
But in the Monadnock location, glacial winds tended
to drop sharply down the sides of mountains, constantly threatening to pull helicopters into a wind
shear and drive them down into trees.

Nonetheless, Hamburger guided his aircraft with a
talent that bordered on genius.

O'Hara asked the pilot to take him as low over
Devil's Glen as the air currents would allow. Hamburger took his craft to three hundred feet above the
trees. He hovered there and did an aerial version of a
crawl.

"I don't suppose," Hamburger said, "you could tell
me what you're looking for." The beer bottle was
perfectly balanced in a side pocket of a leather state
police jacket. The air temperature in the craft was
under twenty Fahrenheit.

"If I knew exactly, I'd tell you," O'Hara said. "I'm
after those abandoned cabins. Those structures that
were put up back in the WPA years."

"You mean if the bears haven't knocked them down
yet."

"That's close to it," O'Hara said. "It would help if
I found one with a blue jeep parked nearby."

"It would also help," the pilot said, "if we weren't
fighting a down draft."

The craft shuddered as if it might go down to stay.
Helicopters always spooked O'Hara since Vietnam
was always his point of reference. Nothing good ever
happened with choppers.

As Hamburger worked the gears, O'Hara worked
with a pair of binoculars, visually searching passes
between trees for any sort of structure. The glen was
thick with trees in this area, so thick that even the

snowy ground was dark. Sometimes the thaw here didn't come till late April.

"We've got about an hour of safe flying time," Hamburger said. "After that we risk going into a stall due to a rotor freeze. In a stall—"

"Yeah. I know. We go straight down."

"Those trees are a lot harder when you hit them than they look from here."

"I get your point. And I'll take your word for it."

They flew back to the main state highway which O'Hara had turned off several nights earlier, the night the man—the suspect—in the blue jeep had stopped when the Pontiac had been stuck.

O'Hara found the road that cut through the glen, the road that had brought death to Stacey Dissette. "See that route right there," O'Hara asked, indicating the road to the pilot.

"Got it."

"Follow it slowly until it hits Route 31," O'Hara asked. "You do the flying, I'll do the looking."

"That'll take about the full hour if you want it slow enough to do a thorough search," Hamburger said. O'Hara glanced at him. There was a picture of a blonde woman in a bikini bottom pasted to his dashboard controls. Wishful thinking on a day flying through glacial air? Or a souvenir from a vacation?

"Use the full hour," O'Hara answered.

"You got it, Detective," the pilot answered. Crawling slowly through the low sky allowed Hamburger to put down his beer with ease. He didn't even share with the woman on his controls.

O'Hara had a much less enjoyable trip. He searched the snowy glen scrupulously with his binoculars. He came away with nothing. He found two structures standing that looked like they could have been habitable, but when the chopper came in low on them, they were clearly wrecks.

Nor could he find any tire tracks or anything to support his nascent theory that Gary's former partner, the killer of several women, lurked somewhere in these woods.

When the hour was up, O'Hara folded his glasses into a case. They flew back to Concord and set down. Hamburger, even in cold, strong gusts of wind, had a velvet touch at setting down his craft.

Then O'Hara drove back to Nashua to find more bad news waiting for him. A thorough search had been entered for the license plate on the blue jeep. New Hampshire VPY-643T. The license plate was nonexistent as well. No such number had ever been issued.

Another damned ghost? O'Hara thought back. He was sure he had seen footprints. He was sure this man was real. But he had little more than his instinct to help him pursue.

O'Hara sat in the living room of his home that evening. Outside the night was still. He held a tumbler of Scotch in his hand and stared pensively across the room.

From a distance of ten feet away, Gary sat at the piano. O'Hara had made peace with his guest. So the ghost played softly, his hand drifting across the keys with the lightness of a leaf in a summer breeze.

You won't find Sandor's home from the air, Gary said, playing some Chopin. *It's not visible from the air.*

"But it's out there?"

It's out there.

O'Hara pondered the point. "How do I get there?" he asked.

Gary played a soft musical elegy to the women he had helped murder.

Maybe never.

"Don't fuck with me, Gary!"

Gary's eyes came up. *You want to go?*

"Of course I want to go."

Gary shifted from Chopin to Stephen Foster to Mozart then to Scott Joplin. O'Hara found himself thinking: Death must be an interesting place. So many magnificent people are dead. He wondered if Gary could communicate with all those composers. Then O'Hara found himself analyzing his own thoughts. Was he preparing to die by thinking this way?

O'Hara mused further to himself: Yes, Captain Mallinson. The job will kill you or render you insane. And in my case, it will do both.

Gary took a Beethoven sonata and dissected it, making it discordant, perverting the melody. Even with a piano, Gary enjoyed an occasional kill.

When you visit Sandor, Frankie . . . will you be shocked at what you find?

"After this many years, nothing will shock me."

You'd be surprised.

"I won't be."

Will you go now?

O'Hara looked at the clock. Not just midnight. A frozen, icy midnight. Twelve degrees and holding steady. Steady as the iceberg that sank the *Titanic*. "Go now? Why now?"

Gary tinkled the alto notes. *Sandor is getting ready to depart this state,* Gary said. *Packing his bags, he is.* Gary's blue eyes came up. *Saw your stupid helicopter, Frankie. Not very smart. Got some money from the people who paid him. Got some money to get out of the state. You're a fool, Frankie. He knows you're after him.*

"Jesus, Gary—" O'Hara put down his drink.

Chicken.

"Look, I'll go," O'Hara said. "But how do I . . . ?"

Drive, Gary said firmly. The ghost lifted his hands

from the piano. The music continued. *Follow your instinct. And my friends will follow you there.*

"Your friends?"

You've spent an adult lifetime looking at these forests. You know exactly who I mean.

O'Hara shuddered. He *did* know exactly who. He stood and gathered his coat, which he had left draped over the sofa.

"And you were never innocent, Gary," O'Hara said. "I've labored over this in my mind for years. Back when it happened and now, recently, when you got into my head. You were made to pay the penalty for two men. But you were never innocent."

Gary grinning: the glowing blue eyes. The million-kilowatt smile. The original dirtball Adonis who could charm the bark off a tree, even in death.

Yeah, I lied, Frankie, my man. But I sure got your attention.

Chapter 23

From the start, it was an act of insanity.

O'Hara holstered his weapon, pulled on his coat, and walked from his house. The Pontiac sat in his driveway. The car door was frozen, and O'Hara needed to bang it hard with his fist to force the lock to give.

Then it opened. He climbed in. The engine turned over. He sat for a moment, letting the engine idle and allowing the car to warm up. The night was as black as a grave. The cold would have done the Yukon proud.

O'Hara closed his eyes as the car's engine rumbled.

Tired, man? Gary speaking. From somewhere in the night.

"Yeah. I'm real tired."

I'm tired, too, man. I want to rest.

O'Hara drew a breath. The car was warming. He opened his eyes but didn't see Gary directly, but he had an image of Gary that was as big and as dark as the night. O'Hara closed his eyes again, but the image pursued him.

Hesitating, aren't you?

"No."

You're the homicide man. Big shot death dick. Gary's laughter. A pause. *He killed Carolyn, too, you know.*

"What?"

Sandor killed your lady. She was my sister, man. Came looking for Sandor. Wanted to turn him in to the police. Want to see?

Gary forced a vision upon O'Hara. O'Hara averted his head, twisting it around in the car like a man trying to escape a nightmare. But a man can escape from a bad dream. There was no escape from this.

Before him in his mind was an isolated cabin in the glen. He saw Carolyn. She looked much healthier here. More alive. More color in her face and body. Then he saw Sandor Clay pushing Carolyn to the floor. Clay held a sword above her. Carolyn was screaming, pleading for her life.

Just like Karen Stoner.

Just like Abigail Negri.

Just like. . . . How many others?

Clay raised a sword above his head and. . . .

O'Hara bolted forward in the front seat of the car, a scream of horror in his throat and ears. He gunned the engine and hit the accelerator.

That's it, man. Tonight. You have to do this tonight. Bizarre: Gary's voice had merged into O'Hara's own.

O'Hara drove through the frozen night until he hit the highway that led to Devil's Glen. Then he turned onto the bad road that led through the narrow valley. He took the Pontiac too quickly up hills and much too fast down the other side of the same hills.

The car tenaciously held the road. For a while. Then, suddenly, he was in the place where he'd met Clay in the pickup. O'Hara's instinct took hold, something he had developed from being out in the snow too long.

Here, man.

He hit his brake. The car fishtailed to a stop. The next thing O'Hara knew he was outside the Pontiac, and gazing into the forest.

Was that woodsmoke from a fireplace that he smelled? Could that pinpoint of flickering light among the trees be the cabin he was looking for?

Again O'Hara followed his intuition, wondering if he had finally lost his mind. And for some reason as he entered the woods, O'Hara was able to walk on top of the hard snow without sinking into it.

He walked among the trees and into the darkness. And as he moved, as he passed the frozen wintery trunks of the trees, he realized that he was not alone.

He was with a small army. The forest ghosts came up out of the Earth and were all around him, accompanying him out into a mini-wilderness, following a path which O'Hara knew he could never find again.

Dozens of these dark figures. Then hundreds, all moving in his direction, acting as his escort. He wondered if Gary was somewhere among them. Not that it mattered any more.

He lost track of time. A feeling of exhilaration gripped him. He passed through a clearing. No trees, but the forest ghosts continued to escort him. Then more woods.

The next thing he knew, he was standing before a small cabin in the middle of nowhere. The structure was dark and looked as if it were abandoned.

But something told him again to follow his instincts.

Instincts? Or was it another act of insanity that followed? He pounded at the door. The cabin door opened. A man came into view, silhouetted by electric lights from within.

"Yes?" the man asked.

"Sandor Clay?"

"Yes?"

"The 'S. Clay,' " O'Hara muttered.

The man was blondish and good-looking, much the same as Gary, but without the white trash harshness. O'Hara stared at him. Yes, indeed, it was the same man as the other night. The man in the blue jeep who had stopped on the road through the glen.

"Do you have a problem?" the man asked. A solicitous voice. Charming in its way. Like Gary.

"Yes," O'Hara answered. "Can I come in?"

Clay didn't say anything. O'Hara stepped into the cabin. Clay stepped back, understanding nothing. But O'Hara did see a flash of recognition in his eyes, a flash that told him that Clay now recalled him from their previous meeting.

Clay stared at the intruder. "Are you sick? Are you injured?" Clay asked. "I don't understand what's going on."

But O'Hara's attention was on the floor of the cabin. He saw boards that were not as old as others. Clay didn't seem pleased.

Gary speaking from somewhere. Or again, was it O'Hara's own intuition? The two were almost inseparable now. *That's where he buried her,* Gary said. *She's down there. Want to see?*

O'Hara felt his rage building.

"Look. You can't just come charging in here," Clay protested. "I think I know you from the other night. You're a policeman? You should know that—"

O'Hara's gaze came up to meet the eyes of Clay. "Shut up," he said. "Where is she? Where did you bury her?"

"What in God's name are you talking about?"

"You and Gary. Used to kill people. What was the connection in Concord? And what about Gary's sister? You did it to her, too, didn't you? You—"

"You're crazy! You're absolutely insane."

O'Hara stared at the floor. "She's down there, isn't she?"

Clay turned. He took two steps. O'Hara's eyes widened when he saw that Clay was going to a shotgun that stood by a door frame.

"Mr. Clay?"

Clay wouldn't stop.

"Mr. Clay!"

The man's hands reached for the weapon. He picked it up and turned. O'Hara's hand was busy, too, lunging under his parka, groping for a weapon that he hadn't fired in years outside of the range . . . except in his own home.

"Clay! Stop!"

Clay raised the shotgun to protect himself. "You're a psycho!" Clay said. But as he raised the shotgun he saw that O'Hara already had his thirty-eight up and ready.

Gary intruded again: A mental image of Gary standing behind Clay. Gary giving O'Hara a final vision of Carolyn, kneeling before Clay and begging for her life and Clay raising a sword over his head and. . . .

O'Hara squeezed the trigger. The weapon erupted with a single blast.

From a range of six feet, O'Hara's mark was perfect. The bullet smashed into the center of Clay's face, and O'Hara then had another image, one that would last forever . . . that of Clay's face exploding in red pulp as the force of the single shot threw him backwards against the wall of the cabin.

The body tumbled violently and hit a table as it hurtled toward the floor. Clay fell facedown and was dead before the sound of the shot that had killed him stopped echoing in O'Hara's ears.

O'Hara had no idea how long he stood there, but it seemed like several minutes. Then, with a gloved hand, he turned the heat off in the house. He touched nothing else. He holstered his own weapon and walked out into the night, leaving the door open.

Snow was falling. Gently this time. He knew his boot tracks would be covered by morning.

He walked into the forest and had no idea where he was. But the forest ghosts appeared again. Black figures among the trees. He followed them. He didn't know how far he walked, but eventually they brought him to a clearing.

He looked around, still lost. Somewhere in the night, he heard a whistle. He looked straight ahead. A joyful Gary was with one of those forest creatures, beckoning him ahead. O'Hara figured he would freeze to death if he stopped.

So he trudged forward. Minutes later, he bumped up against something large and cold. His car. The contours came into focus. He climbed in and started the engine, leaning back in his seat.

How could he ever drive home? How could he ever find his way out of this place? He felt a deep tumbling sensation coming up out of the horror of this night.

He closed his eyes and leaned back.

And, as blackness came in on him, he was aware of himself thinking, if this was freezing to death . . . if this was dying of carbon monoxide poisoning . . . man, it certainly was easy!

It wasn't very difficult at all.

Same as murder. A cinch.

His eyes flicked. Gary emerged from the night and was near him. O'Hara was so cold, so tired and so exhausted that he couldn't move.

Gary laughed. Then Gary smiled.

Ledbetter stood outside the car. He leaned downward and his physical being passed through the door. He kissed the detective on the forehead.

Thank you, man.

O'Hara wanted to answer, but his throat wouldn't work. Instead, he closed his eyes and the blackness came over him like a mortician's blanket.

* * *

The rapping came sharply. A hard set of knuckles on metal.

"Detective? Detective?"

O'Hara's eyes flickered and came open. He was still in the Pontiac. The harsh sunlight of a bright morning poured through the windshield.

The voice came again.

"Frank! Hey, Frank! Jesus! You okay?"

Consciousness came across O'Hara. He felt as if a shroud was being lifted. He was aware that he was in his car, but not where he last remembered being. He was home. In his driveway. Somehow he had driven home. Or so he figured.

Philip Reynolds stood outside the Pontiac and stared. His neighbor. His friend from the local town police.

A few profanities bubbled out of O'Hara's mouth. He pulled himself up in the seat and opened the car door.

"Jesus fucking Christ, Frank!" Reynolds said. "I thought you were—"

"Dead?"

"Yeah."

Coming awake, O'Hara shook his head. "No such luck. What the hell? What's going on?"

O'Hara stepped out into another frigid morning. He felt like he had been drugged. Or was it an ugly hangover?

"You're working too fucking hard, man," Reynolds said. "I know it's been that way since Mallinson went into the hospital. But you got to be more careful."

"Yeah." O'Hara stared at his car.

"You fell asleep in your car, man. Must have spent the night there. Would have frozen to death if the engine hadn't been running."

"Hey, it's a dependable old beast," O'Hara answered, looking at the car. "That's why I keep it."

Then he looked at Reynolds. "What are you doing here?" he asked.

"Your office tried to call you. No answer on your phone. They called me. Asked me to come over and take a look."

O'Hara nodded. The events of the previous night resonated in his head. In a nanosecond, all the events replayed themselves.

"Is there a problem?" O'Hara asked.

"If you're the acting head of homicide in this state, Frank, yeah. There's a *big* problem."

"I might have known."

"We got a telephone tip. Found a man dead. I'll take you," said Reynolds.

They climbed into Reynolds's four-wheel, and while Reynolds drove, O'Hara saw the route of the previous night repeat itself. They took the state highway westward until they neared Devil's Glen, then cut down that familiar side road that had already figured into too much death.

O'Hara felt his heart beating harder as they neared the area where he must have been just the previous night. And then he had a sense of déjà vu when he saw the assemblage of police vehicles at the side of the road, and an obvious path leading far into the woods. He knew exactly where he was being taken. But this time there was a snowmobile to take him.

Minutes later, he stood before Sandor Clay's cabin. He looked upward to see why the cabin had never been visible from the air via Sgt. Hamburger's helicopter. One of these weird little quirks in the universe, he wondered. He had no explanation, other than that the trees shielded it perfectly.

Then two harness bulls in parkas showed him into the cabin.

"Nothing's been touched, sir," one of the men said to him. "We waited for you."

"The murder looks like it's pretty fresh, sir," the other one said.

O'Hara gazed at the body of Sandor Clay, lying facedown exactly where O'Hara remembered him falling.

"One bullet to the head, sir. Someone just walked in here and popped him."

"I can see that," O'Hara answered.

"Looks *real* fresh," the first cop repeated.

"Can't tell that, kid," O'Hara growled. "In the damn cold. Everything gets preserved. No heat in this place. Who knows how long he's been lying here."

A team from forensic arrived, stumbling through the snow, ready to obliterate as much evidence as their usual carelessness would allow.

After making his own inspection, he told them, "Go to it."

"Yes, sir. Right away," one of them answered. It was a young team. Inexperienced. O'Hara was confident they would make a mess out of this.

With a booted foot, O'Hara found some play in the floorboards. As he toyed with the planks, there was a terrible creak in the wood. The creak reminded him of his own place and the events that had transpired there.

"Officer?" O'Hara said to one of the forensic men.

"Yes, sir?"

"I'm going to take personal charge of this case. I want you to submit every bit of evidence directly to me."

"Yes, sir." The uniformed man gazed at O'Hara. "We have some shovels and axes in the truck outside, sir. Do you want us to pull up these floorboards? We might find something down there."

The younger man looked at the suspicious spot.

"No. Leave the floor alone," O'Hara said. "I'll take care of that part."

The younger man nodded. "Yes, sir," he said.

Then O'Hara stepped back and let the investigation begin around him. He thought again of the previous night, or at least his memory of it. He drew a breath and tried to relax. Two words came into his mind pertaining to his own involvement. Two words that would always remain with him.

Innocent, man!

Chapter 24

Several hundred miles to the south, Adam Kaminski still lived a life that was filled with perplexity. Sure, over the years he thought he had developed a keen sense of tenants and which ones would be trouble, but nothing had ever prepared him for the intrigue that had involved Carolyn Hart.

Young women. Psychiatrists. Apartment leases. Police. A combination of any of those two always meant trouble in his business. Why couldn't anything just fall neatly in place? Why was his life such a continuing series of contradictions and inexplicable events? Particularly this last series, which continued to bedevil him.

February came and went. March arrived, and Kaminski fell into a sharp depression, despite the fact that the weather in the mid-Atlantic broke very mildly. An early spring was in everyone's forecast, which somehow only made Adam more depressed.

He had taken to not eating on his lunch hour. Rather, he took long walks around the city, wallowing in his loneliness, trying to sort out his lack of understanding of any of the events surrounding the Carolyn Hart intrigue.

That was how he thought of it: Carolyn Hart intrigue. What else could he call it? He had no way to otherwise define it.

Continually, he replayed the final events leading to her ultimate disappearance that past December.

How else could he explain what those psychiatrists had told him?

Here he had wanted to lead a young woman who had been in their charge back to them. So Kaminski had gone to Oswell Street and had confronted her on the doorstep. In response, Carolyn had frozen on the spot and stared at him without speaking. Several seconds passed. Then Carolyn had fled into the house and slammed the door.

Reluctantly, Kaminski produced a key, hoping that he could talk to Carolyn and convince her to return to Northeastern Pennsylvania State Psychiatric. He entered the residence. He searched every nook of the house, every closet, and every part of the basement.

And no Carolyn.

She had just plain disappeared. How she had slipped out of the house was something that Kaminski would never understand. And the funny thing was, all of her small possessions were gone, too. As if she had anticipated her departure.

Then over the telephone, the shrinks had given him that bizarre story—completely unbelievable, though they did have records to back it up—that Carolyn *had* been in their care, yes. But one story had reached them that she had died under suspicious circumstances in New Hampshire in June of 1990.

Three years ago.

Kaminski had heard that shrinks underwent psychoanalysis themselves. And that many of them were crazy. This episode did nothing to dissuade him. And yet, wherever Carolyn had been, she was now somewhere else.

Kaminski sighed as he looked back on these events. Life was becoming tenfold too complicated for him. His father, a millionaire who could easily have retired, stewed daily about increased municipal taxes. His mother worried about her only son. Adam couldn't wait to get out of the place every noon for his walk. So what that he had lost ten pounds due to his new non-lunch lunch hours?

Hell. He felt rotten.

The walk usually took him in the direction of Oswell Street where a certain house of note (one of the best in their portfolio) was up again for rent. It had sat empty since Carolyn had last disappeared into it.

Or disappeared from it, as the case may have been.

Some days he entered it for no reason, other than trying to catch the vibrations within. The strange thing was that walking around in that building, he still had a vague feeling of her. There was a scent to the place, and he associated it with Carolyn. Foolishly perhaps. It was probably nothing more than an old house smell and he dismissed the notion that he could still pick up a piece of her spirit therein. Kaminski was, after all, the sort of guy who could fully believe in only what he could see.

And he couldn't see Carolyn. Though one day he thought he did.

It was a day in early March as he took his noon walk. Kaminski turned the corner onto Oswell, looked down the narrow street and stopped short. Here it was on an afternoon much like the one several months ago. And there, standing in front of the very house, looking for all the world like she had a few months earlier, was a woman in a light navy raincoat. She had brown hair and beautiful legs and Kaminski's heart leaped upon the sight of her.

She was standing right outside his property, gazing

up at the FOR RENT shingle that had blossomed on the house over the winter.

By all that was holy, it was Carolyn Hart! Her. Again. In the flesh. Or what again appeared to be in the flesh.

Kaminski looked at her as a flood of conflicting emotions overtook him: fear, attraction, excitement, terror.

Lack of understanding. Then he moved steadily forward. No flirtation this time. No nonsense. Just bold confrontation. Just what type of games were going on here?

He was tired of his head being scrambled over those impossible tall tales being told by the psychiatric center in Bryn Mawr. Some of the accounts suggested that Kaminski himself was dealing with a few cards short of a full deck. Adam was owed some answers and, by God, this time he would have them!

The woman turned toward him and smiled as he approached. It was only when Kaminski drew within a few feet of her that he realized that he had been badly mistaken.

From a distance, this woman looked like Carolyn. But up close, the physical similarity was so barely fleeting that he was convinced that he had caught this new woman in a strange light. Or that his eyes were playing tricks upon him. This girl was very plain. More studious than sensual, more a homebody than a home wrecker.

"Hello," she said, looking at him. Her demeanor was warm. She continued to smile.

"Hello," he answered. He remained near her.

"I don't think I know you. Do I?" she asked.

Nonplussed, Kaminski answered the only way he could. With indecision. "I'm not sure," he said.

She glanced up again at the FOR RENT sign.

"I've always liked this house," she said. "I see it's available."

"Apparently," he said.

"Do you know anything about it?" she asked. "Is anyone living in it now?"

"It's empty."

"Do you know anything about the ownership?" she asked. "I might be interested in renting. Or even buying."

He stared at her for several seconds.

"*I* own it." He grew a little on the spot.

She turned with greater surprise. "*Do* you?" she asked. "I'm afraid I didn't introduce myself properly. I'm Bernice Lang."

He felt a tingle at the base of his spine. "Pleased to meet you," he said. He looked at her left hand. No ring.

"And you are . . . ?" she asked.

"Adam Kaminski. I own several buildings in the city. And a few in the suburbs." He grew even more, at least in his own estimation.

"Ah. I see," she said.

"I can show you the house if you like," he said.

"Could you? Now?"

"I have a key," he offered.

The door opened. The house accepted them easily. Kaminski gave her the tour, downstairs first, then the middle room, then the upstairs. The house was a little musty again. Disuse during the late winter. And he really did have to get rid of Paula Burns's furniture, he reminded himself. There was almost something incestuous about all these women living on top of each other.

But the house gave him a very receptive feeling on this visit, one he liked. He wasn't picking up the somber vibrations of his other more recent visits. But just the same, Kaminski was relieved that this visit had

gone well and without incident. He was glad to lead
Bernice back downstairs and out to the street, after a
pleasant moment admiring the rear garden.

"Well?" he finally asked.

"I loved it," she said.

"Are you looking for a place to live right now?" he
asked.

She explained that she was getting a business degree
at Temple University. Her roommate was getting married, and she could use a new place as soon as she
found one.

"A business degree, huh?" he asked. "Any specific
area of concentration?"

"Real estate."

His knees wobbled slightly. Kaminski puffed up his
courage. Somewhere out there was just the right lady
for him. There had to be. And maybe, just maybe, this
Bernice was she.

She looked at the facade of 565 Oswell Street. "It's
just a beautiful, old place," she said.

"The last two tenants were both single women, too.
They loved the place."

"Why did they move?"

"Career changes."

"What sort?"

He shrugged. "I have no idea," he said. "I never
understood. And they never told me."

She smiled again.

"The house has a bit of a history, though," he said.
"If you're interested, I'd be happy to tell you all about
it."

"I'm interested," she said. There was a new espresso
bar around the corner. Adam guided her in that direction.

"That would be nice," she said.

He locked the front door of 565 Oswell. And as he
did so, a feeling of relief came over him. And then a

funny thought: Wherever Carolyn Hart had gone, she was finally somewhere else. The Oswell Street residence seemed finally back in his possession.

"Now, *this*," Adam Kaminski found himself thinking as he walked with Bernice Lang, *"this* really could be *the* girl."

Captain William Mallinson died the same day that Adam Kaminski met Bernice Lang. It was March 10, four days after Mallinson's fifty-eighth birthday. The New Hampshire papers were filled with stories. The prevailing motif was that Mallinson had been a good man in a tough job. And that the job had eventually eaten him alive.

He was buried outside the town of Henneker in a burial plot that he had bought many years ago, back during the early days of his marriage, back when he was a young man, filled with optimism and noble aspirations, unblemished by the job, his psyche not yet bearing the collateral damage of nearly a thousand violent deaths. By a curious coincidence, fifty-eight people stood at his graveside as his casket was lowered. It was a wicked winter day, and the ground had to be broken with jackhammers. He was then returned to the frigid earth of New Hampshire. All of the mourners knew each other.

Mallinson's death cast a pall across Henneker, where the captain had lived. Friends sat at Leary's Tavern and lifted many glasses to him. It is said that great minds discuss ideas, medium intellects discuss events, and small minds discuss people. At Leary's, the faithful discussed people. An individual person. Bill Mallinson. They discussed him at length, but they did so with reverence.

When a man dies, there is much summing up to do, an accounting of a man's years on Earth. The locals at

Leary's were inclined to see Bill Mallinson in terms that ranged from workmanly to poetic: a stand-up, old-fashioned guy who did honest work every day of his life. The notices in the newspapers followed this same theme, usually accompanied by his name and picture.

The one discordant reaction, however, came from his successor. Frank O'Hara saw the man's life more in terms of condemnation and claustrophobia. To him, Mallinson had been a man whose worldview had never travelled beyond the towns and counties of New Hampshire. He had aspired to nothing higher than investigating the tags on the toes of corpses. Then, after a lifetime of this, chopped short by political pressure, too many winters, and endless cheroots, Bill Mallinson was returned to the same rocky soil that he had trod throughout his lifetime. He would lie beneath the dark New England winters for eternity.

Never to escape.

There but for the grace of God. . . . O'Hara might have remarked. But in his mind, he would never finish the thought. It was too frightening.

After the funeral, there was a reception at the Henneker firehouse. Mallinson was recalled more cheerfully there. A day or two later, a marker was placed upon his grave. Two days after that more snow covered the marker.

In keeping with the state law, Frank O'Hara was elevated within the state police hierarchy. He became Captain of Homicide, the job he had never wanted. Inexplicably, he also agreed to stay on for four extra months, or until a proper successor could be found. He agreed for several reasons.

Two were salient.

First, he had been absorbed in the Negri and Stacey Dissette slayings, both of which remained officially open. Then there was mopping up to do from the strange discovery of Sandor Clay's body out in the snows of Devil's Glen.

Second, O'Hara had made virtually no plans to move out of state. He had never had the opportunity, having been so busy in the days before he would have retired. So, since he was staying, since he felt needed, he might just as well draw a paycheck.

And who better to fill the job?

The winter, however, remained relentless. Blizzard followed blizzard. In some cases, the snowbanks by the side of roads reached ten to twelve feet.

Drifts covered sides of houses, two people died when a roof collapsed in Derry, and—sure enough— an entire family was found frozen in Franconia when their power had failed. In March, there was a little bit of a thaw, right around the time of the big police funeral for Bill Mallinson. Then winter returned with a wallop. Two back-to-back, don't-fuck-with-Mother-Nature ice storms put a nice hard coating on everything.

To O'Hara, despite the fact that he had agreed to stay on, winter was still akin to death—either a fast one or a slow one—but a death nonetheless. Sometimes, he insisted, even the distinctions between the two were vague.

Some people thought him a little nutty on this point, but he had his reasons. Even if he didn't explain them.

He missed his old boss. Missed Mallinson's insight. Missed his inspiration. Missed his foul-spirited crankiness, in fact.

So on some days when the roads were clear, O'Hara would drive past the cemetery in Henneker where Mallinson lay. O'Hara would stop his car and gaze across the tombstones.

"Talk to me, Captain," he would say. "You once told me this job would slowly kill any man who took it. And I said I'd be certifiably insane the day I accepted it."

He'd pause. "Now look what's happened. You were a more sagacious old goat than I ever imagined."

O'Hara asked these questions and said these things aloud and unabashedly. Those who passed in cars and trucks could see their new homicide chief carrying on an animated conversation with the tombstones. But was there any surprise there? Frank O'Hara had been talking to the dead for many years, since he first partnered with Carl Reissman and studied those faces staring down from their bulletin board of open cases.

"What do you think now, Cap?" he would press.

"Same opinion as ever. You're dead and I'm nuts."

Sometimes, if O'Hara listened with something more than his ears, he thought he heard the captain answer. And not always with pleasure.

Then there was another reason O'Hara stayed on. The state had been awash in homicide again. The department needed leadership and a firm hand on top. Those in authority felt Frank O'Hara could supply that hand, even if it was common currency that Frank O'Hara seemed a little wacky these days.

So what? The long winters and the career as a death dick would turn anyone into a nut case.

Wouldn't it?

But in private, O'Hara had even expanded on his ulterior reason for staying to two deputies. The Abigail Negri case. Everyone else might have considered it closed, but he didn't. And as the captain of state police homicide, he was free to kick asses wherever he so desired, within reason.

O'Hara had this theory that the money that financed Sandor Clay's low art had come from a respectable source in Concord. So O'Hara spent much time hanging around that area of the state, falling into chance meetings with Wilhelm Negri, making the radio commentator and publisher jittery as a dozen spooked cats, and casting accusatory suggestions and glances his way whenever he saw fit.

"You're nuts, O'Hara," Negri had finally told him one day. "Everybody knows it. It's a matter of time before people lock you up."

"The guy who's going to be locked up," O'Hara steamed, "is you. And I'm going to do it."

So it continued.

As the events of December receded, O'Hara continued to see Dr. Julie Steinberg. They developed an excellent relationship. They spent some time together. They had a brief affair. And in May, when the longest winter on record finally broke, and as the Negri investigation continued to occupy O'Hara's thoughts, four months were up.

O'Hara had his retirement papers processed. A successor was in the offing. All that remained was for Frank O'Hara to take the release that he had so badly wanted for these last few years.

As a sad commentary on his nuttiness, he didn't grab it.

"I have my reasons," he said. And no one walking the Earth would understand them.

To some, it was comprehensible:

He was still having an affair with Julie Steinberg, they said, and wasn't going to leave the state now that he had finally found domestic contentment.

He was on the verge of blowing the lid off the Negri case, the reporters in Concord and Nashua whispered, and would stay until that business was completed. Even a few of the big-time national media had sent reporters to the state to see if there was anything to the rumors.

Some big-name reporters sought audiences with O'Hara, but he wasn't talking. One writer left New

Hampshire the day after he arrived, referring to Frank O'Hara as "a madman."

Then there was a third school of thought. There wasn't a damned other thing in life O'Hara could do, this theory went, other than investigate murders. So, like a dog who chases cars and finally catches one, O'Hara, faced with freedom, had no plans for it when he finally had it.

All of those theories made sense. There were elements of truth to all three accounts. But none had hit the center of the target.

Fact was, O'Hara had found love. But in a way that no man could imagine.

At the end of the Ledbetter case, O'Hara had envisioned many times a huge face superimposed against the winter night. Sometimes he saw this face upon his house. Other times, in the sky. Always, he had identified it as Gary. The face of a dead man watching him.

But actually, the face had belonged to a woman, though maybe in truth the face did represent a different aspect of the larger Ledbetter psyche.

On cold winter nights, and later on chilly spring nights, O'Hara would come home from his day on homicide. He would make his personal phone calls and fix himself dinner. Then he would have a few drinks.

He would not get drunk. Instead, he would have just enough of one sort of spirits to raise another sort. He would bring himself to a certain alcoholic haze and then stop. He wasn't even sure whether the booze was necessary. But this was the way he had always done it. So this was the way it would continue to be.

Then he would go upstairs to his bedroom. He would wait. He would wait until a visitor would come forth, beckoned from God-knew-where, caught between God-knew-where.

Joining him on a trip God-knew-where.

He would do this in the dark or with the light on. Either. It made no difference, other than the fact that Carolyn could be summoned only during the night, much the same way her brother could be summoned when his spirit still inhabited the Earth.

O'Hara would close his eyes. He would drift.

Then he would feel the weight of a female body settling onto the bed. He would open his eyes, and Carolyn would be there. She would be there because he had never sent her back to that place where she had been.

The mental institution. The grave. And beyond.

She wasn't going back, it was clear, until that day in the near future when O'Hara was coming with her.

His home was her refuge. As long as he was there, he kept open a room for the dead.

"Hello?" she would ask, her hand settling upon him.

"Hello."

"How was your day, lover?"

"This is the best part of it."

"Put down your drink," she would say. "I'm here now. You don't have to drink any more."

He would set it aside. Her hand was on the glass, guiding it. He would reach for the tape player. "Do you mind some Sinatra?"

"Why would I? I love Sinatra."

"You're the only one who does besides me."

"Who needs anyone else?"

Some days Carolyn would be beautifully attired in silk, an elegant lady from the city. Other times she would wear gingham or blue jeans skirts. A Southern gal.

She would wear whatever he wanted. And she would listen to whatever Sinatra he wanted.

Moody Frank. Or snap-brimmed, jaunty Frank. Frank with the blues. Frank in love. Or all the different Franks, one after another.

"You *are* a ghost," he would whisper sometimes. "I know that. But I can still be in love. And I can still be safe with you."

She would lean forward and kiss him. In the midst of the glacial coldness of New England, her kiss was as soft as an ocean breeze from a warm place. And it was faintly scented with orange blossoms. This scene would repeat itself as often as he wished. Gradually, other rooms in his home were given over to O'Hara's relationship with Carolyn . . . and his love for her. He knew the day was coming when all the rooms would surrender . . . and he would depart with her.

"Seen Gary?" he asked her once.

"Gary's content now," she assured him. "Gary's gone."

"I won't ask to where."

"Please don't."

She smiled. Her smile was like music. Sinatra sang, too.

Sometimes on evenings like these, friends phoned O'Hara to see how he was doing. He seemed fine, although sometimes it sounded like he had company. No one ever heard a voice in the background, however. And he never invited anyone to his home any more.

Julie Steinberg took an interest in his welfare. She had a sense that over the course of the Ledbetter case, both installments of it, O'Hara had made a descent from light to darkness and back up to light again. And now, it seemed, he was on his way back down to darkness. She knew he was drinking again. And she wasn't sure what she could do about it.

Nor did she even know what he was still doing in the state.

Her professional opinion wasn't too far from that of certain friends who observed O'Hara's behavior and were troubled by it.

These friends said that O'Hara had gone completely crazy.

But he knew better. For the first time in two decades, he was at peace with himself. And, during the final months of his life, Frank O'Hara was as happy as he had ever been.